A PARTI

The sunlight glistened off
nal, arrayed for public vie
in his throat.

Viviane bit her lip and
more through the doorway before beseeching Niall with a
luminous glance. "Could I wish upon my father's stone?
Would it trouble you overmuch?" Her words faltered and
she seemed suddenly very young. She did not stand so tall
now that her optimism had deserted her. "I . . . I might never
have the chance again."

She most certainly would not. And Niall could not see
what damage it would do to indulge her. 'Twould only take
a heartbeat and the archbishop need never know.

She took a deep breath and tipped her head back, squared
her shoulders and squeezed her eyes closed. Her pose tore at
Niall's hardened heart, and for an impetuous moment, he
wished he might have had the opportunity to know more of
this Viviane.

"I wish," she said softly, but with passion, "I *wish* I were
far away from here as ever a person could be."

And no one could have been more surprised than Sir Niall
of Malloy when the lady shimmered right before his
eyes . . .

Praise for the novels of CLAIRE CROSS

Once Upon a Kiss

"A wonderful tale that fans . . . will devour . . . exhilarating
story line . . . enchanting." —*Painted Rock Reviews*

The Last Highlander

"A delight." —*Toronto Star*

"Time travel at its best." —*Romance Communications*

Love Potion #9

"Ms. Cross's style is irresistible . . . fast and exhilarating."
—*Rendezvous*

THE MOONSTONE

Claire Cross

JOVE BOOKS, NEW YORK

TIME PASSAGES is a registered trademark of Penguin Putnam Inc.

THE MOONSTONE

A Jove Book / published by arrangement with
the author

PRINTING HISTORY
Jove edition / October 1999

The Penguin Putnam Inc. World Wide Web site address is
http://www.penguinputnam.com

ISBN: 0-515-12654-3

A JOVE BOOK®
Jove Books are published by The Berkley Publishing Group,
a division of Penguin Putnam Inc.,
375 Hudson Street, New York, New York 10014.
JOVE and the "J" design
are trademarks belonging to Penguin Putnam Inc.

PRINTED IN THE UNITED STATES OF AMERICA

10 9 8 7 6 5 4 3 2 1

Chapter 1

SIR NIALL OF Malloy was not in a good mood.

'Twas the kind of rainy winter morning that made his knee ache in memory of a battle wound he would prefer to forget. His belly growled in mighty protest of the fact that he had not had even the time to break his fast before he had been summoned. 'Twas only made worse by the reason *why* he had been summoned so early this morn.

Because Niall sorely disliked executing prisoners.

He particularly disliked executing female prisoners.

But that was precisely what he had to do this morn. At least, he had to go down to that miserable pit of a dungeon and accompany some poor misbegotten soul to her demise. There were finer ways for a man to start his day, Niall was certain.

Indeed, 'twas in moments like these that he found the employ of the archbishop particularly onerous. Of late, there were just too many days beginning like this one. Niall had a difficult time believing that the hearts of so many men and women in this corner of the land were rotted with evil.

Indeed, he was heartily skeptical that witchcraft had any

truth to it at all. As much as he hated to even consider such a traitorous thought, Niall believed his patron was wrong. Sorcery was the stuff of tall tales alone.

Yet 'twas the plain truth that a scarred old warrior like himself had few other options for earning his keep. Niall was not more than eight and twenty, though his soul felt shrivelled beyond all since his injury.

How he missed being in command of his own fate!

Those days, however, were gone for good. The cold in the nether regions of the castle brought the ache in his knee to a bellow, which was fitting enough for his circumstance. Niall limped along the old stone corridor grumpily, hating that he was no less fettered than the many prisoners moaning within their damp cells.

'Twas no consolation that the old hag who was to die was likely more uncomfortable than he. Niall's heart twisted in a most unsoldierly fashion at the task before him.

One bad fall and he had gotten soft.

Niall could not have said why he felt particularly troubled by the women condemned by the archbishop's court, for he was quite certain that he had been completely spared his comrades' weakness for the fair sex. Either that, or his trying sister had cured him of any such inclinations.

Women were, after all, a powerful amount of trouble.

Niall growled and crumpled the parchment beneath his tabard, a telling reminder of that truth if ever there was one. 'Twas a letter he had received this very morn from Majella and his mood soured yet more at the recollection of its contents.

One would think after seven children, Majella would have the wits to know how she had come by them. Or to at least consider the unholy cost of supporting them before she parted her thighs once more.

But thinking had naught to do with the life of his sister. It never had. She was a creature of passion and impulse, though so warm and charming that even Niall could forgive her many sins. Twice widowed, Majella and her brood would be virtually penniless—were it not for her brother's consistent support.

'Twas a support he felt he owed Majella's children, for there were no others forming a line to fulfil the duty. And 'twas not the fault of the children that they had no father.

'Twas also a support that depended upon Niall continuing to do the archbishop's will. Even when he did not agree with it. He ground his teeth and did not trouble to hide his foul mood when he entered the guard's antechamber.

"Number seven," Odo declared without even glancing up from his ledger. The half-eaten round of bread resting beside Odo's book prompted Niall's innards to complain once more at their neglect.

Perhaps after this deed was done . . .

But Niall knew he would have no taste for a meal by the time he had looked into the eyes of a condemned woman. Sooner begun, sooner finished, he reminded himself. Niall retrieved the appropriate church key and stalked down the hall.

"Oho, and mind yourself, Niall," Odo called after him, with a cheer that was far from welcome. "Do not be letting our witch cast a spell upon you! The archbishop intends to watch this one twitch in the wind himself."

Niall grimaced at the choice of some folk in entertainment as he made his way down the fitfully lit corridor. Scrawny hands reached through grated openings in the cell doors, voices called in supplication. He swore he could hear the rats scuttling across the floor, and somewhere in the distance, something vile dripped with sickening regularity.

How Niall loathed this place.

How he loathed being dispatched to the dark for even a moment. He expected that most of these troubled souls did not even understand what they had done amiss, nor even how much time had passed since they stepped into these clammy shadows.

Niall suspected that few of them cared any longer.

He turned the key in the heavy lock upon the door of the

seventh cell with purpose, anxious to return to the sunlight. He would not think upon the numbers here who would never feel that warmth again. He would not feel guilty that he did not share their fate.

At the sound of the key grating in the lock, the prisoner within the cell gasped. 'Twas typical enough. Niall nudged open the door, the hinges creaked bitterly at the movement, and the woman seated within glanced up and smiled.

Smiled.

Niall gaped, his boots suddenly rooted to the spot. He had not expected a condemned witch to be quite so young.

Nor indeed, quite so cheerful.

"Good morn," she said in a most friendly manner. A delightful dimple deepened in her left cheek. "I had begun to despair that anyone would come at all."

She was *anxious* to be put to a gruesome death?

The witch's clean but simple garb was markedly at odds with the filth of her surroundings. Her face glowed with good health, though her skin was fair, her auburn locks were gathered in a braid finished off with a ribbon tied in a pert bow. She stood and smoothed her skirt, the move revealing that she was both tall and graciously made.

Niall stared. She seemed a perfectly normal, if uncommonly pretty, woman.

"I had understood that I would be summoned at the dawn, and as you might well imagine, I slept nary a wink last night, thinking all the while of this morn." A merry twinkle danced in the warm hazel of her eyes.

Niall's arrival was never greeted with such pleasure and he was momentarily uncertain of how to proceed.

"I simply could not wait and must say that I am most pleased that you have finally arrived. I cannot wait to begin. Shall we go?"

Niall blinked, but her smile did not waver.

"Oh! Where are my manners? Why, I am Viviane and so very pleased to make your acquaintance."

This was no social moment! The last thing Niall wanted

was to befriend a woman on her way to the executioner's block.

But she stepped forward, her smile unwavering. "You do have a name?" she asked with no small measure of charm.

Clearly, this woman did not understand the fullness of her fate.

"My name matters naught," Niall said gruffly, disliking that he should be the one to grant her the sorry news. "If you would turn about, I must bind your hands behind you."

That should remind her of the trouble she faced this morn.

But she simply smiled and complied, as though there was naught strange about the request. She crossed her wrists behind her waist and Niall found himself unwilling to even touch the roughened rope to such creamy softness.

But he did.

If not too tightly.

"Of course, your name *matters*!" she chided as Niall scowled and knotted the rope. "How on earth could I possibly have a conversation with you unless we are introduced?"

The omission did not seem to be interfering too mightily with that, Niall thought, but he refrained from saying as much.

"Truly! What would I call you? What would I say? There is absolutely no reason for this to be unpleasant . . ."

"Unpleasant?" Niall echoed, incredulity breaking his usual reserve. "You do understand that you are to *die* this morn?"

She glanced over her shoulder to him, her full lips quirking with mischief. "Of course, I understand that that is what people *believe* is going to happen, but I know that things will not come to such a dire end."

Niall eyed her dubiously. " 'Tis true then, that you believe you are a witch? You mean to enchant your way free of these proceedings?"

Her laughter pealed like a bell in the tiny chamber, the merry sound nearly enough to make Niall smile along with her. "Of course not!" She shook her head as though he was the one possessed of whimsy. "'Tis perfectly obvious that this is no more than a horrible misunderstanding and as soon as I have the chance to address the archbishop, all will be set in order."

She smiled into Niall's eyes and his heart took an unruly—and uncharacteristic—leap. Indeed, his mouth went dry.

When had he last glimpsed a woman so fair of face?

And when had such a woman smiled for him alone? Niall could not even remember.

It helped little that she made such good sense.

"Do not fear for my life, sir," the lady murmured and wrinkled her nose playfully. "I do not mean to die this day."

Niall was so disoriented by his own response to her smile, that his mood turned even more surly. "You may not have a choice," he growled, then urged her toward the door.

"Oh, you take this far too seriously," she charged, stepping delicately around a puddle of some nameless substance on the stone floor of the corridor. "My mother always declared that I had uncommon fortune . . ."

"'Twould seem to be less than that in this moment."

"But that is only because details interfere and will be resolved in short order. That is why I could not wait for you to come, so we might begin." Viviane leaned closer, her tone dropping confidentially. "Waiting has never been my strongest gift, I must confess."

Niall harumphed, uncertain why he felt so compelled to try to make her understand the full horror she faced. "You need not wait much longer for anything, from all signs."

The lady mimicked his manner with a wink. "Such dire warnings! You, sir knight, are truly too glum for your own good. There is no point in fearing the worst until 'tis before your own eyes. That was what my mother always said."

"'Twill be before your own eyes soon enough." Niall trudged along the fitfully lit corridor, feeling even older in contrast to his companion's light footfall.

Indeed, she nigh skipped. "Ah, but you do not know that I was born under a blue moon."

Niall snorted at such suspicious nonsense. "And *that* will save you from death?"

The lady tossed her braid over her shoulder, apparently untroubled by his skepticism. "'Twill save me from any trouble that might be sent my way. My mother said as much and my mother knew more than most."

Something about her conviction caught Niall's attention. "What do you mean?" he demanded suspiciously. "Did she believe herself a witch, as well?"

That laugh echoed again, the sound spreading a little sunshine in the dank corridor.

Niall completely forgot to limp.

"Of course not! You are a man looking for witches at every turn, sir!"

Niall's ears burned at the charge, but he strode on stoically.

"She had the Sight," his companion confessed as though there was naught preposterous about that. "She could see into the beyond like no one I have ever known before." The lady's tone turned surprisingly wistful. "'Tis a rare gift and one that ensured we ate more often than we might have otherwise."

Niall urged his charge forward, not liking how she suddenly turned silent. 'Twas evidently uncharacteristic and he had a strange urge to restore her good cheer.

. For however short a time she might have left.

"She is dead, then?" Niall asked, realizing after the words left his lips that 'twas not the most uplifting question he might have concocted.

"Aye." She smiled sadly for him, the smile not reaching her eyes. "She is."

But the lady said no more and her shoulders sagged slightly. Niall's footsteps echoed too loudly in the silent corridor as they walked. 'Twas only the fact that she was to die that troubled him, he knew it well.

"Mind your head here," Niall instructed, touching her shoulder so that she did not bump her forehead on a low doorway. To his delight and surprise, she smiled at him once more.

"You are so very kind," she said in a low voice that made something melt within Niall's gut. "'Tis uncommon in a man so handsomely wrought as you."

"Hardly that," he retorted briskly, hating anew his role in all of this, refusing to take pleasure in her compliment. "Down this way."

Viviane stepped lightly along the way indicated, her footsteps whispering against the stone. "My mother sent me here, you know." His ward tilted her chin proudly as though she feared Niall would challenge her word. "That is how I know that no ill can come to me here."

"That is scanty guarantee."

"And what kind of a mother would send her child to their demise?" the lady demanded brightly. She slanted a sharp glance in Niall's direction. "Would *your* mother have sent you into any place that might have proven a threat to your welfare?"

"Nay," Niall was forced to concede, recalling all too well his mother's distress when he learned to handle a broadsword.

"You see?" she said triumphantly. "'Tis more than clear that no mother could do as much, mine being no exception. Nay, she sent me here for my own safety and protection, and I have only good faith that 'twill be so."

Niall thought it tactless to observe that even a mother could be wrong. "Your mother sent you to the archbishop?"

"Aye."

Niall could not help but raise a skeptical brow. "Then it seems her gift of Sight was somewhat limited."

His companion's eyes flashed in a most intriguing way as she spun to face him. "Surely you do not doubt her gift?"

Niall was certain that his one level glance supplied all the answer necessary. He thought 'twould be churlish to further draw the line between Viviane's assertions and her current situation.

The lady tossed her hair. "You must never have witnessed such wonders," she declared. "It cannot be your fault that you do not believe in the most obvious things, for you seem a most sensible man to me."

Before Niall could consider what to say to that, Viviane cleared her throat. "You see, my mother told me, on her deathbed, that I should come here if ever I was to want for anything. And I must tell you, that matters have not gone well since her demise."

"Have you no siblings?" Niall was surprised to find himself curious, no less that he asked a question without intending to any such thing.

'Twas foolhardy to become interested in those sentenced to die.

Though he most certainly was *not* interested in Viviane.

"Not a one. 'Twas just my mother and I, all these years." A frown momentarily marred the lady's brow. "She told me the tales, and truly, I would have had no trade without her."

"You have a trade?"

"Aye!" The lady lifted her chin. "I copy manuscripts and sell them in the markets."

"'Tis a labor of monks."

Her expression turned arch. "But they do not inscribe the more interesting tales, the ones which people truly desire to read again and again." Despite himself, Niall looked to her in curiosity. "I copy romances, those tales of quests and knights and ladies fair, of bold deeds and fearsome dragons."

"And you earn your keep with that?"

Her delight faded and Niall felt a cur. "I did, for a while. But times are less than good and even those who admire my work have little to spare. I have travelled much since my mother's death, visiting all the familiar towns again, but to no avail." She shrugged. "In truth, the details matter little.

Finally, I had no choice but to take my mother's advice, and so here I am!"

She granted Niall an unexpected smile so sunny it warmed him to his toes. "As soon as the archbishop hears tell of this, I am certain that all will be set to rights." She nodded with a confidence Niall found hard to match.

He frowned as he tried to follow her explanation. "Why should the archbishop provide for you?"

But the lady only smiled more broadly at the question. Her expression was wondrously feminine and launched a queer sensation around Niall's heart. Indeed, it seemed to beat overfast. And he could not haul his gaze away from hers, at least until he saw the gemstone swinging from the chain around her neck.

'Twas a moonstone, its milkiness containing an ethereal sliver of blue, blue light. A more superstitious man would have named it a witching stone. Niall had heard tell of such things, though he had never given credence to those tales.

This stone, though, was odd. It seemed to glow from within and just the sight of it made Niall deeply uneasy. There was something unnatural about its very blueness, as though a shard of the moon had been trapped inside it. Niall tore his gaze away, finding the task more difficult than it should have been.

A kernel of dread took up residence in his gut, though he could not account for its presence. Niall was afraid of no odd stone! He knew as well as he knew his own name that there was no such thing as magic. Indeed, Niall found himself unduly disappointed by the sign that this woman was as mad as he had originally feared.

A quick glance to the stone she proudly wore sent a most uncharacteristic shiver down Niall's spine, however, and he scowled at the illogic of his response.

Magic was a whimsy for fools. The woman addled his wits. Too late, Niall recalled that Odo had warned him against this one's copious charms.

"And that would be your witching stone," he asked with all the skepticism he could summon.

His companion rolled her eyes. "What nonsense! I *told* you already that I am not a witch! I am but a woman, admittedly in a bit of a muddle, but 'tis a muddle that will come clear quickly enough. I have absolutely no doubt."

And strangely enough, a goodly part of Niall wanted to believe her.

His gaze fell on the pendant once more, that uneasiness raising gooseflesh over his skin. Viviane followed his gaze and smiled as she toyed with the jewel.

" 'Twas a gift from my father, on my birth," she confessed, then flashed that disconcerting smile toward him once more. "My mother said he captured the blue of the moon within the stone just for me. Is that not a most wondrous tale? It could almost make up the difference for never having knowing him." She shrugged again. "But 'tis a token of good fortune, if naught else, and never have I been parted from it."

She was a whimsical one, that much was for certain. And dangerously beguiling. Niall harumphed, thinking it poor timing to question her illusions.

"My mother told me once that if ever I had a wish to be made, I could wish upon this stone from my sire's hand and all would come right for me." The dimple danced engagingly when Niall dared to glance her way. "Is that not a wondrous gift?"

Niall could not keep his lips from twisting wryly. "One might think your current circumstance would well suit such an appeal."

But Viviane laughed merrily again, the sound making Niall think of a brook splashing through an emerald glade. He was becoming overly fanciful, there could be little doubt of that.

"There is no need to waste its power. Indeed, I have only to tell my tale to the archbishop," she insisted. "There is naught to worry about, for once I have had my hearing . . ."

In that moment, they reached the threshold of the prisoner's gate to the courtyard. Niall caught a glimpse of the archbishop, his hands braced on the arms of the high seat, his expression grimly exultant, the black and red of his garb a striking sight. Thousands gathered in the courtyard, pennants snapped against the azure sky, the smell of smoke in the air.

The sunlight glistened off the executioner's gruesome arsenal, arrayed for public view, and Niall found a lump rising in his throat.

Then the crowd caught a glimpse of the prisoner and roared for blood.

Viviane jumped back against Niall in alarm. She breathed quickly, her gaze dancing over the view accorded to them from here.

And when she turned to Niall, her smile was banished. A fearful light claimed her eyes and the tint of roses that had colored her cheeks faded to naught. There was no longer any merriment to be found in her hazel eyes.

"He does not mean to hear me," she whispered, as though she could not believe it.

Niall could not lie to her in this moment. He shook his head heavily, wishing he could tell her otherwise. "Nay."

"They said he would give me a final audience," she said wildly. "They said I would have a chance to plea my case. They said . . ." Viviane's eyes filled with helpless tears and she stared up at Niall, searching his visage for the truth.

He did not have the heart to keep it from her. He held her gaze and let her see the truth in his own.

"They lied to me," she whispered hoarsely.

Niall looked to his toes, wishing he could tear the archbishop's insignia from his back and run. 'Twas always thus, but usually the prisoners were either deserving of their fate or driven mad by their time in the dungeons. Niall cleared his throat, knowing that this time the archbishop had erred.

Not only was this woman no witch, but Viviane was too delightfully alive to die this day. Indeed, the sparkle of her company had briefly made Niall forget how his knee ached, how far his life had fallen from his own dreams.

Yet there was naught he could do about the matter. Niall hated the powerlessness of his situation, such marked contrast to what his life had been before. His task was to fulfil his duty, no more than that.

Yet, against every rule he knew, against every pledge of loyalty he had sworn, Niall hesitated to lead the woman out into the screaming throng of people. 'Twould be an ugly confrontation, it always was, rotten fruit and vulgar language taking the air. 'Twas a humiliating way to die and one this woman far from deserved.

He liked her, regardless of the addled state of her convictions.

Viviane bit her lip and blinked back her tears, glancing once through the doorway before beseeching Niall with a luminous glance. "Could I wish upon my father's stone? Would it trouble you overmuch?" Her words faltered and she seemed suddenly very young. She did not stand so tall now that her optimism had deserted her. "I . . . I might never have the chance again."

She most certainly would not. And Niall could not see what damage it would do to indulge her. 'Twould only take a heartbeat and the archbishop need never know.

But he could not risk untying her hands, lest someone unexpectedly appear. Without a word, Niall reached for her chain, noting how heavy his hands looked against the finely worked silver, against the flawless cream of her throat.

There was no time to seek a clasp, so he simply took the chain within his hands and lifted it over her head. Her glossy hair caressed his hands like the finest silk, the faint scent of her reminding him of sunshine in dancing meadows of wildflowers. Niall slipped the gem into the waiting cradle of her slender fingers and his mouth went dry as their hands brushed in the transaction.

She took a deep breath and tipped her head back, squared her shoulders and squeezed her eyes closed. Her pose was a curious blend of vulnerability and strength that tore at Niall's hardened heart and for an impetuous moment, he wished he might have had the opportunity to know more of this Viviane.

"I wish," she said softly but with passion. "I *wish* that I were as far away from here as ever a person could be."

And no one could have been more surprised than Sir Niall of Malloy when the lady shimmered right before his eyes, shimmered with the same strange blue light as was trapped in the gemstone. A flash blinded him and he heard a tinkle as he instinctively closed his eyes.

When Niall looked a mere heartbeat later, there was naught before him but a single moonstone, tangled in its silver chain, lying on the floor before him.

And the crowd beyond, baying for the spectacle of execution.

The knight spun but there was no one behind him, not a sound in the corridor. Niall bent to retrieve the glowing pendant, a shiver dancing over his flesh when he touched the fragile chain. The odd sensation made him draw his fingers briefly away, for 'twas unnatural beyond all else.

'Twas witchery.

Against all odds.

'Twas then Niall knew that he had been wrong. He cautiously picked up the pendant and considered anew its eerie light. There *were* such creatures as witches for he had just seen the truth of it. Niall had been not only in the company of one, but had been lulled into granting her the chance for freedom.

'Twas clear that he had made a grievous error in doubting his patron's knowledge.

Niall lifted his head and surveyed the roaring crowd, inadvertently catching a glimpse of the archbishop's impatient expression. The sight made his blood run cold, his hand closing instinctively over the wicked gem.

'Twas equally clear that this particular mistake would cost him dearly.

Chapter 2

Viviane cringed at the sudden blinding light that leapt from her moonstone. 'Twas silvery and blue and cold as death. She could not see anything, not even the stalwart knight directly beside her, not even her own hand. She reached for his solid strength as fear stole her pulse, but her fingers closed on emptiness.

And suddenly she felt as though her body was not her own, as though 'twas scattered to the four corners of the earth, spread thin and laid bare to the chill of an angry moon.

No sooner had Viviane formed that thought that she felt a sense of gathering. The farflung parts of her seemed to hasten together, though they did not fit as well as they did before. She felt dishevelled and disoriented, dizzy and uncertain of what had happened. The cool moonlight faded, the chill left her flesh as abruptly as it had descended.

Viviane cautiously opened her eyes, only to find herself on completely unfamiliar turf. She blinked and looked again, though the scene did not change. Then she gasped aloud, for clearly, she was not where she had been before.

Her father's charm had worked! Oh, he must have loved

her dearly to have left such a magical gift in trust for her. Viviane nearly hugged herself in delight.

But where *was* she?

Viviane was standing at the end of a dirt road, surrounded by wondrously tall pine trees and facing a marvelous span of sparkling blue water. The sky was perfectly clear, the air was warm and she could hear the birds calling. She spun in place just to be certain, but the archbishop and his palace were not to be seen.

Gone was the foul odor of the dungeons, the tang of smoke. Instead her nostrils filled with the smell of flowers, the scent of a salt sea. The air was warm, the breeze gentle, the countryside etched in glorious hues. Viviane took a deep breath and smiled.

This might have been paradise, but the great handsome knight with compassion shining in his green eyes was gone as well.

That realization made Viviane's smile disappear. Oh, to be sure, he was gruff, but there was a heart of gold secreted beneath that man's mail, Viviane knew it well. He was like one of the great knights in the tales she copied over and over again, a tawny lion, both bold and gentle, a knight worthy of serving at King Arthur's own court.

Aye, Viviane could readily imagine him atop a stomping charger, his standard held aloft, while he departed in search of the Grail itself. He would ride with deft strength, she knew it well, he would lead with authority. She wondered how he would smile.

Slowly, to be sure, with a deliberation that would heat a woman's blood.

Indeed, Viviane wished she might have had the chance to know more of this man. Aye, it could not be an easy labor her knight had in the archbishop's dungeons, and he must have a good reason to take it on, for a woman could tell with a glance that he was a knight of fearsome ability.

Viviane sighed and glanced about herself one more time,

just to be completely certain he had not been flung from that foul space along with her.

'Twas then she saw the orchard.

Off to one side of the road and continuing over the rolling land, 'twas filled with trees hanging with ruddy fruit. And this was no orchard such as those Viviane knew from home. Nay, these trees were young and vibrant, not twisted and old.

The fruit was larger than she knew possible, easily three or four times the size of the apples she regularly saw in the markets of Cantlecroft. It was redder than red and Viviane could nearly smell the sweetness of that fruit, even from this distance. She knew she had never seen trees so heavy with bounty.

And she knew that no earthly tree could bear as a single one of the dozens before her did.

Which could only mean they were enchanted.

Or unearthly.

Viviane looked to the blue water, to the sky, took a breath of the perfumed air and suddenly guessed where she had come.

As far from the court as possible.

From earthly hell to unearthly paradise. Her gaze strayed to the apples one more time and the answer came to her with perfect clarity. Nay, 'twas not Paradise in the Christian sense.

This must be Avalon.

Viviane smiled and breathed the name in wonder. Avalon! The hidden island of the ancient Celtic gods, the refuge secreted in the mists to the west of Ireland, the home to all immortal beings weary of the world and its ways. Avalon, where all was possible; Avalon, as far from the false justice and worldly wealth of the archbishop's court as anyone could ever hope to be.

Avalon, the isle of magical apples.

Viviane's pulse quickened. Though she was no bold knight herself, 'twas clear that she had found herself an adventure fitting of a grand tale. She had fallen right into one of the old stories she so loved! Could anything be more perfect? Oh,

Viviane had always wanted to visit foreign lands and exotic horizons, and Avalon was the most exotic of them all.

She was indeed a most fortunate woman! 'Twas just as she had told her knight—she was luckier than lucky and none could contest the truth of it.

Well, her mother had taught her to use her wits to make the best of what she was granted, and Viviane was not going to discard that good advice now. Indeed, she had grown adept at providing for herself these past two years since her mother's death—she considered it to be a fitting tribute to her mother's memory.

The rope her knight had knotted around Viviane's wrists was not tight enough to hurt—there was a hint of his noble character!—and some sustained wriggling let her work one hand free. 'Twas easy then to free the other, a deed she managed just before a man appeared from the woods on one side.

He was oddly garbed and she had the impression that he was a minstrel, though she could not have identified why. Perhaps because there was a disreputable air about him. He had not troubled to scrape the dark stubble from his jaw, his hair hung lank and dark, his gaze was pixie-bright.

Viviane straightened, uncertain what language might fall from his lips and wondering who the first occupant of this blessed realm to cross her path might be. His face brightened at the sight of her, though, and he looked amiable enough. He quickly strode in her direction and waved.

He wore a strange manner of chausses wrought of a dark green cloth and cropped above the knees, and a chemise that looked like purple sheepskin with teeth lining its front. Beneath he wore another chemise of some fine cloth dyed a vivid yellow hue and inscribed with script that insisted *"Just do it."*

This Viviane could not fathom. Do what? And why?

Or considered another way, what precisely did the Just do? Just deeds, she supposed, though that was hardly worthy of such acclamation.

But then, she could not be surprised to be greeted by mystery in Avalon. Wisdom was oft shrouded in riddles such as these. She knew this from the old tales.

'Twas another proof of where she was, no more than that.

"Hey, are you with that historical re-creation group?" he called by way of welcome. "Cause if you are, you're like *way* lost, honey. They're on the other side of the island today."

Island! She was right! Avalon was an island, as any fool knew. Viviane's flush of victory was quickly followed by confusion. She supposed they spoke the same tongue, though his words and his accent made it difficult to be sure.

And what did he mean?

Was his query a test of her eligibility to remain? Viviane caught her breath. Aye, 'twas said that the immortals dearly loved to play games of wit and 'twas not uncommon for them to test those whom they might indulge.

But Viviane could not risk failure. Indeed, to be returned from whence she had come would only mean certain death. She squared her shoulders, determined to prove herself as clever as could be.

There was too much at stake to even consider the alternative. "I do not understand," Viviane said carefully.

The man grinned, revealing an array of remarkably white teeth, then cocked a finger at her. "Right, I get it, you're like staying in character." He nodded with what might have been appreciation. "Cool."

Viviane perceived naught intemperate about the weather. The air here was, in fact, delightfully warm and the sun was lovely. 'Twas quite unlike the damp overcast days so typical of Cantlecroft.

Viviane eyed her companion and wondered whether she should question his conclusion. 'Twas important, she knew, to not let magical beings and sorcerers underestimate one's wits.

But before she could decide, the man continued, his gaze as bright as a cat's. "So, like where are you supposed to be from, anyhow?"

Honesty also was key, as any child knew, for the magical ones could see directly through the most artful lie. "I was raised in the midlands of England," Viviane supplied, "and 'twas 1390 when last I was told the Lord's date."

"Really?" He pushed a hand through his hair and left it yet more disheveled. Viviane supposed 'twould be easy to lose track of the years when one was immortal and living in a timeless realm.

"I had no idea you people were, like, so *specific*." He scanned Viviane from head to toe while she again tried to make sense of his words. Surely he knew that all mortals kept track of years from the Lord's birth? Or knew from whence they came?

His gaze was more forthright than she appreciated and Viviane stiffened. "I guess your costume is authentic, but it's like a bit dull, don't you think?"

Oh!

"My mother wrought this kirtle with her own hands!" Viviane declared indignantly before she could consider the wisdom of speaking her mind. "And we dyed the cloth together. 'Twas woven by the old woman in Kiltyre who knows best to spin the wool and the woad was plucked from the hills not far from town, where 'tis said to grow best. 'Twas the last labor we completed together and a fine piece of workmanship for mortal hands, and I will thank you to not belittle the result."

The man flung up his hands in surrender and took a step back. "Hey, *easy*. It was just like constructive criticism. How would I know you had so much baggage with it?"

Viviane kept her mouth closed, for 'twas clear she had no baggage at all.

Were there madmen in Avalon? She could not recall such a detail, though in this moment she most assuredly tried.

He leaned closer and his manner became confidential. "Really, though, you should like work on that accent. I don't want to hurt your feelings, but it sounds really, really fake. I'd ease up on the *'twas* action. It's just a bit over the top, you know?"

Viviane folded her arms across her chest, more than done

with this man's manners and his mysterious allusions. "Nay, I do *not* know," she said as crisply as she dared. "You speak most oddly yourself and make little enough sense, sir, in addition to the strange manner of your own garb."

"This, strange?" He laughed as though she had made a fulsome jest, though Viviane found naught amusing about her comment.

"Aye, strange 'tis and there can be no doubt of that." Viviane pointed to his outer chemise, annoyed that he would pretend otherwise. "What need has a chemise of teeth? And what whimsy turns the fleece of sheep to such a violet hue?"

He visibly preened and she wondered if his garb was some fanciful invention of his own.

Could he be one who shifted shapes?

"Hey, this is polarfleece, the good heavy-duty stuff." He lifted a fistful and shook it at her. "No sheep died for this, honey, just a few polyesters." He fiddled with the front of his chemise as Viviane wondered precisely what a polyester might be.

"Teeth," he echoed with a grin and a shake of his head. He then meshed both sides of his chemise together by means of a little bar, clearly proving the extent of his magical powers. Viviane gasped when the two edges fastened and remained together. Then she narrowed her eyes, glancing about herself cautiously.

He was not mad. He was a *sorcerer*! She would do well to not cause offense, lest he cast a spell upon her. Too late Viviane wished she had not been so quick to speak her thoughts, but then, she ought to be used to such regrets. She was not known for her silence.

She had best bide her tongue. Severely.

"Zipper," he informed her archly. "Like, hey, we may be out in the sticks, but you can't be that amazed."

Viviane was indeed amazed, but considered it unwise to say as much. Her chattering had gotten her into considerable difficulties in places much less wondrous than this.

Perhaps he—remarkably—did not realize that she was a

stranger here. Perhaps 'twould not be clever to draw attention to that fact. Perhaps if she could merely blend in, no one would think to evict her from Avalon.

Or send her back to the archbishop's court.

'Twas worth a try.

Her companion seemed to be waiting for her to say something, so she chose what she deemed the safest topic possible.

"My name is Viviane," she said with a smile. "I do not believe I have made your acquaintance."

"Monty Sullivan," the man asserted and stuck out his hand in the manner of knights pledging no harm to the other. It could not be a bad import. Viviane took his hand and shook it, as she had seen the knights do at home. "And spare me the Monty Python jokes, okay? And no, just to get it out of the way, I don't do the full Monty either."

Viviane was only too happy to nod agreement, since she could not fathom a guess as to his meaning. He seemed well disposed toward her, despite the oddities of his manner.

And her mother had always said to take fortune wherever 'twas found.

Viviane smiled her best smile. "Could you possibly aid me in finding accommodation on your enchanted isle, Monty?"

"Just arrived?"

Viviane demurred. "I seek a change."

Monty grinned. "Oh yeah, you were like probably camping out with those reenactment types. Sure, there are B&B's out here or a hotel back in town. What's your price range?" Viviane must have looked blank, because Monty leaned closer and frowned. "You know, your *budget*. Like how much cash do you have to spend every night?"

"Oh." That could be a problem. Viviane knotted her hands together. She had naught in her pockets and no purse any longer—hers had been seized when she was cast to the dungeons.

'Twould undoubtedly be better to not mention her incarceration, the charge against her, or indeed her sentence.

Convicted criminals, however innocent they claimed themselves to be, were seldom welcome arrivals in any realm.

"I have no coin."

Her companion winced sympathetically. "I know that tune. Do you like have a job?"

Viviane knew her incomprehension showed.

"You know, what you usually do for money."

"Oh! For coin, I write manuscripts . . ."

"A writer!" He clapped one hand on his forehead. "Man, I knew you were like a kindred spirit. Waiting on royalties, huh?" He hunkered closer beside her, his manner yet more confidential. "Jeez Louise, but publishers are a stingy bunch of bastards, don't I know it. Keep your money forever and a day before they finally ship it off to you, and everyone thinks cause you've got your name in print, you're a millionaire." He clucked his tongue. "Been there, done that, got the T-shirt."

He looked most earnest and Viviane did not trust herself to say anything of intelligence when she understood so little of what he meant.

Monty fortunately was undeterred by her silence. "Hey, look, take it from me. If you're gonna survive in this biz, you like gotta get a day job. There's no way around it."

"I see," Viviane said slowly, even though she did not.

Monty studied her for a long moment, then grinned. "No clue what you're going to do, right?"

Viviane smiled. She was getting used to his strange manner of speaking and considered that it might be her very good fortune that had ensured she met this sorcerer. Indeed, he did not seem troubled by her ignorance, which was most fortuitous.

"None," she admitted.

Monty pushed to his feet. "Well, lucky for you, I have connections. I think Barb's looking for someone and with my endorsement—" he snapped his fingers "—you'll be like in. I've known her forever, after all."

Forever. She *was* then in the company of an immortal—if

not under his protection—and undoubtedly going to meet another one.

Monty grinned and Viviane smiled back. "Then, we must seek out this Barb with all haste and beg her indulgence."

"Absolutely. Hey, look, I like rode my bike out here. You mind walking back to Ganges? It's about three miles."

Viviane could not imagine how else one would travel such a small distance. "A pittance." She shrugged and watched Monty retrieve a two-wheeled contraption from the edge of the woods.

"Great, then let's go, man."

Man? Viviane lifted her nose in the air as she marched to his side, knowing no one with eyes in their head could have doubts as to her gender. She itched to correct Monty, but was still leery of his magical powers.

With an effort, she kept her tone carefully neutral. "Although I appreciate your aid in this, Monty, I do not understand why you refer to me as a man."

Monty laughed as though she were the wittiest jester in the archbishop's own court. "Hey, there's not a doubt in my mind which team you play on." He eased closer to her as they matched steps. "Which is like a nice little segue into what I'd like to talk about while we walk."

Viviane met his gaze and didn't trust the light in his eyes. "Aye?" she said cautiously.

"Aye," he echoed and grinned in a most cocksure manner. "How about dinner?"

"And what of it?" Viviane frowned as they started down the dirt road. "I am hungered each and every evening, as any person of good health must be."

Monty roared with laughter. "Man, you are really something else." She fired a glance his way that sobered him. "What I meant is, would you have dinner with me?"

From his manner, Viviane guessed that this was a matter of import, though she could not fathom why. She supposed 'twas a concession that they were not to be adversaries, for 'twas vulgar to break bread with one's enemy.

But they had already shaken hands. And indeed, if she was without coin and patron, how else might she ensure that she ate at all?

"I should be honored."

"Great!" Monty fairly bounced along the road. He was a most odd man, in Viviane's eyes, all lean limbs like a young boy, yet his visage showed the passage of some years.

But then, what did one expect of sorcerers? Wise eyes and a youthful visage, if naught else. Perhaps a measure of eccentricity and a tendency to laugh.

Monty more than fit the description.

"There's a terrific vegan place in the village—they have a pad thai that is like awesome-licious . . ."

His words so quickly made no sense to Viviane that she let her thoughts wander as they walked, her gaze dancing over the beautiful pines lining the curving road. She heard seabirds calling overhead and turned to watch them, quietly marvelling. She raised one hand to brush her fingertips across her pendant, as she was inclined to do.

'Twas only then that Viviane realized that the moonstone pendant was gone.

Panic flicked through her, for Viviane was not one to lose anything, certainly not anything she held as precious. She spun and darted back along the road, ignoring Monty's cries.

But there was naught on the path where she had first arrived.

Viviane's pendant was gone.

It could have taken no small magic to wring such a great change in her circumstance, she reasoned. Perhaps the very act of making her wish had wrought the pendant's destruction. Perhaps it was a gift intended to save her but once.

Indeed, if she kept her wits about her, that should suffice.

She smiled for a puzzled Monty and returned to his side, mumbling some excuse that seemed to put his concern at ease. Moments later, they rounded a curve in the road and Viviane spied the crescent of the moon riding high in the midday sky. It looked like a sliver of silver hanging there,

the shape of it reminding her of the light that had danced
within her pendant.

Perhaps her gift from her father had become one with the
moon again. Viviane smiled secretly, rather liking the idea
of that.

Monty teased Viviane as they walked that she was "rubber-
necking something fierce" but she could not help staring at
the town they eventually entered. Avalon was so different
from anything she had ever seen before, each glance filled
with inexplicable wonders. The people were of every hue it
seemed, their garb of every shape and description, their
words impossible to catch in the wind.

Some whizzed about on "bicycles" like that of Monty,
their heads encased in brilliantly hued helmets and their
garb tight. Some rode four-wheeled carts of every shape and
colour which evidently had no need of either oxen or horses,
and made a fearsome noise as they passed. It was all very
strange yet they all took it in stride.

Viviane was clearly beyond the beyond.

Barb owned a shop perched on the edge of Ganges Harbor. It was painted in vivid hues that made Viviane feel more
at home than anything else thus far, the columns on the
porch brightly patterned in green and blue and yellow. There
were flowers growing in front of the house and little plants
tangled alongside the path, an orange cat sitting in the sun
on the porch as it cleaned its paws.

Yet the true marvel of this day of marvels proved to be the
contents of Barb's shop. Unlike the merchants' stalls to
which Viviane was accustomed, in which a counter was
opened on one wall of a workshop, the potential client actually entered Barb's shop. And there, that client was con-
fronted by a wondrous array of books for sale.

Books! The single word did not do them justice. These
manuscripts were unlike anything Viviane had seen before.
Some were filled with text and others contained marvelous-
coloured pictures of lifelike detail. And the quantity of them!

Indeed, Viviane knew with unshakable certainty that such books could only exist in a magical domain. Her conviction that she had arrived in Avalon took root and blossomed tenfold. For she already knew that Avalon was a place of learning and wisdom—it made only good sense that 'twould be rife with the most wondrous books she had ever seen.

And one would have to be immortal to even begin to read them all.

Aye, Viviane hoped that she too might have eternity in this place! The very walls were filled with crowded shelves, that alone telling Viviane that this Barb was a wealthy woman indeed. How else could she have afforded such largesse, even here?

How else could she so graciously admit strangers to finger the manuscripts that comprised her wealth?

Viviane cringed at the casual air of one woman in the shop as she rifled through a volume filled with wondrous illustrations of food. Even from this distance, the dishes looked real and Viviane knew that single volume must be worth a king's ransom. Barb must have so much coin to her name—a veritable duchess or queen!—for the damage inevitable from such careless handling to mean naught to her.

Or she might be a sorceress of untold power. This interview might prove to be Viviane's true test. Her mouth went dry at the thought.

To be certain, Barb was not dressed in the fine garb Viviane might have expected—she wore no samite nor ermine, no silk nor expensive hues. Surprisingly enough, she wore chausses of faded blue, and a dark green chemise all of a piece with a hood. She had snatched her long dark hair up in a band—no doubt to keep those long tresses from wreaking havoc all the day long—and her feet were bare, although her gold-rimmed spectacles were another unmistakable sign of affluence.

'Twas not uncommon, Viviane knew, for people of means to adopt odd habits or styles of dress. Both Monty and the other occupants of Avalon Viviane had already seen certainly challenged her ideas of appropriate apparel.

This Barb had skin the hue of honey, another marvel, and her eyes were narrow and dark. Viviane had never seen such strange and exotic features, and she tried not to gape. Certain 'twas appropriate, she bowed deeply upon making Barb's acquaintance.

Barb and Monty seemed to find this amusing.

"She's like got this fourteenth-century thing going," Monty whispered, though his words were loud enough to be audible to all.

More than once in all her days, Viviane's tendency to idle chatter had been her ruin. She recognized that Monty had brought her to a potential patron and bit back any reply that she might have made. She clasped her hands together, met Barb's gaze steadily and let Monty explain.

Though it nigh killed her, especially when she didn't quite understand his explanations.

"But, you see, the real deal is she's stranded here at this medieval fair, waiting on royalties from her publisher."

"Without a return ticket?" Barb asked skeptically.

"Hey, I can hardly criticize poor financial planning."

Barb rolled her eyes at that.

"And like who *wouldn't* want to be stranded here, it's a great place to work. You know it can take forever for publishers to ante up . . ."

"I've heard you whine about it often enough," Barb acknowledged. "Though they don't seem to have the same casual manner with their billing."

"See? Capitalists! All those suits in Toronto . . ."

"Monty, spare us the lecture," Barb chided softly. "What do you want?"

He shoved his hands into his pockets and looked more like a child begging a favor than he had thus far. Clearly Barb was his superior in terms of power and influence. "Viviane needs a job. I thought you said you needed someone in the shop."

Barb's lips pursed and she pushed her spectacles up her nose as she looked hard at Viviane. "What do you write?"

Monty did not seem inclined to answer that one, but turned to Viviane in turn, his lean face alight with curiosity.

Viviane swallowed and tried her best to not make a muddle of matters. "Romances, tales of chivalry and knights and quests afar." She did not trust herself to say any more, for she truly did not understand this matter of publishers.

It must be some fabrication of the realm she had entered—but surely knowledge of great tales of chivalry would win her some favor here? Viviane could only hope!

To Viviane's relief, understanding dawned on Barb's features. "Right! They sell really well." She gestured to one wall, the myriad books there adorned with colorful pictures and flowing type. For the thousandth time that day, Viviane fought the urge to stare.

"All right," Barb continued with a nod of resolve. "Look, here's the deal. You seem like a nice enough person, a bit down on your luck, but that's how a lot of people end up here. Since romance pretty much pays my rent"—she smiled fleetingly—"let's call this one good deed for another. Think you can watch the shop?"

Viviane glanced to either side. The shop did not look inclined to do anything unexpected, though one could not take appearances for granted when one mingled with sorcerers. "Aye," she agreed cautiously.

"I can show you the cash and credit card stuff in a few minutes. Six bucks an hour is about the best I can do, but you're free to read when it's not busy or even work on your writing. How's that?"

Viviane parted her lips, prepared to accept whatever terms were offered, even fall on her knees in gratitude, but Monty interjected. "Come on, Barb! Go to like at least *seven*. She's gotta get a place to live."

Barb folded her arms across her chest. "Off-season's practically here. The rents will get cheap."

"Right. And you'll give her less hours when business slacks off." Monty rolled his eyes. "Come on, give her a break."

"Six is it," Barb maintained with a resolve Viviane was

already beginning to associate with her. She fixed a bright glance on Viviane that made that woman straighten. "But you can have the room over the store for two hundred dollars a month if you help me clean it out. Separate entrance." She put out her hand. "I'll need a deposit. One month's rent."

"Barb! She's like outta cash!"

The woman looked skeptical. "I'm supposed to grant a complete stranger a room in my house *and* a job in my shop with no show of good faith on her part. I don't think so. Maybe you ought to ease up on the homegrown, Monty."

Viviane had no idea what this meant but her companion colored. "So like, give her an advance on her wages."

"On the basis of your sterling endorsement?" Barb folded her arms across her chest, her expression telling.

Monty swore—though the words were unfamiliar to Viviane, their meaning was more than clear. He dug in his pocket and came up with some brightly colored parchment. "Here's fifty bucks. My life savings. And if I can bend a bit for Viviane, then so can you. You're already like taking advantage of her on the wage."

Viviane understood that this was their currency, by Monty's manner and Barb's attempt to take it from his hand.

But he snatched it back. "Utilities included?" Monty prompted.

"What are you, her agent?" Barb demanded more sharply than she had spoken thus far. "I'm not made of money, you know. Season's nearly over, sales are going to go down the drain."

"But Christmas is coming, every retailer's dream . . ." Monty teased.

Barb folded her arms across her chest and glared at Monty. "She's not supposed to live off this wage, just be getting by until she gets paid. That's the best I can do—otherwise I'll just hire one of the local kids."

"I think it is most generous," Viviane interjected hastily, her years of trade telling her that the deal was on the verge of collapse. Goodness knew, even the most wealthy patron could become testy if their largesse was assumed boundless.

Monty parted with his parchment with obvious reluctance and Viviane knew she would have to repay his generosity. "By Goddess, it's even real," Barb muttered.

"Thank you very much." Monty's manner turned haughty and Viviane moved quickly to ensure the arrangement did not falter at this point. "I should be delighted to aid you in clearing the room above."

Barb surveyed her appraisingly. "Hmm, well, I've been meaning to drag a lot of that stuff down to one of the charities. Anything you can use, feel free to make your own. You don't seem to have a lot of baggage"—she punctuated that with a glance to Monty and fingered the parchment—"and there are some old clothes up there that might fit."

Viviane bowed so low that her nose nearly touched her toes. "I am overwhelmed by your generosity and shall ensure you find no disappointment with my services."

"One of those medieval freaks, eh?" Barb mused when Viviane straightened. "Well, maybe it'll bring in business. Check the section when you have a chance and let me know if there's anything in particular your friends might like. Can you start today?"

"Your wish is my command," Viviane acknowledged with a bow, her move making her miss Barb's fleeting smile.

"But she has a dinner date," Monty insisted, then grinned rakishly for Viviane. "I'll meet you here at seven."

The Gulf Islands are sprinkled between the east coast of Vancouver Island and the west coast of British Columbia. The largest of those islands, Salt Spring, has a considerable reputation as a haven from urban hassles, an enclave of artists and artisans, a destination for meandering sailboats. Although Salt Spring was originally settled because of the comparatively low price for the land—thus making settlement there an option for various Australians, ex-slaves and other adventurers—those days of economical real estate and comparative seclusion are long gone.

Viviane was not the first to believe she had discovered paradise the moment she set foot upon Salt Spring's shores. The island has been "discovered" by tourism, a fact that has driven its population to an all-time high, its privacy (and water table) to an all-time low and generally created stress where once there had been virtually none. In this case, the island's unique distinction of three harbors—all with regular ferry service—has proven to be its bane.

It's just too easy, in opinion of many, to get there.

And so, Salt Spring Island finds itself in the midst of a battle familiar to "discoveries"—that of striking a balance between the soul-pleasing pleasures of privacy and the earthy delights of a robust local economy.

Ganges, Salt Spring's main town, is a bustling haven of activity, particularly in the summer. The ferry from the B.C. mainland stops here, disgorging tourists, bicyclists and locals returning from shopping sprees in Vancouver. Ganges's harbor for visiting and resident sailboats is the largest on the island, and thus similarly busy. Restaurants, coffee shops, bakeries and art stores abound, their embrace of visitors (and those visitors' credit cards) whole-hearted.

One of the benefits to Viviane of this constant influx of people was that no one paid much attention to her arrival, nor even was interested in learning precisely how she had arrived. The population mix on the island, and the many eccentricities among those individuals, also ensured that no one cared about whatever Monty meant by her "fourteenth-century thing". On Salt Spring, it not only takes all kinds—most of them are already there.

Indeed, it was rather startling to discover how well she fit right in. Viviane marked this to the incredible tolerance of those wise beings deemed worthy enough to populate the mythic wonderland of Avalon.

The obvious wealth might have been surprising to another, but Viviane expected nothing short of perfection from the fabled land of which she had so often written. With each passing day, she was more convinced of her conclusion. Avalon this was and Avalon 'twould eternally be.

As Monty was teaching her to say, Viviane had lucked out.

And by the end of her first week in this island paradise, Viviane had developed a plan. Her primary objective was to do naught that might prompt questions, or even worse, lead to her expulsion back to where she had come. After all, any fool knew that powerful sorcerers and immortals could be testy and the archbishop had no plans for Viviane that she shared.

Here she would stay, or die trying.

Secondly, interaction with Barb's clientele had made it clear that Viviane's speech was unduly odd. She resolved to say as little as possible, lest she make a grievous error.

Viviane was not good with silence, however; it was against everything within her to not chatter fairly incessantly. All the same, there was little choice to be had. And she did watch her speech diligently, declining to use 'twas and trying to utilize the patterns she noted here.

Viviane increasingly felt as though the words she bit back were going to spill through her skin at some future, much dreaded and quickly approaching point. It was as though they welled up inside her, like a river trapped behind a dam. Viviane supposed that even in paradise, there are prices to be paid.

If she was surprised to find Avalon so focused on mundane commercial activity, she quickly found a rationale—was it not said that idleness led to wickedness? Clearly, those powers in charge of this isle had no need of trade, but used it to provide productive activity for their occupants.

'Twas reassuring to consider that perhaps 'twas not so different in Avalon from all Viviane had known.

Viviane managed to read when business was slow and was delighted to find these romances much the manner of tales she was so accustomed to inscribing on parchment. Indeed, 'twas marvelous to learn that those who inscribed the tales were yet paid as she had been, but here, they were evidently paid "royally."

Paradise indeed.

Though she labored as hard as she could, Viviane knew that she could not rely upon her patroness's indulgence forever, nor indeed upon Monty to feed her each evening. Nay, she had to earn coin of her own, and mercifully, she could still ply her old trade. Her head was full of tales, and she had but to put them to vellum once more. 'Twould ensure that she did fit in with this markedly industrious population.

And also, that she could perhaps afford a residence more private. Then she could chatter to herself, or to the very walls, in order to let out those held-back words, and that with no fear of being overheard.

'Twas her best hope of not saying something she would regret.

So, Viviane decided that she would begin with one of her favored tales, that of Gawain and the Green Knight. She could blend in the other tales of Gawain—as always she had wanted to, but could not as a copyist—and create one fine volume of that most chivalrous and noble knight. 'Twould be a tale uniquely her own. Then she would seek out these publishers, evidently so necessary yet held in such disdain by Monty and Barb.

That decided, Viviane bought markedly fine parchment—wrought of chipped wood, of all things!—and a magical quill which never needed to be dipped in ink. Each night, when the store was closed and the town fell quiet, as the stars slowly appeared in the indigo sky and the moon rode high, Viviane wrote and wrote and wrote.

And if her Gawain bore the manner and visage of a certain kindhearted handsome knight parted from her forever by magical seas, then none but Viviane would guess the truth of it.

Chapter 3

THE ARCHBISHOP HIMSELF read the Mass.

The cathedral was crowded on this morn, for most had heard the tale of Niall's pending mission in the three weeks since Viviane had vanished before his own eyes. If naught else, they were curious to see the knight who had been fooled by a witch.

'Twas not a reminder that the man in question appreciated. Niall's ears burned when he stepped into the cathedral and the whispering began.

Niall's patron—waiting serenely ahead—was a lean man, though his formidable will tinged the air even from this distance. The archbishop of Cantlecroft had an air of command that drew every eye to him, even when he sat back behind the altar as he did now. Indeed, the hair rose on the back of one's neck beneath the weight of his regard.

As Niall's did when he stepped into the central aisle. Oh, he had failed his patron in the worst way and no one was more aware of that than Niall of Malloy.

He had failed his overlord, he had questioned that man's wisdom, he had broken his oath of fealty. The archbishop owed him naught.

But that man, in his grace, had shown Niall marked compassion. He had showered Niall with gifts once that knight had declared his intent to set matters to rights. Niall's new chemise and chausses were wrought of the finest wool, his trusty blade endowed with a new scabbard heavy with jewels. A stallion of untold magnificence awaited him outside the church, that steed festooned in ribbons and caparisons befitting the glory of his intent.

And indicative of the archbishop's endorsement. It took a great man to be gracious when his command had been specifically denied. The archbishop even deigned to bless Niall's mission with his own hand.

'Twas humbling, and Niall was suitably humbled.

He was also sorely irked with the witch in question. Viviane had tricked him and that was no small matter. At least now, there could be no doubt of her guilt, for to disappear at will was no mortal feat.

Aye, Niall would fetch her back to face her rightful fate or die trying. He strode forward with purpose and knelt before the altar, savoring in a strange way, this unexpected return to the life he had once called his own.

Niall's knee complained mightily when he knelt, but he ignored its fleeting groan and kept his features impassive. The air was thick with clouds of incense that would carry the assembly's entreaties to the very ear of God. A bevy of monks brought purely to incur the Lord's favor sang like angels all around him.

The archbishop intoned the ancient words of the Mass, Niall answered in kind, then that man laid the eucharist upon the knight's own tongue. The chalice was cupped in the older man's hands and lifted to Niall's lips. Niall closed his eyes, bristling with impatience to be done with ceremony, as the chorus swelled to its final triumph.

The archbishop raised his hands, and the entire assembly fell silent of one accord.

"On this day, we gather to offer our prayers to Sir Niall of Malloy, a trusted knight in the service of this estate, and one bold enough to venture into the unknown. He pursues a witch of great wickedness and cunning, a thorn in the side of righteousness, but one of a vast number whose plague spreads across the land and darkens the sun."

The archbishop laid a cool hand upon Niall's brow. "This man knows not what he shall encounter, what challenge shall be cast before him, what obstacles he must surmount, yet he goes nonetheless. 'Tis no small thing for a heart to be as valiant as his, for a man to know what is right and pledge to do it, regardless of what the cost might be to himself."

Niall straightened, well aware of the weight of every eye upon him. In a corner of his heart, Niall dared to hope that he might be elevated beyond sentry of the prison if he succeeded in fetching the witch.

When he succeeded.

The archbishop smiled down at Niall, looking like a benevolent father. 'Twas as though he could discern the knight's heart hammering in anticipation. "This knight may well walk in the valley of darkness before his quest is complete—he has the full measure of my prayers behind his quest."

The older man cast a glance over the assembly, his expression turning stern. "And so, we dispatch this knight, surrounded by all our prayers and goodwill, that he might be protected by the grace of God wherever his path may lead."

The archbishop dipped his thumb into the holy water brought immediately to his side. "And so I say to you, Niall of Malloy, go with the grace of God"—he traced a cross on Niall's brow, leaving a damp trail—"and do His will in His creation. Render justice and defy the darkness of false idols. Return triumphant to us, Niall of Malloy, as our own Savior did return triumphant even from the clutch of death. Go forth, knowing that your heavenly reward is assured."

Niall hoped that it did not come to such a dire circumstance.

The monks sang an exultant chorus as the sun pierced the stained glass high above the altar. A beam of sunlight fell on the archbishop's bent head and seemingly enclosed him in a halo of the Lord's own favor. For all his skepticism of the unseen, Niall swore he could feel the heat of God's own will running over his flesh.

Aye, he had underestimated his patron's understanding of great mysteries once before and would not be so foolish again.

The archbishop spoke to the assembly again, lifting his hands in supplication. "I entreat you all to share in the victory over the shadows, to aid this noble knight in his mission. Raise your voices, join me now in the prayer Christ taught to those who followed him."

The assembly rose to chant the Lord's Prayer in unison, the censers swung with new vigor as the archbishop stepped back. A white tabard was passed over Niall's shoulders, its front emblazoned with a fiery red cross like those of the crusaders.

He rose at the archbishop's behest, his knee creaking loudly at the move, though the music veiled the sound. The archbishop kissed Niall's sword, which had been lying upon the altar, and returned it to the knight with a flourish. As the chant rose to a crescendo, the archbishop led Niall down the aisle of the cathedral. They stepped out into sunlight together, the glint of the archbishop's fine garments enough to blind a man.

The crowd spilled down the steps behind them and cheered, clearly in a festive mood. The last of the incense rose to mingle with the few clouds scattered overhead. Niall's belly rumbled, discontent at its emptiness after three days' fast in preparation.

Niall accepted the aid of a servant and mounted the chestnut destrier that he was now to call his own. The beast tossed its head proudly and pranced with an impatience not unlike Niall's own. He rode the beast to the steps of the church, pulling the reins up short so the archbishop's volley of holy water fell over him.

"Go then!" the archbishop cried. "Go forth, Niall of Malloy, and may you return with all good haste!"

The crowd roared approval as Niall gave the steed his spurs and rode through the throngs clustered along the street. He waved once, as regally as he thought appropriate, then looked to the road ahead, letting himself grin outright as the town fell behind him.

It had been three long years since he had ridden a destrier, three years since his knightly oath had seemed to have anything to do with his days and nights. Niall stifled an urge to simply ride forever, reminding himself that he had accepted a quest, and was pledged to clear his own name.

Aye, fulfilling that vow and resolving Viviane's mysterious disappearance would do much to retrieve what he had lost. Niall did not intend to let her influence his ability to fulfil his duty yet again.

Sooner begun, sooner finished, as his father used to say.

Outside the gates and well beyond the shadow of the village walls, Niall pulled his steed to a halt. He dismounted and gave the beast a pat, for with fortune, he would have no need of it on his journey. Indeed, his need mattered little—he doubted he had the means to take the beast with him. He took a deep breath and reached into his purse to retrieve the moonstone pendant that Viviane had dropped.

Aye, there was something wicked about the stone, of that a man could have no doubt. The sunlight was swallowed by its milky depths, the glint of light turned to fey silver. It felt alien in his hand, unwelcome and foul, as though its unnatural beauty was naught but a deception.

Niall wondered now why he had not shown the gem to the archbishop. That man would have been better able to assess it, but in the hue and cry after Viviane's disappearance, Niall had forgotten about the token stuffed into his tabard. Indeed, the archbishop might have been able to explain matters better, had he known the truth of it.

Niall turned the stone thoughtfully. 'Twas as though the gem itself did not want to face such goodness, as though it toyed with his thoughts and made him forget to reveal its presence.

There was a troubling possibility.

Niall fingered the stone, then slipped its chain around his neck. 'Twould not do to lose it, as Viviane had done. Aye, if 'twere to escape his grip, he would never be able to return from the netherworld to which she had escaped.

Indeed, Niall wondered now whether she lured him with the token to some heinous fate, whether she would toy with him when he was securely within her clutches. He had never believed in matters he could not see, but he had seen Viviane disappear, right before his eyes. The truth of that could not be denied.

However it had been contrived. Niall frowned at the stone, instinctively disliking that its abilities defied reasonable explanation.

Would it work for him?

Niall was so focused that he barely noted the sound of footsteps. Then his name was called and he looked up, his frown melting to astonishment.

For a woman trailed by a brood of children ran closer, waving madly. "Niall!" she cried again. "Wait!"

Majella? 'Twas remarkable to see her here, for she lived in a village still within Cantlecroft's domain, but a good ten miles from the main town.

Surely she had not walked this far?

In a heartbeat, she had latched onto his arm. "My baby brother!" she cried, landing a wet kiss on Niall's cheek before he could duck her embrace.

Niall noticed immediately that his sister was as beauteous as ever, though there was markedly more of her than before. Her hair was yet the same ruddy gold, her eyes sparkled, her breasts nigh spilled from her bodice.

And she was quite decidedly with child.

Just as her letter had confessed. Niall's heart twisted at this evidence of yet greater financial burden.

"Oh, I am so very glad that we managed to find you in time!" Majella breathed, taking a trio of quick breaths. She pressed a fist between her ample breasts and inhaled quickly. "We were too late for the ceremony and they said you had ridden this way, but without a horse, well, I had *no* certainty at all that we would find you in time."

We? 'Twas then that Niall realized all seven of his nieces and nephews surrounded him. A handsome brood of children, they smiled up at him with mingled admiration and exhaustion.

"You have *all* come, all this way?" Niall demanded, horrified at the cost. "What seized your wits, Majella? You have no coin for such a journey!"

And he should know the truth of that.

"Of course! How glad I am that we are in time to see you off on such a journey as this!" Majella pinched Niall's cheek as though he were but five summers of age. "The children have not seen you of late, after all, Niall. A man cannot depart on such a quest without a fair sendoff from his own blood. And besides all of that, I have brought you provisions . . ."

She began to rummage in her bag.

"Majella, there was no need for you to do this," Niall began sternly. "You should not have travelled so far . . ." As his sister's eyes clouded with tears, Niall felt his annoyance with her weaken dangerously.

Oh, women were a fair bit of trouble!

"How could we *not* come?" she cried. "You depart on a dangerous mission, one from which you may never return."

"I but right an omission," Niall said firmly. "'Twill be done quickly enough and there was no need . . ."

"No need! And you did not even write to tell me of it!" Majella wailed. "My only brother hastens to fight a wicked and Godless foe, yet does not trouble himself to say farewell! I had to learn the truth of it from a leatherworker in the marketplace, who heard it from the shoemaker, who heard from the alewife, who . . . who . . ."

With that, Majella began to weep in a most noisy fashion. Niall shuffled his feet, hating that she did this and hating even more how much it troubled him.

Majella *knew* he could not bear to see her weep.

"I did not wish to trouble you," he began in a cajoling tone.

"*Trouble* me?" she cried. "When you are about to die?"

"I do not mean to die, Majella." Niall used his most reasonable voice, to no visible effect. "I have but a mission to fulfill . . ."

"To retrieve a witch who has already enchanted you! Oh, Niall, we shall never see you again." Before Niall could think of a suitably reassuring comment, Majella fell on his shoulder and sobbed as though her heart was breaking. "The entire realm is talking of naught else than how brave, and how *doomed*, you are! You will be lost to us forever! How could I not come to see you one last time?"

Niall patted her shoulder awkwardly, scowled, and knew not what to say.

Curse women and their displays!

"Majella, compose yourself."

To Niall's enormous relief, Majella abruptly straightened and took a deep breath, her face still streaked with tears. "Aye, you speak aright. This is no time for tears." She sniffled and wiped her nose. "Niall, I brought you vittles for breaking your fast, though you may never indeed have the opportunity to savor them."

She wiped determinedly at her tears, then opened that satchel again, proceeding to empty its contents into Niall's arms. "There is pastry filled with sausage, I know how you like that, for you always did say that I made them as Mother did."

"Aye," Niall conceded.

Majella sighed and half-smiled in reminiscence. "Do you remember how we used to steal them when Mother was not heeding us? You always took mine and feigned to eat it yourself, though I knew you would return it to me."

She granted him a smile so affectionate that Niall flushed before she turned back to her satchel. "I had little enough time and the children did consume some of them on the journey, but there are a good half dozen of them left to you."

She gave Niall a hankerchief knotted around lumpy contents. The scent of meat escaped the bundle and tempted Niall's empty belly to roar anew.

"And bread from the bakery, his last three loaves this morning."

As those plump loaves were added to Niall's burden, Majella met his gaze with anxiety. "How long will you be gone? Is three loaves enough? I cannot imagine that there is a good bakery to be found in the realms of darkness."

"I would not know," Niall admitted.

Majella bit her lip, clearly concerned. "Well. There are apples, though they are from the last harvest, you can cut around the bruises and they eat well enough. If you are hungry, you will scarce note that they have shrunken . . ."

A dozen apples were piled haphazardly onto the goods Niall already held. Two escaped and rolled in opposite directions, yet when Niall bent to retrieve them, all but one of the others also leapt to the ground.

The children scattered to retrieve them, two of the younger boys making a game of kicking one apple down the road and back.

"I found some wine," Majella continued, evidently unaware of the boys' doings. She pulled a bulging wineskin from the bag, but Niall raised a hand.

"Majella, you should not have troubled yourself." In truth, Niall was much concerned by how much coin she had expended. "I shall manage well enough while I am gone."

"Oh! Now, you do not even need me!" Majella's tears welled again and her shoulders shook. "No wonder 'tis that you never told me of your departure!" she wailed. "You do not care for us at all!" Her tears began to flow with renewed vigor, and the children eyed Niall as though he were the worst criminal alive.

'Twas a most unreasonable charge she made, considering what healthy measure of his earnings went to support his nieces and nephews, but Niall knew Majella would not take well to sensible argument. He had tried oft afore to reason

with her. Instead, Niall patted his sister's shoulder awkwardly, then held her close as she wept with abandon.

He could not help but wonder whether other knights departed on noble quests under such odd circumstance.

It seemed most unlikely.

"There, there, Majella," he said gruffly. " 'Tis not that I do
not appreciate all you have done."

His sister sniffled and glared at him accusingly. 'Twas
progress of a kind.

"And I shall miss you all, of course." Niall forced a smile.
" 'Tis only that I expect to return with all haste—I did not
wish for you to worry overmuch."

To his astonishment, this confession did little to reassure
his sister.

"Oh, Niall! Of course I will worry overmuch! In all honesty, you are such a *man* sometimes!" Majella poked him in
the chest with evident dissatisfaction.

Niall was not at all certain what else he should be.

"I will miss you, Uncle Niall," declared Matthew, the eldest child at ten summers.

'Twas a most timely interruption and Niall turned to the
child with pleasure. Matthew fingered Niall's new scabbard
with awe. "Am I big enough yet to learn to handle a blade?
Will you teach me when you return?"

"And what of me?" crowed Mark, a year and a half his ju-
nior. The boys had grown markedly since Niall had last seen
them, tow-headed troublemakers both. "I can do anything
Matthew can do!"

The children, boys and girls, immediately broke into a
chorus of "me, too!" that coaxed Niall to smile. He ruffled
Matthew's hair, but before he could speak, Majella did.

"Your uncle may never come back!" she cried. "Say your
farewells, children, and remember the courageous knight
that your own blood uncle proves himself to be."

Niall frowned. "Majella, there is no need to upset the children with such whimsy."

"Whimsy!" Majella's eyes flashed and her tears disappeared. She gave his mail-covered shoulder a smack that likely hurt her hand more than it wounded Niall. "'Tis whimsy now, to show concern for the last of one's own family? 'Tis *whimsy* to endure hardship for a last glimpse of a loved one? Wasteful of coin to show such sentiment?"

As always, her rapid change of manner surprised her brother. He would never understand women and their emotional flights, he was certain of it.

He was even more certain that he did not want to.

"'Twas good of you to come, of that there is no doubt," Niall said as soothingly as he could. "But the expectation of my demise is overstated."

"Uncle Niall can best any witch!" Matthew insisted loyally. The children cheered assent, though their endorsement did not dismiss the shadows from their mother's eyes.

Majella sobered and Niall now saw the fear that fed her emotional response. "Truly you will return?" she whispered, her fingers falling of their own accord to the curve of her belly.

And there was the crux of the matter. She was reliant upon him, Niall needed no reminder of that obligation.

Just as he knew that asking after the father of this one would win him naught but more tears. Joseph, Majella's second spouse, had been dead four years. The youngest child and this one on the way could not be wrought of his seed. As for the next eldest, well, Niall did not want to count overly closely on his fingers.

The last thing he needed was more tears.

And the last thing his sister needed was more worries.

Niall looked Majella dead in the eye and smiled for her. "Aye, Majella," he said with soft determination. "You may rely upon me, as always you have." He squeezed her hand. "Never doubt that I shall return."

His sister managed to give him a tremulous smile. "As always," she echoed softly and touched her fingertips to his cheek. "Oh Niall, why have you never found a woman to appreciate you?"

She had the look about her of a woman about to land a

kiss upon him, which could only lead to more copious tears, and Niall knew better than to encourage her.

He squatted down amongst the children to deflect his sister's intentions, noting how this one had grown, and that one cut a tooth. He spoke to each, knowing all too well that they too were reliant upon him.

Even though they might not understand the truth of it yet.

"What is that?" three-year-old Elizabeth demanded, her chubby fingers reaching for the moonstone pendant. She would want it for her own if she deemed it pretty, this one.

Niall quickly snatched it away from her grasp and covered it with his hand. "'Tis a token abandoned by the witch, and one that she used to make her disappearance."

"A charm!" Mark breathed, his eyes wide.

"Aye, and one of great potency." Niall slipped it inside his tabard that the children might not be further tempted to touch it. Who knew what evil a mere brush of the fingertips might spawn in these innocents?

"Is that how you shall find her again?" Matthew demanded.

"Aye." Niall nodded at the boy's quick wits. "'Tis my hope that 'twill take me directly to her side, then back here with all haste."

Matthew frowned. "But Uncle Niall, 'tis said that witches are most cunning."

"That they are," Niall agreed. "And this one already has tricked me once, so I am doubly wary."

The children's eyes rounded in awe, likely as much at this confession as the fact that he had been in the presence of a witch.

Majella had doubtless filled their ears with too many outlandish tales. Niall frowned. They had need of a father in their lives, a man whose good sense would counter Majella's whimsy.

He thought no further before Matthew tugged on his sleeve. "In all the tales, a knight must match wits with the foe he faces."

"Aye, 'tis true enough."

"And in the tales, the knight must choose his words carefully, lest his foe turn his own words against him. 'Tis said that witches are doubly deceptive in this."

Niall smiled for the clever boy who was oft too serious. "That is uncommon wisdom, Matthew. I shall keep your good counsel in my thoughts."

But his nephew was not yet reassured. "And you must speak in a rhyme, Uncle Niall, when you use her charm. The old tales say 'tis so."

Niall did not think it fitting to observe that the witch had departed without any such rhyme to her benefit.

"'Tis sage advice you grant, and I shall heed it well." He ruffled the boy's hair and hoped with all his heart they would fare well while he was gone. "And you, young Matthew, would do well to listen less to tales and more to your labor. Have you found an apprenticeship as yet?"

Matthew's face fell and he looked to his mother.

Majella wrung her hands. "Niall, I have not had the chance . . ."

Niall fixed his sister with a stern look. "He has need of a trade, Majella, need of a way to earn a living with his hands. You owe him no less than to find a suitable apprenticeship, and 'tis time one be found for Mark, as well. You must use good sense in this."

"But I am going to be a knight like you, Uncle Niall!" Matthew declared.

"Me, too!" Mark cried. "Me, too."

Majella smiled indulgently. "Their hearts are set upon it, Niall."

Niall met his sister's gaze steadily, for he knew well enough the expense of a knight's training. So would his sister, if she had ever deigned to heed his counsel. "Then you had best wed a far wealthier man than I will ever be. I have neither the coin nor the associations to win this for even one of them."

His sister looked away, her eyes again clouding with tears. Her hand strayed to her ripening belly and Niall sighed. 'Twas neither the time nor the place for their ongoing argument.

On his return, he would resolve all of this as well, though the thought alone made him feel as though he carried the weight of the world itself. Indeed, none other would ensure these children had trades, had means of seeing food in their mouths long after Niall was gone.

Well, the sooner he departed on his quest, the sooner he could return. Niall straightened with purpose, smiled at the children, then clasped his sister's hand.

"Be well, Majella," he muttered, deliberately avoiding a downward glance as an unwelcome thought crossed his mind.

How many months would this task of his consume?

Who would ensure Majella's welfare, the safe birth of her child, the meals in the mouths of these seven, without him here? 'Twas his honor at stake and his duty to fetch the witch Viviane back again, yet all the same, Niall dreaded what would occur in his absence.

He would not consider whether his pledge to return would have any power in whatever place his witch had fled.

"We shall be fine, Niall." Majella squeezed his hand, as though she divined his thoughts, and landed a wet kiss on his cheek. She took a deep breath and forced a smile, though the shadows lingered in her eyes. "Think only of your welfare. Your victory will not be easily won."

Niall nodded, for there was naught to be said to that simple truth. He handed her the knotted hankerchief and the bread and smiled, hoping she would not take offense. "The children must be hungry, Majella," he said gently, "and we both know that they have greater need of sustenance than I."

She chewed her lip, unshed tears shining anew, and clutched her precious provisions.

"Ride the steed back to town, if he does not come with me, for 'twould be better if you walked less." Niall kissed her cheek before she could argue with him. "I thank you for your thoughtfulness," he added gruffly. "Now, eat of this fine fare yourself, as well. Your babe has need of it."

"Oh, Niall." Majella's tears streamed down her cheeks as her mouth worked soundlessly. Her hair had crept free of her braid and she looked suddenly very much like the young sister whose pastries he had feigned to steal.

The children gathered around her skirts, though, belying that impression of maidenly innocence.

"Go to the archbishop," Niall urged with sudden inspiration. "You have come this far—go and tell him that you are my responsibility. He will not let you go without."

"Oh, Niall!"

Matthew clasped his mother's hand, his eyes solemn, and Niall guessed he was of an age to understand more than the others.

Niall looked his eldest nephew in the eye. "See it done, young Matthew. I place my trust in you in this matter. Ensure the welfare of your mother and siblings in my absence."

Matthew's chest puffed up and his eyes brightened. "Aye, sir!"

Before Majella could fall upon him and weep again, Niall gripped the moonstone with one hand. He grasped the hilt of his blade with the other, knowing 'twas past time to depart. He winked at Matthew with a confidence he was not quite feeling, then closed his eyes, tipped his head back and wished aloud.

"By all that is good and holy,
Grant me but one wish fully:
Place me so near witch Viviane
That I might grasp her right hand."

It has often been said to be wary what one wishes for—in case that wish is granted. Niall, unfortunately, was unfamiliar with the expression.

Although he did get his wish.

Chapter 4

FOR VIVIANE, ONE of the great joys in Avalon was the Saturday market in downtown Ganges. It was endearingly familiar—in concept if not in product—to stroll through the stalls of local artists and farmers. The market could be overwhelmingly busy on a sunny Saturday, but Viviane found a bittersweet familiarity in its hustle and bustle, no less its handmade treasures, a familiarity that reminded her all too much of what she had left behind.

She talked every week to the man who made his own cheese from the milk of his own sheep, she regularly admired the flowers a woman had grown from seed, she watched the skilled leatherworker; she was always awed by the array of obviously magical and mysterious masks. Such was Viviane's obvious enthusiasm for the market that Barb indulged her request to have Saturday mornings off.

And so, despite Viviane's interest in the bobbing white sailboats and the way they raced across the ocean, and despite Monty's considerable persistence, it was a full three weeks after her arrival that he finally convinced her to join his friends for a jaunt in their sailboat.

And only then because he chose a Sunday.

It was a perfect day, the sky as clear as could be, the sunlight glinting off the water, the sail snapping in the breeze. There were four of them aboard the sailboat—Monty and Viviane, along with the older couple who commanded the obviously magical craft.

If their host and hostess were inclined to leave Monty and Viviane alone together more often than might have easily occurred, Viviane failed to notice that, much less guess its import.

Certainly, Monty was in fine spirits—he looked to have laid hands on a new green chemise and odd footwear for the occasion. These "Tevas" as he called them seemed no more than black slabs secured to his feet with colourful straps, though those straps magically meshed together at Monty's dictate.

It seemed that fastenings of all sorts, particularly for garb, were his magical domain. Viviane thought it a rather humble speciality and considered for the first time that Monty might not be a particularly skilled sorcerer.

Once it became clear that sailing was new for her, Viviane was treated to a tour of the gleaming ship. Derek's proud claim that he and Paula lived aboard the boat for the entire summer amazed Viviane, as did the gaggle of mysterious shiny implements secreted below. She did not dare insult her host by asking him to explain his magic, though Viviane was suitably impressed.

The drinks quickly served up were even more impressive. Dark-haired Paula bounced around the little galley like a mad pixie, periodically handing out large cups filled with frothing cloudy green liquid. Though Paula's face was lined and full of character, her hair was a resolute raven hue, unthreaded with silver, and her enthusiasm was that of a woman younger even than Viviane. Her partner, Derek, was a spare and soft-spoken man who gave a great impression of strength, his silvered temples and the glint of humor in his blue eyes hinting at a considerable wisdom.

These two were proof again to Viviane that she had taken

up residence among the fey. When Derek declined Paula's margueritas, insisting that he was "driving" though he did no more than toy with the sails, Viviane wondered what manner of concoction this might be.

Although Monty accepted his with enthusiasm.

Viviane sipped cautiously, her first taste so tart that it puckered her lips. She wondered fleetingly what magic the brew would wreak, but found the second sip was markedly better. And truly, what could befall her? Naught but good fortune, Viviane was certain.

She was uncommonly lucky, after all.

Instead of cheering her, the thought reminded Viviane of her mother. In fact, the hue of this marguerita echoed that of a peridot her mother had worn. The gem had been locked in a ring her mother had once been granted as payment, Viviane recalled.

The memory was saddening. Viviane remembered having to sell the treasure, the recollection more vivid than she would have preferred. She took a deep gulp of her drink.

The ring had been her last token of her mother and not one readily released. But now it was gone, handily sold, the coin spent in turn, the ring lost to Viviane forever across a chasm that could be transversed only by a select few.

Viviane felt suddenly flat. She slipped away from the chatter of her companions and leaned against the rail, letting the wind tousle her hair as she watched the verdant green of the islands slip past.

It had been two years since her mother fell ill and died, two years in which Viviane had not grown accustomed to solitude. In Avalon, it seemed, she missed her mother even more than she had in Cantlecroft. What would her mother have made of immortality? What if she had survived just those two years and accompanied Viviane here?

But if she had been alive, then Viviane would not have been at the archbishop's court. Viviane frowned. What if she had used the power of her pendant sooner? Could she have saved her mother, then?

She drank again and her mood sank yet lower.

Perhaps such doleful memory was the price of the beverage.

Indeed, Viviane realized that she had never been quite so alone on mortal soil as she was here in Avalon. Here, she was the different one, the sole mortal.

And here she was compelled to be uncharacteristically silent. All those words she had bitten back in the last three weeks rose in her throat, as though they would choke her. Viviane took another swallow of Paula's potion, hoping it would ease some of her anguish.

Viviane knew that she could never risk confiding the truth of her arrival in another here. She could not guess what they would make of someone who had not been chosen and guided to the hidden isle as was the traditional way.

Would she be expelled from Avalon, if she was thought to have no right here? Viviane shuddered despite the sunlight, just the memory of those cold dungeons enough for her.

Yet despite the threat full honesty posed, the prospect of infinite silence was not appealing.

Not in the least.

Would Viviane *always* be alone? She could not help but conclude that she would never be enough like these rightful occupants of Avalon that she could become great friends with any of them. She still missed chunks of any given conversation, although she had studied and tried to blend in.

These Avalonites simply thought differently than she. It was a mark of the fact that they were chosen to be here, she was sure of it.

What good was Avalon if she were doomed to solitude for all her days?

What if she also was immortal, simply by stepping on these enchanted shores? Viviane gulped at her drink.

What if she spent all of eternity in virtual isolation here, selling Barb's books by day and writing fanciful tales alone in her room by night? What if she were doomed to live like this *forever*?

That was a grim prospect.

Viviane thought glumly of the knight she would never know, an indulgence she was granting herself with greater frequency of late. Perhaps she should have never made that wish upon her pendant.

What would have happened if she hadn't? Would her knight have saved her? Swept her away? Defended her life and her honor?

Viviane liked to think so. He had certainly looked like a man who would do such a noble and bold deed. She smiled slightly, the realization that he was far, far beyond her horizons sweeping that smile away.

Viviane took another hearty gulp of her drink and watched the sunlight sparkle on the sea. She gripped the rail with her right hand as the boat sliced through the waves. Her drink was safely held in her left, and she turned to glance over her left shoulder when Monty called her name.

"Viviane! Does Barb have any Thai cookbooks in stock? Paula wants to learn and I'm sure I saw one there."

Before Viviane could answer, something flashed to her right. She pivoted in time to see her knight—*her* knight!— jab a gloved finger through the air at her.

Viviane gasped.

"Aha! At your own right hand!" he bellowed, then dropped with a resounding splash right into the sea.

Viviane dropped her drink. She lunged after her Gawain but caught only a fistful of his cloak as he sank like a stone.

A thoroughly mail-clad stone.

And one that threatened to pull her overboard right after him. Viviane hooked her toes beneath the rail and yelled for help.

Derek knew his eyes weren't deceiving him, because he'd declined one of his soul mate's near-lethal margueritas. Someone had to be sober, in his opinion, and as skipper, he was his own first choice.

All the same, he couldn't explain the sudden appearance

of a medieval knight to starboard. The guy seemed to pop right out of thin air. That knight hovered briefly in the air and, remarkably enough, seemed to know Viviane.

It made absolutely no sense.

But what happened after that made perfect sense. Medieval knights—men of any time or occupation, in fact—seldom levitated successfully above the surface of the ocean.

At least not for long.

The knight fell into the sea with a perfectly predictable splash.

"Man overboard!" Derek roared. "Trim the sails!"

Paula knew the drill and dropped her drink posthaste (he'd always suspected that she never really drank much of hers) and set to the task of lowering the sail out of the wind. He heard the splash as she cast an anchor overboard, but he was on the run.

"Please hurry!" Viviane begged. Derek was glad to see that she had a grip upon some part of the man.

Derek grabbed the life preserver and dove off the side of the boat. The ocean was cold enough to nearly make his heart stop, even at this time of the year. Derek kicked off his old deck shoes, surrendering them to the sea, and forced his eyes open. His heart stilled at the way the knight drifted bonelessly below the surface. The man's cape was snared by Viviane, yet he just hung from her grasp.

Like a dead weight. He wasn't even fighting.

Definitely easier to haul aboard, but not a good sign.

Derek broke surface, his lungs bursting, took a gasping breath, then dove down one more time. He quickly lashed the life preserver to the man's waist and was relieved to see him rise slightly, despite the obvious weight of his chain mail.

It was the real thing, amazingly enough, and one hell of a bad choice for swimwear. Derek caught the man around the neck and lunged for daylight once more, his lungs aching for air, his muscles screaming at the man's weight.

Monty and Paula cheered when he broke the surface, Viviane looked as though she might faint in relief.

"He weighs a ton!" Derek shouted, then began mouth-to-mouth resuscitation.

To his enormous relief, the big man almost immediately sputtered and shook his head. His eyes opened, then he turned to choke out all the seawater he had swallowed. Derek hung on grimly, one arm locked around the man's chest, the other clutching the rope lashed to the sailboat's side.

The knight's gaze swivelled back to meet Derek's, that green stare surprisingly hostile. "What manner of man are you to lock your mouth upon mine?" he demanded hotly.

Derek sagged with relief. The guy was going to be okay.

"A man who doesn't like drownings to happen on his boat." Derek grinned, then turned the knight toward the boat. "Go ahead, haul yourself up, cowboy. You can tell us later where the hell you came from—and maybe explain your choice of bathing suit."

To Derek's surprise, the knight *did* manage to haul himself up the side of the sailboat. It was no mean feat, given the weight of his mail and his wet clothing, which looked like it was made of really thick wool. That sweeping cape alone had to weigh more soaking wet than Derek did himself.

Derek followed suit, glad that everyone was fussing over the knight and missed the fact that it took him two tries to pull himself up over the rails.

He had to start doing those sit-ups again. A man looking at fifty couldn't assume that the old body was going to take care of itself any longer. Derek had always been long and lean without worrying much about it, but—he surreptitiously pinched the flesh around his waist and grimaced—years of living well seemed to be finally catching up with him.

The knight stood in the middle of the deck, his feet braced against the polished wood as he made a puddle of tremen-

dous size. He had presence, you had to give him that, and
Derek doubted he was the only one wondering at the breadth
of his shoulders and chest. He looked as though he had
stepped out of a Shakespearean play.

This guy *really* worked out. Derek hoped that his wet
T-shirt wasn't showing the little ripple that had taken up residence around his middle to serious disadvantage. He
plucked at the wet cloth, trying to keep it from clinging too
tightly.

Suddenly the knight fixed Derek with that piercing green
glare. "You ask how I come to be here"—he boomed, then
looked about himself with obvious skepticism—"wherever
this might truly be." The knight arched one brow as he
locked gazes with Derek again. " 'Tis the doing of the *witch*
harbored among you."

And he pointed one thick, wet-leather-encased finger at
Monty's new friend.

Matters were not proceeding precisely as Niall had expected, even after he had stepped away from Majella and her
provisions.

He supposed he had not fully expected the pendant to
work its magic again. A lifetime of skepticism took more
than even Viviane's unexplained disappearance to be completely dispelled. But any lingering doubt had been dismissed when the eerie light enveloped him as the last word
of his wish crossed his lips.

That light was blue and chilly and altogether unnatural.
Niall had been unable to see anything at all. 'Twas as though
he had been struck blind and left on a windy hilltop in the
same moment, a far from delightful sensation.

Added to this was the very unusual sense of having been
taken apart and put rather inexpertly back together again.
Niall felt all jumbled and tousled even before he opened his
eyes and glimpsed Viviane's familiar features.

Aha! His heart had leapt with painful enthusiasm at first
glimpse of her smile—a triumphant skip, no more than that,

for he could not be glad to see the woman otherwise. Aye, 'twas the portent of fulfilling his quest that sent pleasure searing through his veins.

Was it not?

Niall had little chance to consider the matter before his unexpected fall into the salty sea. The lean man's unwelcome embrace was the next puzzling event in this rapid succession, followed by a complete lack of censure from these strangely attired people after his damning announcement of Viviane's occupation.

Last but not least, was the witch's own response.

"You're here and safe!" Viviane cried and flung herself into his arms. Niall could do naught but catch her, though he stared dumbfoundedly down at her delighted smile. Indeed, he could not seem to shake the last vestige of moonlight from his thoughts.

She was *glad* he pursued her? What madness was this? Had she not heard what he had just said?

But then, he recalled she had been anxious to meet her fate before.

And she had insisted upon her innocence then. Niall stared into her marvelous eyes, and once again acknowledged an unwelcome seed of doubt. There was something in this woman's clear gaze, in her delight, in her very presence that made him question anew all he knew of her.

Nay, she was guilty, as the archbishop decreed. He had seen the truth with his own eyes. Niall frowned, but the lady did not seem affected by his manner.

"I have been thinking of you ever since that day," Viviane confided with that smile that could warm him right to his toes. "Though I never imagined that I would see you again, and certainly not here!"

Ah, she did not expect a God-fearing mortal to be able to visit her dark domain. That was telling!

Yet instead of feeling triumphant at this hint of proof, Niall was disconcertingly aware of the fullness of Viviane's breasts pressed against him. Her auburn hair was loose, obviously designed to ensnare a man within its tangles, yet her gaze was as clear and golden as he recalled.

And as trusting. Niall's heart clenched.

"I *knew* you were a gallant man," she breathed, "a true knight if ever there was!"

Viviane stretched to her toes and granted Niall his second kiss in quick succession. This one was markedly more pleasant, though her lips barely brushed across his own. He told himself sternly that it should *not* be welcome in the least.

'Twas only that 'twas from a woman that reassured him that matters were as they should be. Aye, that was the way of it.

And he must remain vigilant against temptation, lest he fail to complete his task once again. Niall thrust the witch a discreet distance from his side and resolved to keep his thoughts firmly fixed upon his responsibilities.

Sadly, his gaze strayed over the witch's alluring legs, which he could not help but note were bare to mid-thigh and beguilingly curved. Her kirtle was craftily constructed to display her charms—which were copious—and indeed, there was markedly little of that garment. She wore some flimsy manner of footwear which left her feet nigh fully exposed to view, and her toenails were crimson.

Blood red.

Niall swallowed, certain he had never seen any feminine frippery as alluring as those crimson-tipped nails. He stubbornly lifted his gaze, only to note the wisp of naught that flowed around her hips. Her kirtle was not only short, but 'twas uncommonly thin. A man could tear that garment off with his teeth, of that Niall had no doubt, and he felt an unruly desire to volunteer.

Of course, that was *not* why he had come, regardless of how delightful the legs of his prey might be.

This time, he must keep his mind upon his task.

With an effort, Niall forced himself to consider the remainder of the company.

A man there was, besides the one who had kissed him so

fully, and another small woman. Niall scanned his surroundings hastily—though he did not intend to linger long, he was curious as to where Viviane had fled.

But Niall could not name this place. Indeed, 'twas so perfectly wrought that it could not be real. It certainly was unlike any corner of England he had ever seen.

Niall's eyes narrowed. The archbishop was right—Viviane had fled beyond the beyond. And this place could not be all that it pretended to be. Nay, this was but an alluring guise cast over the darkness of the netherworld. 'Twas intended to deceive the unwary.

Just as Viviane's beauty hid her traitorous heart.

Well, Niall was wary enough for two. He skeptically surveyed the sky of vivid blue, the water as radiant as a glinting sapphire. The land stretched in great curves around them, though Niall could not guess whether 'twas a morass of islands on all sides or some single jut of land that twisted like a serpent.

The trees that clung to the land were starkly drawn, their boughs drawn to grow in one direction by an evidently strong and prevailing wind. They gripped the veined grey of bare rock with great presence and no small measure of stamina. Seabirds cried overhead as the waves lapped at the sides of their craft.

For they five were aboard what was clearly a ship, though 'twas unlike any vessel Niall had yet seen. 'Twas all wrought of gleaming white, the glimmer of the sunlight upon it so bright as to make a man wince.

"You know him?" demanded that second man. He was as sparse and bedraggled as an unkept dog, his manner little better. Niall assumed him a servant or a beggar of some kind, though his tone was most haughty.

"Well, sort of," Viviane acknowledged, with a sly smile to Niall. Her grip tightened on his arm and her eyes glowed. His heart skipped a beat, though Niall told himself 'twas only because it had been overlong since a woman regarded him with such welcome.

Save his sister.

And Viviane herself on that fateful morn.

Niall scowled, hoping the witch would be dissuaded by the fierce expression that had sent warriors fleeing from before him in the past.

But Viviane was unaffected.

"He *did* save my life," she purred and nestled yet closer to Niall. "Just like Gawain, from King Arthur's court, who so nobly saved the besieged lady in his adventures."

A murmur of appreciation echoed across the deck. The drenched man nodded and the other woman smiled. The bedraggled man folded his arms across his chest and looked displeased.

Niall felt the back of his neck heat beneath their admiration and felt the need to correct the witch's false conclusion. "'Twas naught . . ." he began to protest, but the witch interrupted him.

"You see, he's so wonderfully modest." Viviane sighed and treated him to a smile so warm it could nigh melt the bones of a man unprepared against her allure. Even Niall's resistance wavered. "He *did* save my life, he did!"

"And now you've saved his," the tiny dark-haired woman declared with approval. She clasped her hands together and sighed rapturously. "Perfectly closing the circle and sealing your entwined fates. How wonderfully romantic!"

The man who had hauled Niall from the ocean cleared his throat pointedly. "*Some* others were involved," he commented with a sharp glance to that woman.

They were a pair, Niall immediately concluded, for the woman's eyes widened and she scampered to the man's side to make amends. "Oh, of course! You were *heroic*, Derek, just the way you dove over the rail . . ." She sighed as though much enamored of the man's deeds and Derek exchanged an amused look with Niall.

He winked and Niall knew not what to do.

In ordinary circumstance, Niall would have assumed they

shared a manly jest over a woman's approval, but still he
could feel the imprint of this Derek's kiss.

'Twas a situation rather outside of his experience.

And one of little import. Niall had a mission to fulfil. As
Matthew insisted, 'twould be prudent to see matters resolved with all haste. Sooner begun, sooner finished.

Niall caught Viviane tightly around the waist, refusing to
consider the price she would pay upon their return. 'Twas
sympathy for her that had led him awry in the beginning and
Niall was not a man to make the same error twice.

Niall closed his free hand around the moonstone pendant
and took a deep breath, trying to compose a verse to wish
them back where they belonged.

"Oooh, you're soaked and cold," Viviane complained as
she pulled away from him with a shiver. Niall was tem-
porarily disconcerted by the bold display of her nipples, taut
beneath the thin and now wet cloth of her chemise.

Nay! He would not be tempted! Niall gritted his teeth and
made to wish.

But the witch crowed with delight before he could summon a verse to his lips.

"You brought it!" She pried the moonstone free from a
startled Niall's fingers as her eyes widened in awe. "Oh, you
wonderful man! I just knew that you had a good heart, I just
knew that you were a true hero."

She flung her arms around his neck and kissed his cheek
yet again. Niall caught a disconcerting whiff of the scent of
her skin, more feminine than anything he had smelled in
years. The wind and sun had filled her hair with the smell of
outdoors, yet a perfume reminiscent of the finest flowers
teased his nostrils. His eyes closed, his hands fell of their
own accord to the neat indent of her waist.

How long had it been since he tasted a woman fully?

Niall inclined his head to kiss her fully, his eyes drifted
closed before he considered the wisdom of his impulse. But
Viviane lifted the chain of the pendant over his head with
nimble fingers and proudly dropped it over her own.

Niall gasped but she had turned away to show the others.

"You see? Isn't this just perfect? First, he saved my life, then he returned my pendant, then, oh"—she turned a shining glance upon Niall—"you show up just when I'm thinking about you and wondering about you, almost as though you heard my thoughts!" Viviane rewarded him with yet another dizzying kiss.

Clearly she had discerned that he could be twisted to her will in this way, for this kiss fell leisurely upon his mouth. Niall tried to fight his response, knowing 'twas no coincidence that her soft lips so adeptly coaxed his response, that her tongue nudged against his own lips.

But he lost. His fingers tightened, gathering a fistful of that bewitchingly sheer cloth and brushing against the ripe curve of her buttocks.

She fit perfectly against him, her lips soft and alluring beneath his own. Aye, his blood was roaring, though he fought to remind himself that she sought only to manipulate him.

Charm or nay, he *wanted*. Niall might have tightened his grip upon the temptress's waist, slanted his mouth possessively across hers, intent on thoroughly sampling all she offered.

But Viviane danced suddenly out of his grip, taking her talisman distinctly out of his reach. Niall instinctively snatched after her and the pendant, and she laughed.

Zounds, she was more unpredictable than Majella!

Viviane's cheeks flushed prettily as she shook a finger at him, clearly savoring his frustration. "Not in front of everyone!" she chided, mischief in her eyes. Her kirtle lifted in the breeze, as though 'twould tease him with a greater glimpse of her slender thighs. Their gazes locked and a heat rose between them, a heat that Niall longed to turn to his own advantage.

How he wished he could show this sorceress the fire she awakened!

And how he wished he yet had a grip upon that talisman. He took a deep breath. Somehow Niall must win it back from her, and with all haste. 'Twas clear enough that he could not trust even his own response in this woman's presence.

But Viviane seemed intent on reminding him that 'twas she who would call the tune. She held the pendant out for the perusal of the others, the chain dangling from her fingertips, the stone winking in the sunlight.

"Look? You see?" She was as delighted as a child with an unexpected sweet. "My mother gave this to me, it was a token from my father, but I lost it on the way here. I was so disappointed." Viviane turned a dewy smile upon Niall. "But my very own knight brought it back to me. Just like an old tale of lovers true."

It seemed that 'twould be churlish to snatch at the woman in this particular moment and be gone. Niall folded his arms across his chest and resolved to await his chance.

"What a guy," the disreputable-looking one said sourly. "You should have told me you'd lost it—I would have found you another one."

"But not *this* one, Monty," Viviane insisted. "You couldn't have brought this one. He had it, he kept it safe for me. There's a special bond between us . . ."

Monty of the poor grooming grimaced. "So, does *he* have a name?"

Viviane blushed so demurely that Niall felt his own flesh heat.

A maidenly temptress. 'Twas an intoxicating combination. He resolved in that moment that he would have one thorough kiss from this woman before he returned her to the archbishop.

'Twas only fair, after she had kindled such a flame within him.

One kiss. Just the prospect tightened his chausses.

"Well, I . . ." Viviane hesitated, casting a glance Niall's way through her lashes.

"I am Sir Niall of Malloy," he declared with resolve, "and

I am pledged to the service of the archbishop of Cantle-croft."

"Niall!" Viviane echoed with a smile that made Niall's belly warm. "The champion of champions. You see, it suits him perfectly. My champion, too."

But Monty rolled his eyes. "And who is this archbishop? And where is *Cantlecroft*? I've never heard of it! And where the hell did you even come from?" He snapped his fingers. "People don't just like pop out of thin air, you know."

The other couple eyed him with undeniable curiosity and Niall knew none would let him evade this question. "The witch brought me to her side with the power of her magic," he said slowly, feeling the explanation was hopelessly inane, but not wanting to reveal the truth of her token when it was out of his own grip.

"Magic! What a bunch of crap!" Derek flung out his hands in obvious exasperation and Niall warmed to the man immediately. The world could not have enough men of good sense! "Witches! Circles closing and entwined fates." He shoved a hand through his hair. "Jesus! Spare me the rest of this. It's all a little too familiar for my comfort level."

"But Derek . . ." the tiny woman protested.

"But *nothing,* Paula. I tell you, when the talk turns to magic, angels and horoscopes and who knows what kind of garbage can't be far behind." He made a sweeping gesture with one hand and glared at the small woman. "I'm over my threshold for this stuff for the year, maybe for the decade."

He wrung out his sodden chemise as he strode to an opening that Niall had not noticed. There were stairs leading to below the deck and he halted there to shake a finger at his woman. "Didn't we make a deal for this trip? No mumbo jumbo?"

She shuffled her feet. "Oh, but Derek, this just *happened . . .*"

Derek arched a skeptical brow. "You mean you're not going to insist that it's fate or something similar?"

The little woman flushed guiltily and Niall suspected

these two knew each other too well to be fooled. "Well . . ."
she began tentatively, flicking a glance to her man.

"Fate!" Viviane breathed and danced toward Niall again,
her eyes shining. "That's exactly what it is! You followed
me here because we're destined to be together. In all the old
tales, it's exactly that way—the people who are destined to
be together forever find each other over and over again, despite the odds against them." She smiled in a way that truly
did make Niall feel like a champion. "Oh Paula, isn't this
just perfect?"

The two women grinned at each other, Derek and Niall
exchanged telling glances.

Derek flung his hands skyward again. "See? *See* what I
have to deal with? Every day more of the same. Crystals and
runestones and dreams of import and tarot cards." He
snorted. "I'm going to change into something dry." Derek
cocked a finger at Niall. "You want to escape this conversation, you're welcome to borrow something and do the
same."

Niall, though, was not entirely certain he wanted to be
alone in a small space with this kissing man. He bowed and
summoned his best manners. "I thank you for your hospitality . . ."

"Yeah, well, thanks for not drowning on my watch,
wherever the hell you came from. Paula, if ever a man
needed one of your concoctions, Sir Niall here would be
my prime candidate." He granted the little woman a stern
look. "Maybe you could remember our deal by the time I
come back."

With that, Derek stomped down the stairs in obviously
poor temper. An unrepentant Paula stuck out her tongue at
his back and Monty laughed.

"What deal is this?" he asked.

"Oh, Derek would only sail up here if I didn't go all
woowoo on him," Paula explained breezily, then rolled her
eyes. "His term. Don't worry about him. If he just learned to
trust his inner voice, he'd be much more at peace in this

life." Paula dropped her voice confidentially. "It's an Aries thing, you know, it's not like he can help it."

Niall blinked at this incomprehensible claim, his gaze rising of its own accord to meet Viviane's. She looked as confused as he was by this reference and shrugged when their gazes caught. Niall almost smiled at the sudden sense of camaraderie between them, but managed to catch himself and scowl instead.

It still did not halt Viviane's smile.

Monty tapped his toe. "But I don't get it. So, like, what's the whole story here? Have you got magical powers or something, Viviane? You holding out on us? How'd you make this guy just show up *poof*?"

"She is condemned as a witch and sentenced to die," Niall felt it pertinent to explain.

Both Paula and Monty looked alarmed by this, but Viviane lifted her chin. "I'm not a witch." She looked directly at Niall. "I told you that before," she added, her voice soft with accusation, then her eyes filled with a hurt far more compelling than Majella's tears. "I thought you believed me."

Niall felt an unwelcome jab of what could have been guilt.

Aye, he wanted to believe Viviane; indeed, when she turned that tearful gaze upon him, Niall *did* believe her.

And that was the root of the problem.

Before meeting Viviane, Niall had believed himself to be a good judge of another's heart. Now, he *knew* he was wrong about her, knew it without doubt, yet his heart insisted he should believe her still.

He hesitated too long, for Monty moved quickly to console Viviane, sliding one arm around her waist and shooting a triumphant glance at Niall. "Hey, babe, don't you think this fourteenth-century thing is like getting a bit out of hand? Sentenced to *die*?" He grimaced and Viviane smiled wanly.

When she leaned against his shoulder, this Monty's expression turned smug.

Niall felt his lips thin. So that was how 'twould be. Not that it mattered to Niall where the witch granted her favors. Nay! 'Twas a better thing to be so clearly reminded that her temptation of him truly meant naught.

He folded his arms across his chest and let his voice turn stern. "Aye, I was fool enough to believe your tales afore, and indulge your request. Now the price must be paid in full, and that at the archbishop's command."

Viviane's head snapped up. "The archbishop lied to me!"

Niall could hardly argue with the simple truth of that.

Before he could decide whether to debate the matter or simply seize the witch and be done with it, Paula laid a hand on his arm. "Derek's right, you've *got* to get changed. With this wind, you'll have pneumonia in no time."

"My garb is perfectly suitable."

"It's wet!"

"I shall don dry garb upon my return homeward."

"You can't wait that long!" Paula caught at Niall's elbow when he did not move, leading him to the small ship's hatchway. "You have to get into some dry clothes before you catch a chill, then I'll make you a nice marguerita."

"Nay, I will not be parted from the witch," Niall argued. "I cannot let her from my sight!"

"Viviane isn't going anywhere." The small woman pushed him toward the stairs as Niall found himself unexpectedly confused by the sweet smile Viviane suddenly bestowed on him. "I promise."

Niall hesitated, caught between duty and comfort.

"Where would she go? We're out at sea," Paula chided. Her words were little reassurance, for Niall knew well enough that the pendant Viviane fingered could take her anywhere she so wished.

He pivoted to face the witch, not surprised to find her gaze locked upon him. And once again, Niall was tempted to trust her.

"You must grant me your pledge that you will be here when I return." he demanded of her.

Viviane sobered and straightened, though she could not or did not quell the expression of feminine delight lingering in her eyes. Niall wondered what conclusion she had made now, then her words fell low and filled with conviction. "I do. I swear it to you."

Niall's heart thumped at the way Viviane's luminous gaze clung to his, but her pledge, whatever 'twas worth, was likely all the guarantee he would win.

And, yet again, as much as he might have preferred otherwise, Niall believed her.

Curse women and their wiles!

Paula rapped an authoritarian finger on his arm. "Derek won't let anyone drown on his boat and I won't let anyone catch pneumonia. Come on, don't fight me on this." Paula grabbed Niall's tabard and pulled him hard toward the stairs. "Derek must have something that will fit you."

Niall spared the witch one last glance, and the moonstone pendant winked in the sunlight, as though to remind him of his own pledge. 'Twas true enough that Viviane affected his thinking, but Sir Niall of Malloy was not without a certain charm of his own.

He would win possession of that pendant and return to the archbishop's court, or die in the attempt. 'Twas a quest he had committed to fulfill, after all.

And he would have one lingering kiss to call his own before all was said and done. 'Twas only reasonable, given how Viviane seemed determined to tempt him.

One kiss surely could hurt naught.

Chapter 5

Her KNIGHT HAD followed her!

Viviane could hardly believe her luck. Oh, her fortune had changed for the better when she met Sir Niall of Malloy, there was no doubt about that! She had always been lucky, but this man seemed to bring out the best that Dame Fortune had to offer.

Or maybe Dame Fortune—in concert with the blue moon watching over Viviane's birth—had picked this knight out just for her. Oh yes, Viviane had made the right choice in having her Gawain look just like Niall—he was a perfect hero. Niall's pursuit of her, his return of her beloved pendant, it was just like an old tale and proved the kind of man he was beyond any doubt.

Viviane hugged herself, impatient for him to make a reappearance from below. Niall was every bit as big and burly and gruff as she remembered; oh, he roared, but she could see that enormous heart of his just shining in his eyes.

It was pretty obvious that Niall was what Monty called a straight-and-narrow kind of guy, someone who was concerned with following the rules and upholding justice.

It was what made him such a wonderful knight.

But, of course, that meant that he was troubled that she had been found guilty as a witch. It was only natural. Anyone could see, though, that he didn't quite believe it. After all, he had followed her, even with that cloud hanging over her name.

The only possible explanation was that he was in love with her. That was the only reason men overlooked things like that.

It wasn't such a far-flung thought. Viviane was sure that she was pretty much in love with Niall already. What woman wouldn't be? If not all the way in love, she could certainly get there from here. And the way he looked at her—she shivered in delighted recollection—well, it made her tingle right to her toes.

As soon as Viviane explained the truth to Niall, as soon as he knew that the archbishop was wrong and that she wasn't really a witch, well, it would be obvious to him as it was to her that they were meant for each other.

And clearly, since he was her knight, then she was his lady, which could only mean that he would defend her to his dying breath and all that good stuff. It was always that way in the tales and it was certainly that way in Viviane's book.

Absolutely perfect.

When Niall's head appeared at the top of the stairs, his golden hair glinting with the sunlight, Viviane's breath caught in her throat. He stretched, not unlike a great cat and turned his face up to the sun, as though he savored the heat of it upon his skin. It was not Viviane's imagination that he seemed to grow stronger beneath those caressing rays, bigger and more thoroughly golden.

Gawain, after all, was linked to the sun, Viviane remembered that. The legendary knight's strength waxed until midday, then waned to midnight. He could only be defeated in the afternoon, and that on the shortest day of the year, the blackest night of winter.

And Niall of Malloy obviously belonged in the sunshine. Viviane had a sudden insight into his grumpiness in the archbishop's dungeons. It must have nearly killed him to be trapped away in the darkness like that, and no wonder it affected his mood. Well, he wouldn't want to go back there any more than she did!

Niall had to turn slightly sideways to ease his shoulders through the narrow opening. The red T-shirt he had evidently been loaned was stretched slightly to accommodate his breadth. His arms were tanned to a rich golden hue, he wore a thick golden bracelet upon his left wrist. Derek's shorts outlined the muscles of Niall's thighs and left his strong legs bare.

Viviane swallowed, certain she had never seen a man so powerfully built.

Or so very alluring.

As though he heard her thoughts, Niall glanced up and their gazes locked once again. Viviane's heart pounded and she was completely unaware that Monty left her side, despite his sour comment.

There was only Niall. They might have been alone in the world when he came closer, purpose in every step.

Viviane's pulse began to flutter in her throat. She could remember the imprint of his lips against her own, the warm salt-tinged taste of him when she had kissed him in gratitude. He gripped the handrail with a broad, strong hand, the same hand that had rested heavily on the back of Viviane's waist and urged her closer.

If she hadn't stepped away from him then, Viviane knew she would be kissing him still.

She had a funny certainty that the next kiss they shared—and there would be one!—wouldn't be nearly so fleeting as the last.

Niall marked the distance between them with decisive steps and Viviane suddenly felt very, very warm. She couldn't have said a word to save her life, a fact that would have shocked anyone (besides the residents of Avalon) who had even a passing acquaintance with her.

He braced his arms on the rail beside Viviane, so close

that his bare skin brushed against her own. She watched him squint as he absently surveyed the distant shoreline. Viviane could feel the heat of him so close beside her, and she wanted to touch him more than anything in all the world.

"You kept your pledge," he murmured, pleasure and surprise mingled in his low tones. "You are yet here."

"Yes," she managed to say.

Niall turned to face her. "'Tis not a trait one might expect from a witch."

Viviane saw the blond hair on his forearms stir in the wind from the sea and caught the scent of his skin. Her mouth was completely dry. "I suppose not."

Niall met her gaze steadily, unexpected humor dancing in the emerald depths of his eyes. "I have never known you to be without words," he teased, an equally unexpected smile curving his firm lips. "Has something gone awry?"

Viviane felt herself blush and knew she would never find another word again. She stared as that smile widened, ever so slowly, as tantalizing and warming as she had expected it to be.

No, it was definitely more tantalizing than she had expected. In fact, Viviane felt a bit dizzy.

"Why did you come?" she whispered, her voice a faint shadow of its usual strength.

"To fetch you," he murmured, his eyes glinting. "Why else?"

Viviane's knees melted. He *had* come just for her. She was right.

Perfect!

Niall lifted one hand to ease an errant curl back from her cheek. There was a heat in his eyes that made Viviane's heart stop, yet she stood rooted to the spot, as though she had been turned to stone.

Her heart hammered as he leaned closer, she closed her eyes when the warmth of his fingertips slid down the length of her neck. Viviane lifted her face and parted her lips, wanting only Niall's kiss. His lips neared, her heart raced, his breath fanned her cheek, she trembled.

"Refills!" Paula chirped so close behind that both she and Niall jumped. Their hostess smiled cheerily and shoved the frosty glasses into their hands before she danced away.

Viviane blinked, licked her lips and let the frost of the glass disperse the fire smouldering within her. She took a deep breath and reminded herself that they weren't alone.

Yet.

But she could fix that, as soon as they returned to Ganges. She would take Niall to her room, Viviane decided impulsively, she wouldn't let him stay anywhere else. He had ridden into the unknown in pursuit of her and now they wouldn't be separated again. Her breath caught as she wondered whether she would take him to her bed tonight, let alone what he would do about it if she did.

Viviane slanted a glance through her lashes at her knight and made a fairly good guess.

Niall meanwhile sniffed his drink suspiciously. "And what is this concoction?"

"It's good, really."

"Aye? And what will it do to me? Is it a potion to cloy my wits?"

"No, nothing like that!" Viviane laughed and her words spilled forth with haste now that she was reassured. "It's kind of tart, both sweet and sour, and very cold. Like ale, but different"—she pursed her lips—"so not really like ale at all. And that's salt on the rim, which makes an oddly pleasing tingle in contrast to how sour the drink is. It's called a marguerita, although I don't know why."

"So you have not been struck dumb after all," Niall mused. He shot her a quick look. "Though your speech has become most odd during this time."

Viviane felt herself blush scarlet again, but she couldn't stop talking now that she had begun. "Well, I didn't really have a choice, you know. I have to at least try to blend in, or not arouse suspicions that I don't belong here. What could I do but dress as they do and speak as they do? I'm not a fairy or a sorceress myself and you would think that even a lesser immortal could tell that with just a glance, but still there's no reason to draw attention to myself."

"Indeed." Niall's gaze lingered on her as though she were a puzzle he was trying to solve.

"Indeed!" Viviane nodded firmly. "You know, you should try your marguerita, you wouldn't want to hurt Paula's feelings. It's not precisely what you would expect and, to be honest"—she lowered her voice and leaned closer—"I did wonder at first just what to expect, since our hostess *is* one of the fey."

"The fey?" Niall repeated tonelessly.

Viviane had the sense that he was trying to keep his surprise from showing, though why he would be surprised by such a statement, she just couldn't imagine.

What other explanation could there possibly be?

"Yes! Why, it's perfectly obvious." Viviane hastened to explain as he looked across the deck. "She seems both old and young at the same time, which is, I understand, one of the characteristics of the little people. Not to mention, of course, her tiny build."

Viviane sipped beneath Niall's watchful eye.

In fact, he watched her so carefully that it was almost as though he was ensuring her response before he drank of the brew. She took another swallow, purely to reassure him that it really did taste good, and felt a languor steal through her body.

"You believe our hostess is one of the fey, merely because she is wrought small?"

It was clear from his tone that Niall did not share her conviction.

But then, he didn't know the whole truth about this place.

Viviane was more than happy to explain.

"Oh, it could be," she insisted. "After all, Paula believes in every manner of strange thing! Already she has spoken of great mysteries with authority, though I can't even guess at what she means. Did you understand what she meant by calling Derek an Aries?"

Niall shook his head slowly.

"You see? She must be one of the initiates, to just casually refer to things beyond everyone's understanding. And everyone here *is* an immortal of some kind or another—you can tell with just one glance, even when they don't tell you so. Monty said he has known Barb forever, and he said it just as easily as that, as though there was nothing remarkable about it at all. I have met people who say that they're eighty years of age!"

Niall's fair brows lifted in surprise and Viviane nodded. "Imagine! They say they're eighty years *young* and then they laugh, which just goes to show what kind of expectations they have. I wonder whether they just start counting over at some point, though I really can't imagine when that would be." She frowned in thought. "Maybe when they arrive here. What do you think?"

Niall's expression was impassive. "I could not fathom a guess."

"No, well, neither could I, really." Viviane smiled. "Of course, it's because they're immortal that they're so different from us. And so incomprehensible."

She gulped her drink again and thought that maybe it was helping her to explain matters. "Although I don't think that Paula has any malice toward us, not at all. She must be a good fairy. Not that I know very much about fairies, but my mother always talked about them and it seems to me that she said things like that about them, that there were good ones and bad ones, and the good ones would aid you and the bad ones would vex you. And that, of course, if *you* vexed a good one, well, then even they could act like bad ones, just to get even."

Niall chuckled beneath his breath and shook his head.

"What?" Viviane demanded.

He gazed steadily at her. "I do not believe that the fey exist."

"Shhh!" Viviane pressed her fingertips to his lips. Her heart skipped a beat when her fingers touched his flesh and their gazes met with sudden intensity. Viviane tried to chatter on as though she was unaffected, for her mother had always said it was unwise to let a man see his effect upon you.

"Don't even think such a thing! That's the very worst thing you could possibly do. You don't want to insult them! Who could tell how they might turn upon us, then. My mother used to tell stories of offended fairies that would keep one awake half the night, and play tricks upon mortals and all sorts of maliciousness. It's only sensible, really, because even mortals can be malicious if they feel that they've been insulted or treated poorly."

Niall nodded, then took a cautious sip of Paula's concoction. He rolled it around in his mouth as Viviane watched, then nodded as he swallowed. " 'Tis not all bad."

She drank again as though to indicate her agreement. "I wouldn't be surprised if Paula knew most of the other fey that are resident here . . ."

"*Other* fey?" Niall interjected.

"Well, of course! There are hundreds if not thousands of fairies here, it's so hard to keep track of them all, never mind the wizards and sorcerers. They don't live alone!" She cast a stern look to her companion. "Honestly, you have to use your wits here if you're going to blend in."

Niall's eyes narrowed and he leaned closer, his sombre manner bringing Viviane's tirade to a sudden halt. "And where *are* we, that there are so many fey at large?"

There was a glint in his eyes that told her he wasn't prepared to believe the truth, at least not yet. Viviane knew she had to persuade him to at least be careful, before he made a mistake and was evicted. It wouldn't be fair if her knight was snatched away from her, right after he arrived!

"Niall—do you mind if I call you Niall? After all, it seems as though we've known each other for a long time, probably because of all we've shared, and besides, they don't use titles here, at least not as much as I can tell."

He lifted one brow in acknowledgement and Viviane hastened on, liking how his name rolled over her tongue. "Well, Niall, you just have to believe me. And keep your thoughts less skeptical, because you never know who could be listening. My mother aways said that the fey had sharp ears, that they could even hear your thoughts if you weren't careful, and that they never missed a chance to straighten out the thinking of a skeptic . . ."

"Viviane, where *are* we?" Niall interjected calmly.

Oh, it was an unexpected delight to hear him utter her name!

Even if he sounded a bit impatient when he did.

But it seemed so vulgar to just blurt out the truth and Viviane didn't even know if it was supposed to be a secret, or whether it was forbidden to even say the word *Avalon*.

Niall wasn't looking away, though, just waiting for his answer as though he'd wait for it all week if necessary. And she supposed he did have a right to know. Viviane licked her lips. She glanced to their companions, who seemed markedly disinterested in their conversation, although you could never be entirely sure.

"This place is"—Viviane dropped her voice, glanced around to ensure once more that no one was listening, then leaned dangerously close to Niall—"*Avalon!*"

He choked in the act of sipping his drink then. "Avalon!"

"I know!" Viviane nodded sagely. "Isn't it amazing? I could hardly believe it myself when I ended up here. And now we're both here and everything . . ."

"Avalon!" he muttered through clenched teeth. "Are you mad?"

Viviane straightened. "Shhh! Don't get them upset!"

"Them?"

"The immortal ones! I *told* you! They're all sorcerers here and who knows what kind of hexes they might loose upon us, especially if they thought that we didn't appreciate their hospitality."

"I would have expected more from great sorcerers," he mused with a significant heft of his drink.

Viviane barely stifled the urge to swat him.

"Your irreverence could cost us dearly!" she hissed.

"Nay. There is no such place as Avalon," he insisted, with all the flexibility of a mountain. "And there are no such things as fairies."

Viviane tossed her hair over her shoulder, not caring for his tone at all. "Of course, there's such a place as Avalon. There must be because it's where we are."

"Aye?" Niall challenged, his voice low. "Prove the truth of it to me."

Viviane lifted her chin, intent on doing precisely that. She ticked off points on her fingers. "The island where we sailed from lies in the west. It's shrouded by mist and invisible to those mortals on the mainland, except on a day of rare clarity, and people on the island say that the mainlanders are always trying to come to the island. But they can't—because they have to shed their love of material possessions and greed to enjoy the spirituality of the island life. That's what Monty says and he should know—he's a sorcerer after all."

Niall glanced across the deck at the sorcerer in question, his expression speaking volumes.

But Viviane pressed on. "And it's hard to navigate a safe passage through the islands, although they say that it's just people getting lost in unfamiliar waters, it's probably a protective spell. Immortals do that, you know, to maintain their privacy. All the myths say so." She took a fortifying sip of the marguerita, watching Niall sip long and slowly.

"And there is no poverty on the island; the elderly come there when otherwise they might die; the shops are full of inexplicable marvels that anyone can buy for themselves. The land is blessed with bounty, the hills are wondrously green, the sky is flawless blue, the weather is perfect. *Apples* grow in unnatural abundance on trees that hang to the ground with massive fruit."

Viviane punctuated this with a stern glance, for it was not

insignificant. Her heart skipped to find Niall watching her avidly.

"And women abide upon that island in great numbers. They are revered. Barb says that there are many priestesses there, though I've yet to meet one. Finally, books are so common that every man and woman can collect the most beautiful manuscripts themselves."

"And they all are in agreement with you?" her knight asked, shrugging toward their companions. "They too believe themselves to be in Avalon?"

Viviane had the feeling that he didn't believe her explanation. "Well, not exactly," she had to admit. "They call the island Salt Spring, for some reason. Perhaps there is a magical spring that I have yet to see. Springs are always of freshwater, after all, so that would be a marvel."

Niall did not look persuaded.

"They say that we are off the west coast of British Columbia, which I can only imagine is another name for Ireland. Wasn't it claimed for the English king? And didn't Saint Columb come from there?"

Niall did not look suitably impressed by this assertion. He sipped his drink. "I believe he was of Scotland."

"It doesn't matter! Don't you see—they wouldn't tell just *anyone* that this was Avalon! Maybe they've altered the names of places so that Avalon can't be easily found. It has to be some kind of a secret, otherwise everyone would just come here and there wouldn't be anything magical about it at all!"

Niall levelled a glance at her that effectively communicated his doubts.

But Viviane lifted her chin. "You can be as skeptical as you like, but I know the truth. We're on an isle to the west of all the world, a mystical magical enchanted place that exists on no known maps. And that *is* Avalon." Viviane waved off any further objection he could make.

Niall took a quick gulp of his drink. "And what have you told them of your own deeds?"

"As little as could be contrived." Viviane sighed. "Monty tells everyone that I have a 'fourteenth-century thing.' They don't seem very interested in the passage of time in the mortal world."

Viviane dropped her voice and practically leaned on Niall's shoulder. "Actually, I was afraid I might say the wrong thing and prompt too many questions, so I've tried to be quiet. You see, I don't think we've come here the usual way and they might not let us stay if they figure it out."

That snared his attention. He considered her, his gaze sober, then glanced to her pendant. "And you came here with the aid of your witching stone."

"It's not a *witching* stone, because that would mean that I was a witch." Viviane rolled her eyes. "Or that my father was a witch, which makes no sense at all. In all honesty, Niall, how can you be so gullible as to believe those false charges against me?"

Niall arched a brow. "Yet we are in this place, without explanation, by virtue of that stone."

"A father's love is a powerful thing," Viviane insisted. "There's nothing more powerful than love—my mother taught me that. And what parent wouldn't want to see their child saved from execution?" She shook her head as she fingered the pendant, then shook her head. "I don't care exactly how it worked; my father's love saved me and that's explanation enough. We're here and alive and that's a good thing."

And she smiled at Niall, letting him see that his presence was a big part of everything that was good. "Thank you for returning my pendant. I was upset to have lost it, because it's all I have left from my mother."

"Aye?" Niall demanded softly, and arched a fair brow as he leaned closer. "Then, if you are so well pleased, perhaps you might grant me a small token of your gratitude."

Viviane knew exactly what token he had in mind. She didn't even need a whisper of her mother's Sight to recognize the meaning of that purposeful gleam in Niall's eyes.

Nor did she have to guess why a quiver took up residence in her belly.

And she was in absolute agreement with him.

Viviane nodded mutely and leaned closer. She shivered when Niall's arm slipped around her, she arched toward him when he splayed his fingers across the back of her waist, she tipped up her face when Niall bent closer and blocked out the sun.

And Viviane sighed when his mouth closed possessively over her own.

Perfection.

Monty pounced on Derek as soon as that man appeared on deck again. "Look at them," he muttered, jerking a finger toward the embracing couple. "Talk about a flying liplock!"

Derek looked supremely untroubled by the sight. "And so? Obviously they know each other. Nothing like a happy reunion." He shrugged and made for the rigging with purpose.

"Well?" Monty demanded. "Aren't you going to do something?"

"Like what?" Derek shrugged. "Green's not your color, pal. Let it go." And he turned away once more.

But Monty wasn't going to let him get away that easily. "Yeah, but like where did he come from? Did you see? He just"—Monty snapped his fingers—"like *appeared* out of thin air!"

Derek met his gaze levelly. "I didn't see a thing," he insisted flatly.

"What do you mean, you saw *nothing*?" Monty flung out his hands in frustration. He was really annoyed; just when he thought he was making progress with Viviane, when he'd blown a fortune on dinners, this guy had to appear out of the blue and ruin everything! "Come on, Derek! You were like looking right at him! You saw what I saw, which was a guy just *poof* appear from nothing."

"I told you that I didn't see a thing."

Monty stepped into his friend's path and propped his hands on his hips. "Then where did he come from?"

Derek shrugged. "He must have been hidden on board." He nodded, the idea obviously gaining appeal as he thought about it. "Yeah. A stowaway. He popped up and jumped overboard to get the lady's attention. Seems to have worked." And he started to whistle as he tugged the sail back into the wind.

"Come on!" Monty surveyed his friend with disgust. "You don't believe that any more than I do!"

Derek flicked a serious glance Monty's way, his voice dropping low. "And what's the alternative?"

"That something truly weird is going on."

"Right, truly weird. I need that like a hole in the head." Derek rolled his eyes and turned back to his work. "Like this guy just appears out of midair for no reason at all. You can't say it happens all the time. Think about it, Monty."

"But it *did* happen! Right here, right now."

"Nope. Can't have. No way. It's impossible and we both know it."

"Can't be impossible if it happened," Monty felt compelled to comment. He stole another look at Viviane and noted that the killer kiss showed no chance of stopping anytime soon.

He was jolted back to the conversation when Derek poked a finger in his chest.

"Look. You're going to just let this go, understand? I don't know what happened, I don't really care. There's got to be a perfectly rational explanation, so I'm sticking to the best one I know."

Monty grimaced. "He stowed away and suddenly appeared."

"You got it."

Monty watched his friend work for a few moments, knowing that Derek was fiddling more than necessary. "What if there's like a perfectly *irrational* explanation?"

Derek pivoted and propped his hands on his hips to glare

at Monty. "You know, I put up with this shit all the time. Power of the unseen, the magical mystery of runes, on and on and on it goes and frankly, I've had enough. I don't appreciate you even hinting that you might encourage Paula with more of it. I've always thought it was bunk and I'm not changing my mind."

"Even if it means closing your eyes to what's going on?"

"Monty, there's *nothing* going on." Derek pointed at the couple still embracing. "You tell me what's unnatural about that, hmm? Have a marguerita, put your ego back on ice, and just enjoy the fact that your friend is happy."

The older man smiled. "In a couple of days, my friend, you'll get over the fact that her happiness isn't with you. And eventually, you might even be glad. These things have a way of working themselves out."

Then Derek winked and headed back to his work.

But Monty turned to watch as the pair finally parted, something ugly in his gut twisting when he noted Viviane's flush of delight. It wasn't just jealousy, he knew it.

Nope, there was something screwy going on, whether Derek admitted it or not.

And Monty was going to get to the truth of it.

For Viviane's sake, of course.

The potion of Paula's reminded Niall of the tales the old crusaders told of Greek fire. It slipped over a man's teeth without much noise, indeed, 'twas almost pleasant. He had just enough time to savor its tang before it hit his empty belly.

And exploded.

'Twas a thousand times stronger than the strongest ale he had ever imbibed and it shot through his body like wild lightning. Matters were helped naught by Viviane's torrid kiss which left him dizzy—Niall had downed almost the whole of the green brew before he realized its potency.

And then, 'twas too late to save himself.

Worse, he did not care.

Even worse than that, he completely forgot to wish. He

had had this thought that he would accomplish two matters
at once, by having his kiss of Viviane and making his wish
while she was in his arms, holding the pendant by way of
holding her. But as soon as her soft lips parted beneath his,
as soon as her breasts were pressed against him, as soon as
she made that irresistible little sigh of satisfaction, Niall just
forgot.

Savoring was the only thought he had.

And in the wake of that kiss, naught made sense to him,
not the way Viviane's smile set his very flesh afire, not
the easy command Derek had over his strange craft, not the
thousands of lights that erupted along the shore as the sky
grew dim. Certainly not Viviane's conviction that they had
come to Avalon, a place that did not even exist and certainly
not one that would tolerate intruders even if it did.

He could not even sort the proof of Viviane's witchery
from his belief in her pledge of innocence. Indeed, 'twas impossible to believe ill of her when she smiled at him just so,
never mind when she kissed so sweetly.

There had to be a reasonable explanation for all that had
transpired. The tiny sober bit of his mind was convinced of
that, even as it was banished to a corner. That sober bit of him
was equally convinced that he could sort matters through,
given some time and a good bit less "marguerita."

But the greater part of Niall was oblivious to such concerns. He was simply having too much fun. 'Twas the first
time since the wounding of his knee that he had celebrated
anything, and though he did not precisely know what 'twas
he celebrated now, he did so with gusto.

He drank more of the brew, he sang with abandon, he consumed "grilled steak" until there was none left to consume,
he kissed the woman back who was so determined to make
herself his own. He let her talk and did not correct her illusions, for indeed, he could not have summoned a decent argument to save his life.

And when they stood in a moonlit harbor and she shyly
invited him to her abode, Niall accepted without a second

thought. Viviane took his hand and led him through the quiet streets, the weight of her slender fingers in his own giving Niall more pleasure than he had known in years.

And 'twas then he realized the truth.

'Twas not because he had been fasting that he was so intoxicated. 'Twas not because of some fearsome ingredient in Paula's brew. 'Twas not because anyone had bewitched him against his will, 'twas not even because he was in the presence of a fearsome witch.

Nay, nay, nay. Those were the obvious answers. The truth was simply that the loveliest lady he had ever met thought he was wonderful.

And that was heady stuff indeed. Indeed, to be believed a hero had a tendency to make a man want to fulfill such expectation, not to shatter it. Niall was not quite ready to prove to Viviane that he was somewhat less than wonderful, certainly not that he had come to collect her presence for her execution.

Nay, not when she smiled at him shyly as she did now.

Indeed, Niall of Malloy smiled back.

Chapter 6

NIALL AWAKENED TO a persistent thudding.

He winced and buried his head deeper beneath the linens, though that earned him no respite. He realized that the pounding came from within his own head and groaned softly at the recollection of Paula's powerful potion.

'Twas indeed some foul brew, and he could only hope that this was the worst of the damage done to him. Niall wiggled his toes and fingers, did a quick check to ensure that all was as it should be, and knew some relief.

Indeed, this pounding between the ears was not unfamiliar and in a way, that was reassuring. It had been years since Niall had drunk too much ale, and he winced anew at the souvenir he was likely to enjoy all the day long. He tried to recall events of the night before, without a great deal of success.

That, too, was typical of a night of overindulgence.

Niall was fairly certain there had been singing, and given the thunder between his ears, would hazard a guess that it had been particularly loud and off-key singing, undoubtedly of vulgar verse. Niall did recall, now that he pondered the matter, that Monty had not participated, and that Derek, despite his tendency to be overly affectionate, had proven to be quite a decent sort.

He also remembered that there had been naught magical about the cuts of beef Paula conjured from the ship's tiny kitchen, except perhaps the speed with which they disappeared. Aye, he had had four chunks himself and could have consumed that again, had there been more available. The recollection of good food made the pounding in his head recede, just as it made his belly growl.

And Viviane had lingered close by his side all the night long. Niall smiled, his eyes still closed, not wanting to dispel the memory of the many soft smiles she dispatched in his direction, or the way her eyes shone.

'Twas then he recalled his intent to wish while he kissed her, and his failure to do so. Niall caught his breath and rolled to his back at his inevitable realization.

She had fooled him again!

Aye, the moment his lips touched hers, Niall had forgotten to take Viviane back to Cantlecroft! How could he have forgotten his pledge? How could he have failed in his task, again?

He had been bewitched.

That was the simple truth of it. Niall could find no other explanation, though this one made his innards writhe. Nay, he was neither a man who did not cleave to his duty, nor a man who could not be relied upon. Niall always did what he pledged to do.

The fact that he had not could only be due to forces beyond his control. His lips tightened to a grim line. Aye, 'twas no coincidence that the two times Niall had not fulfilled his intent had been in the presence of Viviane.

Nor that she was a convicted witch.

In his heart, Niall did not believe in potions and hexes and spells, he did not believe in fairies and witches and sorcerers, he did not believe in Avalon, nor even heaven or hell. He did not believe in magic, yet magic was apparently complicating his days and confounding his intent.

The evidence was inescapable.

'Twas clear he was to learn something in this, yet equally clear that Niall's habit of believing in only what he could hold within his hands would not be readily dislodged. He tried to persuade himself of Viviane's guilt, of the fact that he had been enchanted, and failed.

Utterly.

Niall scowled and tried again, without success.

Truth be told, he had fine if somewhat hazy recollections of Viviane's company the night before. The way her eyes sparkled when she told him tales, the way she leaned against him, the way she looked at him as though the sun rose and set in him alone could certainly be borne without complaint. She made Niall feel alluring, she coaxed him to believe in his own charm, she made him feel a man of power again.

Though her tools were of the most earthy kind. Was this witchery? Niall had a difficult time persuading himself so. He was quite certain that the dark arts could only be practiced with the sacrifice of various livestock, the chanting of spells and general misdeeds undertaken in the dark of the night when the moon was veiled.

Not on a ship, in the sunlight.

Niall's head throbbed at the challenge of reconciling what he had experienced with his beliefs, and had to admit that this spell of Viviane's must be cursedly strong. He winced anew at the realization of what he must do this morn. Indeed, he felt a measure of guilt that he had to seek out Viviane and immediately return to Cantlecroft.

After all, she still had the moonstone talisman.

Sooner begun, sooner finished, after all, Niall concluded with a sigh. He had best be about his labor before she enchanted him yet more fully.

Though it could hurt naught to linger abed a little longer. Clearly, Niall had somehow found a perfect place for repose. He could hear a faint patter of what might have been rain, the pallet beneath him was soft and he was too gloriously warm to leap willingly from his repose. And his head ached, after all.

When he shifted slightly, his leg bumped against the heat of another.

Niall's eyes flew open, his heart skipped a beat. He belatedly recalled Viviane's invitation, then wondered if the "memory" was but an invention of his own desire.

A desire born of witchery.

His head was buried beneath a pillow which was lighter than a cloud, and as a result, he could see naught but markably luxurious linens of a creamy hue. He caught a whiff that could only be feminine skin, then his heart galloped with the certainty of which particular woman curled beside him.

Viviane. Sorceress, temptress.

Witch.

Niall slid his toe across the mattress once again and caught his breath when he encountered soft, smooth flesh. A part of him responded to the news with enthusiasm, though Niall knew he would be wise to be wary.

Surely, he reasoned, it could hurt naught to *look*?

Aye, a single glimpse was well worth whatever price he might have to pay. Niall eased from beneath the pillow and peeked at the woman beside him.

The breath left him of one accord when he saw that he was right. 'Twas indeed Viviane.

And the lady was a beauty. Viviane slept on her back, as trusting as a child, her auburn hair cast in disarray across the pillows. Her rosy lips were parted, her breathing deep, her cheek nestled in her own delicate palm. The linens were caught beneath her underarm closest Niall, cast over her opposite shoulder.

Even in sleep, she seemed to smile softly, as characteristically sunny in outlook as when she was awake. Only now, while she slumbered unaware, did Niall dare to admit to himself how very compelling he found this lady's cheerful confidence.

Viviane believed the world to be a good place, she believed in her own good fortune, she was convinced that naught ill could truly befall her.

Though ill certainly had. Niall had certainly never been so unfortunate as to be sentenced to die, and he heartily hoped he never would be. He certainly would not have continued to believe in his own good fortune if he was.

Niall wondered whether that conviction alone was what held everything dire at bay for Viviane. And he was the one sworn to bring the ultimate bad fortune to her. His gut chilled, though Niall knew a pledge made was a pledge that must be kept.

He was a man of honor, after all, and his very reputation hung in the balance of making what had gone awry come right.

He was not, however, in a hurry this morn. That should have surprised him, but Niall was instead reassured to find himself less cold-hearted than he might have feared. Aye, he might have gotten soft, but he grew accustomed to it, and 'twas less dire a fate than he had once believed.

For 'twas no crime to think, just for a moment, that Viviane was still too lovely, too vivaciously alive, to die.

Niall eyed the bare shoulder nearest him and swallowed at the knowledge that lovely Viviane was nude. Indeed, her flawless skin lay bare whenever he could see it and certainly there was no chemise obstructing his exploring toe.

He thought of the long, sleek legs that had tormented him the day before, the ripe breast that had pressed against his chest, the smooth buttock that had fallen beneath his hand. He recalled her delightful smile, the shine of her eyes, the mischievous dimple that dinted her cheek.

One look. One glimpse alone would satisfy him, he knew it well. Niall eased back the linens, his headache nigh forgotten.

He was not disappointed.

First he learned that Viviane had a mole on that bare right shoulder, then another came to light, nestled amidst the intriguing hollows below her throat. A third was secreted above her left breast, temptingly close to where the nipple must be. Niall had a playful urge to trace a line between the three with his fingertip and awaken her with a featherlight kiss.

Indeed, 'twas impossible to believe ill of her when she looked so beguilingly innocent.

So *trusting*. Viviane was not only a beauteous woman, but one who had evidently welcomed him to her bed. They had slept nude, side by each, her faith in his good intent so great that she curled up with the contentedness of a cat.

'Twas enough to humble a man.

Especially when that man was pledged to bring the lady in question to her own execution.

Niall's mouth went dry as he stared and, even knowing all he knew, he yearned for yet another of this lady's kisses.

Surely 'twould not be unwelcome?

And who would know?

Viviane had not protested the day before. If an ache between his ears and slumber in a fine bed was the worst due extracted for a kiss, Niall could bear the burden that would be earned by another. He leaned closer, convinced that brushing his lips just once across her lips would pass undetected.

But the lady suddenly stirred.

Niall froze and watched as Viviane stretched in her sleep, arching her neck as gracefully as a swan. Her lashes fluttered but her eyes did not open. Niall did not dare to breathe, so certain was he that his conclusions would be proven wrong, that she had not actually invited him to be here, that she would awaken and cast him out of her bed.

Viviane made a wordless sound of contentment in the back of her throat, a breath that fanned across Niall's skin and warmed him to his toes. Her hand fell upon his arm as though she knew she would find him there and he jumped. Her touch was so light that he might have missed it had he not been avidly watching her every move.

And Viviane smiled, her fingers sliding across his arm, back and forth again. She was not disappointed, nor even surprised! Niall thought his heart might burst, it clamored so loudly.

Viviane eased the linens lower with a sigh and turned toward Niall in a soft tumble of femininity, wriggling her shoulders as she nestled contentedly into a hollow beside him. Niall's mouth went dry as the move revealed the sweet curve of her left breast fully to his gaze.

As well as the moonstone pendant she still wore.

Niall stared at the odd stone. He knew he should snatch at the pendant and make his wish, he knew he should seize this chance to see his quest complete, but that taut, ruby-hued nipple so temptingly displayed distracted him.

'Twas so very, very beauteous.

Just like the lady herself. Niall swallowed, the weight of his pledge heavy on his shoulders.

He much preferred to think about Viviane's bare flesh. Indeed, he was certain her breast must be soft and sweetly scented, perhaps even more so than her delightful kiss.

But he knew what he should do. His hand lifted but hesitated before him instead of moving decisively toward the pendant. Caught between desire and duty, Niall closed his eyes and reached, trusting Fate to guide his hand.

And Fate, as she has oft been known to do, betrayed him.

Niall's fingertips brushed over the ripe curve of Viviane's breast and she sighed contentment. She arched against the roughness of his hand like a demanding cat and Niall could not help but close his hand over her. Her jutting breast fit perfectly beneath his palm, tempting his fingers to curve around its softness. His gaze slid to her mouth in time to watch the tip of her tongue appear between her parted lips and his desire raged like an inferno.

Just one more kiss, Niall insisted to himself.

And *then* he would do his duty.

Niall's thumb slid leisurely across that nipple, and it puckered quickly. He bent without a moment's pause, cup-

ping her breast in his hand and ducking his head to kiss that
errant mole, then moving across the warmth of her flesh to
take the pert nipple in his mouth.

Viviane's eyes flew open when his breath slid across her
skin. Niall halted as though caught at a crime. The sleepy
scent of her inundated him and curled his toes, time stood
still while the lady eyed him.

This was it. Niall feared anew that Viviane would chastise
him for his familiarity. If naught else, she would scream and
shout. She would clutch the gem and flee his side, leaving
him alone in this place. Worse, she might weep! Niall's gut
clenched.

But all the same, he could not willingly move away.

To his astonishment, Viviane smiled, confounding his expectation yet again.

"Good morning," she murmured, a welcoming glow taking up residence in the depths of her eyes. Her smile
widened and that dimple appeared in her cheek. Her fingertips brushed his jaw, wonder dawning in those marvelous
eyes. "So, I didn't dream you after all," she murmured and
the thunder of Niall's pulse drowned on the pounding between his ears.

He found himself smiling back at her, filled with a sense
of potency that he had not known in years. Her hand fell on
the back of his neck, her fingers curled into his hair and she
urged him back toward her breast.

Niall could not resist. He let his thumb move across her
nipple again, savoring how she gasped when the roughness
of his skin snared that turgid peak. Viviane fell back against
the pillows, arching her back as she clenched his hair. She
gasped and writhed, her delight making Niall want only to
please her more. He bent to suckle her.

He began gently, loving how she moaned when he flicked
the peak with the tip of his tongue. Her immediate response
fed his own desire, the silky warmth of her skin prompted
his fingers to drift ever lower and lower in exploration. She

was lean and long, all supple curves and satiny skin, soft and feminine and seductive.

And she desired him. The way Viviane moaned in pleasure and stirred beneath Niall's touch fed a newfound confidence in his own allure, a confidence that had been shattered along with his knee and his knightly life.

If this was the magic she wrought, Niall only wanted more. He wanted to please her in exchange for this feeling she gave him, to make her cry out and scream aloud.

Niall knew that he would have to finish the quest he had begun. He knew this and he deliberately forgot, pushing everything from his thoughts to focus solely on Viviane and her pleasure. He knew that he had never felt this way with a woman before, be there a spell cast or nay.

He knew without a shred of doubt that he would never forget her.

'Twould have to be enough.

Niall caressed the indent of each rib, he flattened his hand to slide his palm across her belly, he gripped the curve of her hip possessively. His other hand slipped beneath her, lifting her breast to his hunger as he feasted upon her. He gently grazed his teeth across that nipple, then laved his attention upon its partner, his every touch making Viviane writhe.

He trailed kisses up the length of Viviane's throat, he kissed the wild pulse visible beneath the creamy perfection of her flesh. He kissed those moles, drawing a line between them with his tongue and blowing softly upon it, making her shiver with delight. Viviane locked her arms around his neck and pulled him closer, her kiss filled with all the urgency that Niall felt.

His tongue slipped between her teeth, and he swallowed her sigh, his fingers dipping into the slick mystery between her thighs. He cupped her head in his hand and kissed her thoroughly as his fingers coaxed her response. He watched the flush rise over her flesh, the glitter of desire dawn in her eyes. Viviane twisted beneath his touch, but he granted her no escape, teasing her, drawing her further, urging her to the heights.

And when she cried out, her fingers clutching him, Niall swallowed the sound of her release greedily and held her while she trembled in its wake. She whispered something he did not catch, then her lashes fluttered to her cheeks again. She sighed and cuddled closer to him, a smile of contentment curving her lips as her breathing deepened.

Yet again, she slept against him, her legs entangled with his, her trust in him complete. A nigh unbearable sweetness flooded through Niall before practicality checked its course.

Indeed, his bile rose that the lady should have judged his intent so wrong. He was a knave of the lowest order to have fed her illusion. He was a liar and a thief, for 'twould be Niall who stole this woman's life and freedom away from her.

He felt suddenly dirty, unworthy of sheltering her sweetness against his chest.

Niall rolled abruptly from the bed and put the width of the room between them. He shoved a hand through his hair and scowled, then turned back in time to see Viviane settle into the warm hollow he had left. His heart contracted painfully and he could not stop himself from stepping closer, if only to gaze upon her.

The cursed moonstone glinted at him as he drew near, rising and falling on the lady's breast as she dozed, a tangible reminder of his pledge. Niall knew what he should do, just as he knew that in this moment, he could not do it.

One fall had indeed made him soft.

Niall swore under his breath, spun and snatched up the red shirt of Kissing Derek. He hauled it over his head and made impatiently for the door.

'Twas just the call of nature clouding his thoughts. Aye, that was the way of it. He had need of a garderobe, 'twas no more than that.

Then, Niall would keep his word.

•   •   •

Barb plugged in the kettle, chose Lemon Zinger from her array of herbal teas and yawned mightily as she waited for the water to boil. She leaned one hip against the counter and rubbed her eyes sleepily. Another day, another dollar.

Another day older and deeper in debt, more like it.

Her laugh was more of a snort. She wasn't going to think about Payables so early in the morning when they'd kept her up half the night already. She deliberately went to the window, trying to let the gentle sprinkle of the morning rain calm her with its soothing echo on the roof.

Barb loved the patter of falling water. She closed her eyes and listened to the rain hitting the glass, feeling as though the sound alone could ease all the kinks out of her neck and straighten out all the tangles in her thoughts.

One of these days, she really had to get that garden planted. Barb could see it in her mind's eye, her imagination helped by the pages of horticulture magazines dutifully earmarked and piled on her nightstand. There would be a little fountain splashing into a pond ringed by irises and lilies. It would be filled with private shadows, a world apart from everything else. It would be Barb's own haven to retreat from the world, close her eyes and listen to the splash of water.

One of these days, she would work less and play more.

But not anytime soon. Barb heaved a sigh and admitted that planting a single Siberian Iris hadn't been much of a start or an inspiration. It was probably a bad omen that the reputably tough plant had shown itself discontent with Barb's garden.

The withered little thing couldn't be said to be thriving.

Barb looked ruefully in the direction of the little cluster of iris leaves, hoping that the plant had made a miraculous recovery in the face of adversity. That was something she was going to have to do soon with the shop and she could use a mascot.

But the plant wasn't any better. And how could it be? There was a great big blond guy peeing on it!

Barb was out the door in a flash, scooping up a loose sneaker on her way. *"Hey!"* she bellowed, not caring about the early hour or the sleeping habits of her neighbors. "Hey, *you*! What do you think you're doing?"

The man seemed intent on finishing what he had begun. His head moved slightly, but he didn't turn, the yellow stream running unrestrained on the defenseless iris.

Well, it wasn't completely defenseless. Barb chucked her shoe at the guy's head and hit him squarely in the back of the neck. He jumped in a most satisfactory manner and the stream was momentarily dammed.

Ha! Barb bunched up her bathrobe in both hands and marched across the wet grass to do battle.

"Who the hell do you think you are?" she raged. "It's bad enough that I have to pick up after everyone's cats, but I will not tolerate human waste in my garden!"

The man turned, his manner that of a monarch acknowledging the lowest serf of his realm. He glanced skeptically across the weed-infested stretch of greenery that some—specifically Barb—generously called a lawn.

"Nay, this can be no garden," he said evenly.

Barb's eyes widened when she saw that he was only wearing a T-shirt. She didn't want to look, but it was hard not to notice exactly where the hem ended.

And what was right below.

Even looking past *that* didn't help when the guy had the legs of a gladiator. He propped his hands on his hips, his move mercifully driving Barb's gaze upward, and she felt relieved only until she meet the keen green of his eyes.

There was a hunk pissing in her yard.

Barb felt suddenly very withered. It had been a while since she had had—or even wanted—a man in her bed, but the sight of pure beefcake half-naked awakened a few forgotten urges.

Unwelcome urges, to boot.

Barb folded her arms across her chest and glared at the intruder, doing her best impression of a woman unaffected by his actor looks. "It *is* a garden. It's my garden and you're pissing on the only flower in it."

He looked back at the iris, which didn't make much of a proud showing. "*This* would be a flower you hold in esteem?" he asked, with a point of one finger.

Barb lifted her chin and changed tacks, figuring that a good offense was better than a poor defense. "Haven't you ever heard of a toilet? Or are you one of those biker-hiker kids who crashes drunk on the beach?"

He didn't look like much of a kid, but then, lots of men never passed the intellectual age of two.

Barb glanced at those legs again without intending to do so.

But most got stuck at sixteen.

She shook her finger at him. "If you think you can sleep outside then come hang around here, using my garden as a toilet, then hoping for a meal like all those other eco-tourist bums, you've got another think coming."

"I did not slumber outside." His gaze strayed to the second story of the house—the room over the shop—and Barb suddenly had a very good idea where he had crashed.

The accent should have given her a clue.

"Don't tell me." She held up a hand. "You're a friend of Viviane's."

His gaze meeting hers once again. "'Twas Viviane who welcomed me to her bed last eve."

Oh boy. That was more info than she needed.

"Well, there's a toilet up there and I'd appreciate your using it," Barb snapped. "However long you're staying." She turned and marched back to the door, glancing back to find that he had picked up her shoe. He was looking at it as though it was an enchanted slipper or something, instead of just a plain worn red Ked. "And you can tell Viviane that the rent's for one, not two. If you're staying, we'll have to talk."

His expression turned grim. "That should not be a consideration. I do not intend to linger long."

Well, wasn't that typical? They really were all the same.

Barb contented herself with a shrug and retreated to her chaste kitchen where the kettle was whistling merrily away.

For the first time since she had bought this place, the floral wallpaper border annoyed her. It made the room look so exclusively feminine, as though it would tattle to anyone who had listened that no man had ever crossed its threshold.

Which was exactly how Barb wanted it to be. She mutinously poured a steaming mug of tea and sipped it so quickly that she burned her tongue.

She stiffened when she heard the back door open and knew that half-naked man was coming into her house. He was going to chase her into her kitchen, Barb just knew it, and she could make a pretty good guess of what would happen after that.

Or what he would *try* to make happen. Oh, it had been a long time since she had had the chance to set a man straight about how irresistible he was, and she'd thought of a lot more compelling arguments since that last one.

She braced herself and turned, a warrior princess at the ready for anything at all.

Except for what did happen. The clear sound of a shoe dropping onto the mat echoed through the little hall. The door closed with a resolute click and Naked Man's footsteps faded away. The faint creak of Viviane's separate entrance opening, then closing again, was barely audible beneath the whisper of the rain.

Barb leaned against the counter one more time, sipping Lemon Zinger that wasn't quite steeped without even tasting it. She couldn't be feeling disappointed. The last thing she wanted was a guy, particularly one who had been with Viviane just last night.

No, what she felt was a *yearning*, a sense of incompleteness that she'd been ignoring for a long time. She stared through the rain-streaked window at the swordlike leaves of the iris and felt a sudden sympathy for it. They were both vulnerable—lonely, wounded, but making a good show of doing just fine.

Barb frowned and decided she just hadn't had enough sleep.

And that was mucking with her mind. By Goddess, she was happy here and that was all there was to it. She'd made her choices and hoed her own row and she'd be damned to hell and back before she admitted that there was a single thing wrong with the life she'd chosen.

Barb put her mug down with a thump. She gave herself a shake and strode to her own bathroom. What she needed was a good hot shower, and some revenue rolling in the door.

She certainly wasn't going to think about what kind of rolling was going on in her rental unit right now. No way, no how.

She'd much rather think about Payables.

Chapter 7

VIVIANE AWAKENED WITH a smile. She snuggled deeper into the sheets, taking an intoxicatingly deep breath of Niall's scent lingering there and sighed contentment. Her knight had come, he was more than even she had dreamed he would be and everything was going to work out beautifully.

Her smile broadened in recollection of Niall's gentle touch, the way he leaned over her, the way his eyes darkened as he gave her pleasure, and she shivered with delight. She had never guessed she could feel that way, but her knight had given her the gift of it.

Everything was just perfect.

Well, not quite everything. Viviane reached one hand across the mattress and found herself alone.

Her eyes flew open, but Niall was nowhere in sight. Viviane sat up and pushed her hair back, wondering where he could have gone.

And why. Surely he wasn't gone, surely she hadn't just dreamed him up? Her imagination could get away from her, that was for sure, and Viviane nibbled her lip in consternation.

Then she saw the shorts Derek had loaned to Niall, crumpled in a pile on the floor. She sighed with relief, knowing he couldn't be far. Maybe he was going to bring her a surprise. Maybe he was going to come back to bed and seduce her all day long.

Maybe he hadn't expected her to awaken so soon. Viviane smiled and hugged her knees in anticipation.

But nothing happened.

She listened, but Niall wasn't in the bathroom. Hers wasn't a room filled with secretive corners and she could see it all from here. Niall wasn't present. The house was quiet, so Viviane rolled out of bed. She folded her arms across her nakedness and peered out the window.

No sign of him.

Viviane was just going to look for a note when heavy footfalls sounded on the stairs. Niall! She spun with delight just as the man of her dreams entered the room.

"Niall, you're back!" Viviane danced across the room and cast her arms around his neck. "Good morning," she purred, walking her fingertips up the damp expanse of his shirt. "Did you sleep well?" And she tipped her head back to meet his gaze, fully expecting another soul-stirring kiss.

But Niall wore a pensive frown. His gaze flicked over her, even as Viviane smiled, and his arms did not close protectively around her. She might have been embracing a statue. Viviane stepped back, uncertain what was wrong and watched as he scanned the room. It was almost as though he was avoiding looking at her.

He was shy! The realization almost made her laugh out loud. How could this bold knight be shy after what they had shared?

Maybe he was afraid she hadn't been pleased. Wouldn't that be just like the hero she knew Niall to be?

Well, Viviane would ease that doubt from his mind. She ran her hand over his shoulder and smiled. Niall looked into her eyes, swallowed, then looked away.

Her heart clenched that he should be unsure of his talents—and too shy to ask. She pressed a kiss to his shoulder. "I have to thank you, I've never woken up that way before. It was absolutely wonderful," she breathed.

He didn't say anything, though his breathing quickened and Viviane hoped she was making progress. She stretched to her toes and brushed her lips across his, noting how Niall closed his eyes. His hands had clenched into fists and there was a dull red rising on the back of his neck.

Well, this was working! Viviane could feel the tension building within him and knew she was getting somewhere. She ran a fingertip playfully around his ear, loving how he shivered, and knew she had to please him as he had pleased her.

She wasn't exactly sure how to do that, but Viviane had no doubt that they'd sort it out. They were destined lovers, after all.

"Won't you come back to bed?"

"Nay!" The word exploded from Niall and he flung himself away from her. He paced to the window, his agitation obvious, then folded his hands behind his back. He didn't turn to face her, though his hands worked, opening and closing into fists.

Viviane bit her lip. Had something horrible happened this morning?

Oh, he had been out! This Avalon could be a perplexing place, Viviane knew from her own experience, and there was no telling who or what Niall might have encountered this morning.

Just as she knew that Niall was not the kind of man who would volunteer any story.

She'd just have to work it out of him.

"I wondered where you had gone." Viviane kept her voice as toneless as possible, hoping he would confide in her.

"Even a dog does not soil his bed," Niall said grimly and glared out into the rain as though he was angry with it.

Viviane realized then that he was wet and that he had only troubled to put on his shirt. She bit back her laughter in sudden understanding, doubting that he would appreciate her amusement.

But it was funny that he had gone out into the rain to relieve himself, unaware of the washroom—or its purpose—so warm and dry and close at hand.

That would start anyone's day off wrong! Viviane stepped closer and ran her hands over Niall's shoulders, massaging the knot of tension in the back of his neck.

"You didn't really need to go outside, although there's no way you could have known." She kissed his shoulder blade, surprised when Niall stiffened. "They have indoor facilities here that are truly a marvel. You can relieve yourself and wash and groom, without ever leaving the chamber."

His quick glance was somewhat less than romantic, his words even less so. "I am told I must use the toilet. What and where is this?"

Oh, nature called again. Well, that explained *everything*!

And once such details were resolved and Niall was feeling his usual self again, maybe they could have a nice, long shower together and pick up where they left off. Maybe then, he'd get that intent gleam in his eye, maybe then he'd really *look* at her again.

That was a tempting enough possibility to reestablish Viviane's cheerfulness. "A toilet is what they call a privy here," she explained, claiming his hand. Niall extricated his hand quickly, though he followed behind her.

Viviane tried not to read too much into his gesture, knowing that he had something on his mind.

He grimaced. "And 'tis inside the chamber?"

"It's in its own chamber, in the washroom over here, which is a room for washing and for doing other things as well. There's a wonderful looking glass which could only be magically wrought, it's so very clear. I try not to look into it too much, for my mother always said that there were pixies lurking in looking glasses, waiting to snare those who stared too long."

She cast a smile over her shoulder at Niall from the

threshold of the washroom and his gaze flicked downward. A reassuring heat dawned in those green eyes when his gaze fell on her bare breasts. His determined expression softened slightly, and Viviane's heart skipped a beat.

But then Niall's gaze rose to her pendant and his eyes narrowed. He straightened and once again looked grim and cold.

Viviane raised one hand to her pendant, wondering why he was looking at it that way. "Would you rather I took it off?" she asked hastily. "I can put it away."

Niall's eyes flashed. "Nay! You must wear it at all times!"

Viviane must have looked surprised at his vehemence, for Niall took a deep breath and pushed one hand through his hair. His words sounded strained when he spoke. "'Twas a gift from your parents, after all."

Viviane smiled. He was so determined to not take credit for the generosity of what he had done. "And one that you returned to me." She kissed his cheek, a little disappointed when he didn't even incline his head to touch his lips to hers.

"You should garb yourself," he growled. "There is a chill in the air this day."

And he pushed past her into the small room.

Viviane's shoulders sagged for only an instant. He was a man with a mission, that's what he was. She shouldn't be disappointed. No, he was just being protective of her. It *was* cold in here, but Viviane didn't plan to linger around naked for long.

She was looking forward to that shower.

Maybe he was still feeling uncertain. Barb was always saying that men were unbelievably dense about such things, which Viviane understood to mean that they missed subtlety.

She discarded subtlety, right then and there, and followed Niall into the tiny room. She pressed herself against his back and smiled to herself when he caught his breath. She wrapped her arms around his waist and pressed her hips against his buttocks, running one toe over his foot and up his leg.

"Viviane!" Niall whispered, his voice wonderfully strained.

Viviane decided subtlety was overrated. She flattened her hands beneath his shirt and ran them over his chest, closing her eyes as the thick pelt of hair ran through her fingers. She felt the outline of each rib, she inhaled deeply of his scent, she felt her own desire stir once more.

"I think we should return to bed," she whispered. "I think I should touch you the way you have touched me. I think we should spend this morning learning all there is to know of each other."

But when Viviane looked past his shoulder into the mirror, fully expecting to have the man's avid attention, Niall was frowning at the sink basin as though it was personally offensive. He didn't even glance up at her reflection, his lips were drawn tight, and he stood as taut as a bowstring.

"This is no garderobe," he said tersely, reminding her that he had other priorities. "There is no course of water, no means of disposal . . ."

First things first.

"Yes, it is! You see?" Viviane reached around his waist and turned on the taps with a triumphant flick of her wrist. Niall's features brightened and he hunkered down before the taps, moving easily away from her and stepping out of her embrace as though he was unaware of it.

Her presence was apparently forgotten and Viviane didn't welcome the change.

It was absolutely no consolation to recall that she had spent half a day herself playing with the taps when she first arrived. Theirs was a fearsome magic—yet one that in a mere month, she had come to take for granted.

Viviane folded her arms across her chest, a very feminine part of her not liking being upstaged by the washroom, however marvelous it might be.

Niall tried to peer up the spout. "From whence does the water come?"

So, he hadn't *completely* forgotten her! "It's conjured up by magic."

Niall cast her one of those skeptical glances she was starting to associate with him. "Magic," he muttered, then snorted, his attention on the taps again.

Viviane waited, but Niall might as well have been alone, for all the attention he was going to give her. Clearly, she was going to be part of this discovery only if she explained things.

Well, she could do that. Viviane stepped forward, summoning her best smile, and put herself firmly between Niall and the current object of his fascination.

"You see, you just turn these knobs. On and off, hot and cold. This one plugs the hole—see? You just pull it up and down and it holds the water as long as you like. There's the most wonderful soap right here"—she passed it under his nose for him to smell—"and behind the looking glass— you'll never believe this!—there's a secret cavern."

She opened it with a gesture. "It opens with only the merest touch of the fingertips. Obviously, it's there for offerings for the pixie of the looking glass. She doesn't seem to be interested in my offerings, though." Viviane removed the wilted flower left there a few days before, as well as the piece of chocolate that she had been so sure the pixie would like. She frowned. "Maybe it's a boy pixie, or maybe what I leave there isn't good enough for an offering. What do you think?"

But Niall's eyes narrowed as he leaned closer to the taps. He was busy, turning the water on and off, on and off, his attention fixed on the changing flow. He played with the plug, he peered up the spout, he watched the basin fill and the water spill through the overflow.

Viviane waved the piece of chocolate at him, just to get his attention, but Niall ignored her. Her shoulders slumped as she wondered whether he had heard anything she had said.

And then she wondered what she could have done to have

so lost his attention. If only her mother had told her more about things between women and men, this would have been a lot easier. Viviane wondered whether there was something she should have done this morning to please Niall, and hated that she didn't know the answer.

Just when Viviane thought the taps couldn't occupy him any longer, he opened the little cabinet beneath the sink.

"Aha!" Niall murmured at the array of gleaming metal there, and fell to his knees. He tapped and listened, managing to fit his head into the tiny space to study the pipes.

Viviane might as well have been part of the wallhangings. She thought rather longingly of the way they had begun the day. Well, maybe she could solve the basic problem and get them back to where they had started.

It was worth a try.

Viviane cleared her throat pointedly, though Niall didn't look up—at least not until she lifted the lid of the toilet. He bumped his head on the top of the cupboard and winced, though that didn't seem to affect his interest.

In the toilet.

Viviane flatly refused to believe that any magic serving bodily functions was more interesting than she was. At least not for more than a few moments.

"And this is the toilet you were looking for. You see, it really is very clever, you sit and well . . ." She felt herself blush. "Well, you can guess that part, but then it all goes away."

"Aye?" He peered at the bowl, then looked behind it.

"Like this!" Viviane flicked the lever, pleased with her showmanship when Niall jumped backward at the noisy flushing of the bowl. A heartbeat later, he swatted beside it, unceremoniously laying claim to the lever and flushing it himself. He chuckled to himself, repeating the deed.

Then he leaned close to listen and did it again. And again. And one more time.

He might as well have been alone. When he murmured to himself, that was enough.

"You're not supposed to flush it unless you have to," Viviane said a little more snippily than she had intended. "Barb says it's bad for the water table, though how you could make a table of water, I don't know. It must be some kind of magical trick they do here in Avalon and the flushing affects how well it works . . ."

Viviane's words caught in her throat as Niall's fingers fell on the lid of the box at the back. Before she knew what he was about, he had removed it, displaying the innards of the magical device to the eye. Viviane cried out in dismay, certain some vengeful being would retaliate for the intrusion, but Niall took no notice of her whatsoever.

And the toilet didn't seem inclined to take vengeance for Niall abusing it so.

Viviane crept closer and looked at the array of bars and balls submerged in water there, curious despite herself. She couldn't see any sign of a being in charge, vengeful or otherwise, but then, it had probably hidden away in the blink of an eye, once it had known that Niall was going to expose it. The fey didn't like to be spied upon or have their dwellings invaded. Everyone knew that.

Except apparently Niall. He plunged his hand into the water there and flicked at the innards with one fingertip.

"You shouldn't touch them!" Viviane hissed, clutching his arm. "You'll muck up the magic! Who knows what will happen to you? You could be struck with lightning or banished from the realm, cursed for all your days and nights."

Niall cast her a telling glance. "You fret overmuch. This is no magic."

Before Viviane could argue, he pulled on something with a fingertip. The toilet flushed, even though he hadn't touched the flushing lever.

This time Viviane jumped backward, though Niall almost smiled.

He shook his head and pursed his lips, looking as satisfied as a large cat after a hot meal. "Now, where does the impulse begin?"

He straddled the seat, both hands in the tank, water up to his elbows as he explored. Some of the water splashed on the floor, but Niall was as oblivious to that as he was to Viviane. A frown marred his brow as he touched and wiggled, his concentration complete.

She had lost him to a magical garderobe.

His obliviousness to her naked presence was a startling contrast to earlier this morning and Viviane didn't much like the change. She thought she had a good idea how to get his attention back again, although it was her last real possibility.

"Well," she said with a breezy confidence she wasn't quite feeling "if you think that is a marvel, you will be amazed by this!" Viviane hauled back the drape over the shower stall, feeling triumphant when Niall glanced up.

She turned on the torrent of water, making sure the blend was nice and hot, then sent a victorious look his way. "You see, it's a small room made specifically for washing, like standing beneath a waterfall, but right in the warmth and comfort of this room. It's perfect! And people here take it for granted so much that they bathe within it once or even twice a day."

Viviane was uncertain how he would respond to her bold suggestion, but was still intent upon making it. "It has always seemed to me that the room is large enough to be shared, but perhaps we could find out for certain this morning."

Niall stood up and leaned into the stall, toyed with the taps, eyed the drain, then shook his head.

"'Tis just as the smaller one," he concluded, shook the water droplets out of his hair, and bowed his head once more over the innards of the toilet.

"But this one is for washing all over." Viviane waited, but to no avail. "You climb into it naked and there's plenty of room for two. I'm sure of it!"

Niall's brow furrowed with concentration. He didn't even answer her. Viviane tapped her toe, she let the steam fill the washroom.

But Niall didn't even look up. She danced her fingertips over his shoulder, but he just shrugged off her touch.

Well, it was clear enough that just about anything was more interesting than she was this morning, though she had certainly tried to set matters to rights. Viviane couldn't solve Niall's mood alone, particularly when he wasn't helping her any.

Maybe he just needed some time alone.

Well, she had to go to work anyhow.

Viviane lifted her chin and marched into the shower, taking great delight in generously using her favorite shower gel. She wasn't about to let him forget she was here, that she was naked, that she was willing, and that this shower could be shared. The washroom filled with the perfume of roses and Viviane knew it, but Niall's shadow still hunkered over the new object of his affection.

Viviane hummed, loudly and off-key, just to make sure he didn't completely forget she was there. She "inadvertently" got him wet, when she had to reach past him for a nail brush, making good and sure in the process that he couldn't miss seeing her naked and wet.

Niall barely glanced up.

She brushed her hip against him, laying a hand on his shoulder and practically poked her breast in his ear when she reached for the soap beside the sink. She apologized prettily, citing the small confines of the room, knowing full well that she had left a dribble of scented shower foam on the nape of his neck.

Niall wiped it off without glancing her way.

And Viviane finally became angry.

How dare he treat her with such disinterest? How dare he follow her all the way to Avalon, prove himself her own knight in shining armor, then simply forget about her?

That was not the way any of the books proceeded and certainly not the way hers was written. No! Niall should have been right here in this shower with her, running his big hands over her body, lathering up that shower gel and making her moan.

Well, it wasn't as though she hadn't made things crystal clear!

Viviane scrubbed with rising annoyance, wondering what else she could have possibly done. Her temper had just about come to a full simmer when Niall cried *"Aha!"* and the toilet gurgled as it flushed with gusto.

The water in the shower turned so scalding hot that Viviane screamed.

She jumped out onto the mat, trembling from head to toe, and earned herself only the most cursory glance from the man of her dreams.

"You end this ritual most hastily," he commented with an innocence that made her wonder whether he truly had no idea what he had done. She glared at him, but he was supremely oblivious, his tinkering fingers back at his self-appointed task.

He even whistled slightly under his breath.

Curse him! Viviane scrubbed herself off, then threw the wet towel at his head. She stormed off to dress for work without wasting a backward glance. She wouldn't give him the pleasure of any more of her attention. After all, few hours of being alone would show him the delights of her company and remind him of all he was missing.

Wouldn't it?

The toilet flushed once more as Viviane descended the stairs, her anger rising another notch at the certainty that Niall didn't even know she was gone.

Men!

But Niall knew.

Oh, he knew and he wished he did not. 'Twas only after the door slammed behind Viviane and the chamber echoed with silence that he heaved a sigh of relief. It had nigh taken every vestige of determination within him to not lunge into the shower after Viviane and take her against that shower wall.

Even now, he was not convinced he could trust himself to not run after her and beg for another chance to lay claim to her many charms. Aye, Viviane was a dangerous beauty, one whose witchery was readily forgotten when she smiled and chattered with such easy charm.

Niall released a shuddering breath. He could nigh see her with the torrent of water pouring over her lovely breasts, her neck arched back, her hair in a wet rivulet against her neck. He had glimpsed her silhouette through the curtain and clenched his teeth; he had smelled that potion she used within that place, and known that he could not endure the temptation much longer.

But he had.

And she—sorceress that she was—guessed his torment and sought only to make it worse. She leaned herself against him, ensuring that he felt the ripe perfection of that breast, no less the way the nipple beaded with the cold. She left a dollop of that infernally seductive mixture upon his own flesh to torment him with the knowledge of what could have been his own. Even now, Niall could smell it and, with each inadvertent turn of his head, he was inundated with a desire that weakened his knees.

Aye, Viviane had cast a spell upon him and addled his wits. Though it took all within him to not take what was offered, Niall of Malloy still ached with desire denied.

How was a man to think sensibly when a beguiling woman stood naked before him and sought to tempt him? What was a decent man to do when he tried only to keep his pledge, and hurt flashed in the eyes of that same woman as a result? Even if that hurt must be feigned, intended to twist his heart with guilt, 'twas no less effective for all of that.

How was a man to forget the way that very woman writhed in his arms, how she trusted him, how she tasted, how very innocent she seemed?

Niall turned the taps and concentrated on them, desperately trying to push the lady from his thoughts. On and off, hot and cold. Up and down, flush and fill. These devices were not nearly so interesting as he would have had Viviane believe.

But they had kept his hands busy.

Aye, the way she pressed those breasts against him, the way she kissed him, the way she persistently invited him back for more—'twas enough to drive a man of principles mad with desire.

A desire Niall dared not fulfill.

He had no place taking pleasure from the woman he had sworn to return to the executioner's block. 'Twould be wrong, 'twould make his task even more difficult. Niall reminded himself of that, even as his body argued the lady's own case.

The very fact that she desired him was telling. Aye, 'twas not the way of women to seek out such intimacy, unless they were in the trade of earning a living that way.

And Viviane was no whore.

Nay, she was a witch, which meant she sought to seduce him for other nefarious means, for her own means. There was one tale of witches that Niall recalled, for 'twas the one that chilled him to his very bones.

There was a token they desired, these witches, one that made men fall thrall to their twisted will. Aye, 'twas a token that must be won willingly from a man, then could be used against him and all his brethren with dreadful power.

For a mortal man to plant himself willingly within a witch was a daunting prospect, by the telling of this tale. To be sure, there was a part of him that Niall would prefer did not shrivel and fall off. Whether 'twould be mounted and used as a powerful talisman thereafter or not.

Niall would simply prefer to keep himself intact.

Viviane must have guessed his true objective in pursuing her and sought to turn matters to her own advantage. Indeed, Niall recalled little of what he had said the night before be-

neath the assault of Paula's potion. He might well have told
her of his mission himself.

One could never be certain. Viviane intended to render his
quest a failure, 'twas as simple as that.

'Twas far from reassuring that the better part of Niall was
more than prepared to surrender to the lady's ardent demands, the consequences be damned. Aye, 'twas not reason
guiding his impulse here!

Indeed, he had come dangerously close to joining her as
she laved herself so close beside him. So great was his distraction that Niall had barely been able to distinguish what
was before his own eyes. He had not found the flushing
lever on purpose, though in hindsight, he was glad he had.
Niall had been close to succumbing to the lady's allure, her
exit saving him just in time.

He was honest enough to admit that he was disappointed,
however foolishly. Niall toyed absently with the water device, watching the water flow when he turned the handle one
way, then stop when he turned it the other.

'Twas only then he realized the import of what was beneath his hands.

He was no sorcerer and yet he readily made the device
conjure the water. Hot and cold, on and off. Niall could see
the hand of man in this. Though he could not fathom what
made the water run, he knew that he controlled its tempera-
ture and pace with perfect precision.

No spells, no rhymes, no incantations or slaughtered
poultry were necessary to ensure the device did its task. The
good sense of a clear-thinking man was behind this or Niall
would eat his armor.

Ha! A reasonable explanation!

It made perfect sense. Niall had heard of marvels of the
East in many matters—men of afar oft had other ideas, other
cleverness that could be understood once explained.

But that did not make those marvels *magic*.

Aye, he could not explain the mechanism of the mill that
ground the flour, though he knew well enough that it did.

And he had not the skill to make ale from water and yeast, though he knew it could be done.

What if no magic governed doings here at all?

He straightened, stunned by the next clear step in his thinking. What if this was *not* Avalon? What if Paula was not a pixie and none of the others were sorcerers? What if they were but *people,* albeit people of some unknown and exotic locale, people with skills beyond those of the archbishop's court?

Foreigners. With foreign ways and advanced mechanisms.

Niall dropped the lid and sat down heavily, his thoughts flying like quicksilver. 'Twas perfectly reasonable, an explanation that deeply appealed to his sense of how matters should be.

And, if he could learn some of the marvels of this exotic place, then he could bring new prosperity to Cantlecroft! He would be like one of the old crusaders, returning from an arduous quest with exotic marvels that dazzled those who had remained behind!

And vastly improved their lot. Oh, had they not learned much of the machinery of war from Outremer? And what of the marvel that was silk? The spices they now used to flavor meat, the cloves and pepper, both were once unknown on England's chilly shores.

Then, he truly would be a hero.

Niall turned on the shower as Viviane had done and watched the water flow, an even more appealing possibility taking shape in this thoughts. People like the archbishop would pay dearly for this marvel in their homes. Aye, the man who held the secret of this cleverness would be in high demand.

With understanding of these devices, Niall could create labor for his nephews that would see them gainfully employed for all their days.

'Twas perfect!

But all hinged upon his ability to prove that this was a mechanical marvel, that this was not Avalon, but some distant realm of men. Niall stripped off his garb and stepped beneath the stream of water, knowing his mission had just taken on another wrinkle.

First and foremost, he had to discover where precisely this was.

'Twas only then, as Niall turned his face to the beat of water, that he let himself savor the sight of Viviane, gloriously nude. He smiled to himself in recollection of her hasty departure from this shower, droplets over her skin, her nipples beading, her eyes flashing sparks.

He recalled how she had looked when she gained her pleasure, the little wordless sound she had made as she crested the pinnacle, and part of him awakened with a vengeance. He had been overcruel in letting her believe that he was not achingly aware of her beauty—'twas no wonder she was annoyed.

Surely 'twould hurt little to make amends with her first.

'Twas just his sense of chivalry, Niall knew. Aye, 'twould be churlish to leave the lady irked with him for no better cause than his own distrust of his impulses.

Or perhaps 'twas a desire for his own welfare. There was no telling, after all, what a vexed witch might do to a man. Niall told himself that he had a duty to set matters to rights, to ensure that Viviane was not irked with him. Then he would avoid her company—at least until he had discovered all he needed to know—lest she tempt him to forget himself.

And *then,* he would return them both to Cantlecroft.

Chapter 8

Barb TOOK ONE look at Viviane and headed for the tiny kitchen off the back of the bookstore. "You look like you need a cup of tea," she said in the same moment that she plugged in the kettle.

"Oh, Barb!" Viviane's hands bunched into fists and she made a little growl of frustration. She looked like a riled pussycat, one who was so seldom riled that she didn't know quite what to do with her claws. "I could just *kill* him!"

"Sit." Barb pulled out a chair and pointed to it, characteristically in no mood for avoiding the point. "Who is he?"

Viviane dropped onto the seat and knotted her hands together in her lap. Her teeth were obviously gritted and her color was high.

She had it bad, Barb immediately decided. The guy after all, had said he wouldn't be here long. She didn't need a map to see where this conversation was going, although she didn't like the view. Barb reflected that, sadly, it had only been a matter of time before a really nice woman like Viviane found some jerk to take advantage of her.

Viviane was almost too nice. In fact, business had improved a lot since Viviane came on board, mostly because the younger woman was so genuine. She was a bit shy, but once people asked her about books—especially romances!—well, she had lots to say.

She was really interested in the constantly changing condition of Mrs. MacAllister's gout. She listened to all of Mr. Ramsay's adventures, or at least the adventures of his amorous billy goat who wouldn't stay home and Mr. Ramsay's ongoing efforts to foil the goat's escapes.

And Viviane loved books. Barb was starting to think that hiring Viviane was one of the smartest things she had ever done. People came just to visit with Viviane, just to see her smile and hear her talk about the books she was reading.

The woman read like a demon—she seemed obsessed with reading every single book in the store. And she was ready to tell anyone about her latest favorite, always with such enthusiasm that her listeners invariably bought books.

A lot of books. Barb was beginning to wish that Viviane was twins.

As unlikely as it might have seemed to the casual observer, even prickly and private Barb had become very fond of her new employee. Viviane had a tendency to bring out Barb's deeply buried maternal impulses, as she did right now. Viviane was such a peach—she deserved better than some love-'em-and-leave-'em type.

A type who had apparently left Barb with the fun job of explaining the truth to Viviane.

What a rat!

Viviane took a deep breath and unknotted her fingers, clearly choosing her words with care. "I knew Niall before, where I used to live."

"And he followed you here." Barb tossed tea bags into the old brown teapot, not liking the sound of this at all.

"Well, yes." Viviane frowned and propped her hand on her elbow with a sigh. Barb noted that it was not the sigh of a happy woman. "And I thought it was so romantic, that he came after me and that he brought me back the pendant I had lost there and that he seemed so *glad* to have found me . . ."

"And . . ." Barb prompted.

Viviane shrugged and toyed with a spoon left laying on the table. "I thought it was like one of the books, and that everything would be wonderful, that we were destined to be together and that he loved me. And when he kissed me, well . . ."

"So you slept with him." Barb grimly filled the teapot with boiling water.

Viviane lowered her voice to a scandalized whisper as her cheeks pinkened. "We didn't just *sleep*, Barb."

"Well, *duh*!" Barb sighed in exasperation. "I figured that out."

Viviane bit her lip and frowned at the stray spoon as she spun it around the tabletop with one fingertip.

Barb had seen enough of regret to recognize it when it showed up in her shop, guns ablazing. And she had given the "Get Real" talk enough times to have it memorized, not to mention her own extensive on-the-ground experience.

Might as well get it over with. Barb poured tea which was pretty thin and plunked the two mugs down on the table. She sat down opposite Viviane and willed the younger woman to look at her.

She deliberately kept her voice unemotional.

"So, now it's done and you're worrying about biological souvenirs and thinking that maybe you made a big mistake. You can't imagine what you were thinking last night, that maybe you jumped into the pond too fast. Maybe you're half worried he's going to boot it."

Barb turned her steaming mug in the wet ring it left on the table. "On the other hand, you don't really know anything about him, not nearly enough to be making any sort of commitment and what you've seen so far isn't changing your mind. And that part of you is wondering how you're going to get rid of him if he *doesn't* boot it."

Barb sipped, certain she had nailed it in one.

"Oh, no! Niall won't leave."

That was news to her, but Viviane seemed convinced. In

fact, her whole face had brightened. "I mean, we're meant to be together." She smiled with a sunny confidence Barb didn't share. "I just know it."

Hmmm. Barb sipped her tea and decided to try another tack. Let him do his own dirty work! "So, how well did you know him before?"

"Not very well," Viviane acknowledged with a dreamy smile. "But there was a force between us, right from the beginning. And you know, when he kisses me, well I just forget all about everything else. He tastes so good and he feels so . . ."

"Spare me the play-by-play." Barb waved her mug. "What's the issue here?"

Viviane sighed. "We had a wonderful time last night and a better time this morning. I fell back asleep, but when I woke up, Niall was different."

"How different?"

"As though he didn't want to be near me." Viviane appealed to Barb with a glance. "I just couldn't seem to get his attention. He started fiddling with the toilet, trying to figure how it worked or something. It was as though I wasn't even there!"

"Did you say anything mushy to him?"

Viviane looked perplexed.

"You know, did you make any reference to, say, your being destined to be together."

"Well, of course!" Viviane looked at Barb as though she was the thick one. "It's perfectly obvious, after all. That's why he's here!"

Barb leaned across the table, losing the battle to bite back a smile. "But Viviane, he's a *guy*."

"I *know* that."

"Do you have brothers?"

"No."

"Well, if you did, you'd know that they're just *different*. Guys think different from us, they talk different from us, but sometimes they mean the same thing. And when emotion shows up"—Barb rolled her eyes—"they do their damnedest to duck and run." She gestured with her mug. "He's being evasive. He's not sure what you expect from him and doesn't want to talk about it."

Or he did know and didn't want to let Viviane down right to her face? Barb's usually unsympathetic heart twisted just a little.

Because anyone could see that Viviane was an incurable romantic. Barb didn't want to be the one to tell her that some men never fell in love. Nope, Mr. Tall, Blond and Handsome could clean up after himself.

As much as Barb hated the thought of him doing it. She heaved a sigh and tried to be helpful as well as protective. Because if anyone could reform a rat, it was sweet, genuine Viviane.

She forced a smile for her troubled employee. "Take a look in the relationship section when you have a chance and you'll see different. Men are from Mars and all that jazz. They're like a different species."

"I had no idea . . ."

"How would you?" Barb patted her employee's hand. "See, you've been reading too much in the romance section. Great stuff, but written *by* women *for* women, if you know what I mean Kind of how we'd like men to be if we got to design them from the ground up, instead of the way they really are."

Viviane seemed to be thinking about that.

"They don't read romances, Viviane, so they don't have a clue. In fact, they don't read the relationship books, either, though they whine enough about not understanding women. Goddess forbid that they did anything to solve that!"

Viviane smiled, just a glimmer of her usual enthusiasm but it was enough for Barb.

"You've got to look at what he's done. Guys put more value in deeds than words."

"You sound like Niall," Viviane charged and Barb couldn't stop her chuckle.

"Years in the trenches. Three brothers—I was trained from the cradle, after all. Or maybe I should call it trial by fire." Barb leaned closer when Viviane didn't seem to follow the reference. "You said he followed you—was it far? Expensive? Hard to do?"

Viviane's eyes rounded. "Oh yes!"

"And he brought you a gift?"

Viviane fingered a pendant she was wearing. "I dropped this when I saw him last and he brought it back to me."

Barb was impressed, despite herself. "That was nice of him. Give credit where it's due—most people wouldn't have bothered."

Viviane smiled. "I thought it was a gallant gesture," she said softly, that smile broadening to make her features glow. "Something fitting for a knight of old to do for his lady."

Oh boy, she was smitten.

"Well, he must have wanted to see you again," Barb acknowledged reluctantly. "Maybe it was an excuse. They like that—covering up a sweet gesture with what seems like a logical one." Or a horny one. Barb couldn't bring herself to say that when Viviane looked so hopeful. Instead she reached out one hand. "Let me see it."

The pendant was a moonstone set in silver, an old piece and obviously of some value. There was a lot of silver in the heavy setting and the stone was probably the biggest and bluest moonstone Barb had ever seen.

She touched it with one fingertip and shivered at the coldness of the stone. "It's beautiful and unique."

"My mother gave it to me," Viviane admitted.

A sentimental piece. The guy had played a sentimental card and, judging by Viviane's softened expression, he had played it well. Barb frowned—that wasn't the gesture of a guy determined to cut and run.

Maybe, just maybe, he was smitten as badly as Viviane but did a better job of hiding it. Barb ran her thumb across the stone and wondered.

Maybe.

"Right." Barb released the pendant and gave her employee a smile. "Maybe you should cut him some slack. If he's a creep trying to take advantage of you, you'll know soon enough. That kind of thing is hard to hide." She shrugged and finished her tea.

But Viviane didn't look away. "Do you think he's a creep?"

Barb turned her empty mug in that wet mark again, but she found it impossible to lie to Viviane.

"I don't know." Barb shrugged. "He could just be Grade A prime male, right to the bone."

The younger woman flashed an impish grin. "Or maybe he just doesn't understand that we're meant for each other." Before Viviane could say anything more, the man in question appeared on the stairs to the room above.

"Viviane?" he said, the low rumble of his voice filling the shop. His gaze fixed on Viviane and he smiled the kind of slow, sensuous smile that would make every woman with a pulse ready to surrender.

He was almost better looking dressed than half-naked, though it was a close call. He was certainly all man. Barb took a good look to confirm her conclusion and silently sighed with almost forgotten longing.

"Are you not hungered this morn?" Niall asked, the direction of his thoughts as obvious as the perfect nose on his ruggedly handsome face.

Barb snorted at her own reality check and took her cup to the sink. "One hundred percent prime beefcake, all right," she muttered.

Niall frowned and Barb felt his gaze follow her. "I must apologize to you for this morn. I did not know the marvels of this washroom . . ."

Barb waved off his apology. "What's done is done." She stopped and turned to him. "I and the Siberian Iris would appreciate no repeats."

Niall bowed and Barb disliked that she was so easily impressed by his manners.

Viviane looked between the pair of them with obvious confusion. "You know each other already?"

"We met in the garden," Barb supplied crisply, unable to resist tossing one hard look at the man in question. He held her gaze steadily and she credited him with not wincing.

But it wouldn't hurt Viviane to have all the facts. "Funny what you said about not staying long," she said flatly. "Viviane seems to think you're here to stay."

He inhaled sharply and Viviane gasped, her smile banished. She turned to Niall with dismay and Barb felt a surge of satisfaction that at least she'd moved everything out into the open.

"Go on, take the day," she said with a cheerful wave and a wink for Viviane. Her employee was busy looking daggers at Niall, who was glaring at Barb. "Get your boytoy fed. It's going to be slow today, anyhow, what with the rain."

It would probably take them all day to sort that one out.

Barb almost wished she could watch.

To Niall's relief, Viviane seemed disinclined to chatter, which could only mean that she was hungered as well. She marched along beside him, with nary a glance his way. And 'twas easier to not be tempted by her charm this way, that much was certain.

Though after a few moments, Niall began to wonder whether there was more at root than hunger.

"You seem less than amiable," he ventured. "Did this Barb complain of my pissing in her garden?"

Viviane flashed a lethal glance at him. "So, *that* was how you met. Did you have a nice long chat?"

"Nay."

The lady sniffed and hauled open the door of a shop, and the expression on her face would have made a lesser man cringe. "Then isn't it strange that you had time to tell her of your plans, when you haven't told *me*."

She let the door close right behind her, leaving Niall to open it again and stride after her.

"Viviane!"

"I have nothing to say to you," she snapped, then made a show of examining the pastries on display. "After all, you're not even staying." She smiled deliberately for the man behind the counter, her manner turning sweet as honey. "Good morning, Joe."

A burly man with thinning hair and perspiration on his pate smiled a greeting from behind the counter. "Morning, Viviane." He jerked a thumb toward Niall. "This guy giving you trouble?"

Her smile broadened, though she did not even glance at Niall. "In a way, yes, but there's no need to worry yourself." For the first time, she looked at Niall, though the characteristic warmth in her eyes had faded.

That hurt lingered there again and Niall knew that he was responsible for it.

"I'm sure it's just a misunderstanding," she added softly, the hint of vulnerability in her tone twisting a knife in Niall's heart.

Oh, if she had not been a witch, he would have been a base villain! He could not help feeling the part, though he knew that she deliberately toyed with him.

The baker looked doubtful. "If you say so."

Niall's belly knotted at the smell of fresh bread and he knew he would not be able to think matters through without a good meal. He eyed the goods on display and his hunger grew a thousandfold. They even had pastry filled with sausage meat, his favored treat, though the pastries were oversmall.

Niall frowned. Though 'twas not uncommon for merchants to cut portions to ensure higher profits. Surely even here there was a master of the market to ensure the measures were being met?

But no one seemed prepared to complain besides Niall.

"What would you like today?"

Viviane stepped forward and opened her mouth, but Niall did not like the gleam in the man's eye. Why did this one take Viviane's protection upon his own shoulders? And what would he desire of her in return? Niall could readily imagine and did not like the thought.

Indeed, he would win her favor once more by showing himself respectful of her honor. Then she would be irked with him no longer. Niall immediately stepped up beside Viviane and asked for a dozen of the small sausage-filled pastries.

After all, he wanted to ensure that they had enough.

Viviane caught her breath and the look she turned on him was frosty. Niall realized that his plan to win her favor was not working overwell.

"Anything else, sir?"

"A measure of ale would be most welcome."

The man behind the counter snorted. "Not here. No need for a liquor license in a bakery."

Niall was astonished. "A man cannot break his fast with ale?"

"Only in the tavern, and on some days, not before midday," Viviane confided in an undertone.

Niall shook his head. "And you call this paradise," he muttered, earning a sympathetic grin from the man behind the counter.

"I'm with you. Nothing like a cold brew first thing in the morning to start the day off right." He winced. "And nothing like the old L.C.B.C. to take the fun out of that."

Niall knew of no Elsie Beesie, and thus knew not what to say. How could a woman keep a man from selling ale in the morn? He could not imagine, but dared not ask Viviane under this merchant's scrutiny.

The baker propped an elbow on the counter, clearly warming to a favored theme. "Nothing like the government putting their dirty fingers into everything, taxing the life out of us, that's what they're doing. I say they should get out of the liquor business, privatize the selling of booze like they've done in Alberta. They'll never do it, though, bunch of weenies, because they're making too much money to bear to give it up."

He nodded emphathically and Niall slanted a glance to Viviane. She looked as confused by this monologue as he, and he was startled to find himself again feeling a sense of kinship with her.

Niall nodded, because it seemed some acknowledgement should be made. "You speak good sense," he allowed, and the baker sniffed approval.

"*Then* you'd be able to have your brew in the morning, because you can be sure I'd have it right on tap, right here." He winked. "Though it wouldn't be the most profitable enterprise I ever took on, if you know what I mean."

Niall did not, but refrained from saying so.

"Usual for you, Viviane?"

"Yes, please, Joe."

"And what is this concoction?" Niall asked her as the balding man bustled away to mix things together. He couldn't help but wish that she would at least look his way, even knowing 'twas her spell that left him yearning like a pup.

'Twas most disconcerting to have her resolve to ignore him before he could apologize, then proceed to keep his distance from her.

"Is it of the same ilk as Paula's potion?"

Viviane smiled for the balding man, but not—Niall noticed with disappointment—for him. "Joe's café au lait is so good that you'll believe it's made by magic alone." She tossed her hair over her shoulder and smiled again for the baker Joe. "You should have one, too."

That man beamed as he set a cup on the counter. The warm gaze he spared for Viviane was duly noted by Niall.

Who heartily disapproved.

Aye, this man wore a ring upon his finger, a gold band of import that could not be missed. And Viviane was not his spouse!

Niall was prepared to dislike his concoction on principle alone, at least until the steam rising from the frothing cup teased his nostrils. It smelled so exotic and unlike anything else he had known that he immediately decided to take Viviane's advice.

Perhaps that would win her favor.

But nay, she seemed not to note his choice, not at all.

Niall's mood soured yet further. When the tally was made, he tried to pay with one of the coins he had moved from purse to pocket on Derek's vessel, but the baker frowned at it.

"We don't take foreign money," Joe said crisply and handed it back. "U.S. dollars at par, unless you go to the bank. Sorry"—he shrugged—"but it's so busy that I don't have time to screw around with exchange rates."

Niall looked to Viviane, embarrassed by his inability to pay for their victuals. She dug in her own pocket, producing an odd array of colored coins and paper.

The balance was paid while Niall's ears burned, though none seemed to find him less of a man for so relying upon his female companion's largesse. Indeed, friendly greetings were exchanged as they gathered their purchases, and the shop filled with familiar talk about the weather. The merchant had provided small tables and chairs in his shop, perhaps the reason for his small portions.

Niall followed Viviane's lead with brown powders she called sugar and cinnamon, his first sip of this beverage making his eyes close in wonder. 'Twas marvelous and he could quickly see that he would have need of another.

Niall consumed several sausage rolls in silence before his belly was appeased, then met Viviane's cautious gaze. The deed could be avoided no longer. "I would apologize to you, for 'tis clear you are angered with me this morn."

Her lips tightened and she avoided his gaze. "If you're leaving, it doesn't matter whether I'm angry with you or not."

"Viviane . . ."

She put her cup back down on the board with force. "*Are* you leaving? And if you are, how could you tell Barb but not me? You don't even know her! And why did you ignore me this morning?" Her lovely eyes clouded with tears, which must have been the only reason Niall's innards clenched. "What's wrong? How could you even think of leaving? I thought that we . . ."

Niall reached across and snared her hand, wishing the others in this establishment were not so interested in their conversation. He looked into Viviane's eyes, knowing he could not lie to her despite her witchery, but needing to reassure her.

And zounds, he had to ensure she did not cry!

Some parts of the truth would simply have to be avoided, there was naught else for it.

"Viviane," he said in a voice low with determination. "If I had joined you in your showering chamber, we should still be there."

That was true enough.

She caught her breath, her eyes widening slightly as she stared at him. Her gaze was so full of hope that he could not imagine the expression was contrived.

Niall held her gaze and smiled slowly, liking how her hand relaxed in his and her gaze softened. He stroked the back of her hand with his thumb, unaware he intended to do so before he felt the smooth sweep of her skin pass beneath his touch.

"And if I had but looked upon you," he murmured, "then I would have joined you. Matters might well have moved too quickly and we might have done what would later be regretted."

"Oh, Niall!" Viviane smiled at him then, for the first time since he had come down to the shop seeking her and Niall's breath caught. "Trust you to be worried about something like that!"

And she reached across the table, framed his face in her hands and kissed him soundly.

Niall's heart leapt, but Viviane did not pull back, her lips soft against his own. He could smell the sweet scent of her skin, of that cursed lotion she had used in the shower, and his body responded with vigor.

When she flicked her tongue against his lips like a thirsty kitten sipping milk, desire raged hot through his veins. Zounds, he would take her right here and care naught for the consequences!

Niall caught at her wrists, and with a herculean effort, lifted her hands from his face. He broke their kiss, knowing his gaze simmered into hers but unable to stop it.

His breathing was ragged, the sight of Viviane's flushed cheeks doing naught to ease his state.

Then, she smiled.

'Twas only because he had affirmed the effect of her spell upon him, Niall was certain. Though now he realized the folly of what he had done, too late to undo it.

At least, the tears had disappeared from her eyes.

Indeed, she leaned closer and Niall's heart skipped a beat, his mouth going dry. "Oh, Niall, I just knew that everything would come out right. I knew that you had to desire me, just as I want you and now that I know that you're not leaving, well everything will be just fine! Barb said you would be shy about confessing your emotions, but I think you've done a wonderful job already and now"—she pinkened in a most delightful way as she smiled at him—"now, I'll just have to convince you to love me. Don't worry, it will be perfect!"

And she sipped her beverage, as content as a cat by the fire.

Niall swallowed. He had put himself back in the position he most wished to avoid. He had to say something to keep Viviane at distance, something to undermine her conviction that they would shortly share a bed, something to make her forget her intent to charm him.

So, Niall said the first thing that came to mind, prompted as it was by the smell of a warm sausage pastry.

"Aye, I should be sorely hungered if we still were in this washing room. 'Tis good indeed that we were not delayed there overlong."

Niall bit into his pastry with gusto.

Through his lashes, he watched Viviane stiffen and deliberately decided to make matters worse.

"Indeed, I cannot imagine what a man could love more than a warm pastry such as this one." He finished it with one hearty bite, quickly claiming another, smacking his lips and feigning indifference to the lady's presence.

Viviane glared at him, her lips tight, then sat back in her chair. Her eyes shone oddly but Niall refused to let himself be swayed by the prospect of tears.

Nay, he had a mission. And he could only complete his mission by ensuring Viviane's desire was not achieved.

Surprisingly, his own desire to kiss her did not ease.

Indeed, Niall felt newly guilty for disappointing her. 'Twas an irrational impulse and he would do best to not linger upon it.

"What is the coin of this realm?" Niall asked, in a bid to distract her and prompt her chatter once again. The woman loved to talk, after all, and she was uncommonly good at explaining matters, even if she was prone to attribute all to magic. "Let me see it. I would not err so again."

Viviane obligingly poured it onto the table between them, though her manner indicated that she was unimpressed by the chance to explain it to him.

'Twas unlike any currency Niall had ever seen before, the rims of the coins unnicked. There were coins of all hues of metal, instead of simply gold or silver, and they were most finely minted. There was a regent on one side—a queen, no less!—which was familiar enough, and an animal on the reverse, much like the emblems Niall knew well.

The images upon them however were more crisp than any Niall had ever seen. This he suspected was a function of a skilled die-maker.

"Tell me of it," he asked.

The lady folded her arms across her chest mutinously.

"Viviane, 'tis all I ask of you," Niall murmured and saw her heave a sigh.

"Are you leaving?"

Niall held her gaze. "Not without you."

'Twas true. Just uttering the words restored Niall's glum mood, just as the deed clearly delighted the lady.

"I knew it!" she cried and smiled for him again. Niall's heart began to pound. "I'll teach you to love me," Viviane pledged as she leaned closer, a tempting smile playing over her full lips. She wrinkled her nose and shook her finger at him playfully. "And it has been said that I can be irresistible."

Niall's mouth went dry. Indeed, he believed her claim well enough and could think of several ways to succumb to her charms right here and now, though he fought to keep his expression impassive.

Viviane barely noticed his response, her cheerful manner restored. "This one is a dollar." She fished out a copper-hued coin and handed it to Niall, the brushing of their fingers in the transaction sending a tingle over his flesh. He frowned that she might not guess his response. "They call it a loonie, though I don't know why."

Niall turned the coin in his fingers. Viviane spoke with good sense—there was naught about it that resembled the moon. Its color was wrong, too brassy for even a harvest moon and there was a waterbird of some kind upon its back.

"And this one is worth two of those," she separated another from the pile and handed it to him. 'Twas distinctive in that it was wrought of two different metals, one encircling the other in a most skilled fashion. "They call it a toonie."

Niall glanced up, puzzled, and she shrugged.

"I don't know why." She picked through the pile of smaller coins, laying them out in order. "These ones are worth fractions of the loonie or the dollar, whichever you want to call it."

"Like shillings and pence."

"Yes, but they divide the dollar into measures of a hundred called cents. So, this is a quarter of a dollar, and this is called a dime and is worth ten cents."

"Ten to the dollar."

"Um-hmm. And the nickel is five cents and the penny is a single cent. Then there's the paper money." She unfurled vellum so brightly hued and embellished that it made Niall gasp. These pictures he could not so readily explain, though it was clear there was real talent in the making of them. The green one labelled 20 even had a square upon it that gleamed like gold when held one way, and with the shiny green of a beetle's back the other.

He could not blame Viviane for calling this magic, though Niall hoped he could prove 'twas otherwise.

"They call it paper," Viviane confided in an undertone. "Barb says it's made of wood and they use this paper for everything, including books."

Niall glanced up with surprise. "What of vellum and parchment?"

"Very expensive here." Viviane shrugged. "Paper is cheaper."

Niall arched a brow, the idea of goods being expensive having little to do with his idea of an otherworldly paradise. His pulse quickened, his certainty growing that he was right. "And whence does it come, this currency?"

"You work for it, just like in Cantlecroft, but get it at the bank." She pointed to a building with a large blue sign and Niall marked its location.

"Moneychangers."

Viviane nodded and Niall shook his head. They were everywhere, with their exorbitant interest rates and fees for services, worse than whores for cheating a man.

Their presence did not mesh with his expectation of paradise either. All the same, he would visit there later this day to have his own coin changed, though he would ensure the moneychangers did not cheat him. They were well known for such thievery, even in Cantlecroft, and Niall was even more convinced that this place was more like home than not.

"Barb pays me to be in the shop and help her clients. She even lets me read the books so I can suggest which ones people might like to read and oh, Niall, it's so interesting! I never imagined that there were so many books in the world and so many stories being told, and so many marvelous kingdoms being described."

"Though indeed"—she leaned closer and Niall echoed her gesture before he caught himself—"there is much that I do not understand."

Viviane wrinkled her nose in a most fetching manner. "They must all be tales of this magical realm, or perhaps of other magical realms. 'Tis more than a little confusing, though I must confess, my interest is in the romantic deeds. That I can *always* understand!" Her eyes shone in a most beguiling manner as she talked and Niall had a hard time keeping his skepticism in place.

Aye, he could have simply watched the woman all the day long. No doubt that was her scheme, for 'twould keep him from learning all he needed to know.

Niall snorted. "I was not aware that any tales of paradise included the concept of labor for coin."

Viviane sipped her drink. "Well, I don't work very hard."

"But you are not there this day."

Viviane shrugged. "Then Barb won't pay me."

Niall was a practical man. Even this small meal had cost considerable measure of Viviane's coin. They must eat thrice a day and oft more than this small feast. He could see the limitations of this system already, particularly as he was uncertain how long 'twould take to gain the knowledge he now desired, let alone what measure these moneychangers would give him in exchange for his own coin.

He and Viviane might spend a good bit of time in each other's company. Niall's heart skipped a beat at the prospect, though he knew 'twas just Viviane's spell working its witchery upon him.

Nay, his sole desire was to win good apprenticeships for his nephews. And he must remain in the lady's presence, ideally sharing her quarters, to ensure that she did not flee or use her charm to disappear.

'Twas only the prospect of success that made his pulse quicken.

Niall scowled. "And your chamber? You pay for this with coin or labor?"

"Money. Two hundred dollars per month."

"And how much are you paid by this Barb?"

Viviane ran through the numbers for him, Niall calculating sums in his head as ever he had done. She explained her wage and her mode of payment, which meant she had to explain the odd manner of keeping hours in this place. He added and subtracted, and was somewhat reassured that they would not starve.

'Twas then that Viviane told him of the healthy tithe taken from her earnings.

"It's a tax," she explained. "From the government."

"What government? I have seen neither king nor court!"

"Well, there isn't actually one here . . ."

"Nay? And what do they do with your coin? I see no knights, no steeds, no armory. Is all this hidden away from the eye? What of the master of the market?" He poked at his over-small pastry. "Does no one police the measures?"

Viviane dropped her voice and leaned closer. "I haven't seen any signs of anything like that," she admitted. "And they say the money goes away to Ottawa, wherever that might be."

"Distant kings, who take coin and grant naught in return! They are no better than thieves in the night!" Niall roared so loudly that others turned to look. He shook a finger at Viviane. "You should refuse to pay their tithes, for no one should pay a due without winning something in return."

"You can't do that. They take it from your pay before it's given to you."

Niall was appalled. "What manner of dishonesty runs amok in this land that none are trusted to pay their tithes and taxes?"

"It's just the way they do things here." Viviane shrugged. "You'll have to get used to it."

"I shall never become accustomed to having my purse

raided." Niall fixed her with a skeptical glance. "One would think that *Avalon* would be spared the drudgery of labor, coin and taxes. It has always seemed to me that those were the inventions of kings of men."

Viviane looked surprised. "I never thought of it that way."

"There is no other way to think of it," Niall said sternly. "You had best return to your labor this day, for you will have need of the coin."

Viviane straightened, that hurt flashing through her eyes once again. "I thought we would spend the day together."

"I have matters to tend," Niall said gruffly, staring at the table instead of into those wondrous eyes. Indeed, he did not dare risk too much of the lady's companionship, for he knew already how she could make him forget his sworn word.

"I see," Viviane said frostily. She put her cup firmly on the table, pushed to her feet and left, without a backward glance.

Niall watched her walk away through the rain and felt a nigh overwhelming sense of failure. It seemed he had done little to ease the fact that she was vexed with him. 'Twas a conundrum to not be able to lie to the lady, yet at the same time to seek her favor.

Niall sighed and sipped from his cup. Aye, he knew that confessing that he was the one dispatched to retrieve her would do little to improve Viviane's current opinion of him.

But she was a witch. And she had enchanted him. And the guilt he felt was not only magically induced but kept him from fulfilling his duty.

When Niall thought of matters that way—without the distraction of a lady's lovely face—all made good sense.

Even if it made his innards writhe to know that Viviane would be the one to suffer the price. Niall determinedly finished his pastry, being certain to consume every single crumb.

Sooner begun, sooner finished, he concluded and pushed to his feet with purpose. Niall's lips tightened to a grim line.

First, the moneychangers.

Chapter 9

DEREK MOSEYED INTO the bank that Monday morning to do his weekly cash run and was surprised to find Viviane's friend there. Niall seemed to be in the midst of an argument with the teller at the service counter, but Derek deliberately minded his business.

He'd better not mention this to Paula, he reasoned as he counted his bills again at the teller's counter. She'd kill him for not eavesdropping on the details.

Derek had no sooner had that thought than there was no choice but to eavesdrop.

"You would cheat me!" Niall roared.

Everyone in the bank turned to look and the reedy man behind the counter turned red to the tips of his ears. He tried to apologize, but Niall gave him no choice.

In fact, the man in Derek's clothes shook a finger at the clerk. "This ploy of taking my coin for appraisal is an old one, indeed. I know well enough that you have an accomplice who will trade the gold for some folly that deceives the eye yet holds no value. Nay! My coin remains in mine own hand until you offer the coin of the realm in exchange."

The clerk looked a bit desperate. "But sir! I'm sorry, sir, but . . ."

"Maybe I can help," Derek suggested, his smooth tone designed to even tempers and ease attention away from the exchange. He had practiced it to perfection, but was still delighted every time it worked.

As it did right now.

The clerk nearly fell on him in gratitude, just for the intervention. "It's a procedural thing, sir, really. We can't evaluate gold coins here, so we have to send them to the city . . ."

"To the city!" Niall snorted. "Even better—your accomplice is a *foreigner.* Do you think me witless enough to wait days for your response, while my coin travels farther and farther afield?"

"Sir! We issue a receipt . . ."

"A receipt for what? For theft of my coin? And will you grant me another equal coin in exchange?"

"Well, well," the clerk's gaze strayed agitatedly to the gold coin laying on the counter between them. "That would be hard to do, sir."

"Aha! 'Tis a trick, I knew it well." Niall stood back and folded his arms across his chest with the satisfaction of a man who had proven his point. "I would suggest," he said silkily, "that you exchange this coin for the coin of your realm with all haste."

The clerk's mouth opened and closed, he appealed to Derek with a glance.

"May I?" At Niall's nod, Derek picked up the coin for a closer look. It was gold, or at least it looked like gold to him. Derek had fingered more gold than most men, but still he couldn't be sure without an appraisal.

But the interesting thing about the coin was that it appeared to be old. Really old. It sure wasn't Canadian or American currency, although the date on it was a bit tough to read. It could say 1390, but Derek wasn't sure.

Sure or not, his heart made a little pit-a-pat. 1390! He could be holding a numismatic treasure in his hands.

And if he was, Niall wasn't going to get anywhere near its real value from a bank. Of course, there weren't a lot of options on an island like this.

But Derek could solve that. He handed the coin back to Niall and smiled. "You're right, they won't give you nearly its value here."

Niall gave a triumphant look to the clerk.

"Especially if it's antique, as I think it is."

Now Niall's eyes narrowed and he studied Derek again. "Antiquity is long behind us."

"Yeah, yeah, I know, but there are people who collect old coins. Like this one."

Niall ran his thumb across the gold, his voice low and considering. If Derek didn't know better, he'd think the guy was trying to drive a better price. "This coin is not so old as that."

"Well, maybe not to some collectors." Derek shoved his hands in his pockets and met the taller man's gaze. "Look, we can go back to the boat and I'll contact a collector I know. He's a reputable man—if he wants the coin, he'll pay a fair price for it."

Niall nodded. "Referrals are of import in the business of changing money."

"You better believe it." Derek flashed a smile at the still-rattled clerk. "I live and die by my reputation every day."

Niall's gaze sharpened. "You are a moneychanger?"

"No, no. I'm a financial analyst." At Niall's puzzled look, Derek explained. "I'm an independent. I invest people's money for them, manage their assets, ensure that they make a nice profit or secure their retirement funds." He shrugged and grinned. "You could say that I'm a numbers guy. I do the math."

"Ah!" Understanding dawned on the other man's face. "I also do the math." He tapped his temple. "'Tis my great gift."

"You have a gift with numbers? You can do the math in your head?"

"Aye. I had a patron once who found this most useful and consigned me to the counting room." Niall shrugged and almost smiled. "It saved him much vellum and spared him much cheating, though did little for my own studies."

"I can imagine." Derek studied the other man with new eyes. A numbers guy. That was the most interesting thing Derek had heard in quite a while. He was always looking for new talent, someone to follow in his shoes, and lately had been bending Paula's ear about the sad state of the education system.

"Aye. Though as is the way with most gifts, 'tis honed to a keen edge only by diligent practice."

Derek liked the sound of this better and better. A numbers guy who wasn't afraid to work. Now, there was a novel proposition!

"Hey, look, we've got to talk. Why don't you open an account here, just in case this all goes through? Horace is pretty fond of just transferring funds. Saves a lot of trouble."

"Ah!" Niall's opinion of the bank seemed much improved. "Is this establishment associated with the Templars? They are great facilitators of the transfer of coin between realms." He shook a finger at the bewildered clerk. "You should have told me this sooner."

"I don't think the Templars are involved here," Derek acknowledged as the clerk dropped a form on the counter.

"Perhaps the Hospitaliers, then," Niall acknowledged absently, gaze scanning the form. "Either are equally adept, though I profess a fondness for the Templars. 'Tis more manly, in my estimation, to wage battle against the infidel than to bind the wounds of the fallen."

Fortunately, Derek was spared from responding to that bit of oddness by Niall's questioning of demands of the form.

He didn't have a speck of I.D., which complicated things quite a bit. Derek refused to think too much about why, because then he would have had to think about Niall's odd appearance and all of that was better left unexplored.

There was always a reasonable explanation for anything worth explaining. The guy must have left it somewhere when he changed into his knight's gear to stow away on the sailboat. Yeah, he was one of those anachronism types, the ones who dressed up in medieval gear and had fake battles, much like Viviane. Obviously that was how they knew each other.

Perfectly reasonable. Derek reminded himself that he liked people with a little bit more dimensionality, people with interests outside of their work, no matter how weird those interests were. Medieval dress-up might be strange, but it was harmless.

Come to think of it, Paula had made a couple of comments about how sexy Niall looked in his gear.

Sexy. Hmm.

Derek and the clerk exchanged a glance when Niall professed his lack of drivers' license, in silent agreement that they not rile the bank's new customer yet again. Derek suggested they use Viviane's address as Niall's, which seemed to only make sense. The clerk was visibly relieved by this suggestion and took over the task of filling in the form for Niall.

He waved off the lack of drivers' license, saying he had only needed it for the address.

He was, though, not nearly so ready to concede the matter of a social insurance number. Damn government, with their fingers in every pie! Derek couldn't see what the hell difference it made, since Niall hadn't a dime to put in the account, but the clerk wasn't backing down.

Niall looked more than willing to rumble. He easily outweighed the little guy and was clearly all out of patience for bank procedure.

Before he could question his impulse, Derek grabbed the pen and countersigned for Niall, personally vouching for him as a respected bank customer. Effectively, it was his account, though he insisted on giving Niall signature on it. The clerk ceded on that, though unwillingly and only after checking Derek's balance on his other accounts.

They made a quick exit, by Derek's plan. It was definitely time to check out that coin.

Preferably elsewhere.

• • •

There was a little room in the sailing vessel that Niall had not been privileged to see the previous day. Ingenious slatted doors along one wall below the deck hid a desk that had been built right into the wall. A swivelling chair was tucked beneath, the desktop pulled out to make its surface larger. Derek gestured to the gleaming boxes reposing in the hidden space.

"Fax, laptop, laser printer—all the conveniences of home." One slim box had a hinged lid, which Niall noted when Derek opened it. The bottom of the box was covered with buttons, each labelled with a letter; the top was a big square. Derek pressed a button and Niall jumped at the note that the box sang, his eyes widening in astonishment as the top box lit up with color.

"Yeah, it's one of the new Mac PowerBooks," Derek said with a nod more fitting of a proud papa. "Impresses the hell out of me every time I boot it up. Beautiful display." He recounted what were evidently statistics but his words fell on deaf ears.

For Niall was marvelling at the little pictures. Derek steered a little arrow around somehow, his hands moving so fast that Niall had a hard time seeing precisely what did what. In a moment, there was a white box displayed and Derek was hitting the little buttons in succession.

And words appeared in the white box. Niall watched closely and realized that each button Derek struck put the matching character on the white box.

'Twas a marvel, but a machine all the same.

Derek laughed beneath his breath. "Old hunt and peck school, that's me. You'd think after all these years, I'd learn, but I never have. Drives Paula crazy." He winked. "Maybe that's why I haven't—this way, she does the lion's share of my typing."

Niall smiled fleetingly at the older man's jest, his interest fixed by the words appearing on the screen. 'Twas a letter, as any fool could see. Derek was writing to one Horace Thorogood, asking after his interest in gold coins. This made good sense to Niall, though he acknowledged that 'twould be inconvenient to be without coin until this Horace replied and any transaction could be made.

It could take weeks, even if the Hospitaliers transferred the funds.

But to Niall's astonishment, when Derek finished the letter, he pointed the tiny arrow at a little box labelled "send". The cabin filled with a series of tones that made Niall jump and look around.

Derek laughed at his reaction. "Hey, this is *my* ship! All the bells and whistles and modcons. Paula's comments notwithstanding, I can't be unconnected for weeks at a time. There's two phone lines here"—he looked up and Niall was sure he looked suitably impressed—"and a sweet little dish on the mast to get me onto the 'net." He gestured at the box, which displayed a dizzying array of messages. "Look, there it goes."

Niall looked.

Message sent. Waiting for reply.

Niall leaned closer, peeking around the back of the box and finding naught but a few cables. Certainly no boy had scooped up the missive and run with it, for there was no means by which that could have been done without Niall seeing it. "I do not understand how this message was dispatched."

"Don't you use e-mail?"

Niall shook his head.

"Ah, well, you see, it's pretty simple stuff. Uses phone lines to relay messages, but a lot quicker than actually talking on the phone." Derek turned the little box around, pointed to a variety of cables and quickly explained matters, even taking Niall up on deck.

Niall did not follow all of the explanation, though he understood that the little disk on the mast beamed the message into the sky, from which another disk far way snatched it up and passed it on, eventually to this Horace.

'Twas a marvel.

And the work of man. Not magic, but sophisticated machinery.

Not Avalon, but some place of man. Niall looked around the harbor and wondered once more *precisely* where they were.

Fortunately he had a good idea where an answer might be found.

"Have you a map of this place?" Niall asked, trying to keep the anticipation out of his voice. "You must have need of one to guide this vessel through these islands."

"Oh, yeah, regular mare's nest around here." Derek led him back below and unrolled a map across the top of a table. 'Twas intricately detailed, more elaborate than any Niall had ever seen, with sweeping blue lines all across it. Indeed, 'twas a thing of beauty, and as fascinating as the one map Niall had seen before.

"See here's the prevailing current." Derek traced a line with his fingertip, explaining the course he charted here in such detail that Niall was almost immediately lost.

Niall's ears pricked up only when he heard the word "home."

"You do not live here?"

"No, no. Most of the year, we're down in the condo in Seattle. The sailboat is a summer thing."

"Seattle?"

Derek tapped a town marked at the bottom of this map, one that Niall hadn't noticed before. "It's a bit of a haul, gotta cling to the coast a bit because I'm not the most experienced sea captain going. I'd like to change that though, take some time when we retire and really do some sailing." He looked at Niall. "Course, I can't retire until I find someone to take on the business."

"Ah. An apprentice."

"Right. A real numbers guy."

Derek paused and Niall realized that his question had not been answered as yet. "Could you sail this craft to England?"

"England! Whoa—do you have any idea how far that is?"

Niall shook his head, his pulse leaping that the information he desired could be so close.

"Need the other map for that." Derek rummaged and pulled out another, unfurling it on top of the first and weighing down the corners. Niall leaned over it, astonished by the amount of land shown. It had been quite a while since he had seen a map of the known world and it had been only the barest glimpse of a precious treasure held by the archbishop, but he was certain Christendom had not been shaped like this.

Or been so extensive.

Derek poked a finger at a markedly small island, its shape heartwrenchingly familiar. Niall could even make out the name of the town of Carlisle, not so far from all he knew.

"There's merry olde England right there. And we're over here. But it's even worse than it looks, because you have to go around the continents. Now, once upon a time, you had to go all the way down here, by Tierra del Fuego, but since the Panama Canal opened in 1914—a little marvel of modern engineering—you can zip through here . . ."

But Niall wasn't watching the course of Derek's finger anymore. He was staring at his companion in shock. "In *1914*? This was the year of its opening?"

The older man didn't even look up, despite the tightness of Niall's voice. "Yeah, it's hard to believe it's only been there for eighty-five years or so, we've gotten so reliant upon it . . ."

The year 1914 was eighty-five years past? Niall's head nearly spun at the implication of that. He must have misunderstood. "What is the date this day?" he asked hoarsely.

"Um, well, it would be the twenty-seventh of September, come to think of it."

"And the year?"

Now, Derek glanced at Niall. He grinned crookedly. "Been on the island long enough to lose track of time, huh? Or were you really getting into your historical reenactment?" He snapped his fingers in sudden recollection. "Look, your chain mail is in a hockey bag there, don't forget to take it along with you. Hope you don't mind but I had a look—it's really great stuff. Looks like the real thing. You probably ought to hang out that cape to dry before it wrinkles all to hell." He cleared his throat. "Where do you buy stuff like that, anyway? If for example, I was interested . . .?"

"At an armorer."

"Right. Gotta go to the medieval faire."

"The year," Niall said through gritted teeth. "What is the year?"

"Easy, cowboy! It's 1999, of course. Everyone knows that."

Niall sat back in astonishment, for he had not known any such thing. Where they were had not surprised him overmuch, for he had guessed they must be at a distance from Cantlecroft. Perhaps not this far, but still.

'Twas *when* they were that shook him to the core.

Because Niall could not imagine how any mechanism of man could hurl them across six centuries on the power of a wish alone. He thought of Viviane's moonstone and his innards curdled. Could that talisman be magic after all?

Or was it some cleverness of the men of this time, that only seemed magical to Niall in his ignorance of its mechanism?

Six centuries! 'Twas a long time.

Suddenly Niall realized the import of hurtling so far into the future. All he knew were wormfood, and wormfood long forgotten. Majella had not only had her child, but they were all long dead, babes and she.

Niall sat down heavily. The archbishop was no more, indeed Cantlecroft might not even stand any longer. The bile rose in his throat at the thought. Every soul to whom he had made a pledge was dead.

What had they thought of him, as they lived out their days, awaiting him to keep his word? Had his only sister thought him faithless? Had his patron thought him trapped in some netherworld? Or dead by some horrific fate? But a day since Niall had tousled his nephew's hair and they were lost to him forever.

'Twas enough to sicken him.

"You all right?" Derek's concern interrupted Niall's thoughts. "You look a bit pale. It *is* a bit choppy today."

"I am well enough," Niall insisted stoically, his fingers gripping the table so tightly that his knuckles were white. He glanced down at them and saw the inscription in the corner of the map.

Based on survey data from 1989 A.D.

Niall's stomach rolled. This made no sense! 'Twas impossible, it defied belief.

Yet he was here.

And it was 1999. Mathematics came to his rescue, his mind tabulating the difference by habit. Six hundred and nine years, gone missing in the blink of an eye.

With nary a reasonable explanation in sight. Niall tightened his grip on the table, uncertain whether 'twas the vessel swaying or him.

"Yeah, well, you don't look so good. As soon as we hear back . . ." The little machine sang out once more, distracting Derek. "Ha! There's a message from Horace."

Niall pushed to his feet and leaned over the man's shoulder to read along. Now that he thought to look, he noticed the dateline, complete with its damning year. Niall deliberately took a deep breath, trying to steady himself, the numbers wavering slightly before his disbelieving gaze.

There had to be a rational explanation, he merely had to find it. Indeed, six hundred years of clever men could well explain all the marvels surrounding him. If naught else, he knew now that they were not magic.

And that this was not Avalon. Nay, 'twas Salt Spring Island, according to the map.

The missive revealed that Horace was very excited about the coin. With Niall's permission, Derek dropped it on what he called a scanner, which apparently dispatched an image of the coin to Horace.

Moments later, Horace professed himself delighted, listed a sum that made Niall blink and offered to transfer half in good faith, the remainder on receipt of the coin. 'Twas only reasonable that he would confirm of its authenticity—Niall had been known himself to bite a gold coin with his own teeth to ascertain that 'twas real.

"Suit you?" Derek asked.

Niall rolled the numbers through his head and had no qualms whatsoever. Surely by the time his four coins were sold and all the resulting coin spent, he'd know how to return to Cantlecroft, his task completed?

Niall could only hope.

"The agreement seems one of good sense," he agreed, appreciating anew that this man had vouched for him. He was, however, skeptical that Horace would truly pay such a sum in the local currency for a single gold coin.

Even a fraction would suit him well enough.

"Yeah, Horace is a bit of an oddity, but a straight shooter. Look, if you like, we'll go back into town and courier the coin to him, after we've checked that he's transferred the payment."

"This also seems of good sense to me."

Derek stood and stretched his legs. "So does a celebratory beer."

"Beer?"

"Ale, wine, the hard stuff, your choice." Derek winked. "Tell you what, I'll buy and you can tell me about your gift with numbers."

Niall nearly fell on his new friend with relief. "An ale would be most welcome," he said heartily and Derek chuckled.

"Yeah, I know that feeling. It's good for what ails you." He struck a succession of buttons once more, asked Niall for his new passbook, then sent an agreement off to Horace. When that man replied, they headed for town.

Coin and ale, in that order.

Niall had no quibbles with that.

Niall could not have known that his parting with that single gold coin would prompt serious repercussions. You see, the coin was not where it should have been, a fact which became of particular import when it left Niall's fingers and lost all reasonable hope of returning to medieval Cantlecroft.

Which was, of course, where it belonged.

The coin was the first tangible thing that either Niall or Viviane parted with in their new location, and as such, its movement cast strong ripples across the surface of ensuing events.

For starters, the coin's sudden appearance in the late twentieth century Pacific Northwest exactly doubled the world's known supply of Cantlecroft gold coins. That rather severely affected the value of the formerly sole Cantlecroft coin, a fact which directly impacted the financial circumstances of the man who owned it.

He was the same man who bought Niall's coin through Derek. Horace Thorogood III loved coins with a passion that had irked every one of his three ex-wives, even the last one, who had been a coin collector herself.

It is an oddity of human nature that few women take kindly to having their spouse find dirty bits of metal more fascinating than their own company, particularly at the *exclusion* of their own company. Horace had never cared for much of anything other than coins—though he liked women well enough—and his passion only intensified as he grew older. By the age of fifty-three, he was thrice divorced and had reconciled himself to the reality that no woman would tolerate him.

By then, he didn't much care. He had his coins and they filled his days and his nights with pleasure.

Derek managed Horace's other investments, so knew exactly the man to call when the subject was coins. Horace was so excited by the possibility of there being another Cantlecroft gold coin available that he had to have it.

He probably paid too much, even given the information available at the time. He didn't care though, once the coin—in such good condition that it appeared freshly minted—fell into his hands.

His third ex-wife, however, did.

For the sudden expense of acquiring Niall's coin cut rather deeply into Horace's liquid assets, making it impossible to pay that ex-wife's monthly alimony installment on time. She did not take kindly to this omission, having rather too many credit card collectors calling her by her first name, and showed up at Horace's bedraggled estate toting her gun.

Now, Horace was quite used to Esmeralda's theatrics—they were, in fact, a contributing factor to that divorce since such theatrics interrupted the peaceful contemplation of coins—so he paid little attention to her show. He chose instead to enthuse over his new acquisition. If Horace thought she would be swayed by this news as a fellow coin-lover, he was sorely mistaken.

Just as Esmeralda was mistaken when she thought the safety was still on. She pointed the gun at Horace and demanded her money or else, quite certain she'd put a little fear into him when she pulled the trigger and not much else.

Horace had time to look up and no more.

In the ensuing unscheduled drama, the coin in question fell unnoticed from Horace's fingers. It rolled under his desk and secreted itself in a crack in the parquet floor.

More than one Cantlecroft gold coin would not be found amongst Horace's possessions—although the receipts for both were readily accessible. The resulting legal battle—among Horace's various children by those terminated marriages—would outlive his three ex-wives and consume so many legal fees that in the end, there was precious little of Horace's hard-won fortune for the victorious heir.

The elusive gold coin would be found some eighty years later by a construction worker involved in demolishing the house, thereby putting him on the front page of every paper in America and convincing his recently departed wife to move right back in.

But as important as where Niall's coin was, was the issue of where it was *not*.

It was not in Cantlecroft, it was not passing from Niall's fingers to a butcher, a baker or a candlestick maker in that fair burg. Nor was it even slipping to the fingers of his sister Majella, where no coin lingered long.

And that was equally problematic.

For it is the nature of man to keep track of what he deems precious. There are tallies made of coinage minted and tables kept of the weight of silver and gold passed from one tradesman to another, and so there always have been. And when the sum was made in Cantlecroft, it was clear to the archbishop's chancellor that the man responsible for melting the archbishop's gold bars and transforming them to Cantlecroft coins had shipped short of the measure.

The weight of one coin and one coin exactly was missing.

The archbishop was not one to overlook this sort of thievery and Aaron Goldsmith was summoned to make an accounting. Aaron, unfortunately, could offer no decent explanation for the missing weight.

Indeed, he insisted that he had counted and delivered all of the coins. It was an obvious lie—for the numbers in the ledger did not lie. The archbishop and his chancellor knew that Jews *did* lie, however, for they had the example of Judas in the great book itself as a reference, and they were not inclined to be lenient with Aaron Goldsmith.

It was suggested that those Jews in Cantlecroft might be overdue for a lesson on their real place in Christendom, particularly if they had become so bold as to believe they could cheat the archbishop himself.

When Aaron's wife vouched for her spouse's honesty and swore even upon the Old Testament that she had counted the coins herself, the court shook their heads in disgust.

The Goldsmiths hung together.

That might have been that, if Aaron had not been so well-liked and respected in Cantlecroft. He had been God-fearing, if not Christian, he had raised his sons well and he was a man who could be relied upon.

Additionally, Aaron was oft teased for his soft heart—he was known to discount his prices on wedding bands when couples could not afford them. Nay, the consensus was that Aaron Goldsmith was a good-hearted man.

He did not cheat his customers, though many of them knew they could have been cheated as easily as not. The acquisition of jewellery was beyond the opportunity of most and certainly not something one could acquire often enough to show real skill in choosing stones or assessing the weight of a setting.

The people of Cantlecroft trusted Aaron, so when he pledged a thing was true, they believed him.

He had sworn that he had made the full shipment and all of Cantlecroft knew it.

It was therefore believed in Cantlecroft that Aaron had been falsely accused and falsely convicted, that he was innocent of the charge brought against him, and that his death had been unjust.

The archbishop had clearly made a mistake.

Furthermore, it was sinful to execute the innocent, this was widely agreed in the taverns of Cantlecroft in the weeks after Aaron's execution. And sins, as every good Christian knew, had a way of attracting the vengeance of God. Sin and the killing of innocents could not be tolerated.

So, because of the journey of one gold coin, Horace Thorogood III died before his time, as did Aaron Goldsmith and his wife.

And even more importantly for Niall, Viviane and all those they held dear, the murmuring in Cantlecroft began.

Chapter 10

VIVIANE COULD HAVE just spit. Niall ran more hot and cold than the taps that interested him so much!

She nearly growled the whole way back to the shop and was glad when her patroness didn't ask any questions. In fact, Barb welcomed her with undisguised delight.

The store was uncommonly busy that morning, precisely the opposite as Barb had predicted. The rain seemed to have driven everyone on the island out in search of a book and a cup of tea. Viviane took a deep breath, forced a smile and started to work. Her usually even temper was quickly restored by visits from a few of her regulars.

Barb must be right—Niall wasn't nearly as disinterested as he'd appeared to be. After all, he'd touched her so gently this morning and been intent on giving her pleasure. And, he had followed her—of course, he was her own Gawain!

He just had things on his mind.

Although Viviane couldn't imagine what they could be. What could be more important than spending time with her, now that they were reunited again? She puzzled over it all morning, until inspiration struck.

He was preparing to court her, of course. He must be

planning a surprise, or acquiring a token of his affections, or doing something similar that required Viviane's absence. What better excuse than to send her back to work?

The very thought put Viviane's mood back on an even keel.

By lunchtime, she was ready to let Niall persuade her to kiss him again. In fact, she was starting to get a bit curious as to what he would do, or what he would bring her. What kind of gesture would a knight like Niall make? Viviane didn't know and curiosity gnawed at her.

But Niall didn't show.

By mid-afternoon, Viviane was starting to be concerned. Niall had absolutely no tendency to miss meals. What had happened to him?

Still Niall made no appearance. Viviane kept glancing out the door, but there was no sign of him at all.

Just before closing at six, Viviane finally had a moment to herself and decided to make use of it. She headed straight for the relationship section of the store, determined to find out what to do when Niall did come back. She rummaged through half a dozen books, and quickly found the common thread.

In matters between men and women, in questions of love, the real issue was communication, according to the wisdom recorded here. Because men and woman effectively spoke different languages, these books insisted, it was critical to be blunt.

A woman must tell her man exactly what she wanted of him.

Viviane was quite certain she could do that. That must have been what happened this morning—they just had a misunderstanding, as apparently countless other couples did. Viviane's spirits soared. And if Niall didn't understand what she wanted at this point, well, she would have to be really blunt!

Fortunately she not only knew what she wanted, but she had a really good idea of *how* to tell him, too. What better way to communicate her expectations than to let Niall read her book? It was a terrifying proposition, because no one had read that book yet besides Viviane, but she knew that was the perfect solution.

After all, it was a romance and Niall—or her version of him—was the hero of it. Vastly reassured now that her course was clear, Viviane smiled and started to put the book back on the shelf.

"Hey, witchy woman," Monty said so close beside her that Viviane jumped. "Like, what's happening?"

"Oh, it's been a really busy day." Viviane busied herself with putting the book away, blushing when Monty tilted his head to read the title.

His lips had thinned with disapproval by the time she looked up again. "So, like, where's your *friend*? The big guy?"

"He had things to do today and I was working anyhow." Viviane smiled, hoping Monty wouldn't ask for more details. She would have stepped past him and returned to the counter, but Monty moved directly into her path.

His expression was remarkably grim. "What about last night? Did you really bring him home?"

"Monty!" Viviane's cheeks were hot and she was very aware of the last few customers glancing their way. "That's not for you to know!"

"Isn't it? Jeez Louise, Viviane, I thought we had something going!" Monty scowled at her and shoved his hands into his pockets.

"Something?"

"Yeah! We had dinner together! A lot."

Viviane was confused. People didn't eat with their sworn enemies, she knew, and the sharing of meals considered companionable. Beyond that, she had no idea what Monty meant.

"Yes," she acknowledged hesitantly.

He cast out his hands. "I thought we were like *friends*!"

Relief washed over Viviane. "Of course, we are friends, Monty. Why would you question that?"

For the first time since his arrival, Monty grinned. "All right! Well, then, I wanted to ask you about something. See, it's almost the full moon, and you might not know this, but there's lots of witches on the island."

"I haven't seen any." Viviane was intrigued to hear of the witches here—having been condemned as one, she thought it quite natural to want to know more.

"Yeah, well, you might be surprised. Anyhow, they have a sabbat on the full moon, and since I like have connections, I've gotten us an invitation." He winked. "This coming Saturday night. What do you think?"

Viviane was intrigued. "But what's a sabbat?"

"It's a celebration, kind of a party, maybe dancing and food and drink. Some kind of Goddess stuff involved that I don't understand, but hey, live and learn!" Monty's grin widened. "Wanna go?"

Live and learn indeed. That seemed to be Viviane's new motto. "Oh, yes, I'd like that."

"Great!" Monty's eyes narrowed slightly. "Just *us*, okay?"

Viviane laughed, immediately seeing his meaning. "Oh, Niall doesn't believe in magic. I'm sure he has no interest in joining us."

"Cool!" Monty leaned closer. "How about dinner tonight?"

Viviane's gaze strayed tellingly to the door. She did want to be here when Niall came back, especially if he had spent the day planning some surprise for her. "Um, no, I don't think so."

Monty looked annoyed and she hastened to make things better. Monty had been a great help to her and Viviane didn't want him to be angry. "But thank you for your offer . . ."

Monty waved her off. "A guy's gotta make do with what he gets, I guess," he muttered.

"But Monty!"

"Forget I said anything!" He strode out of the shop just as

Mrs. Haggerty came in for her weekly allotment of romance novels.

"Oh, Viviane, don't lock the door on me yet!" Mrs. Haggerty cried. "I need my fix and I need it tonight. Nothing like a rainy night to turn a body's thoughts to"—she winked boldly as she stepped into the shop.—"*you* know!"

Monty disappeared down the street, his shoulders hunched, his hands shoved into his pockets. Viviane couldn't very well go after him, not since Mrs. Haggerty did come specifically to talk to her.

Reluctantly she closed the door and smiled. "I've put a few new ones aside for you, ones that I thought you might like."

"Oh good!"

Half an hour later, Viviane waved from the doorway as Mrs. Haggerty headed on her way, a thorough discussion of new books having been completed. That lady left with a good dozen more than the ones she had ordered, all those additions based on Viviane's recommendations. Barb was whistling as she put the cash register through its nightly ceremony.

As Viviane locked the door, she took a good look at the quiet road and empty sidewalks. The rain fell on the silent street and trickled down to the harbor.

Monty was long gone and Niall was still nowhere in sight.

Had something happened to him? Viviane folded her arms about herself, Monty forgotten, and worried.

"You're wrong, you know," Barb said and Viviane jumped.

"About what?"

Barb smiled wryly as she tallied the totals for the afternoon. "About Buns of Steel."

Viviane had no idea what her patron was talking about.

"Niall," Barb clarified. The cash register clattered away and spewed a length of tape into her waiting hands. "He's not going to stand by and let you go to a sabbat with Monty alone. I'd bet my last dollar on it."

"Well, he's not going to stop me from going." Viviane picked up a stack of books to be reshelved and absently stuffed them back on the shelves. She looked out the windows again and again, wondering where he was.

Barb grinned. "Then you can count on him going with you. Party of three." She raised her eyebrows expressively and shook her head. "Could be more of a crowd than Monty has in mind."

But Viviane didn't want to hurt Monty's feelings. "Well, I'll just tell Niall not to come, as simple as that," she declared and hefted a stack of books from the counter, smiling confidently for Barb. "He's not interested in magic or witches, anyway."

Barb was far from persuaded. "He's interested in *you*, though."

Viviane clasped the books to her chest, savoring her patron's conviction of that fact.

Barb didn't look up. "If you tell him not to come, he'll just follow you, like a stubborn old dog—if you'll pardon the analogy—tracking his favorite bone." She shrugged, her shrewd glance falling on Viviane, her voice falling low. "Unless he's already got another favorite bone."

It took Viviane only a heartbeat to understand and then she was outraged. She dropped the books back on the counter. "Barb! Niall isn't like that! He said he came back for me and that he wouldn't leave without me. Why, he must be upstairs already, waiting for me!"

"Uh huh." Barb counted bills as though she wasn't paying attention, but Viviane knew her employer wasn't convinced of Niall's good intentions.

It was some consolation that that was only because Barb was worried about her. Viviane knew that her employer wasn't nearly as hard-hearted as she liked to appear, and she appreciated Barb's concern.

"You don't have to worry about me, Barb," Viviane said softly. "I know that Niall is the man for me and he knows it too."

Barb looked up, shooting a telling glance over her spectacles as Viviane leaned on the counter. "You see, you just don't know how he is. He's a man who keeps his word, a man who honors women and keeps his promises. He's a knight . . ."

"You mean, *like* a knight," Barb interrupted tersely. "There aren't any real knights anymore. Those reenactment types or men's fraternities don't count."

"Right!" Viviane straightened after her slip and continued carefully. That was what she got for chattering on! "Niall's *like* a knight, like one of the knights in those stories, a knight who rides in to sweep a woman off her feet."

Barb looked wry. "And you would be the damsel in distress?"

Viviane smiled with confidence in her role. "Oh yes, I think so."

The older woman shook her head and braced a hand on the counter. "There are no men like that anymore, Viviane." She gestured to the wall of romance books, her expression deadly serious. "Don't confuse real life with fiction. I'd hate to see you get burned."

Viviane frowned, but Barb returned to the task of counting money and she knew better than to interrupt.

How could she be burned when there was no fire in her room?

And what did fire have to do with Niall?

Other than the heat he awakened with his touch. Viviane smiled and finished shelving the books, more than looking forward to finding him upstairs.

Of course he would be there. She knew she could rely on Niall.

And he would have a wondrous surprise for her, one intended to win her heart and make her his own.

It would be perfect.

It is the way of a flagon of ale to tempt a man to have another. Niall wasn't helped by the fact that each time the coinage of this realm passed under his nose, he saw the date stamped or printed upon it, yet more evidence that he was not where he belonged.

And perhaps beyond the possibility of return. His word might be broken irrevocably, his solemn pledge as ashes in the wind. That knowledge, too, drove him to have another, if only to bolster him against the assault of the truth.

Derek proved to be a man well versed in how matters worked and had no qualms about explaining all and sundry to Niall. They talked and talked as they drank and drank. Niall tallied vast lists of numbers in his head, laughing when Derek was clearly impressed.

He divided, multiplied and subtracted with equal alacrity, although those talents were somewhat adversely affected by the ale as the night went on. Derek's explanations also began to suffer, but neither man particularly heeded the change.

Indeed, they toasted each other's cleverness and called for another round.

'Twas well past midnight when they were cast from the tavern for their poor singing. They waved good night to each other, two men who did the math and were now far better friends than they had been just hours past, then stumbled in the directions of their own pallets.

Niall made his uneven way toward Viviane's abode, hauling the bag filled with his mail with no small effort. He sincerely hoped she would let him in. The rain was cold, his knee was aching. He wanted only to sleep on the floor, sheltered from the downpour, although a smile from the lady would not be unwelcome.

Niall's steps fell a little faster at the prospect. He found the door unlatched and leaned his brow against the frame in relief, his heart thudding that this lady should show him such compassion. Niall's loins tightened in recollection of Viviane's smile. She did prompt a feeling within him, a sense of power that recalled the days when he had not been a lowly sentry. He felt bold and brave in her presence, he lived again as a knight who was honored.

Niall barely crossed the threshold before the lady herself gasped aloud.

"Niall! You're here!"

As he looked up, Viviane came flying down the stairs, her hair unbound, her feet bare and her eyes wide. Niall saw the traces of her tears just before she cast herself into his arms and he caught her, instinctively holding her close. Her heartbeat fluttered beneath his palm like a wild bird, she clutched at his neck as though she had to reassure herself that he was real.

She had been worried for him. Affection flooded through Niall and he cradled her against his chest, wanting only to ease her concern.

It had been a long time since a woman who was not his kin had worried for Niall of Malloy.

"I was so afraid something had happened to you! I was worried when you were out so late and you didn't come back even for a meal and I was afraid something might have happened to you." Viviane pulled back, her eyes luminous yet lit with fear, her fingertips grazing his cheek. "Are you all right? Were you lost? Did anyone take advantage of you or trick you? Don't tell me that you were robbed!"

And in that moment, staring into her wondrous eyes, 'twas all so perfectly clear. Niall held the most beautiful woman he had ever known in his arms, she was concerned for his sorry hide, she made him feel like a hero returned victorious.

Viviane was a woman who desired him, and Niall was a man who desired her.

It could be no more simple than that.

Niall enveloped Viviane's delicate jaw in his hand, he tipped her face up to his. "You have no need to fret," he murmured. "I am here and all is aright."

The lady parted her lips but Niall granted her no chance to speak before he indulged his completely natural desire for her kiss. He bent his head and slanted his lips across the sweetness of hers, claiming her and silencing her in one move.

If she had turned him away, Niall would have stepped

back, but Viviane did not. Indeed, she sighed with such contentment and leaned against him with such abandon, that Niall thought his heart would burst with its thundering.

Niall dropped his bag, swept the lady into his arms and kicked the door closed behind them. He carried her up the stairs without breaking his kiss or heeding the complaints of his knee.

Aye, he could find that fine pallet in the dark this night, he knew it well, and neither of them would regret it.

Viviane twined her arms around Niall's neck and returned his kiss with abandon. This was the best surprise of all.

Maybe he wouldn't even need to read her book.

His tongue slid between her teeth in that instant and drove coherent thought from Viviane's mind. She sighed and opened her mouth, surprised to find herself on her own bed, Niall's shadow looming over her. They knelt there for a moment, wavering against the tide of their desire, then Niall broke their kiss.

"Viviane," he said simply, his voice low with desire. The way he said her name stole Viviane's breath away, the tenderness in the hand that rose to caress her jaw made her mouth go dry.

She melted when he rubbed the rough edge of his thumb across her cheek and understood when this perfect knight shook his head, as though incredulous that she was not only before him but welcoming of his touch.

"Tell me," he urged. "Tell me what 'tis you desire."

Viviane framed his face in her hands and smiled. "Niall," she whispered, leaning closer to barely touch her lips to his. She opened her eyes in the act of that kiss and found his bright gaze fixed upon her. Her nipples grazed his chest, she could feel the heat of his erection near her thigh even through her nightgown.

But he waited, granting her the chance to decide.

Viviane's smile widened. "I want you," she whispered. "In every way I can imagine."

Niall's eyes gleamed like emeralds in the shadows for a heartbeat before he caught her against him once again. The purpose in his touch made Viviane tingle in anticipation. This time there would be no halting short of the finish.

She could hardly wait.

Niall's strong hand slid into her hair to cradle her nape, his mouth settled on hers once again as his other arm locked around her waist. Her curves moulded to the hard lines of his body as though they were made to be together. She could smell the distinctive scent of his flesh, the hint of ale, the wind and sun that clung to his hair.

Viviane was captive within his embrace and could think of nowhere else she would rather be. He held her with that tempered strength that was so characteristic of him, of a strong man striving to be gentle with an infinitely precious gift. She could feel the thrum of desire running through him—and was well aware of the answering cry within herself.

Niall's lips grazed her jaw, her temple, her earlobe. Viviane closed her eyes and surrendered to his sure touch, savoring the sweet brush of each butterfly-light kiss. His hands roved over her, ceaselessly gentle, as though he would memorize every mole she had, as though he would seek them out and taste them each in turn. His hot kisses trailed down her throat and Viviane arched her back, sighing then shivering, when he pressed a languorous kiss into the hollow of her throat.

Then Niall was kissing her moles, each one in succession, running a line between them with the heat of his tongue, his breath fanning her desire ever higher. He caught her waist in his hands, the span of his fingers nearly surrounding her and lifted her to his questing lips, his mouth locking around her nipple. His tongue and his teeth teased the peak until Viviane squirmed, but there was no escape.

And Niall only teased her more. Viviane buried her fingers in the thick silk of his hair and urged him closer, leaning back in unbridled delight. This was her knight, after all, the man by whose side she was destined to be. There was no need for secrets between them, no need to hold anything back.

Niall flicked his tongue against her, making her shudder from head to toe, and Viviane forgot everything except his touch.

He treated the other breast to the same thorough attention and Viviane heard herself moan aloud. She thought she heard Niall chuckle, but couldn't be sure. His questing kisses slipped lower and when his tongue flicked into her navel, Viviane felt her knees buckle. Niall eased her back onto the mattress, his hands cupping her buttocks and lifting her hips to his kiss.

Viviane wasn't sure exactly what he was doing, until the heat of his mouth landed upon her in a most distracting fashion. She gasped aloud and grabbed fistfuls of his hair, but this time Niall did chuckle. And he did not move away. His broad shoulders braced her thighs, opening her to his persuasive touch, his tongue teasing her much as his fingers had the day before. Viviane felt the heat rise beneath her skin more quickly than it had before, though it was hotter this time as well.

Though this time, Niall taunted her. He halted when she was just shy of reaching the summit, pausing for a telling moment, then beginning his sensuous assault once more. Viviane felt herself climbing higher each time, release tantalizingly close but still out of reach.

On the third time, she wriggled demandingly against him, uncertain she could stand it if he denied her this time. Niall gripped her buttocks and lifted her hips off the bed, his tongue dancing with gusto, flicking and suckling in turn.

Viviane writhed, her nipples tightened like beads, her hips bucked of their own accord. The heat rose beneath her skin like a tide and she understood just as the crest hovered over her that this time, Niall would see her through. Her heart pounded at the gift of pleasure he was intent to give her.

And then, suddenly, the release flooded through and over her. She shook to her core, she cried out, she shuddered like a leaf in the wind.

In that moment, Niall dove the length of the bed, capturing her in his arms, holding her fast against the storm. Viviane felt his shoulder against her cheek when the last ripple left her and she leaned against him with a smile.

Her knight was back.

She was beautiful, even in slumber.

Niall held Viviane close, watching her doze against him. She had been pleased, he knew it well. And Niall felt like a victorious king for his role in that.

This 'twas that Viviane gave him. This 'twas that astonished him and made him feel more the man than he knew himself to be. She believed in him, she trusted him, she expected valor and honor from him.

She made him feel whole again.

The lady sighed and stretched contentedly, her lashes fluttering against her cheeks before her eyes opened. Niall's heart clenched—his desire for her was unsated, indeed it raged, but never would he force himself upon a woman.

But Viviane smiled. She curled against him and slipped her arms around his neck, her lips brushing his in that way that fired everything within Niall. Her hand fell upon his erection with a certainty unexpected, the weight of her hand there making Niall gasp.

"We're not done," she whispered, her gaze warm and welcoming.

Niall needed no second invitation. He slipped her fingers into her heat, ensuring that she was well prepared for him. He kissed her, nursing her desire once more, surprised by how quickly she arched against him, every move she made a silent demand.

The musky scent of her was inescapable and infinitely arousing. The floral scent clinging to her flesh from the shower this morn teased Niall with the memory of how she had tormented him. She echoed his slow thorough kisses, her tongue nudging between his teeth and making Niall's blood boil.

He lifted his head, knowing he could not last unless he halted for a moment, but Viviane was not inclined to let him cease. She followed him with her intoxicating kisses, locking her hands around his neck and tumbling across him when he rolled to his back.

Her hunger for his touch enflamed him as naught else could have done. The ripe perfection of a buttock fell beneath one hand, Niall found a turgid nipple with another and he was powerless to escape the lady's touch.

She eased across him as they kissed, her hands running over his flesh, her breasts crushed against his chest, the sweep of her smooth thigh across his erection nigh making him explode. He whispered her name and her laughter fanned across his neck.

"Show me, Niall," she said softly. He looked up to find her eyes sparkling with humor. "I don't know what to do."

Niall gripped her buttocks and lifted her so that she straddled him. He savored how pliant and pleased she was, his heart pounding at the welcome in her smile. The meagre light coming through the window must be of the moon, for it painted her in ethereal silver, making her look like a fairy lover come to make Niall her own. She looked gossamer-wrought, as delicate as a cobweb, as silky smooth as a white flower opened beneath the moon.

He hesitated anew, afraid he would hurt her. But Viviane framed his face in her hands and kissed him soundly, wriggling her hips until his erection encountered her softness. 'Twas so easy to shift his hips, to find his destination, to ease against her welcoming warmth.

Niall had a fleeting impression that something was amiss, that she was too tight for him, too tiny, too finely wrought, but Viviane put an end to any hesitation. She drove her tongue into his mouth and settled herself onto him, a move that could not have been better designed to override his hesitation.

And then, Niall was buried within her, dizzy with sensation and oblivious to all else. There was only Viviane, her sweetness, her silken thighs, her ardent kisses. The wet heat of her seemed to draw him deeper and deeper, her grip upon him and her beguiling tongue forcing all coherent thought from his mind.

Niall was lost and did not want to be found.

They moved together in that ageless dance, temple to temple, whispering incoherently to each other and gasping in turn. The heat was easily conjured between them once more, the lady's embers stoked to a flame. Niall moved his hips to caress the lady, savoring her moans and fleeting smiles. Already he could read her response, as though they had been together countless times, already he could feel her proximity to release.

This time, they would share the pleasure.

Niall slipped his hand between them, his thumb landing upon Viviane with a persuasiveness that made her cry out. She sat up and strained for the sky, a vision of silvered femininity high above him, her knees digging into his waist as they rocked together.

She suddenly threw her head back and moaned, the secret heat of her clutched him with a surety that made Niall bellow in turn. For one electric moment, their gazes held, the world stopped and there was naught but the explosion of pleasure between them.

Then Viviane collapsed atop him and Niall caught her close, rolling against the tangled linens. Their bodies were spent but he was loathe to release even a fraction of her touch.

Even when he felt her drift into slumber once more.

Niall leaned back and closed his eyes as he nestled Viviane more tightly against his side. His thumb stroked the softness of her shoulder, marvelling at what they had shared, as he too drifted off to sleep.

Chapter 11

VIVIANE AWAKENED THE next morning to find sunlight slanted across the floor and birds chirping outside the window. And everything was right with the world, because the heat of her knight was right beside her.

She was tingling right to her toes and lazily satisfied in a way she had never imagined possible. Her mother had been right to insist that it was worth waiting for the right man to savor the pleasures of love.

And now that she had found her knight, Viviane was ready to savor some more.

Viviane propped herself up on one elbow to survey Niall, delighted to find him not only awake but watching her. She smiled at him and to her pleasure, a crooked smile eased across his firm lips.

"You should do that more often," she teased, unable to resist the temptation to trace the curve with her fingertip. Niall captured her finger and kissed it, his intent gaze holding hers as he slid his teeth across its tip.

"Do what?"

"Smile. It makes you look less forbidding." Viviane wrinkled her nose. "As though you're actually happy about something."

Niall chuckled and rolled her to her back, meshing his fingers with hers and stretching her arms over her head as he loomed over her. He braced his weight on his elbows, the move bringing them breathtakingly breast to chest as he slowly smiled. Viviane could feel his erection against her thigh and her heart skipped a beat at the dark hue of Niall's eyes.

She knew what he had in mind.

And she had no objections.

He bent and nibbled on her earlobe, his breath making her shiver. "Aye? And what would I have to be happy about this morn?" he teased, then flicked his tongue against her earlobe.

She caught her breath, then rolled him to his back, echoing his gesture and liking how his eyes twinkled. He let her push him around and Viviane knew it, but still she was enjoying herself.

"I never knew lovemaking was so marvelous," she whispered, wrinkling her nose with delight. "Or is it just that you are so skilled in the amorous arts?" She bent and slid her tongue across Niall's nipple, liking how he shivered.

The man in question snorted amiably as he freed his hands, his thumb moving to slide across the small of her back. The lazy caress made Viviane feel warm and shivery at the same time, the weight of his hand made her feel delightfully feminine.

"Not I," he rumbled, then smiled at her. His dark blond hair was tousled, his emerald eyes gleamed with a sensuality that made her want to blush scarlet. He reached up and pushed a hand through her hair, the warmth of his hand cradling her cheek. He smiled up at her and rubbed his thumb across her temple.

"Beautiful," he murmured, his voice low with admiration, and Viviane felt cherished.

She folded her hands atop his chest and dropped her chin

to rest upon them, hardly able to believe that her knight truly had come. Even though he was right here beside her. Niall stared back at her, the sight of his mingled appreciation and awe making Viviane want to laugh aloud.

Oh, she had lucked out again.

She traced a pattern amidst the hair on his chest with a playful fingertip. "You must have dozens of women clamoring for your touch," she teased, then sighed contentment. "Hundreds of ladies intent on winning the favors of Sir Niall of Malloy."

Niall snorted again, the image of masculine skepticism. "Hardly that."

Viviane tilted her head to consider him. "Why not? You certainly seem to have a talent for . . ."

"I do not couple frequently with women," he interrupted sharply and looked away.

Oh, he was embarrassed! Viviane warmed to this man who was so determined to not trumpet his desirability.

"Well, I can't imagine why not. You certainly have a skill for it." Viviane brushed a fleeting kiss across his flesh. "Not that it's a surprise or anything—I knew the first moment we met that you would know how to thoroughly please a woman. In fact"—she tapped a fingertip on his shoulder— "I wondered even in that dungeon what it would be like to kiss you."

Niall's gaze flicked to hers, then away. His golden brows drew together and his lips tightened, his thumb stopped its lazy caress.

Though he still lay beside her, it felt suddenly as though he were a thousand miles away.

"A knight in shining armor," she teased, but Niall's frown deepened.

"Viviane, I am not the man you think me to be," he said sternly and looked away.

"No, you are much less dour than you would have me believe," she jested, kissing the tip of his nose.

Niall's gaze locked suddenly with hers, no playfulness in

his expression. "Nay, I am not the knight you believe me to be. 'Tis time we had the truth between us."

"What do you mean? You're a knight. Anyone can see that." Viviane snuggled closer. "And you're my knight, I can see that."

Niall shook his head. "Nay, I am a knight in name alone, but not in role."

Viviane frowned. "I don't understand."

Niall sighed. "I am a knight in name alone, for I have earned my spurs and none can take them from me." His lips thinned. "But I do not ride as a knight any longer. 'Tis not mine to defend my patron or his holdings, 'tis not mine to quest and conquer, 'tis not mine to ride to battle."

There was a wistfulness in his tone that made Viviane nestle closer. "Why not?"

He shrugged as though the tale didn't matter but Viviane knew better. "'Tis not a tale worth telling."

Viviane reached out a fingertip to touch his jaw, gently compelling him to look to her again. The shadows in his eyes wrenched her heart. "Tell me," she urged softly. "It's a tale I would like to hear."

"You would hear of my failure?"

"I would hear everything about you." As he watched, clearly incredulous, Viviane stretched to kiss him. Far from a gentle reassurance, the kiss immediately became incendiary, that heat rising quickly between them. Niall opened his mouth to her and bracketed her waist with his hands. He pulled her closer, then rolled atop her once more, his lips both demanding and pleasing. His knee was between her thighs, their limbs entangled, and their breathing ragged when he lifted his head.

"You are a marvel," he murmured, tracing the line of her jaw with one fingertip. His touch made circles on her skin as he frowned in thought, then his gaze flicked to hers. "Indeed, you make me recall those days before my shame."

Viviane looped her arms around his neck. "What shame could you have?"

Niall grimaced and rolled to his back once more. His tone was flat. "I was bested in a tournament before the archbishop three years past. 'Twas my role to defend his cause, for he had chosen me to carry his colors against the champion of his neighbor and rival. All of Cantlecroft gathered for the match and though 'twas in sport, there was an element of truth riding on the outcome. 'Twas a telling responsibility and a trust I dared not disappoint."

Viviane had a good idea where this story was going. "What happened?" she asked when Niall fell grimly silent.

"I rode out, ceremony and fine trappings on every side. We met on a field chosen between the two holdings, the perimeter tight with tents of nobles. Every peasant within walking distance was there, every merchant walked his eligible daughter through the throng. 'Twas a spectacle such as few have the chance to witness—and my match with this champion was the highlight of the fete."

" 'Twas there I showed myself no champion of repute."

"Of course you are!" Viviane cried.

"Nay, Viviane. I failed my patron. I miscalculated the intent of my opponent on the seventh course. He swerved his steed and collided with mine, unhorsing me, wounding both beasts and crushing my knee."

"But you must have been wearing armor!"

He flicked her a wry glance. "Do you know the weight of a destrier? The beast was running at full gallop and fully armed as well. He struck mine so hard that both beasts broke a rib, and my knee had the misfortune to be trapped between."

"That's horrible!"

"Aye, I was quickly defeated after that and the archbishop was mightily displeased."

"But your knee?"

"Healed after a fashion, thanks to the aid of a sympathetic physician. The steeds did not fare so well—and neither did my repute." He stretched out his leg and the joint creaked. "The rain worsens its complaints and it does not suffer me to ride overmuch these days. Nay, Viviane, I am a knight no longer."

Viviane exhaled in sudden understanding. "So, that was why you were a sentry in the archbishop's dungeons!"

"Aye."

She sat up, nodding her understanding. "I just knew it couldn't be an easy labor for you. You were intended to ride on quests, to right wrongs and to save damsels in distress. You're not the kind of man to march people to their deaths and I knew it, right from the moment we met . . ."

She leaned forward to give him a hearty kiss, certain her endorsement would improve his spirits, but Niall abruptly swung out of bed.

It must be that his injured knee needed a stretch, Viviane concluded, for he limped as he crossed the room. He shoved a hand through his hair with impatience and his expression was forbidding when he turned.

Oh, horrible feelings had been dredged up by that memory, Viviane could see. She was doubly honored that Niall had shared it with her.

The books were right—communication between them was key.

"What did you think of *me,* there in the archbishop's dungeons?" She smiled brightly, hoping to lighten the tone of the conversation. "I have to say that I didn't spend a very comfortable night there and I couldn't have been looking my best . . ."

Niall looked up suddenly at that, his expression agitated. "Viviane, 'tis time I confess to you . . ." he began, his tone purposeful.

But then, his eyes abruptly widened and his words halted. Niall stared at her, then at the linens as though disbelieving what was before his own eyes. Viviane followed his glance, catching her own breath at the telltale dried red drops.

Oops.

She noted her own virginal blood smeared across Niall's

flesh in the same moment that he discovered it. He touched himself and inhaled sharply, then his eyes flashed.

Viviane blushed and dropped her gaze, her rush of maidenly shyness a little late to be much help.

"You are a virgin?" he demanded.

Perhaps she had not done so badly with lovemaking as she feared. Any pleasure Viviane might have felt at the implied compliment, though, was quickly shattered by Niall's evident horror.

She shrugged self-consciously, pulling the linens higher over herself as she tried to smile. "Well, not anymore."

Her attempt at humor fell flat.

Niall flung out a hand as he took a step closer. "How could you not have told me the truth?"

"You didn't stop to ask!" Viviane pushed the weight of her hair back from her cheek and lifted her chin proudly.

"You should have told me!" Niall thundered.

"If it mattered that much, you should have asked!"

Niall muttered something that Viviane was quite glad she couldn't quite overhear. "This changes all!" he declared with evident frustration. "Zounds, but what is a man to do?" He paced the room with new vigor, not looking nearly as pleased as he had just a few minutes before.

If Niall had chased her to Avalon to return her pendant, using it as an excuse to see her again, if he was really her one true love and they were destined to be together, then what did her virginity matter?

Viviane straightened, unable to shake a portent of dread. "What do you mean?" she asked carefully. "What does it change?"

Niall shoved a hand through his hair and paced the width of the room one more time. When he pivoted suddenly to face her, Viviane had a distinct sense that he had made a decision.

And judging by his dour expression, it wasn't one he liked.

"We shall have to be wed," he declared flatly. "This very

day. There is naught else for it, though indeed the repercussions may be dire."

It wasn't what she had expected him to say, and certainly not the way Viviane had ever expected the man of her dreams to propose to her. In fact, Niall looked as though he were doing something particularly distasteful, and that he was doing it only because he didn't have a choice.

"What?" Viviane croaked, certain she must have misunderstood.

"We shall be wed," Niall affirmed, then nodded briskly as though all was resolved. "There is no choice."

Viviane gasped at the lack of romance in his attitude. This wasn't how he was supposed to ask for her hand. "You're asking me because you have no choice?"

"Clearly." Niall frowned as he thought. "Surely there is a priest to be found in this place? No doubt the press of coins in his palm will see the matter resolved before midday."

Viviane's mouth fell open and she bounded from the bed in outrage. "I'm *not* a matter to be resolved! And I won't be married by midday, today!"

Niall looked at her then, his gaze fathomless green. "A man of honor must do what is right, Viviane. I have taken your virginity and will pay the price, however heavy that might prove to be."

And he reached for his clothing, as though there was nothing more to discuss.

Viviane had a somewhat different view of things.

"What are you talking about? You said you came for me!"

Niall steadily held her gaze, an apology in the depths of his eyes that Viviane couldn't understand. "Aye, I came for you," he admitted softly, as though he didn't want to.

"And you said you wouldn't leave without me."

Shadows dawned in his eyes. "Aye, 'tis true enough."

"Then, what's the problem? Why don't you want to marry me?" Viviane flung her hand out toward the bed. "You wanted me last night, and again this morning, just as I wanted you. Why is marriage a price to be paid? And what sort of dire repercussions could there be?"

"Viviane!" Niall took a step toward her, appeal in his gaze. "You must understand . . ."

"I don't understand!" Viviane's tears threatened to choke her. She had practically thrown herself at Niall, she had been so sure that they were meant to be together, and he had taken advantage of her offer. She was such a fool! Oh, she had confused the tales in her imagination with the truth, she had mingled the hero of her book with a living, breathing man. "I trusted you. I believed you were my one true knight. Barb warned me about men of your kind . . ."

"Nay, Viviane, 'twas not thus." Niall propped his hands on his hips. "Matters are most simple, if you would but listen to me."

Viviane folded her arms across her chest and hoped desperately that he had a good explanation. A convincing one. Her heart was hammering wildly and she could not steady her breathing.

How could she have been so wrong about her knight?

"I'm listening," she said with as much dignity as she could.

"Your maidenhead is a treasure destined for the man who takes your hand in marriage," Niall said patiently. "'Twas not mine to take, and I apologize for my failure to recall that in the heat of the moment. Further, I would make matters come aright, instead of leaving you in shame."

"So now what we have done is shameful," Viviane said with disappointment. "As well as an obligation."

This was not the way it happened in her book.

Niall's lips tightened as though he didn't like her tone, though he slanted a very green glance her way. "'Tis right for a man to bear the consequences of his deeds. I have taken your maidenhead and will pay the rightful due."

If he had made some mention of passion, or even desire, instead of citing responsibilities like a legal clerk, Viviane's annoyance might have waned.

Instead, his measured words made her even more angry.

"You took *nothing* from me that I wasn't prepared to give!" Niall seemed momentarily astonished, but Viviane wasn't done. "And I'm not going to marry you just because my virginity is gone!"

His eyes narrowed thoughtfully. "You care naught for the shame that will find you on your wedding night?"

"Maybe I'll never marry!" It wasn't such a long shot, given her disappointment in this moment.

"Viviane!" Niall scowled. "Use the wits with which you were blessed. There could be a child from this union, one compelled to pay the price of this folly for all its days."

Oh, it was *folly*. Better and better.

Viviane lifted her chin, irked even more that this practical tack was the only argument Niall thought it suitable to make. "So there could be. If there is, I'll manage on my own. It won't inconvenience you."

Niall straightened. "What is *that* to mean?"

Viviane stared him down, virtually daring him to show some passion over this. "*I* am the one who will bear that child, give birth to it and raise it. It has nothing to do with you."

Now he was angry.

Niall's eyes flashed before he jabbed a finger through the air and roared. "'Tis my obligation to support any fruit I compel a woman to bear! 'Twill not be said of Niall of Malloy that he took what was not his due and did not make matters come right!"

"And what about me?" Viviane demanded. "What about what *I* want?"

The annoyance melted from Niall's eyes, and his puzzled expression caught at Viviane's heart. "But what else could you possibly desire? Viviane, I have seen that you are a woman of sense—how could you not want a spouse to take responsibility for your child? How could you believe there to be merit in raising a babe alone?"

His appeal nearly undermined Viviane's anger completely, because she could tell that he couldn't think of another thing a woman could want, besides a husband to provide for her child.

Besides *him*.

But Viviane wanted more than Niall's pledge to wed her. It was time for a little communication. Fortunately, she was more than prepared to be blunt.

"What about love?"

Niall blinked. "Love?"

"Yes, *love*! I want love," Viviane insisted. "And love is the only reason that I'll ever marry anyone."

It would have been nice if Niall seized this challenge, stepped forward and pledged undying devotion, right then and there—that's what would have happened in Viviane's book!—but he didn't.

Actually, he rolled his eyes. "Love!" he snorted. "Love does not see a babe fed and clothed, love does not see a roof over that child's head. Love heats a man's loins, compels him to make poor judgments, then flees into the night."

Viviane gasped. "Is that what this was? A poor judgment?"

"It would seem so!" Niall roared. "Certainly you are not thinking clearly, Viviane! Love is not to be trusted and no reliable guide for one's choices. Love is a whimsy of poets and minstrels and has naught to do with the good sense of *responsibility*."

"Well, responsibility isn't a good enough reason to be married!" Viviane shouted back at him. "Whether it's for a child or for virginity, it's not enough!"

Niall folded his arms across his chest and glared at her. "Did you find this whimsy in this realm?"

Viviane echoed his gesture and glared right back. "No. I learned from my mother that the only marriage worth having was one based on love. That's what she valued, and that's what I want too." Niall held her gaze stubbornly, his thinking clearly unchanged. "I won't marry you just because you feel guilty, and that's all there is to it."

Niall seemed to have nothing to say to that. He grimaced and exhaled heavily, shook his head and turned away. Viviane thought he muttered something about *women*, but she couldn't be sure.

She was too busy being disappointed. The man of her dreams wasn't supposed to find love a foreign concept.

Well, to live was to learn, as her mother had often said.

And Viviane was learning a bit more than she would have preferred. She fingered the pendant Niall had returned to her and was glad to have that much at least. Viviane was determined to not cry in his presence, so she blinked back her tears and turned to pick up her robe.

Once composed, she shot a telling glance over her shoulder en route to the washroom. "Besides," she said archly, "you don't have a very nice way of *asking*."

Niall's head shot up. Viviane held his gaze for a telling moment, then strode away while she still could, her nose in the air. She wasn't entirely sure she'd make it without Niall chasing her, much less that she could turn him away if he so much as touched her again.

But she did.

And she didn't think about exactly who she was locking the door against. The image of a very nude, very muscular knight—the knight of her dreams, in fact—staring after her, an unexpected vulnerability in his green eyes, was one that Viviane knew she wouldn't easily wash from her thoughts.

She was less sure that she wanted to. She leaned back against the door and let her tears of disappointment rise for only a moment before she straightened and turned on the shower.

Niall opened his mouth and closed it again, certain he would never understand the thinking of women. He had thought Viviane different from Majella, a woman of sense, yet she clung to arguments of passion with the same nonsensical determination of his sister.

'Twas not welcome news.

And just when he thought he had no chance of salvaging the situation, Viviane threw him a tantalizing comment like that last one.

He hadn't asked nicely enough.

There was a sentiment Majella would applaud. Niall rubbed his brow and decided 'twas an arduous task he had taken upon himself when he followed Viviane. Indeed, matters grew more complicated by the moment! She had denied his proposal born of duty, but in typical female fashion, had left more questions in the wake of her decision than before. Niall, though, after years of dealing with Majella, was certain he could think matters through.

Did Viviane mean she wanted only the pleasure he could grant her, without any further ties? 'Twas an odd perspective for a woman so recently a virgin and Niall immediately dismissed that possibility.

Or did she mean she would never accept his offer, regardless of what he said or did? Surely Viviane knew that children had need of hearth and home, of food and security? Aye, she spoke warmly of her own mother, so clearly knew the value of family.

And she knew naught of his pledge to return her to the archbishop—Niall fidgeted with guilt that he had not confessed the truth to her, though he had come close—so *that* could not be a factor in her refusal of his suit. Indeed, she seemed to think that Niall had pursued her for her own company alone, a fact that hinted that she would not be displeased to find that suspicion proven true.

So, Viviane must have some favorable inclination toward him, as the last night so amply showed. Did she mean then that she would entertain the notion of marriage if he asked *properly*?

That sounded most womanly, to Niall's way of thinking, and suitably incomprehensible. Though, indeed, he wondered whether Viviane would be any more comprehensible anywhere he encountered her. He recalled their first meeting in the dungeons and pinched the bridge of his nose.

The lady had a talent for defying his expectations, no less for challenging his convictions.

'Twas what he liked about her, truth be told.

But a woman's greatest treasure should be reserved for the man who took her to wife—Niall had only to look to the example of his nieces and nephews to see where the opposite choice left children. Marriage was the only honorable choice, even though marriage to a woman convicted of witchcraft could only earn Niall a place alongside Viviane on the executioner's block.

A man must stand by what he had done, a man must bear the weight of his responsibilities. Niall's sense of duty tolerated no exceptions for challenging circumstance. A lesser man might have stepped away, relieved that his task was not to be further complicated.

But Niall was a man of honor and he knew what was best. They would be wed.

And with all haste.

To have Viviane decline him, for the sake of that trouble-making folly known as love, did not fit well with Niall's view of his responsibilities.

Clearly, she must first be dissuaded of this foolery that marriage was a matter reserved for those snared in the false trap of love. Niall did not trust love, as it fell into that category of unseen intangibles that were not to be relied upon.

Although, Viviane was certainly not the first maiden to find that siren's call alluring. And truly, if ever there had been a woman capable of seizing a notion and running farther with it than any might have believed possible, 'twas his Viviane.

Niall smiled despite himself. Her tales and her conviction in their truth were appealing, he had to admit. He liked how her eyes flashed when she explained matters to him and how her entire face shone with the certainty of what she knew. He enjoyed how passionately she argued her case, not a shred of doubt within her thoughts.

Even if she was completely wrong. Aye, there was something about Viviane and her manner that a man could watch and savor for all his days and nights.

Marriage was a matter of responsibility, of obligation, of partnership. 'Twas two laboring as one toward their mutual objectives, two ensuring the welfare of each other and their spawn, two building a haven from the caprice of the world.

That was marriage. And Niall knew, with dawning conviction, that if he could but show Viviane the good sense of this, then she would agree.

Both to his view of matrimony and his proposal.

It sounded more simple than Niall guessed 'twould be, but he was well prepared to try.

The shower began to run in that moment and Niall lifted his head to stare at the closed washroom door. 'Twas easy enough to visualize what Viviane did. Niall took a step closer, his blood quickening with the prospect of lending his aid.

'Twas then that Niall realized something truly marvelous. For if this was not Avalon—as he now knew 'twas not— then 'twas not a realm governed by magic. 'Twas a realm of men, governed by the mechanisms of man, just as Cantlecroft was. In fact, 'twas within the *same* world that Cantlecroft occupied, just somewhat later and further west.

This affirmed all that Niall believed, that only what a man could hold in his hands or see with his eyes was truly real.

There was no magic, even here.

But if there was no magic, then there could be no spells. Viviane could not have enchanted Niall. She could not have cast a spell over him to feed his desire or to serve her own, she could not have compelled him to feel anything.

Niall considered this carefully but 'twas unassailable.

No magic meant no spells.

And if his desire for Viviane was not unnaturally contrived, then there was naught wrong with it. He frowned and stared down at himself just to be sure, but naught was shrivelling.

And certainly naught had fallen off.

Indeed, 'twas quite the opposite. He had never been so large or so hard in all his days.

And at the sight of his own enthusiastic arousal, Niall began to laugh. Because his Viviane, the woman he must take to wife, was no witch. The proof was right before his eyes.

Which meant that he could save his lady from a most dire fate. *He* would prove her innocence to the archbishop, he could swear to the fact that she was no witch at all. They could return to Cantlecroft, they could wed, and all would be right in Niall of Malloy's world.

'Twas a dazzling prospect.

But first, he had to persuade Viviane to accept him. Niall also understood enough of Viviane to recognize that she would not be easily swayed from whatever course she had already chosen. His lady was cursedly stubborn.

Fortunately, Niall was more so. He would persuade her now, with whatever means necessary; he would overwhelm her with the power of his argument.

Niall grinned as he crossed the floor, feeling very persuasive indeed.

Viviane knew she was in trouble the minute she stepped out of the shower. The doorknob was jiggling and she had a fairly good idea who was trying to open the door. She froze and stared, her heart hammering as Niall softly swore on the other side.

She had a feeling that the little lock was going to disappoint her.

There was a moment's silence, then a futile click as the knob resisted a hard wrenching. It whined slightly, metal scraped on metal, and the door opened with a jerk.

Viviane took a cautious step back, which was about all the room allowed, and braced herself for the inevitable argument.

She certainly didn't expect the glint of sensuous determination in Niall's eyes, never mind his banner of enthusiasm flying at full mast somewhat further south. Viviane's mouth went dry as he stepped into the small space with purpose.

And they said women changed mood fast.

Niall backed her into the wall before she could make a sound. He touched her jaw with fingers so gentle that she nearly melted on the spot, then brushed his lips across her own.

Viviane forgot any protest she might have made.

"I apologize," he murmured against her flesh, his breath making her shiver, his words making her objections fade. "For earlier, I spoke with undue haste and angered you for no good cause."

Viviane might have gasped in delighted surprise, but Niall's lips sealed over hers so resolutely that there was no room for even that. Her eyes closed of their own accord as Niall backed her into the wall, his lips tempting her to surrender all to him once again. He kissed with a thoroughness that belied anything else in the world. Viviane was certain she had his complete, undivided attention, and she couldn't imagine wanting anything else.

Niall sandwiched her between his gloriously hard body and the equally hard and somewhat more cold wall. The towel Viviane had wrapped around herself fell beneath his persuasive fingers, she arched as his hands closed possessively over her breasts. Her head fell back as his fingertips caressed her nipples and his tongue slid between her teeth.

She couldn't quite remember why she had declined him anything.

Niall's muscled thigh slid between her own, one hand slipped over her flesh to seek out the heat between her thighs. Viviane caught her breath when his thumb slid over that sensitive spot and Niall grazed a line of kisses along her throat. He captured her earlobe in his teeth, his tongue flicked against the tender flesh there, the warmth of his breath driving her to distraction.

"Forgive me, my Viviane," he urged quietly, but Viviane could only moan in agreement.

His fingers caressed her more deeply, his every touch stoking the flames that rose beneath her flesh. The hair on his chest tickled her aroused breasts, the warm strength of him made her feel cossetted and cornered.

Seduced by her lover true. Viviane sighed with satisfaction and surrendered to the moment.

This was more like it.

Viviane opened her eyes and found Niall's gaze fixed upon her with a dizzying intensity, the green hue of his eyes so piercing that it seemed he could see her every thought. A smile curved his firm lips, as though he could think of nothing but pleasing her beyond her wildest dreams. Viviane parted her lips, then forgot whatever she might have said when Niall leaned down to kiss her once again.

She was drifting in a haze of pleasure and had no desire to come back to shore. Niall coaxed and teased, his touch so sure that Viviane couldn't have stopped herself from responding. She shivered and moaned, he caressed and kissed, and just when she thought she could bear no more, he cupped her buttocks in his hands.

He lifted her in one smooth movement and impaled her upon himself, his legs braced against the floor. Viviane could not touch the ground: she was trapped between her golden knight and the wall, she was full of his strength.

Their gazes locked and held, he squeezed her buttocks in his great hands, and he began to move within her, his every motion languid and powerful. He rubbed against her deliberately, making Viviane writhe, his small smile telling her that was precisely his intent.

And she had no complaints.

"You're teasing me," she accused softly, and his grin widened.

"Nay, to tease is to tempt without granting satisfaction." Niall bent and grazed her neck with a searing kiss. "Trust me, Viviane, I intend to grant satisfaction as you have never known it before."

Viviane shivered as he stroked deliberately within her

once again. He shifted to let one hand move between them and coaxed her yet higher with ease. He lifted her against him and suckled her breast, his fingers dancing, his hips thrusting in a persuasive rhythm.

Viviane gripped his shoulders and hung on as the crescendo rose within her again. Niall growled against her flesh. He moved with renewed vigor, his grip tightened upon her. She could feel his own heartbeat thundering beneath her fingertips and savored the knowledge that he too was strongly affected.

She framed his face in her hands and kissed him with abandon, loving the way he buried himself within her. She swallowed the roar that came with his release and held him ever closer as he trembled with the force of his orgasm. When he lifted his head and stared down at her, his eyes dark with passion, and whispered her name, Viviane shook to her core and cried out.

"Wed me," Niall murmured unevenly against her shoulder in the trembling aftermath. Viviane was sorely tempted to do precisely that. "Come, Viviane, be my bride, my partner, my lover."

She pushed a hand through the golden thickness of his hair and smiled up at him. She sighed and ran a fingertip along his jawline, not quite willing to end this magical moment. "I like this way of asking much better."

Niall smiled crookedly and squeezed her buttocks. "I could ask you again," he suggested, a wicked gleam in his eye.

Viviane looped her arms around his neck, very pleased to find that they'd just had a misunderstanding. Barb's books were right. She crossed her ankles behind his back, not in the least bit ready to surrender his warmth. "You can be very persuasive, sir."

Niall half-chuckled, his quick glance revealing his interest in her answer. "And are you persuaded?"

"Not quite," Viviane conceded. She tapped a playful fingertip on his nose. He had a perfect nose, she decided, aquiline and noble. A good straight nose that would suit their children.

For there would be children if they continued at this rate.

Niall's eyes narrowed assessingly. "Not quite?" he echoed with a precision that should have warned her.

Viviane smiled. "Well, it's a great beginning, but you've hardly dropped to one knee and sworn undying love. Shouldn't you depart on a quest to win my favor, or bring wondrous gifts from afar, or wear my sleeve in a tournament to show your devotion to me? I mean, you haven't said a word about *love*!"

Niall stilled dangerously. "I could love you again, if you need further persuasion," he rumbled, but Viviane shook her head.

"No, no, no. That kind of loving isn't the same kind of loving as what I mean and you know it."

He steadily held her gaze, his eyes darkening slightly.

But Viviane was too delighted to pay much attention to such warning signs. She twined her arms around his neck a little more tightly. "People who love each other would do anything for each other, regardless of the risk to themselves. They put their loved one first, they think about their loved one, they think about pleasing their loved one . . ."

"Have I not pleased you and put your pleasure first?" Niall demanded.

"Of course! But it's not just with bodies." She smiled up at him and tapped a fingertip on his chest. "Love comes from the heart."

Niall, though, extricated himself from Viviane's embrace and put her solidly on her feet, his scowl back in place once more. He propped his hands on his hips, the move filling the bathroom with disgruntled knight.

"I had always thought my heart was within my body," he charged, his eyes narrowed.

"Niall! Think about it!"

"Aye, I do think about it and I listen to all you say, as well, even being the nonsense that it is. Indeed, it seems to me that each time I ask your favor, you do change the terms of your agreement!"

"What?"

"You said I did not ask nicely enough," he said savagely. "I ask more *nicely* and still 'tis not enough. Now you would have deeds and tournaments, I must ride to war in your name, sacrifice all for the pleasure of your smile, grant all I have to surrender for your happiness alone." Niall flung out one hand in evident annoyance. "We do not have *time* for such whimsy!"

Viviane had a sudden sense that they were talking about different things again.

And that that wasn't a good thing at all.

Chapter 12

VIVIANE FOLDED HER arms across her chest, feeling suddenly cold. "What has time got to do with anything? Even if I was with child at this very moment, the baby would still not come for nine whole months!"

But even faced with such "good sense," Niall shoved a hand through his hair and growled in exasperation. For some reason, his gaze fell to Viviane's moonstone pendant, the sight obviously doing little to improve his mood.

His annoyed gaze flicked back to meet hers once more. "Will you wed me this day or not?"

So much for his persuasive manner! "Well, if you're going to see it that way, no!"

"Even knowing 'tis the most honorable choice?"

"I don't care about honor, I told you that!"

"I do!" Niall roared, his eyes flashing. "I care about responsibilities. *I care about good sense!*"

"I care about love!"

"Feminine whimsy," Niall said with a dismissive sweep of his hand. "No marriage of value was made on the apparent merit of love."

"Apparent merit? Love might be whimsy to you, but it's

important to me!" Viviane poked a finger into his chest. "And that *counts*!"

"Love is a lie, Viviane, a lie concocted by men of dubious character to persuade women to part their thighs and no more." Niall's brow was dark, his manner intent. "Love is no foundation for a good match and never will it be."

"Don't talk to me about arranged marriages!" Viviane retorted. "Besides, you seem to have found your way between my thighs well enough."

"Viviane!" Niall's expression turned appealing and Viviane's resistance melted. "There is a critical difference, though, for I would stand by my deeds. I would treat you with honor, I would not leave you to bear the burden of what we have done."

Viviane folded her arms across her chest, holding his gaze. "Do you love me?" She held her breath, but didn't have to bother for long.

Niall immediately shook his head. "I do not believe in love."

"Then we have nothing further to say," Viviane said, disliking the little break in her voice. She might have turned away, but Niall snared her elbow.

"I say we do," he insisted.

Viviane froze and waited. She couldn't look away from him, his manner was so compelling, his attention so completely fixed upon her. Could he really not love her? It was impossible to believe.

Niall considered her for such a long moment that Viviane felt like a mouse cornered by a clever cat. Then he smiled, as though that cat had just spied dinner.

He braced his hands on the wall over her shoulders and held her gaze, exuding male confidence. "I shall make you a wager, my Viviane," he rumbled.

"What kind of wager?" Viviane hated how breathless she sounded. It was all his fault for using her name that way, but even knowing that didn't help her catch her breath.

Niall's smile broadened as though he knew exactly his effect upon her. His gaze danced over her, the hue of his eyes a vivid green. "I shall persuade you to put your hand in mine," he vowed so seriously that she shivered.

"You'll only persuade me with love," she maintained breathlessly.

"Nay." Niall bent and kissed her earlobe so slowly and sensuously that Viviane trembled. "I shall persuade you with good sense."

That was so ludicrous that Viviane might have laughed, if Niall hadn't been nuzzling her below her ear in such a distracting way. His tongue traced a beguiling path down her throat and Viviane's toes curled when he nibbled leisurely on her shoulder.

She was melting away, her bones were dissolving, her knees were weak.

"A man of repute will keep his word, feed his family and defend his own hearth," Niall murmured. "Be warned, my Viviane, I shall persuade you that I am such a man of merit. I shall prove the truth of it to you."

Viviane parted her lips to argue that she was already persuaded of that, except for one pesky detail, but Niall kissed her lingeringly instead. In fact, he kissed her so thoroughly that she almost agreed right then and there to marry him, regardless of his ideas.

But she did know better. Love had to be a part of marriage. It mattered to her, which meant it should matter to him.

And she had to be sure *first* because marriage, whether in Avalon or Cantlecroft, was forever.

Niall straightened and pushed one hand through the thickness of her hair, his glowing gaze making her mouth go dry. She wondered if he was going to seduce her again and felt a tingle of anticipation. Niall smiled down at her as though he read her thoughts, and his heavy fingers massaged her nape.

He bent his head toward hers and Viviane knew that if he kissed her again, she'd melt like butter in the sun.

So she poked a finger into his chest and took a step sideways. "And I'll make you a wager," she said pertly.

Niall arched a fair brow.

"I'll reconsider your proposal after you do something for me."

"Aye? Another task?" He smiled ever so slightly, his expression almost teasing. "And what would that be?"

Viviane ducked beneath his arm and darted across the room, picking up her manuscript and offering it to Niall with a flourish before she could change her mind. "I want you to read this. It's a book, one that I've written, and I want to know what you think of it."

Viviane held her breath as Niall glanced at the manuscript, skepticism clear in every line of his being.

"Why?"

Because once he had read this, he would know exactly how Viviane felt about love. And he'd have a good idea how she felt about him, too, she realized, because Niall was clever enough to recognize himself in her work.

Perfect!

But she should probably not tell him that exactly. Barb would say it sounded too "mushy" and Viviane really didn't want Niall to start playing with the taps again.

Much less stop looking at her the way he was looking right now.

"Well, because. Um, it's important to me and I'd like to know what you think of it. No one else has read it and I'd like you to be the first." Viviane offered it with a smile, then caught her lip in her teeth. "You can read, can't you?"

"Of course, I am lettered!" Niall crossed the room, his eyes lighting with curiosity as he lifted the volume and fanned through it.

Viviane felt a pang of worry now that her work was out of her hands. "So, you see, it would be a really good way for you to get to understand me, to know what I'm thinking, what I want, what I expect from love and marriage and everything."

Her words faltered when it became apparent that Niall wasn't listening.

Because he was reading.

Her book.

A frown furrowed Niall's brow as he turned the first page. "This is not the tale of Gawain as I recall it."

"No, I changed it." Viviane knotted her hands together nervously. "It's my story of Gawain. That's what people do here, they start with a story and make it their own, embellishing it and blending it, making it into something different. They don't just copy as we had to. People expect each book to be different."

Niall pinned her to the spot with a glance. "And you would trust me with the first reading of your labor?" he demanded with that intensity that stole her breath away. "Viviane!" he whispered and took a step closer, his eyes gleaming.

Oh, it didn't help that he knew she was trusting him with something important!

She shook a finger at him and backed away. "Just read it, please! And tell me what you think."

Niall bowed. "Your wish is my command," he murmured in a way that made her want to take back the book and do something entirely different. But Niall perched on the edge of the bed, his gaze apparently snared by what she had written, and read.

"I guess I'll go to work," Viviane said pointedly.

Niall nodded and made a murmur of assent, turning another page and laying it aside. He pursed his lips and leaned back on the bed, bracing one foot against the mattress, clearly unaware of how magnificently masculine he looked.

Viviane took one lingering look, knew she should be glad he was interested in her work, and trudged down the stairs.

She hoped he liked it.

She hoped even more that it convinced him of the merit of love.

• • •

Niall had a difficult time putting his lady's book aside, though indeed, he knew there were other matters he must resolve. Aye, he had to think, as well as make a plan to not only prove Viviane's innocence but win her agreement to return to Cantlecroft and set all to rights.

Then he had to figure out how to manage the deed. If all that did not persuade her that he would be a worthy spouse, then Niall could not imagine what would.

Indeed, he trusted in his own ultimate success.

Though, still, Niall wondered at the power of Viviane's pendant. How did it work? Would it work again? Were there other objects here possessing the same power? He did not know and could not fathom a guess.

And how had Viviane come by such a token in the first place? She said 'twas a gift from her father—had he been of this time?

Niall shook his head, unable to solve such problems so early in the day. With reluctance, he put her book aside, knowing that he had much to do this day before he read at leisure.

After all, he must show his lady that he was responsible. That was the greater obligation before him.

Niall scrubbed himself in the washing room, a whistle on his lips, taking great satisfaction in how the water ceased its flow completely as he turned the spigot. The looking glass over the sink was one of incomparable quality, and Niall considered the new growth gracing his chin.

He should look his best if he meant to persuade Viviane of his case. A good man should be fastidiously groomed, 'twas what his own mother had oft declared. Indeed, she had always spared a kiss for her own spouse and Niall's father when that man arrived at the board with a clean-shaven face.

Niall fetched his dagger to scrape the whiskers from his chin and began to whistle as he worked. Aye, he would prove his eligibility to Viviane, convince her of the good sense of wedding him, persuade her that there were pleasures aplenty to be had, and ensure that her innocence was proven to the archbishop. And he would read her book, as well, thereby fulfilling the lady's own demand.

Viviane would not be able to resist such persuasiveness.

'Twas then Niall spied the tiny brush hung above the sink. He fingered its bristles and examined its small size. A useful tool, of that there could be no doubt, and one particularly suited to cleaning small nooks and crannies.

Which reminded him of one particular task which could not be avoided. His gaze drifted across the chamber to the staircase, at the bottom of which reposed the bag Derek had returned to him. It contained the jumble of his discarded mail, a considerable investment that must be protected.

Niall retrieved it, then squatted beside it, pulling the sodden mess of his tabard free. He examined the garment for tears, then hung it in the washroom to drip. His cloak was similarly spread to dry, his chausses and aketon wrung out to the best of his ability before they also were left to drip.

He hunkered down beside the array of remaining metal, scanning the links and disliking the damage already wrought by that salted water. The greaves were well enough—a buff from Viviane's incomparable "towel" put them back to rights. Yet the mail was in sorry shape. Without a squire, there was none to tend it but Niall himself, and were it not tended, his considerable investment would be worth less than naught.

And he did desire to look his best. Perhaps he should have proposed in all his finery, instead of nude before her.

Perhaps that was part of her quibble with matters. Women, Niall knew, were oft fond of a little ceremony. And this red chemise looked increasingly disreputable. He thought of the coin that was now his own and considered that he should acquire new garb. Aye, a man bent on courting would do well to ensure his lady's approval.

But where and how, and what to buy?

Niall shook his head, unprepared for the challenge of a day at the mercy of shopkeepers. Nay, here was a task to keep him occupied while he awaited Viviane's return, a sensible labor and one that would leave him more ready to court affection when 'twas done.

So, Niall fetched the little brush and set to work on his mail.

It hurt naught that such a tedious labor gave him ample opportunity to relive the delightful flash of a certain lady's lovely hazel eyes, or the little sound she made before the pleasure rushed through her, or the wondrous curve of her lips when she smiled for him alone.

Or to plan precisely how he would win those responses from her once more. Niall whistled tunelessly at the prospect of being persuasive.

Aye, there were worse fates than to take a woman to wife who was beauteous, alluring and charming, if occasionally unpredictable. Niall was newly glad that he had won sentry duty on that fateful day and had the good fortune to make the lady's acquaintance.

Viviane would have said 'twas because of her birth under a blue moon, the very idea making Niall grin. Aye, he could grow accustomed to such harmless whimsy, especially when espoused by such a charming woman as his Viviane.

Niall's belly growled as he set to work, its volume growing with every passing moment. He began to wonder whether Viviane had skill in the kitchen, as well.

That would be uncommon fortune indeed.

Barb was boiling water for tea when Viviane entered the shop.

"Let me guess—he came back?" she asked drily.

Viviane laughed. She dropped into her chair at the table and propped her chin on her hands. "Oh, yes!"

Barb shook her head as she put tea bags into the pot. "Judging by the sound effects, you didn't get a lot of sleep last night," she remarked, much to Viviane's confusion. Her employer's knowing expression though quickly clarified her comment.

And Viviane felt her cheeks heat. "Well . . ."

Barb studied the teapot as though it was a lot more interesting than it was. "A little trouble in paradise this morning?" she mused, and Viviane realized their argument had also been overheard.

"Oh, just a misunderstanding." She grinned sunnily as she accepted a mug of tea. "Everything will work out, I'm sure of it."

"Is that right." Barb shook her head and took the other seat, looking the younger woman right in the eye. "Viviane, you do know that men have commitment disease, don't you? They fight like tigers whenever they think they might get snared, and lie like the devil to get loose. Men don't want to settle down, get hitched, tie the knot. They avoid it like the plague—if you'll forgive the medieval reference—and would rather jump off the Golden Gate bridge than propose."

Barb shrugged and pushed to her feet, heading back to the kettle. "It's just the way they are and if your particular catch is trying to bolt into the blue, well, you can't be too surprised. The really good looking ones never stick around."

Viviane shook her head vigorously, both impressed by Barb's protectiveness and anxious to defend Niall. "No, no, you don't understand, Barb. Niall's not like that at all. Niall wants to get married."

Barb pivoted, her eyes wide. "*Married?* Is that some kind of a joke?"

"He seems very serious about it. In fact, he was quite unhappy when I refused him."

Barb frowned at the whistling kettle as though she didn't know what to do about it, then unplugged it and crossed the small room with quick steps.

She folded her arms across her chest and stared down at Viviane. "So, let me get this straight. He followed you, you're glad to see him, and now he wants to marry you? And that's a problem?"

"Well, yes." Viviane smiled. "Obviously."

"Obviously? Viviane! It's pretty remarkable that he's so

ready to get married—I mean this was the guy who said he wasn't staying long—and you did keep saying that everything is *perfect*, never mind that he was your knight and all that jazz."

Viviane rolled her eyes. "Well, it would be perfect, if Niall could stop talking about duty and responsibility and partnership." She stuck out her tongue. "It's not very romantic, is it?"

"Uh huh. Fate worse than death." Barb leaned back, her assessing gaze fixed on Viviane, and Viviane tried to explain.

"Well, it *isn't*! You see, he just doesn't even talk about love and how could I marry a man who didn't love me? He says he doesn't believe in love, and well, I can't even imagine thinking anything like that!"

"Love." Barb sounded a lot like Niall.

"Love." Viviane sighed at the very thought. "It wouldn't be so bad if he at least mentioned love, but he keeps saying that it's his *duty* to marry me. He goes on and on about responsibilities and children needing a father and"—she grimaced then appealed to Barb—"he's just so practical about it all!"

"Duty!" Barb raised her brows. "He sounds pretty medieval." She studied Viviane for a long moment. "Maybe he's the perfect guy for you," she said mildly.

"Not unless he changes his thinking! He only wants to marry me so that people don't question where he's a man of honor. It's all about him and his reputation and the fathering of his children. That's not nearly romantic enough for me."

Viviane waved one hand. "But don't worry, it's all solved now. You said that men didn't read romances, so I gave him mine and he's agreed to read it. And once he does that, well, everything will be perfectly obvious and he'll act like the knight in the story does."

Barb seemed to be trying not to laugh, although Viviane couldn't imagine why. "Viviane," she said and shook her head, her lips quirking. "You are a treat."

Viviane frowned. "I don't understand."

"No, I know." Barb shook her head and folded her arms across her chest. "You see, real live guys can't even say the L-word."

"What L-word?"

"Love. The word tangles up on their tongues and they just can't spit it out. It gets all knotted up in there, maybe it's stuck in their teeth. They know what it is and they feel it, but they'd rather die than admit it."

Viviane blinked. Now, there was a thought. Maybe Niall really did love her but couldn't say the word. That was an interesting possibility! "Really?"

'Really. Wild horses couldn't drag it out of them." Barb shook a finger across the table at Viviane. "They usually can't manage to say marriage either, so count yourself lucky." She grinned unexpectedly and pushed her spectacles further up her nose. "Maybe you shouldn't give up on him just yet. Sounds like he has some unexpected promise."

"Oh, I think so!" Viviane smiled. "Thanks for your advice. You are so wise."

'Mmm." Barb flicked a glance across the table. "Well, here's another bit of advice for free. Do yourself a favor and get some rubbers. I have a feeling you'll be sharing your bed while you decide about this one. Better safe than sorry."

Viviane frowned. "Rubbers?"

"No babies, no STDs. They're cheap and effective." Barb nodded firmly. "Trust me on this, Viviane, you don't want to get pregnant before you know exactly where you stand."

"Pregnant? No, that would only make things worse!" Viviane nodded hastily. If she became pregnant, she knew Niall definitely wouldn't take no for an answer—he'd toss her over his shoulder and go looking for that priest, whether she was persuaded or not.

And Viviane wanted to be *sure* before she pledged to remain by a man's side for all her days and nights.

"Rubbers," she repeated carefully, so she wouldn't forget the word, then smiled for Barb. "I'll find some today."

• • •

"I have to go and get rubbers," the lady occupying Niall's thoughts announced from the doorway. He glanced up in surprise, not having heard her on the stairs, and wondered how he could have forgotten how alluring she was.

She was wearing another of those short kirtles that drove him mad, this one adorned with yellow flowers on a black background. Her arms were bare and her hair loose, that cursed pendant fairly glowing against her fair skin. She reached for a short cloak hung inside the door, hauled it on and shoved her hands into its deep pockets. "Maybe we could buy something to eat on the way."

"I have coin now so there is no need for you to pay," Niall agreed, getting quickly to his feet and brushing off his hands. He laid his tools carefully aside, well aware that kissing Derek's chemise and short chausses were in need of a wash.

And return.

He would have asked Viviane for guidance on acquiring new garb, but she suddenly gasped. She strode across the floor to snatch up the brush he had been using. "What are you doing with this?"

"I clean my mail. 'Tis a most useful implement indeed, for the taint of the salt water is fiercely difficult to work from the links . . ."

Viviane shook it at him. "Do you know what this is?"

He guessed, despite the dawning sense that he was wrong. "A useful implement for cleaning mail?"

"A toothbrush. It's a toothbrush, my toothbrush."

Niall's eyes narrowed. "Teeth have no hair to be brushed."

Viviane laughed and shook the brush at him. "That's what I thought. People clean them here, with this." She leaned closer. "So their breath smells sweeter." And she exhaled slightly, the scent of mint filling Niall's nostrils.

He did not dare imagine how his breath smelled, for he had never conceived of brushing his teeth with mint. He kept his mouth resolutely closed. "I shall return it to you, duly cleaned."

Viviane grimaced at the state of the brush he had used, her expression and the twinkle in her eyes making her look most appealing. "No. I'll just buy another one. And one for you too."

Niall, as always, was concerned about frugality. "Are such tools of great expense?"

"No. A dollar or so."

Niall considered this, reviewed the money reputedly entrusted to the bankers in his name, then decided to stock up. "'Tis a paltry expense for such usefulness. I shall acquire a quantity for future use."

After all, he wanted to ensure he looked his best at all times for Viviane. Though 'twas curious that a time with no use for mail developed the perfect tool for its maintenance.

"And what are these rubbers?" he demanded. "Are they of small expense as well? What purpose do they serve?"

"I don't know how much they cost, but I *have* to have them." Viviane turned to the door once more, as though avoiding Niall's gaze. "Barb said they would keep me from becoming pregnant."

Niall started and stared, unable to hide his astonishment. "Why should you avoid that?"

His lady tossed her hair in a way that did not bode well for the presence of good sense. "That way you won't have to worry about planting your seed, which means you won't have to marry me after all."

Niall was appalled by the very suggestion. "Viviane, what is done is done and my obligation to you unchanged, regardless of whether you acquire these rubbers or not. 'Tis unnatural to tamper with the course of God."

She folded her arms across her chest and lifted her chin, her eyes snapping with defiance. "Well, I'm not *persuaded* that we should be married."

Niall smiled slowly, infinitely reassured by her choice of words. He reached out and captured her hand, tracing a circle on its back with his thumb. "Then I shall have to be more persuasive." He bent and brushed his lips across her knuckles, smiling against her skin when she shivered. "Perhaps, there is no need for haste in seeking a meal," he murmured.

The lady snatched her hand away, but not quickly enough to hide her response from Niall. "Did you read my book?"

"Nay, Viviane, a responsible man does not mark his leisure before his labor is done."

Instead of being impressed by this, Viviane's eyes flashed. "Leisure? Learning about love isn't leisure!"

"Viviane! I mean to show you that I am a man who can be relied upon! I fulfil my obligations first, I heed my responsibilities first, I tend my duties first." He took a step closer, having no intention of putting his persuasiveness aside. "I would do well by you, Viviane, and indeed, there is many a man who would treat you with less than your due."

She backed into the wall, but her eyes were wide, her lips parted, her wisp of a dress driving Niall to distraction. He leaned over her and heard her breath catch in a way that fired his own blood.

"Viviane," he whispered, touching her chin with one fingertip and tipping her face to his. "Let me persuade you of the good sense of this."

She leaned toward him, her eyelids fluttering closed and Niall smiled in anticipation as he dipped his head. But his lips barely brushed across hers before the lady darted away, ducking under his arm, then wrenching open the door.

"I need rubbers," she insisted anxiously. *"Now."* She shook a finger at Niall when he might have argued the case. "No rubbers, no persuasion."

Well, if she was going to put matters like that, Niall had no choice.

The lady would have her rubbers. He ran a tongue across his teeth and wondered if 'twas his unminted breath she found troublesome.

That, too, could be resolved with all haste.

* * *

Monty waited until Romeo and Juliet were out of sight and earshot, then darted into Barb's shop. Barb was sitting at the counter, frowning at a ledger, and barely glanced up at his arrival.

"Psst, Barb!" Monty looked over his shoulder. "Where's he taking her this time?"

"What's it to you?"

"Come on, Barb!" Monty crossed the room to make his appeal, but Barb kept adding the columns. "You and I go way back, you ought to like *know* when I'm hurting."

That made her glance up. "You owe me eight hundred and ninety-four dollars and sixteen cents. Ante up."

"Man!" Monty pushed a hand through his hair in exasperation. This wasn't going to make things any easier, but then, Barb never did. "Come on, Barb, we're in this together. We could have been an item, if you'd like been interested at all . . ."

She gave him a withering glance. "An item?"

"Yeah, you know, you and me, it would have been perfect and it's not like I haven't tried . . ."

Her eyebrows lifted. "To empty my shop without paying for anything you took."

"Hey, that's like an assault on my character! I've sincerely tried to woo you for years but . . ."

Barb pointed in the general direction of her kitchen. "See that red rubber thingy hanging over the counter?"

Monty looked. It was a flat circle and had some pizza joint's logo printed on it. "Yeah. What is it?"

"A jar opener. It's the mark of an officially single woman, a woman who needs a man like a fish needs a bicycle."

Monty scowled. "Women need men for more than opening jars!"

"Yeah, well, several things in my lingerie drawer say I've got that covered, too."

And she went back to her books.

Monty watched for a few moments, guessing that he was

not in any way in line to get what he wanted. He decided on a bald appeal to her feminine pride.

"Hey, come on, Barb, it wasn't such a long shot for me to think of you and me together. We're two of a kind after all—book lovers!—and our species is getting seriously rare. Like dinosaurs, you know, we gotta breed before we're extinct."

"*Dinosaurs!* Thank you for that, Monty Sullivan."

"Okay, okay, bad analogy. Really bad. Give me a second. Crusaders!" Monty snapped his fingers. "*Crusaders* on a quest to save the written word, yeah, I like that. We're fighting undaunted against the adversity of publisher conglomerations and the onslaught of the visual age . . ."

"Cut to the chase." Barb shut him down with a look just when he was warming to his theme. "What do you want this time, Monty?"

Monty tried to turn up the charm. "Hey, Barb, like, take it easy." He smiled.

Barb didn't.

"Hey, you know, about that bill, well, we all know that winter sucks for revenue, but spring will come, it always does. And then royalties roll in, regular as rain . . ."

"I thought royalties came in the fall, too."

Monty squirmed. "Well, yeah, they do."

Barb tapped the list of his acquisitions for the year. "Yet, oddly enough, none of those little pennies from heaven showed up here, posting against your account."

"Hey, Barb, it was less than I thought! And my agent is like a *thief*, man, he hit me for all sorts of fees that I wasn't expecting and then, well, I owed Derek a lump of cash and the feds were after me for my quarterly deposit . . ."

"And I came last. Again. Same story as last spring." She closed the book grimly and held his gaze. "Don't tell me you're back for more."

"Well, just a couple of books." Barb rolled her eyes but Monty leaned closer, intent on making his case while he could. "You see, it's about Viviane and this guy. It's just too weird the way he goes on about coming from Cantlecroft,

like he really did or something. About her being a condemned witch. It's creepy, don't you think, like he's got it in
for her."

Barb snorted and shook her head. "Viviane doesn't seem
to share your reservations. I just sent them out for rubbers."

"Go on! *Already?*" Monty scowled. "And, like, how
could you know?"

Barb almost smiled. "Monty, there are sounds even a
dinosaur doesn't forget."

Monty exhaled mightily. "Okay, so like it's really critical
now. I have a bad feeling about this guy, like a *really* bad
feeling, and you know, I just want to make sure Viviane is
okay. You do, too, don't you?"

Barb's lips tightened, but she nodded.

Reluctantly.

Monty didn't care that she wasn't thrilled to be doing so,
he just wanted his books.

"You see, here's the thing. I called the reenactment people and they didn't know anything at all about Viviane—
nothing!—let alone Niall, and he's not the kind of guy you
miss seeing, if you know what I mean. They never heard of
Cantlecroft either. And that's kind of weird, which makes
me wonder whether he's really who he says he is . . ."

Barb frowned. "But Viviane said she knows him."

"So, maybe she's not who *she* says she is!" Monty flung
out his hands. "Maybe they're part of a plot, maybe they're
like *spies*, maybe she's defected and he's been sent to elim-
inate her before she talks too much . . ."

Barb almost laughed. "You've been reading too many
conspiracy theories. Or too much of your own fiction. You
do know that the Cold War is over, Monty?"

"Barb, this is serious!"

"Because you're crazy in love with Viviane?" She looked
skeptical about that, but Monty couldn't exactly avoid the
question.

And he couldn't lie when she looked him dead in the eye.

"Well, no, not exactly." He fidgeted. "I mean, I *like* her and she's cute and everything, but it's more than that."

"More, but not crazy in love."

"So, I kind of have an investment here and it bugs me that this guy just swept in and scooped her up. There! I said it. Don't shoot!"

"So, you want to prove him to be the spawn of Satan and pick up where you left off."

Monty avoided her gaze. "Well, yeah. It's not like a crime."

"You guys are all the same." Barb sighed before Monty could defend his gender. "How do I fit in to this great scheme?"

"Books." Monty cast a longing glance in the direction of the history section. "I want to look up Cantlecroft, figure out what that reference is all about, read all about it. It might give me a clue."

Barb pushed to her feet with resignation. "So, go ahead and look. Park yourself in the corner but don't bend any of the pages or leave any nasty fingerprints in the stock."

"Actually"—Monty looked nervously toward the door— "I'd like to take them with me."

Barb slammed the ledger on the counter and spun to face him. "Monty! You've confused this with the library again!"

"No, I've *been* there and they have nothing. You know how pathetic the medieval history section is. And I need to know, I need to help Viviane, I need to make sure that this guy doesn't mean her any harm."

"To protect your investment."

"Come on, Barb, give me some credit!"

She squarely met his gaze. "Your credit stinks. You pay this balance first, then we'll talk."

And that, Monty knew, was that. He begged and cajoled, he tried to sweet-talk his way to a better deal, but no luck. Barb was adamant.

So, Barb got a rubber check and Monty got his books. He

scampered down the street, trying hard to not feel guilty about tricking his old friend.

It was all for the greater good, after all.

Next royalty check, he'd pay Barb first.

With interest.

Chapter 13

VIVIANE AND NIALL went to Mouats, because everyone knew that Mouats had everything.

Of course, Mouats had everything for *outdoors* and a
good lot of stuff for indoors, but wasn't a pharmacy by any
stretch of the imagination. Viviane, unaware of exactly what
she was shopping for, missed that critical distinction.

Niall trailed behind Viviane as she wound her way
through the amazing displays of new goods, his interest
snared by all the intriguing garments and tools, much as
Viviane's had been the first few times she came in here. She
lost him a couple of times and had to go back to snag him
by the arm, forcing him to follow her further into the store.

Because there was hope for him, even if he did insist on
practicalities. She'd get the L-word out of him, Viviane
knew it. She was born under a blue moon after all and destined to be lucky all of her days.

But she knew herself well enough to guess that there
might be a few persuasive interludes before things were
resolved.

When Niall did that thing with his thumb and smiled that
smile that turned her knees to butter—like he was doing as

they walked through the store—Viviane got dizzy just thinking about him and lost track of practicalities again.

She had to get those rubbers.

Right now.

If she became pregnant, she knew Niall would carry her kicking and screaming to a priest, regardless of her thoughts on the matter. Viviane had to admit though that it was rather nice that he worried so much about doing the honorable thing.

Mouats was crowded as usual. Viviane had learned to recognize several of the people who worked here and when one greeted her with typical charm, she caught at the girl's arm.

"I need rubbers," she hissed, not wanting everyone to know what she wanted, for they surely would guess why. "Where do I find them?"

"Oh, down in footwear." The girl smiled encouragingly, though Viviane was scandalized by how loudly she talked. "Let me show you. We're kind of running out, what with all this rain lately."

Viviane could not imagine what rain had to do with conceiving children, though Mrs. Haggerty seemed to think it had a certain sensuous appeal. Puzzling over this, Viviane followed the clerk, and was even more puzzled when the girl presented a pair of dark green boots.

"What's your size?"

Viviane wasn't certain what she had expected, but she hadn't expected boots. Niall snorted behind her and she felt her color rise.

What did boots have to do with conception?

Or more specifically, with avoiding conception?

She didn't have to even look at Niall to know he had that skeptical expression again, but she knew to trust Barb. Barb understood things, Barb was wise, Barb was helpful.

Barb said she needed rubbers.

"I don't know my size," Viviane admitted. "I just tried these shoes until they fit." The girl rummaged cheerfully for a silver implement, gestured to a chair, tugged off Viviane's wet sneaker and quickly pronounced Viviane a seven and a half.

Then she was gone, darting through customers to the "back room" from whence Viviane had seen many marvels issue.

Niall picked up one boot and looked at it, doubt in every line of his features. "This is a rubber?" He looked pointedly at her, his question not needing to be uttered, and Viviane shrugged.

"Maybe it's part of a spell," she said hastily. "Barb knows a lot and I'm sure that she wouldn't give me bad advice."

Niall cleared his throat and rolled his eyes. "A spell," he said beneath his breath, as though it was the most ridiculous thing he'd ever heard.

It did sound a bit unlikely, even to Viviane.

The clerk bounced back, dumped boots out of a box and offered them to Viviane. In no time at all, they were pronounced a fit and Viviane walked the length of the small area and back as it seemed what she was expected to do. She chewed her lip as she looked down at them, trying to figure out how they worked.

Perhaps they were intended to make her look unattractive.

She looked to Niall. "Do you find them"—she cleared her throat—"ugly?"

He smiled slowly, obviously discerning the direction of her thoughts. "Nay, my lady fair. They do naught but enhance the beauty of your legs," he murmured, that sensuous gleam appearing in his eyes. "Indeed, I believe the color favors you most admirably."

Uh oh.

Viviane looked back to the boots and the clerk grinned at her, obviously approving of Niall's comment. "They look great on you, they really do. He's right!"

Viviane cleared her throat, hating to appear foolish but needing to ask the question. "How exactly do they work?"

The clerk frowned. "What do you mean?"

Viviane could feel a blush rising over her cheeks, Niall's

wolfish grin doing nothing to ease her embarrassment. "What do I have to do?"

"Oh! Oh, these are really good ones, you don't have to do anything to take care of them. We don't sell those cheapies. They'll last the rest of your life, probably. Just don't leave them in the hot sun for days and days, you know, but that's hardly a problem here."

The clerk smiled reassuringly.

Viviane thought about wearing clumpy green boots that came up to her knees for the rest of her life and wasn't particularly reassured.

"I'm sure you'll just love them," the clerk enthused. "We've never had any complaints. They work just great and you know"—she leaned closer—"there's nothing better in the garden."

In the *garden*?

Niall cleared his throat deliberately and Viviane felt her blush get hotter. "I'll take them," she managed to say.

"Great, should I wrap them up?"

Viviane risked a glance to Niall, only to find his bright gaze fixed upon her with an intensity that could only mean one thing.

"I'd better wear them," she whispered to the clerk, not in the least bit reassured when her knight chuckled and looked very pleased with himself. It seemed an eternity before they managed to pay and escape the store, and Viviane was well aware of Niall's smile the whole time.

"I find myself feeling very persuasive," he murmured as they stepped into the street and Viviane knew she blushed clear to her toes.

She gritted her teeth and seized his arm, practically dragging him to their next stop. He chuckled and slipped his arm around her waist in a companionable gesture that she didn't quite want to shrug off.

En route, Niall pulled her to a halt and made a great show of peering into a neighbouring garden, as though curious as to what the people there were doing.

"Indeed, I cannot help but think somewhat more favorably of Barb's small garden," he mused. Once again, he smiled with the innocence of a child, though a wicked twinkle glinted in his eye.

He was teasing her!

"You have reading to do first," Viviane declared as sternly as she could and Niall's grin flashed.

"I do not believe we agreed that I should stop trying to persuade you in the interim," he said silkily, then bent and kissed her before Viviane guessed what he was about.

She was trembling in her rubbers when he lifted his head and Niall had to know it. He started to whistle, striding along the street as though he didn't have a care in the world. Viviane didn't know whether to kiss him or kill him—he was so sure of her response.

And so good at cultivating it.

In a bittersweet irony that neither of them appreciated, their next stop was at the drugstore.

For toothbrushes.

Niall watched Viviane stride down the street to return to her labor, admiring how those green boots accented the slender perfection of her legs. With a sigh, he slipped back to Mouats, readily finding the woman who had been so helpful. She smiled at the sight of him and Niall knew he had been right to seek her aid.

She easily guided him through the choices of clothing and rendered him not only presentable, but she announced "delish." This apparently was good. She also recommended a restaurant which was "divine" when Niall confessed to wanting to impress his lady.

He returned to Viviane's chamber, fed and well-garbed, then carefully brushed his teeth with his new brush. 'Twas not unpleasant to run his tongue across the smoothness of his teeth, though he quickly thought of running his tongue across the similar smoothness of Viviane's and nigh forgot himself.

Niall considered her book. Aye, Viviane had been irked that he had not read more of it, despite more practical obligations. Niall pushed his mail aside. He sat on the edge of the bed and began to read the volume one more time.

And within moments, he was snared once more, for his lady had a skill unexpected. Each page he turned drew him more deeply into the tale, each scene ensured he must read just a bit more.

Indeed, Niall read until the midday sun slanted through the window, and was surprised to find himself yet sprawled on the bed. His knee was aching at being bent in the same position for so long, his belly was complaining at its empty state, but Niall could not put this tale down.

Nay, he wanted to know what became of Gawain, how the noble knight fulfilled his daunting quest, how he proved himself to the lady whose heart he had made his own. Niall wanted to know how Gawain would show himself worthy of that glorious and gorgeous damsel, no less how he would best the Green Knight at tournament.

He rolled around on the bed and read some more, ignoring more earthy complaints. Each time Gawain and his lady kissed, Niall's loins heated in recollection of Viviane's sweet kisses. When they coupled—a mating filled with too much chatter, to Niall's thinking—he smiled, for his own lady's maidenly naivete was clearly revealed.

Though she proved to have a rare imagination for these encounters. Indeed, he put the book aside after the couple's third mating merely to consider whether the deed *could* be done that way.

There was naught for it, he and Viviane would have to try.

Each time that Niall thought he would stop reading, that he would gather himself and go to the bookstore or that he would labor a little upon his mail, the tale lured him back.

Aye, the battle scenes were clearly penned by one who had never witnessed the filth of war, though they were filled with excitement. 'Twas a weakness quickly forgiven, for the men and women in the tale seemed true to life. Aye, Niall knew better than to trust the chatelain of the court, for that man had a scheme to see Gawain dead, there could be no doubt.

Just when the sky grew darker and he was certain he should put the manuscript aside, the tale surprised him and there was no chance of halting his course. Indeed, Niall sat up straight when the lady gave of herself to ensure her knight's survival. She drew herself into danger to see Gawain safe and, though Niall cried out in dismay, she did not repent of her course.

This could not be!

Yet further reading revealed that in the same moment, far afield, Gawain put himself into similar jeopardy, intending only to ensure his lady's survival.

Nay, it could not be so! They could not *both* die, one could not die and be left without the presence of the other—but indeed, it seemed that death would not be cheated in either case. Niall read in a frenzy, he turned the pages in increasing haste, until he turned the last one, his heart in his mouth.

But the ending of the book was not there.

Niall's eyes widened, he felt abandoned at the lip of a precipice. He scanned the chamber, rifling through the few other papers on the table beneath the window but did not find what he sought. He looked beneath the bed, certain he must have dropped part of the tale, but there was naught.

'Twas then Niall recalled the tale was his lady's concoction.

Which meant she alone knew the ending.

"Viviane!" he roared.

He raged into the bookstore like an avenging angel and every woman froze to stare. Niall of Malloy was a vision in jeans that showed every muscle to advantage and a creamy chambray shirt that only made him look more broad, more tanned and more blond. The broad gold bracelet on his wrist gleamed, his eyes shone, his lips were taut.

Viviane's mouth went dry at the sight. Niall cast one glance around the shop, spied her and cut a path straight to her. Nothing could have stood in his way and she found herself thinking of Gawain in her own book, riding to the rescue of his lady with fire in his eyes.

She hadn't begun to do Niall justice in that scene.

"Viviane!" He halted before her and propped one hand upon his hip, the other cradling her manuscript, blissfully unaware of the whispers that had begun in the shop. "I am reading this book of yours, but there is no ending." He scowled. "Where is the end of the tale?"

"I haven't written it down yet." Viviane tapped her temple. "It's still in here."

"Aye? Tell me of it!"

"I can't. I have to write it down."

Niall shoved a hand through his hair, leaving the waves askew in a boyish fashion. "But what happens to those benighted souls? Tell me that neither one nor the other died alone, much less for naught!"

Mrs. MacAllister eased her gouty leg closer, her eyes narrowed. "You wrote a book?" she demanded of Viviane.

"Well, yes, but it's not finished yet . . ."

"What kind of a book? What's it about?"

"It's a romance . . ." Viviane began but Niall interrupted her.

" 'Tis a sweeping tale of a knight endeavoring to win the favor of his lady fair," he answered firmly. "A tale in which all goes awry despite that valiant man's efforts, a tale which no man with a heart could willingly put aside. 'Tis a compelling tale that snatches one in its grip and does not surrender until the last page is turned." He locked his intent green gaze on Viviane. "And then one learns that the ending is not there."

Viviane swallowed. "I haven't had a chance to write it down, but I will. I promise."

"Aye, you will." Niall punctuated his words with a telling glance. "For I would know the ending of the tale."

"Because of our wager?" Viviane asked, hoping that Niall didn't just want to have a final answer to his proposal.

He frowned. "Nay! I want to know the resolution of the tale! Indeed, you cannot leave me to fret for the hide of that knight, no less the woman he swore to win for his own." He drove his fist into his palm. "They are both in dire peril and I must know the ending of their tale."

"Oh, it sounds so good!" Mrs. MacAllister's eyes were cat-bright. "When do I get to read it, my dear? You know how I love a good story."

"Well." Viviane looked away from Niall with difficulty. Honestly, he looked as though he would stand right there and wait for her to scribble down the end of the book! "I guess I'll have to find a publisher, right, Barb?"

"Uh huh. Look, there's a book right here, a market guide for writers." Barb pulled down a fat volume from another section and strolled closer, thumbing through the back. "There's usually a listing under the index of romance publishers."

Niall put down the manuscript and scooped the book out of her hand, scanning the column under Barb's finger. "Aye? And what does one do?"

"Well, you send them the book. Not the original, a copy, and they decide whether they want to buy it. At the front, it usually talks about format and stuff, and each listing tells what the publisher likes to see."

Viviane reached out a hand for the book, but Niall shot her a dark look. "You have a tale to commit to the page. I shall read this volume while I await the ending of yours."

"And then what, Viviane?" Mrs. MacAllister demanded. "Are you going to be a famous author?" She giggled, looking markedly younger than her years and dug her elbow into Niall's ribs. "She might not even admit she knows us then!"

"Nay, Viviane is not of the kind who believe themselves better than their fellows, simply by dint of a stroke of fortune," her knight insisted, a small smile curving his lips as he warmly considered her. Viviane felt herself blush. "After all, the lady was born under a blue moon and has been uncommonly lucky all her days."

There was no mockery in his tone, not a shred of skepticism, only affection shining in his eyes.

Oh, he had understood!

Viviane's heart began to pound and she couldn't look away from his gaze. "Did you really like it?"

Niall smiled fully and folded his arms across his chest, his gaze turning indulgent. "Do you imagine I am irked at not knowing the ending because the tale had no merit? You did a fine job, my lady, indeed, you are most talented."

"Oooo!" Mrs. MacAllister squealed. "Isn't this *exciting*? We'll have our own author!"

"Well, the book isn't ready to be sent anywhere," Viviane argued.

"'Tis true enough," Niall agreed pointedly. "It has no ending." He turned to Barb. "Do you know the books of these publishers?"

She led him toward the shelves, chatting about this publisher and that one. Viviane followed, she and Mrs. MacAllister pointing out the books they particularly enjoyed. Niall quickly learned where to look for the publishers' addresses and was compiling titles against the listings in the market book in no time at all.

Mrs. MacAllister toodle-ooed and went on her merry way—no doubt to tell anyone who would listen about Viviane's book—and Barb made a run to the bank. Niall hauled a chair across the shop and settled in the romance section. He began to examine the books in turn, focusing on those adorned with knights and damsels, and was busy making sense of it all by the time the store closed.

Viviane was itching to ask him again whether he had liked her book, whether he had recognized himself, but she didn't know how to do it. So, she worked and he worked, and she watched him through her lashes until she couldn't stand it any longer.

Then she took a deep breath and crossed the shop.

And in the end, she didn't have to say anything at all.

"This is of similar ilk to yours," Niall declared without look-ing up from the volume he perused when Viviane came back to his side. "For it concerns a knight, though your tale is finer."

A part of Viviane hated that she was so unsure of her work, but she couldn't help asking for Niall's praise. "You really liked it?"

Niall glanced up at her and smiled. "Aye, Viviane, you have a gift for making a tale take flight from the page. You paint an image with words with rare talent."

Viviane smiled back, three-quarters reassured. She locked her hands together, knowing she had to ask the question she'd rather not. "Is there anything you *didn't* like?"

Niall pursed his lips and considered her, as though won-dering how honest he should be.

But Viviane had to know. "Really. I'd like you to tell me. If I could change something to make it better, I'd do it be-cause I want to send this to a publisher."

She hunkered down beside Niall when he didn't say any-thing, intent only on explaining herself. "I mean, wouldn't it be wonderful to see my book like this! People like Mrs. MacAllister would be able to read it and I'd have a job doing something I really enjoyed. Not that I don't enjoy working in the shop, but I don't want to be a burden on Barb after she's been so nice to me and all."

"This is of great import to you."

"Yes." Viviane's mouth went dry as their gazes held and the silence stretched long.

Then Niall nodded in understanding. "They talk too much abed, to my thinking, for there are more interesting matters to attend with one's mouth in such circumstance."

He winked unexpectedly and Viviane dropped her gaze, remembering all too well the interesting things he had done with his mouth.

Niall cleared his throat, his fingers rifling through the manuscript again. "And your innocence is evident in some of their couplings."

Viviane's cheeks heated. "I can fix that now."

Niall's eyes twinkled when she dared to meet his gaze once more. "Aye, I have little doubt of that," he said warmly and Viviane felt as though she was the only person in his world.

It wasn't a bad feeling.

"Though truly, my lady, you might have need of further *persuasion*. The third time in particular seemed most challenging to me." He coughed into his hand, that wicked glint reappearing in his eyes. "I believe we should ensure the pose is a plausible one."

"Niall!"

He flipped open the reference book, tapping the header on a chapter called "Research." His eyes gleamed, though he tried to take a lofty air. "'Tis your duty as a writer to ensure that all you include is truth."

Viviane tried to look disgusted with him and failed. "And you volunteer to help with my research?"

He bowed slightly. "'Twould only be gallant."

Viviane laughed at him, she couldn't help it. Niall grinned and their gazes held for a breathless moment before Viviane remembered not only that they were in the shop, but that she was trying to get his opinion.

And see if he noticed the most important part of all.

"Anything else?" Now, she tried to not look too hopeful. Niall had shown he was a perceptive man—had he discerned that she was really writing about him? Had he guessed how she felt? Had he understood what she meant about love and its importance?

Viviane held her breath and hoped.

When he spoke, it seemed that he chose his words carefully. "Aye, there is one more thing I noted."

Viviane bit her lip, but Niall suddenly looked at the pen Barb had lent him and discovered the button to retract the nib. He clicked it a few times with obvious delight, then prepared to take the pen apart, doubtless intending to pry at its magical workings.

"You shouldn't do that, you know. No one likes having meddlers in their magic."

Niall's glance was wry. "I meddle with no magic."

"Of course, you do! Everything here is magic and sooner or later, someone won't take kindly to your . . ."

"Viviane, *naught* is magic here."

Viviane sat back on her heels, astonished that he could be so sure of himself, especially when he was wrong. But Niall's gaze never wavered. "Of course, it's magic! What else could it be?"

"'Tis the cleverness of man we witness," Niall confided. "'Tis not true that we are in Avalon, though indeed, you were not so foolish to imagine so. This place is indeed full of marvels."

Viviane frowned. "Well, where is it, if it's not Avalon?"

"'Tis a place called Salt Spring Island . . ."

"Oh, I know they call it that!"

Niall's eyes grew sober and his voice dropped low. "Nay, Viviane, they call it that for that is what 'tis. Truly. 'Tis not Avalon, but a foreign land, thousands of miles from Cantlecroft."

Viviane blinked and looked around herself. "No, Niall, that can't be true. There's magic everywhere here!"

"Nay, these marvels are but the workings of men." Niall unscrewed the pen as she watched, a spring and a narrow tube dropping into the palm of his hand. He fiddled with it for a moment, then put the spring and tube back into the bottom of the pen. He pushed the nib in and out, then showed her how the button at the top pressed the assembly back and forth.

No vengeful sorcerer smote him for dissecting this magic and indeed, when Niall explained it, it didn't seem very magical at all.

"'Tis cleverness, Viviane, no more than that."

But Viviane frowned. "Then, why have we never seen any of these things? Why have we never heard of these marvels? Travellers and merchants leave Cantlecroft all the time, then return with tokens from foreign lands—surely they could have brought these!"

"Only if they had been here."

Viviane flung out her hands. "You know that the merchants leave Cantlecroft for the four corners of Christendom!"

"But they do not leave Cantlecroft's *time*."

Viviane stared at her knight in astonishment, certain he had lost his wits, but he held her gaze steadily. "Viviane, we have come into the days far beyond our own," he explained softly. "'Tis the year 1999, nigh 2000 years since the birth of Christ and some six centuries away from all we know."

Viviane caught her breath. "But that's impossible!"

"Clearly not, for we are here." Niall dug in his pocket and unfolded bills, pointing out the date to her. He showed her coins, with the year—1999—marked on a shiny new penny. Viviane couldn't believe she hadn't really looked at them before.

She'd liked the pictures of the animals and assumed the numbers meant something entirely irrelevant to her.

Niall seized her hand and showed the legends on maps, even the dates in the front pages of books. Viviane gave a little cry when she realized that the "–99" on the cash register tape implied a "19" in front of it.

She turned to Niall, still shaking her head. "But how? How can this be? How did we get here?"

"I do not know. 'Tis some wondrous invention of which we know naught, but clearly one of this time."

Viviane frowned, momentarily uncertain how that could have happened. She fingered her pendant. "But I wished on the pendant and then came here," she said slowly. "Unless someone summoned me here at the very same moment with whatever invention is at work . . ."

Her voice trailed away, that possibility not sounding very likely to her. Niall's gaze fell to the pendant.

"And I wished upon the stone, as well. 'Twas that which brought me to your side, or so I believed."

Viviane's fingers trailed across the stone and she shivered at its chill. "But how could that be? Do you think my father is here, in this time and place?"

Niall shrugged. "Or perhaps he was once. We know for certain that naught from our own days could explain this feat." He met her gaze. "Maybe he came from here."

Suddenly, it all made perfect sense to Viviane. "And loved my mother. That was why I never knew him. But my father did save me! My father did give me a token of his love in this gift!" she said with delight. "He saved my life!"

Niall did not smile.

"Don't you see, Niall? We're as far away from the archbishop and his court as we could possibly be!"

Niall nodded heavily. "Aye."

"But if I have the stone and it's not from Cantlecroft, then no one can ever follow us here! I'm safe!"

"I do not know for certain, though 'twould seem to be the case." Niall frowned, though Viviane couldn't guess why. "Just as I do not know whether we can go back."

But who *wanted* to go back?

Not Viviane! She was ready to sing and dance. In fact, she couldn't imagine why Niall looked so glum.

"That's perfect!" she declared with a grin. "Who would want to go back? We couldn't have planned any better than this if we had tried! I *told* you that I was uncommonly lucky and it seems my father was lucky, too!"

Niall frowned. "Viviane, perhaps you do not understand . . ."

"I understand exactly what you're saying. We're stuck here, which suits me fine. Niall, I don't care whether I can ever go back to Candlecroft or not!" Viviane practically bounced. "I'm here and I'm staying here and you're here and you're staying here—it's perfect!"

Niall got to his feet, frowning at her. "But Viviane, we do not belong in this place."

Viviane arched a brow skeptically. "Niall, I don't belong anywhere where someone is trying to have me killed."

He pushed his hand through his hair and appealed to her. "But Viviane, 'tis not right that your reputation should be maligned! We could clear your name! You are *innocent*, the archbishop would clear the charge against you if he knew the truth of matters."

Trust Niall to want to do something so sweet! Viviane's heart melted that he believed in her innocence so much that he was prepared to defend her.

And he said he wasn't really a knight anymore.

Unfortunately, Viviane didn't share her knight's conviction that justice would prevail at the archbishop's court.

She caught at his hands and leaned close to explain, knowing she could persuade him. "But I'm *safe* here, Niall."

"I would see you safe in Cantlecroft," he said gruffly, his protectiveness making Viviane want to kiss him senseless.

But first she had to win his agreement. "But you know that the archbishop lied to me before. He promised me an audience, but didn't give it to me." Viviane shook her head. "No, I don't care where this is, I'm staying and that's that. It's not worth the risk to go back." She cast her best smile Niall's way.

But he was scowling at his toes and seemed to be summoning an argument.

It was endearing that he wanted to see everything set to rights, but it wasn't important to Viviane that her name was maligned by people who were long dead and gone.

Although she was beginning to understand that Niall was the kind of man who finished what he started, who defended his woman—which is clearly who he had decided Viviane was—and ensured the truth was laid bare.

It was the kind of gallant thing that her Gawain would have insisted upon doing and Viviane decided that Niall's arguments about love were easily outweighed by his deeds. Her heart skipped a beat or two while she watched him.

She certainly didn't want to argue anymore. In fact, she wanted just one more teeny confirmation that this man was the knight for her.

So, Viviane deliberately changed the subject to one that interested her a lot more than the issue of returning to Cantlecroft. It was a shameless effort to resolve the last obstacle between them, so that she could surrender to a little persuasiveness.

"What about my book?" she asked pertly. "What else did you notice about it?"

Niall held her gaze, though he didn't look very pleased. "Your Gawain," he said, his low voice filled with portent.

Viviane caught her breath. He *had* noticed! And he was just shy talking about mushy stuff, just like Barb said. Oh, this was too marvelous! They were stuck six hundred years from Cantlecroft with only each other for all the rest of their days. And no one could follow them to ruin everything.

"Yes?" she asked anxiously, more than ready for Niall to admit that he understood her view on love.

And that he agreed with her, of course.

Niall frowned. "He seems a man of intellect and great loyalty."

Viviane wished he'd get to the point more quickly. "Yes? Yes?"

Niall took a deep breath and seemed to be searching for the words on the hardwood floor. "A noble knight who fulfills his pledge," he said heavily, "regardless of the cost to himself."

"Oh, yes, yes, *yes*! That's my Gawain!" Viviane couldn't wait to hear the acknowledgment fall from his lips.

Niall studied her for a moment, looking for all the world as though he was going to give her the worst news ever, instead of the best.

"But he embarks on this quest without the consent of his overlord." Niall shook his head. "'Tis not done, Viviane, at least not by any man of merit. A pledge to an overlord cannot be broken, not at any cost, and no man is free to choose his course once he has made such a pledge."

He sighed and sat down again as Viviane stared at him. "You shall have to change that, and make it Gawain's overlord who dispatches him upon his quest. There is no other way it can be."

Viviane waited, but Niall returned to his perusal of the books and the listing.

Chapter 14

"THAT'S IT?" VIVIANE demanded.

She had expected a great confession and Niall gave her a lesson on fealty? This wasn't what she had planned!

But Niall glanced up, once again looking like the grim knight who she had first encountered in that damp prison cell. He certainly didn't look inclined to confess anything romantic.

"Aye." He frowned and fingered the pages of her manuscript. "'Tis a fine work, Viviane, and you should be proud of it."

And he opened the market book again.

Viviane stared at him, even as she fought her disappointment. How could he have missed the point? Niall wasn't a stupid man, not by any means, and she had been so sure that he would see through her characterization . . .

Well, Viviane wasn't going to give up that easily. Maybe she could explain it to him.

Over a nice romantic dinner.

Viviane smiled hopefully, the prospect alone cheering her up. Niall was always ready to eat, after all. "The shop is closed," she reminded him. "We could go for dinner."

But astonishingly enough, Niall shook his head. "Nay,

Viviane, 'tis impossible." He shook the pen at her. "You have a book to finish writing and I, I have much reading to complete." He smiled a slow, sexy smile that made her blood start to simmer. "But you have only to summon me when you wish to affirm the possibility of that coupling."

No! Viviane couldn't let Niall seduce her with his touch again, not before he admitted to having some feelings for her.

And admiration for her book didn't count.

Viviane bounced to her feet and scooped up the reference book she had used. She waved the *Kama Sutra* under his nose triumphantly. "Oh, that's all right, I can just check everything in here. You go ahead and read."

"Aye? What is this?" Niall plucked the book out of Viviane's hands before she could hold it away. His eyes widened as he turned the pages. He tilted his head, then turned the book halfway around, his gaze flicking to Viviane's.

"Perhaps we should take another wager on the illustrations in this volume," he suggested, turning the book so she could see.

Viviane blushed.

"Aye, it fair looks impossible." Niall inverted the book again, the twinkle in his eyes when he suddenly looked up catching Viviane off guard. "Shall we try this manner? Indeed, these illustrations seem designed to make a man feel . . . persuasive."

Oh, there wasn't going to be any persuading done around here soon! Especially not when Niall refused to give her the slightest hint of any emotional ties.

How could he *not* love her?

"You're impossible!" Viviane retorted, snatching the book and headed out of the shop.

"You have but to call me," Niall shouted after her.

"I have work to do," Viviane retorted with a toss of her hair. "You said so yourself."

Niall shook a finger at her. "Aye, Viviane, I am much interested in the ending of this tale. Write hastily!"

It wasn't much consolation that he seemed to forget even his persuasiveness after that. In fact, he bent over the market guide with a frown, as though Viviane wasn't there at all.

She turned and stomped out of the shop in her new rubbers, quite certain that this wasn't the way her love story was supposed to work out. If *she* had been writing this story, well, it would have been a lot different.

But all she could do—and incidentally the best way to regain Niall's attention—was to finish her book. It was as good an excuse as any to get back to work.

She wouldn't so much as think about feeling a little persuasive herself.

It didn't help that her argument made sense.

Niall scowled at the market listings, not truly seeing any of them. How could he fault Viviane for not wanting to return to the site where she was condemned to be executed?

Worse, how could he persuade her to do it?

Aye, her argument was reasonable, for the archbishop *had* failed to keep his promise. Though that had been before a man pledged to the archbishop's own service argued Viviane's case. Niall was certain that no man of good character—as he knew the archbishop to be—could condemn an innocent woman to die. Nay, 'twould be wrong.

When they returned to Candlecroft, all could be set aright.

If they returned to Candlecroft. Niall tapped the book with one heavy fingertip. For truly, Viviane had no good reason to return. Her mother was dead, as she had already confessed, and apparently she had no other ties. She certainly showed no inclination to return.

Should Niall tell her of his obligation to his sister? Would that sway her decision?

There was an idea! Aye, he knew that women could be tender about the welfare of children and certainly naught good was likely to occur for his nieces and nephews in Niall's absence.

Save the addition to their numbers.

He drummed his fingers, wondering how he would make this argument. Ideally, 'twould be phrased so that Viviane could not refuse, though he sorely disliked even the thought of deceiving his lady. And he certainly was not a man quick with the sweet words that women found so appealing.

Niall was still pondering the matter when Barb returned to the shop, her keys jingling as she unlocked the door. "Helpful book?" she asked, nodding at the volume in Niall's lap.

"Aye. 'Tis most informative."

To Niall's surprise, Barb crossed the floor and pushed her hands into her pockets as she halted beside him. Her gaze was probing. "Viviane's book is good?"

Niall smiled, recognizing protectiveness when he saw it. "Aye, she has a gift, 'tis clear."

Barb pulled out a chair and sat down beside him. "Look, I want you to be straight with me. I know that you and Viviane have got some kind of thing going here, and that every guy alive would want to tell his woman that she was brilliant at everything she did, if only to make sure she didn't hold out on him, but you can tell me the truth. Is it *really* good?"

Niall held her gaze. "I believe so," he said firmly. "But you would know better than I."

Barb shook her head and got to her feet. "I can't read it unless she asks me to. Writers are sensitive about stuff like that." She pursed her lips and considered Niall. "I just don't want you leading her on." She looked at him hard one more time. "Don't hurt her."

Niall's softened heart twisted a little at the lie of his presence here, but he managed to hold this stern woman's gaze. "I will not."

Barb nodded. "Because this is really important to Viviane."

"Aye. I see that now. 'Tis why I intend to aid her in seeking this publication." Though he had not even thought of doing such a thing, as soon as Niall uttered the words, he knew they were true.

He knew her tale of Gawain was important to Viviane, for her eyes shone when she spoke of it, and doubly so when she spoke of finding a publisher.

Aye, he would aid his lady in her own quest. 'Twas only fitting.

Barb looked surprised. "Really?"

"Aye. She needs to know that I am a man she can rely upon, a man who will attend to her concerns, see her safe and see her fed. 'Tis this role that an honorable man takes in marriage, though Viviane is dubious that I shall do it well." Niall nodded, his mind made up. "I shall aid her in this, to prove to her that her will is of import to me."

And then, somehow, he would persuade her to consider the import of *his* will, perhaps by confessing the tale of Majella. Somehow, he would convince his lady to return to Cantlecroft, that he might both clear the shadow of conviction from her name and fulfill his own pledges.

First, the book manuscript.

Niall fired a glance at Barb. "Have you objections to a change over these ensuing days? I would have Viviane work on her tale while she so desires."

"I need her in the shop."

"Aye, 'tis that I would address." Niall tried his best smile, but Barb's frown did not waver. "I know full well that I am a poor substitute for my lady's abilities, but perhaps there is some labor I can do for you in her stead."

While Niall watched, a curious glimmer dawned in Barb's eyes. Had he not known her as well as he already did, he might have guessed that this stern woman was softening toward him.

"Is this fitting to you?" he prompted when she said naught.

"Yeah." Barb nodded and looked away, folding her arms across her chest. "Yeah, I could use some help with those new shelves and there are a couple of cartons out back to heft in here for stocking. You up for heavy work?"

"Aye, I am capable of this and much more." Niall pushed to his feet and offered his hand. "Shall we make an agreement?"

Barb regarded him skeptically. "You're going to do this, just to give her the chance to work on her book?"

"Aye. 'Tis a simple enough exchange."

Barb stared at him for a long moment, then shook her head. "You are something else, aren't you?" she asked softly as she took his hand. Her grip was surprisingly strong.

Mercifully, Niall was spared the obligation of a reply, for he knew not what he would have said. Barb turned and walked quickly out the back of her shop, flicking out the lights on her way.

Niall stood in the dark for only a moment before he decided 'twas time he returned to Viviane's chamber anyway. He lifted a book that had rested beside that illustrated volume of hers and smiled to himself as he fanned through the pages.

Aye, this wench was as slender as Viviane, though she had not the perfect breasts of his lady. Niall paused to consider a particularly appealing illustration, his desire to be persuasive rising to the fore.

'Twas time, he resolved, for his lady to cease her labor this day.

Viviane couldn't believe it when Niall came back to her room and told her what he had done. He wanted to help her get her book published! His was such a touching gesture that she had a hard time quibbling over his insistence that it was for duty alone, that a man must support the wishes of his lady.

In fact, her resistance to him was sufficiently weakened that when he showed her the book he carried and suggested a little research, Viviane didn't even mind the wicked glint in his eye.

Neither did she mind what happened after that.

And Niall seemed to take the challenge in stride when Viviane insisted on keeping her rubbers on.

It took Viviane the rest of the week to get the book into shape, to make the changes Niall suggested and to sufficiently research her love scenes. Barb typed up the manuscript on that gadget she called her computer when the shop was slow—as it increasingly was—and printed it out on that lovely white paper Viviane found so appealing. It almost looked like a book already when it was finally done.

And Niall had chosen three publishers who might be interested in the work. Barb showed Viviane how to write a cover letter, then on Saturday afternoon, Viviane and Niall took the whole thing down to the little copy shop in town.

Viviane's heart nearly stopped an hour later when the clerk at the postal wicket in the drugstore took the three parcels from her hands and dumped them into the bin behind the counter.

"Tuesday delivery in New York," the clerk chirped, then looked over Viviane's shoulder. "Next!"

Her labor of love was gone, out of Viviane's hands, as simply as that.

Suddenly, she wanted the parcels back. She wanted to go over the story one more time, make Gawain just a little bit more noble, perhaps change one last thing. She knew she could make it better, given just a few more moments. Viviane actually stepped closer to the counter and opened her mouth to ask for them back.

But Niall caught her around the waist. "There is naught to be done about it now," he murmured in her ear, as though he had read her thoughts. "You have done your best and now your tale must fend for itself."

"But oh, Niall, I need to know whether they'll like it! How can I possibly wait?"

"The book declares 'twill be two to three months before you might have a response and Barb is skeptical of even that timing." Niall shook his head and laced their fingers together. "We shall have to find other things to occupy us."

He looked so smug that Viviane could guess what some of those things might be.

She grinned and matched her step to his, more than ready to tease him a bit. "Like what?" They stepped out into a surprisingly balmy evening. Ganges was quiet, the sky was dark blue smeared with the glorious shades of a sunset.

Niall slanted her a very green glance. "We could be wed."

"Because you love me?"

He snorted in a very unflattering way. "Viviane, we have spoken much of love and its overrated charms. I would wed you because we are well-suited, each to the other, and the match would be most sensible."

"I'll only marry a man who loves me and you know it."

Niall growled something in his throat that Viviane was glad she couldn't quite hear. Then he pivoted, clamped his hands on her shoulders and stared into her eyes. He looked more than a little bit determined.

"Would you have me lie to you?" he demanded. "Is this what you wish? Viviane, 'tis not my way to speak a falsehood, but you tempt a man overmuch when you refuse to see sense."

"I would know if you were lying anyway," she replied, then tapped his nose with one fingertip. "It would show in your eyes." She smiled and stretched to kiss him, but Niall stepped away.

"Viviane! You muddy the issue!" He shoved a hand through his hair. "Wed me."

"No. Not until you admit you love me."

Niall shook his head and strode down the street, Viviane hot on his heels. "You are a cursedly stubborn woman," he muttered darkly, which only made Viviane laugh.

"While you aren't stubborn at all," she retorted with a smile. She linked her arm through his, knowing that he couldn't be so annoyed with her if he didn't have some feelings for her.

It was a matter of principle, though—she would have his sweet confession before she gave her pledge.

They had made a wager. And Barb had reminded her that a man should be judged by his deeds. Niall certainly had done the deeds of a man interested in supporting Viviane's desires.

He'd come around to confessing, she just knew it.

Viviane was content to let him take his time mustering up the L-word. Her destined knight was here and she was pretty happy with the way things were working out.

"We should do something to celebrate, though," she suggested cheerfully. "After all, we've both worked hard to see this book on its way." She pressed a grateful kiss to Niall's cheek. "Thank you for your help, by the way. It was very sweet of you to take an interest."

"Sweet," he muttered, a dull glow rising on the back of his neck. "'Tis the first time I have been called that."

"Well, you *are* sweet."

"Would you wed a man for his sweetness?"

"No. Only for love." He shook his head and turned away, but seemed content to let Viviane keep her hand in the warm crook of his elbow.

"Now, what shall we do?" Viviane was very aware that she was wearing her green rubbers, mainly because they had seemed a sensible choice of footwear in the bit of misty rain they'd had all day. Those boots clomped inelegantly on the damp sidewalk now, the sound making Viviane sure that she knew what Niall was thinking. She even started to blush, imagining that everyone else on the street could guess what they were thinking.

But Niall halted in the street and turned to face Viviane, his expression wary. "Perhaps you could return the favor I have done you and do a deed for me."

There was something about his tone that made Viviane cautious, as though he knew that she wouldn't like whatever suggestion he was going to make.

But she couldn't imagine how that could be.

She smiled, sure he had just been flipping through that book again. Who knew what he had found now? "Like what?"

Niall did not smile. "Return to Cantlecroft with me."

The unexpected words shook Viviane to her core. "Cantlecroft!" She danced backward when Niall might have grasped her arms, his expression telling her that this wasn't a joke. "I told you, Niall, that I'll never go back there! How could you even ask me to go to certain death?"

"Viviane, 'twill not be thus." Niall was earnest and was talking fast. "I shall vouch for you, I shall see your name cleared, I shall ensure that the archbishop grants you the hearing you deserve. His is a man of honor! You shall see that all will resolve itself and your name will be cleared . . ."

"But, Niall, I don't care!" Viviane flung out her hands. "What earthly reason is there to go back and to bother with any of it? Let's just stay here."

Niall's lips tightened and he looked away. "Viviane, I cannot."

Viviane stared at him. Something *was* wrong.

Very wrong. Why did Niall have to go back to Cantlecroft? Was she going to lose him, after all?

"Why not?" Viviane whispered, the words barely making it past the lump in her throat.

Niall frowned and pushed his hand through his hair. "I have obligations in Cantlecroft," he said in a low voice, his manner that of a man confessing something he would prefer to hold back.

"What kind of obligations?" Viviane asked, refusing to imagine the worst. He was pledged to the archbishop, that was it. That was why he had gone on about oaths of fealty before.

Maybe he hadn't been released from that man's service. Trust Niall to worry about a technicality like that.

The knight in question heaved a sigh so heartfelt that Viviane's trepidation grew. "I have pledged to return to Majella and to ensure the support of the children . . ."

Majella? Who was Majella?

And *children*? Viviane was quite certain that her knight in shining armor shouldn't come equipped with a woman and dependents.

"What children?" she demanded, her voice rising shrilly. "And who is Majella? What haven't you told me?"

Niall reached for her hand, his eyes shining with sincerity. But how could he be sincere? Viviane had always thought Niall had been honest with her, but his failure to tell her about Majella and these children was telling.

How could this be a misunderstanding?

"Viviane, I can explain, if you but grant me a moment . . ."

"No!" Viviane shook a finger beneath his nose. "There's nothing to explain. There's only *one* reason that children are dependent upon a man's support and that's that he's their father!" She nearly choked on her disappointment. "Oh, Niall, how could you *do* this? How could I have been so wrong about you? How could you deceive me this way?"

"Viviane, nay! 'Twas never my intent to deceive you!"

But Viviane spun away from him, not wanting him to see the sudden rise of her tears. "How could you want to marry me when you're obligated to Majella and the children?"

Viviane didn't really want to hear his explanation. It could only be a lie.

She just wanted to get away.

Those tears ensured that she couldn't see where she was going, so when she spun away from Niall, she promptly walked right into someone else.

"Hey, Viviane, like where's the fire?" Monty demanded, steadying her with his hands on her shoulders.

Viviane took one look at him and started to cry in a most inelegant way. "He lied to me! Monty, Niall lied to me!"

Monty gave her a hug. "Oh yeah, babe, don't I know it." He glared over her shoulder at Niall, who Viviane could feel hovering right behind her.

And exuding disapproval. Well, she certainly didn't owe anything to a man who mislead her about his emotional ties!

"Viviane, I can explain," Niall insisted, his voice sounding strained. "Cease your weeping that we might talk."

"I don't think so, pal," Monty interjected coldly. "Besides, the lady and I have a date tonight and you're not invited."

What date? Viviane glanced up, then realized that this was Saturday. She had forgotten the sabbat until this very moment. Her move gave her an inadvertent glimpse of Niall bristling.

"What nonsense is this?" he demanded.

"We're off to a witches' sabbat," Monty confided. "Not something you'd be interested in, given your dislike of witches."

Niall visibly simmered. "And what," he asked, his voice strained "would be a witches' sabbat?"

"Oh, a little naked dancing under the full moon, a few spells, some drinking and dancing. Sounds like a good party to me."

Monty grinned.

And when Niall turned to her, his eyes flashing like lightning, Viviane would have rather been just about anywhere else on the face of the earth.

Of course, she'd never give him the satisfaction of seeing that. And she had a few things to tell Niall of Malloy, starting right here and now.

Matters could not have progressed worse, if Niall had planned for all to go awry.

"Witches!" he echoed, stunned that Viviane would even consider such a course. "Why would you consort with witches? Why would you even consider such foolishness?"

Viviane tossed her hair with defiance. "You can't blame me for wanting to know more about it," she declared, as though there was naught illogical about her choice at all.

"It's only natural to be curious about witches, since I've been convicted of being one."

"Natural!" Niall flung out his hands and let his voice rise, not caring who listened. The woman risked her very hide! " 'Tis only *natural* to steer a wide course of such types, that you not jeopardize any chance to prove your innocence!"

But Viviane stepped forward, her eyes snapping fire and her finger jabbing at his chest. "What difference does it make to you what happens to me?" The hurt in her voice was unmistakable. "You've got Majella and all your little obligations to worry about!"

"Viviane!" Niall snatched at her hand, but Viviane backed away. "My concern for Majella is as naught compared to that for you."

Viviane rolled her eyes and folded her arms across her chest. "That seems unlikely!"

"How is it unlikely that I should be concerned for the welfare of the woman I would wed?" Niall retorted. He did not like the stubborn glint in his lady's eye. "How is that good sense?"

"You mean you didn't even marry this Majella? How many children has she given you? Or maybe I should ask how many you've given her! Is that why you didn't want me to have my rubbers?"

"Viviane!" Niall roared, desperately trying to get the conversation back on course. "Would you be condemned here as well as in Cantlecroft?" he demanded. "Would you see a repeat of the past?"

Niall's voice rose when Viviane seemed unswayed by this. "Zounds, Viviane! 'Tis said that people of sense learn from all that has befallen them, and truly, I thought you had more sense than this! Do not consort with witches, I beg of you!"

Viviane's features softened slightly, though her expression was still wary. "Are you worried about me?"

"Of course I am worried about your welfare," Niall snapped. "What man of sense would not be?"

Viviane lifted her chin. "Well, you could temper your response a bit. A person could think that you were angry with them when you shout so . . ."

"I am angered with you!" Niall roared. "What manner of witless fool needs to be condemned *twice* to die?"

Viviane froze, her expression less than encouraging, but before Niall could try to repair the damage, Monty stepped forward. "Hey, don't sweat it, big guy. We don't condemn witches here. That's pretty medieval stuff." He smiled so cockily that Niall longed to force the smile from his face.

As though to add insult to injury, that man put his arm around Viviane's shoulders and she did not shrug off its weight. "So, the lady's like safe here with me. Feel free to trot on home to your *obligations*."

Monty smiled at him, Viviane's gaze shimmered with unshed tears though her lips were set tightly. Niall knew he was losing this argument badly.

And 'twas Viviane who would pay the price.

"Viviane!" Niall dropped his voice with an effort, instead of continuing to shout as he would have preferred. He could feel his annoyance with her—or more accurately, her stunning disregard for her own welfare—thrumming through his voice, but he fought for control over his unruly response.

He had to make her understand.

First, about the witches. Second, about Majella. A few moments of levelheadedness and clear thinking would prevail.

Niall hoped.

He met her gaze unblinkingly. "Viviane, you must consider the wisdom of what you would do. To be sure, you have escaped the weight of your conviction, and even if this one speaks aright and there is no such penalty here, a return to Cantlecroft once you are known to have consorted with witches could . . ."

"But Niall, I'm not going back to Cantlecroft." Her lips thinned as she took a step back. "Don't let me keep you from Majella."

"Nay, Viviane, 'tis true enough that I have a commitment in Cantlecroft, for Majella is ripe with child and I fear greatly what shall transpire in my absence. She is not a woman of good sense in the best of times . . ."

"With child?!" Viviane cried, as upset as Niall had ever seen her. "How could you leave her pregnant? How could you, Niall? How could you follow me and seduce me and do all those things with me when Majella was pregnant and alone? Oh, you're not the kind of man I thought you were, not at all!"

Niall frowned. He wasn't quite certain what his sister's state had to do with anything between himself and Viviane.

He growled beneath his breath and attempted to seize his lady's hand. "Viviane, we must *talk,* for 'tis clear that there are matters which I must explain to you . . ."

"Oh yeah, he's like got a ton of explaining to do," Monty interjected so brightly that Niall fell silent.

What did this one have to say? Naught good, Niall guessed.

Monty's eyes narrowed. "You know, big guy, I picked up a few books from Barb and spent some time reading about this Cantlecroft you two are always going on about. Funny thing is, Cantlecroft ceased to exist at Christmas 1390."

"1390?" Viviane echoed, her mouth opening in surprise.

"Christmas," Niall muttered in disbelief. Surely naught could have happened to Majella in his absence? "It cannot be so."

"Oh, yeah, it was so." Monty, curse him, smiled. "Oh, its occupants revolted and slaughtered everyone in the archbishop's palace."

Niall felt the blood drain from his face. He had left near the beginning of October—and he had sent Majella to the archbishop's palace. She was too close to her time to have travelled much further than that so quickly.

Nay, she would have stayed, and delivered the babe there. 'Twas for her own safety, after all, that he had sent her to the archbishop, for Niall knew full well that his patron would not turn his sister aside.

He could not have sent her to her own demise!

And what of the children?

"Nay, this cannot be so," Niall argued, dreading that indeed 'twas. "Tell me the truth of it!" He stepped forward but Monty retreated, that man's eyes widening in alarm.

"It *is* true," Monty insisted. "Everyone killed, even the dogs in the hall. Seems the locals were upset about the death of some jeweller, guy named Aaron Goldsmith."

Viviane gasped. "Not Aaron!"

Monty gave her an odd look. "Yeah. Aaron Goldsmith and his wife—they were convicted and executed for short-shipping the archbishop on his gold."

Niall raised a hand to his brow, for he felt ill. Surely all could not have gone so badly awry so quickly? "This cannot be," he said woodenly. "Aaron is a man of good repute, a man known to cheat none."

"He bought my mother's ring from me when I had no choice but to sell it," Viviane said, her eyes clouding with tears. She clutched Niall's hand and her fingers were cold. "And I know he gave me more than a fair price. You have to be wrong, Monty."

"What precisely happened there?" Niall asked hotly. "Who died? Does this account list their names?"

But Monty's eyes narrowed as he looked between the two of them. "Are you two like confusing real history with your reenactment people? I mean, I could like understand if you knew some guy who took the role of this Aaron dude and didn't want to see anything bad happen to him, but you can't actually know the *real* Aaron. He's been dead for six hundred years!"

"He would never short-ship anyone," Viviane insisted. "Not Aaron. He'd give someone the shirt off his own back rather than see them cold."

"Aye, he is a man of good name." Niall met her gaze and was reassured to see a hint of her usual consideration there.

"My lady, 'tis yet October," he reminded her gently. "If indeed we could return thence, we might be able to ensure that Aaron does not die so wrongly. I, too, would see him thrive."

She wavered. Niall saw the indecision dawn in her eyes, he noted how she bit her lip. "But, Majella . . ."

Before Niall could tell her the truth of it, Monty spoiled everything.

"Yeah, *right*! Going back to the past. As if!" He leaned closer, his tone dropping. "But I'll tell you something really interesting, Viviane, something about this little history lesson that you probably don't know."

Viviane looked alarmed. "What do you mean?"

"Research, man. A writer's gotta research, and I did." He glared at Niall and Niall wondered what this man of no repute had found. "Funny thing is, a lot of people in Cantlecroft thought things had gone wrong right from the moment they dispatched a certain knight to retrieve an escaped convict."

Niall stared in shock. He could not have found that tale!

"A woman named Viviane, condemned as a witch and sentenced to die." Monty licked his lips as Viviane started.

"Nay," she whispered, obviously seeing the path of the tale.

"Oh yeah," Monty said with a nod. "And that knight, who swore before the whole of Cantlecroft at a big shindig to bring the witch back to face her execution, was named Niall of Malloy."

"Nay!" Niall roared, but 'twas too late.

"Nay!" Viviane rounded on him with flashing eyes and snatched her hand out of his. "Tell me 'tis a lie!" she cried. "Tell me that you didn't follow to take me back there! Niall! You couldn't have wanted me to die!"

But Niall could not lie.

Nor could he tell her the truth.

He cleared his throat. "Viviane, 'tis not as it seems . . ."

"No, it's worse, babe, it's a lot worse." Monty pushed his

way into the conversation. "He's just trying to get around you, get you back with the troupe to reenact the last chapter of the scene. It's not gonna be any fun for you Viviane, even if it is just play-acting . . ."

"You deceived me!" Viviane stepped forward, raised her hand to slap him, and Niall seized the only chance he was likely to have.

He had to ensure Majella's safety.

He had to fulfill his pledge.

He had to clear Viviane's name—and he knew there would be no chance to explain all to her here before she fled his side for all time.

Niall caught Viviane in his arms, ignoring her scream of frustration and her kicking. He shifted her weight to one hip, locked an arm around her waist, and closed his hand around the cursed pendant at the root of it all.

He began to chant.

> *"Sea of green and sky of blue,*
> *Let this one wish come true:*
> *To Cantlecroft would we now flee,*
> *A word with the archbishop we do plea."*

The shimmering that Niall recalled started, the coldness emanated once more from the ethereal stone. Viviane whimpered and struggled against him, clearly disinclined to participate in this journey, but Niall held her fast.

She twisted and fought, she bit him as the shimmer grew to a glow. She cussed at him with a vocabulary he had not guessed she possessed. She was crying and Niall hated that he was responsible for the fall of a single tear. He locked her arms around her waist, determined not to let her go, secretly terrified at the prospect of her escaping his grasp during this transition.

Where then would she be left?

Where would he be left, if he was no longer in possession of the stone?

"Viviane! You must hold fast!" he cried.

"Hey!" Monty roared as the light grew to blinding intensity. "What the hell is this about? And where are you like going? You can't just take off with her like this!"

And he leapt on Niall just as there came a blinding flash.

Chapter 15

VIVIANE SHIVERED FROM the chill and kept her eyes tightly closed. Though she would have never admitted it, it was a relief to feel Niall's arms locked around her once again and his heat pressed against her.

Even if she was of secondary concern to some woman he had left pregnant!

She cried while no one could witness it, letting her tears scatter to the four winds, hating her own gullibility. Oh, she had been a fool to believe that Niall was her one true love, following her across all time to win her heart and hand.

He had just been doing his job, and a horrible job it was. And now, she was going back to face that execution that she had so narrowly escaped.

Some hero she'd found.

Viviane had that same sense of being stretched thin, before she finally felt the gathering begin. It was even more disorienting than the last time, and she couldn't seem to get a clear sense of where she was. All she could see when she forced her eyes open was clear blue light.

She heard a man cry out, then footsteps hastily drawing closer.

She heard Monty swear eloquently, then felt the welcome weight of Niall's arm around her waist.

The first thing that she could discern was the floor.

It was made of heavy, rough-hewn planks of wood. Viviane stared at this unwelcome hint of her location as everything else was still lost in that eerie blue light. There were herbs strewn on the floor in a way that wasn't very common on Salt Spring Island.

Viviane reached for her pendant with shaking fingers, her arm still unwilling to quickly do her bidding. Even though she was dazed by the leap through time, she knew that she had one chance and one chance only to escape her dire fate.

But Viviane didn't even have that.

A man's hand brushed her fingers aside and closed proprietarily over the moonstone. She looked up to find a tall man bending over her.

His smile was not friendly.

"I will just take this," he insisted silkily and gave the chain a little tug in case she missed his meaning.

"But the pendant is mine!" Viviane protested.

His smile broadened. "Not anymore. Take it off."

Viviane glanced around herself, only to find Monty shaking his head and moaning. Niall had his fingertips pressed to his temples, his jeans and shirt unlikely to aid them much here. Viviane recalled with a pang that his mail and weaponry was spread over the floor of her room at Barb's.

An impatient tug urged her to look again at the man holding her moonstone. He was a tall, elegantly wrought older man, dark of eye and silver of hair.

They were apparently in his bedroom, which was a remarkably lavish chamber. A massive bed, hung with rich tapestries drawn against the chill of the air, nearly filled the room. Viviane knew she was back in Cantlecroft and she knew she was in the presence of wealth, but she would never have recognized who this man was, because he was naked.

But Niall did. "My lord!" he said in sudden astonishment and the man flicked an impatient glance his way.

"I shall deal with you later," he said crisply and Niall frowned, though he held his tongue.

Viviane gasped. The archbishop! Of course, Niall had asked for an audience in his verse.

She couldn't hold back her question. "*Are* you the archbishop?"

He smiled coldly in acknowledgement and Viviane dared to hope. "The pendant, if you please," he ordered curtly, but Viviane wasn't listening.

Maybe she could have the hearing that had been promised to her.

This was her chance!

"Sir!" Viviane, unable to bow, inclined her head with respect. "Sir, my name is Viviane . . ."

The archbishop frowned. "I know full well who you are. Now, give me this token and give it to me now."

"But there has been a misunderstanding. I was convicted without ever having the hearing promised to me and if you grant me the chance, I can explain . . ."

But the archbishop chuckled under his breath. The laughter, Viviane noticed, never reached his eyes. He shook his head and regarded her as though she was a particularly stupid child.

Viviane's heart chilled.

"There is naught to explain." He gave the pendant a little tug. "*This* is eloquent enough."

Oh, he thought she had created the magical pendant! Viviane hastened to reassure him. "Oh, but that's not my doing. I didn't know that it had such power! I just made a wish and never imagined this pendant would take me across the centuries."

The archbishop's eyes narrowed and he studied her with

sudden intensity. "Across *centuries*?" Viviane nodded and held his gaze, content to let him see that she wasn't lying.

"Aye, my lord," Niall contributed. "We journeyed to the year 1999 and saw many marvels which could be put to use here in Cantlecroft. 'Twould create labor and mechanisms to sell abroad. Indeed, I began to learn of the marvel they call plumbing . . ."

The archbishop lifted one hand to silence Niall. "Marvels from the future," he mused and stared into the stone. "Never did I guess the talisman was so potent as that."

He smiled into Viviane's eyes but the sight was not re-assuring.

All the same, she summoned her best smile and hoped her usual good fortune would see her free of this circumstance. "So you see, there was no witchery about it. I'm not a witch, I didn't even know that the stone did this. It was a gift to me and one whose power I never guessed."

"I know full well where you won it." The archbishop's tone was cold and decisive. He ran his thumb across the stone in an almost proprietary way. "Though I had no inkling of its power until this very moment. Of course, I guessed once you disappeared that there was more to the stone than I had suspected. You may be assured that had I known the truth sooner, it would never have been left in your possession."

She had been condemned because of the stone, but the archbishop hadn't known it was magical? Viviane frowned in confusion, even as the archbishop's lips drew to a tight line.

"Such an oversight cannot be tolerated again." He shook his head and his eyes flashed. "I would have it *now*."

The archbishop suddenly twisted his wrist and snapped the pendant from its chain. Viviane cried out as the chain bit into her neck and Niall stepped forward to steady her.

"There is no need to injure the lady!" he said heatedly.

The archbishop smiled. "And no reason to spare her."

Viviane caught her breath as Niall shook his head. "Nay,

my lord, she has been misjudged," he said vehemently. "The lady is innocent of the charge made against her, and I would vouch for her before you. She is no witch, she is naught but a woman falsely charged. She knew naught of the witchery inherent in this stone."

The archbishop seemed to find Niall's defense amusing. "I *knew* she was innocent of witchcraft."

Niall's face lit up. "Then . . ."

"'Twas never the issue. 'Twas enough that she wore the stone." The archbishop shivered elaborately and glanced around the rich chamber as Viviane struggled to make sense of his words. Without saying more, he turned to walk back to his bed.

Viviane looked to Niall in consternation and it seemed that he could evidently hold his words back no longer. "But my lord!" he protested. "If you knew the lady was innocent, then why was she condemned to die?"

The archbishop tossed Viviane's pendant onto a table and glanced back. She gauged the distance and knew she would never be able to retrieve it. "Because *obviously* I could not afford to let her live." He smiled coolly. "Just as now, I cannot afford to let *you* live."

Niall's eyes flashed as he straightened. "What nonsense is this?"

"It is no nonsense, Niall of Malloy." The archbishop folded his arms across his chest. "You have learned matters that were best left unknown."

"But I am pledged to your service!" Niall argued. "I swore a pledge to you to fetch this woman back to Cantlecroft, and I have fulfilled my task!"

"Against all expectation." The archbishop smiled thinly.

"I defend her honor and her name!" Niall declared. "You must hear my testimony, as a man of honor." He interlaced his fingers with Viviane's. "She is the woman I would take to wife, a woman of good heart and noble intent. You must proclaim her innocence!"

But the archbishop shook his head. "I must do no such

thing. 'Tis regrettable, of course, as you were always competent, but one must do what one must. Indeed, if you match your fate to that of a condemned witch, what else am I to do?"

Viviane gasped in horror. How could the archbishop treat Niall so poorly? Niall was pledged to that man's service and had done nothing wrong.

" 'Tis not right!" Niall cried.

"And of what import is that? You will die, as will the woman." The archbishop smiled. "Together, as you evidently desire to be. Clearly"—his gaze was chilly—"she has bewitched you."

"But you declared you knew her to be innocent of witchery."

The archbishop lifted a hand. "There 'tis again, the evidence that you know too much to live." And he turned his back upon them all as Niall struggled visibly for an argument.

Viviane squeezed his fingers as Monty piped up. "What about me?" He was still sprawled on the floor, his eyes wide and his face pale.

The archbishop considered him with disdain. "And who might you be?"

Monty scrambled to his feet and offered his hand. "I'm Monty Sullivan." The archbishop surveyed Monty's outstretched hand and his lip curled slightly. "I'm not even from here and well, hey, I don't even need to like *know* these people, if you know what I'm saying."

Distaste flickered across the archbishop's features. "Aye, I know what you are saying. You are a man of no account and thus infinitely expendable." He shook his head. "I shall see that you die first."

"But . . ." Monty squeaked.

The archbishop waved off anything he might have said and raised his voice. "*Guards!* Intruders in my chambers! Aid me!"

No less than seven guards burst into the chamber, their

swords drawn and armor rattling. Monty moaned in dismay at the sight and scampered backward until he hit the wall with a thunk. Niall turned and thrust Viviane behind him, clearly ready to fight.

Unfortunately, his armor was safely back in her room over Barb's shop. And those jeans, regardless of how alluring Viviane found them, wouldn't help him much here. Undaunted, Niall faced the foursome who had drawn their blades on them both, as though he was assessing their strength. Viviane wondered whether he knew any of them.

She glanced to Monty, garbed as always in shorts, T-shirt and polar fleece, and decided they must look like a pretty odd group. Monty already swallowed visibly beneath the point of a wicked length of steel. His eyes were as wide as saucers and he seemed uncharacteristically struck dumb.

Viviane stepped forward to argue with their assailants, but as soon as she stepped out of Niall's shadow, the tip of a sword nudged at her chin. It was a large and particularly shiny blade—it looked well-honed and brought her to a full stop. Viviane followed the length of the blade to a grim-faced guard whose steely gaze was far from merciful.

"Niall," she whispered.

He cast a glance over his shoulder and inhaled sharply. "Do not wound the lady."

"Then do not fight us," the guard retorted, pressing the blade against Viviane's throat to make his intent clear. Viviane gasped and felt a warm trickle of blood on her flesh.

"Halt!" Niall insisted and raised his hands. He managed to stand near Viviane and she was glad of his presence.

The archbishop nodded approval. "This is much better. I feel safe indeed with your enviable command of this keep, Gaultier," he nodded to the biggest guard. "Though no man can defend himself against witchery."

"Witchery, my lord?"

"Aye, this is the condemned witch who escaped our own dungeon but a month ago. She has appeared magically in mine own chambers to wreak her vengeance, my emissary snared within her spell and her minion at hand."

"No! That's not true!"

"The lady is innocent!"

"I'm nobody's minion!"

The archbishop raised his hands to his ears. "Gaultier, ensure your men are not so foolish as to listen to their lies! She has turned even Niall of Malloy against me and not a one of them can be trusted."

"What shall be done with them my lord?"

"They shall be executed three days hence. 'Twill give them time to repent of their wickedness and savor our hospitality." With that, the archbishop made to return to his bed and the guards urged the unhappy trio toward the door.

'Twas in the midst of her dismay that Viviane realized someone else lurked within that great pillared bed.

"Oh, Richard!" a woman chortled sleepily from behind those heavy curtains, her voice low and nearly inaudible. Viviane straightened in shock, though she couldn't decide why she should be surprised that this man who broke his word to Niall would also break his vow of chastity.

"I thought I had dreamed of you," the woman cooed, then laughed sensuously. An elegant hand stretched out through the gap of the draperies, the skin flawlessly creamy. "You have become so cold while I slept so warmly here! Did I hear voices? Is something amiss?"

"Duty, my dear," the archbishop purred as he joined his consort. "Duty, as always, must be tended before pleasure."

He did something in those shadows that made the woman cry out with pleasure, the sound enough to make Viviane blush. Then the woman laughed aloud, her voice louder than it had been before.

"Oh *Richard*!" she cried. "You truly are a marvel!"

And Niall straightened with a snap. He pivoted and stared at the draped bed, a dull flush rising over his neck as he resisted his escort. The guards tried to pull him out of the room, but Niall shrugged them off.

"Majella?" he demanded, outrage in his tone. "Is that you?"

Silence came from the bed for a telling moment, then there was a rustling of linens. "Niall?" the woman squealed. "Niall, is that you finally returned?"

Viviane knew the blood left her face. Niall's Majella was in bed with the archbishop? This couldn't be a good thing.

A fulsome beauty bounced out of the bed, her copious charms on full display, and did nothing for Viviane's confidence in her own charms. Majella was gorgeous! Her hair was slightly more red than gold, its thick waves falling over her shoulder in inviting disarray. She was all curves and silky skin, the kind of woman that no man could easily forget.

As Niall clearly hadn't. The stricken look on his face told Viviane all she needed to know. The woman was decidedly pregnant, the sight erasing any doubt Viviane could have had of her identity.

This was the Majella who Niall had been so anxious to protect. This was the woman who held Niall's heart in thrall.

"Venus rising," Monty muttered incomprehensibly. Viviane glanced to him to find him staring at Majella with wonder shining in his eyes. In fact, all of the sentries were similarly enthralled by the sight of this beauty and Viviane felt not only abandoned, but very plain.

But Majella was staring at Niall, her features transformed with pleasure. She smiled, then she blushed scarlet. "Niall! It *is* you!"

Viviane was ready to dislike the woman, though the way her features softened with affection at the sight of Niall made it hard to do so. She looked relieved and delighted, a response to the sight of Niall that Viviane could truly understand.

Majella spun back to the bed, tugging a gossamer robe

over her shoulders. "Niall, *Niall* is here. Oh, Richard, this is the most marvelous news! Niall is returned!"

She flung herself across the room to embrace the knight Viviane had once imagined to be her own. "Oh, Niall, I have been so very worried about you, for one never can tell what might transpire on such an adventure as yours."

Majella planted a hearty buss on Niall's cheek that seemed somewhat inappropriate as a greeting for the father of her child. Then she propped one hand on her hip and looked him over assessingly, her manner almost maternal.

"Look at you! You look to have been eating well enough"— she conceded with a pinch of his flesh—"but your garb is so very strange. Now, you must tell me . . ."

But Niall gripped her shoulders, typically cutting to the heart of the issue. "Majella, how long have you shared the archbishop's bed?"

Viviane's heart twisted. She knew it couldn't be easy for Niall to witness his lover's indiscretions, even if he had been indiscreet himself. After all, Majella carried his child, which wasn't a small thing.

Majella blushed and her gaze flicked away. Viviane knew she was going to lie and was surprised when it didn't seem as though she did.

"Well, ever since I came here, that day you left. Richard just swept us into the castle, it was absolutely marvelous, we have been spoiled to bits. And after all, you had told me to find a more wealthy man to ensure that Matthew has the training he desires . . ."

But Niall set the lady aside, his angry gaze fixing on the archbishop as that man stepped once again from the bed.

"You coupled with my sister!" he charged, incredulity echoing in his voice. "What manner of man are you, to take advantage of a woman in such a state as this?

His *sister*?

The archbishop waved one hand nonchalantly in Majella's direction and chuckled. "She could hardly lose her virtue."

"She is with child!" Niall roared. "I sent her to you for her *protection*!" He slammed his fist into his palm. "I expected you to ensure her welfare on account of my pledge to you! Did my oath of fealty mean naught to you?"

"She is well enough." The archbishop shrugged. "My protection does not come cheaply."

"You are a man of God! You are pledged to chastity! You of all men should be relied upon for good works!"

"I am a *man*," the archbishop said grimly. "And I take what is freely offered. You may rest assured that your slut of a sister was not coerced in any way."

"Richard!" Majella gasped.

"You had no right!" Niall cried and lunged for the older man.

The guards snatched for him, but Niall moved too quickly for them in his anger. He was on the archbishop in a heartbeat, he landed two solid punches, one to the jaw and one to the gut.

The older man dropped to his knees before one guard leaped forward and beat a shield over Niall's head. Viviane's knight slumped bonelessly to the floor as the archbishop stumbled to his feet.

That man spit in Niall's face. "Faithless wretch! Kill him slowly!"

"Nay!" Viviane tried to break free of her captor but was wrestled toward the door. Meanwhile, the guards dragged Niall across the chamber.

"But Richard," Majella protested in obvious dismay. "What are you doing to my brother? 'Twas you who sent him on a quest, and now he is returned. He is a good man and you know it well. What is the meaning of this?"

The archbishop cast a glittering robe over his shoulders. He felt his jaw where Niall had punched him and granted the four of them a cold glance, before addressing the guards.

"My former mistress will join the brother of whom she is

so very fond," he said with quiet authority. "Let them become reacquainted in the dungeons—'tis all the time they will have together before their execution."

"Aye, my lord."

Majella's eyes widened in shock. "Richard!"

The archbishop's gaze hardened though he did not even deign to look at Majella. "And cast her brats into the dungeon as well. We might as well be rid of the lot of them."

Majella paled. "Richard! You assured me that the children were safe here."

"They are no longer." He surveyed her with icy calm. "This would have been a good day for you to slumber long, Majella. 'Tis a mistake you will regret, though admittedly, not for long."

And he climbed back into his bed, hauling the drapes closed behind himself. Majella began to shriek, more guards came running, Niall was dragged out of the chamber. Monty managed to take the distraught Majella's elbow and she clung to him, wailing at Richard's injustice and weeping copiously.

Children were herded from elsewhere in the palace, their protests mingling with their mother's cries. The largest boy took one look at the scene and planted himself beside Niall, his expression grim for a child of his age.

And they were all marched to the dungeons that Viviane recalled all too well.

But through the chaos of it all, Viviane could only think one thing. Majella was Niall's *sister*, not his wife or lover or lady. He had been worried about his sister and her children—and that was an awfully nice weakness for him to have. She worked her way through the throng to walk beside him, keeping an eye on how he was treated.

Maybe, just maybe, Niall was destined to be her knight after all.

Either way, Viviane was going to be the first person he saw when he awakened. And she was going to give him that chance to explain himself. It didn't look as though they were going to have a lot of time left and Viviane wanted to spend it knowing the truth.

Odo looked up from his ledgers at the racket in the dungeon corridor and his eyes nigh fell from his head, so great was his surprise.

Not only had Niall of Malloy returned, and not only was that man garbed as a foreigner, but he had fetched back the witch Viviane herself. 'Twas well worth a look and Odo rose from his stool to peek at the passing party, somewhat annoyed to realize that he would owe Francis at the alehouse a hefty sum. Odo had bet against Niall's return and the odds had been long.

'Twould be an expensive debt.

But then he frowned at the realization that Niall was not only unconscious, but that he was being cast into the cell with all the others. Odo drummed his fingers on his table, not impressed to see a woman heavily with child and a brood of children locked in, as well.

The guard who Odo did not like sauntered back along the corridor and grinned. "Another lot for the executioner. Faith, but that man never goes lacking for labor."

Odo withdrew into his small chamber and retrieved his ledger. "Is that Niall of Malloy among their number?" he asked with all the innocent curiosity he could summon. Hopefully, 'twould pass under the pretence of needing the information for his register.

"Aye. You know him?" The sentry's gaze was a little too searching for Odo's taste.

He shrugged. "I thought he looked familiar. He labored here for a while."

"Ah, before his quest no doubt. Well, the man is a failure, of that there can be no doubt. The one who looks about to calf is his sister, the children her brats, and they are all to die together."

Odo frowned. "And the charge?"

"Sorcery. As usual."

Odo cleared his throat, certain he must have misunderstood. "Surely not the children?"

"Of course, the *children*," the guard sneered. "They teach them young, that kind, and one cannot be too wary." His eyes narrowed. "Are you sufficiently wary, Odo? 'Tis said they have all fallen under the witch's spell." He leaned closer. "She seems to fancy small men, Odo, for her minion is one such. You had best mind yourself this night."

Odo wriggled a little further back into his chamber. "Do you have their names and ages?"

"What?"

"For the register." Odo tapped the book.

The sentry shrugged. "Nay, not I. If you care so much, you can fetch the truth of it yourself. I am to summon the executioner for the dawn three days hence."

Odo nodded numbly, hoping the sentry would not guess how the bile had risen in his throat. The sentries marched away, jesting amongst themselves and Odo considered what he should do.

He liked Niall of Malloy, always had. A man could smell a man of honor and Niall had been one. Niall had insisted on taking responsibility for the disappearance of a witch who had surely beguiled him, a deed that many a man would not have done. And Niall had sworn to make matters come right, to fetch back the witch.

Contrary to the sentry's insistence, Niall had not failed. Nay, Odo recalled the face of that very witch and he had seen her in that party. Niall had succeeded, and he was to be rewarded with not only his own demise but that of all his blood.

Charged of sorcery, a laughable pretence to any who had ever known Niall of Malloy. The man believed in naught that could not be held in his own hands. *Sorcery!* Odo rolled his eyes before his hand stilled at the price Niall would pay.

First, Aaron Goldsmith had died, along with his loyal wife.

Now, Niall of Malloy was to share that fate.

And *children* were to die! Innocents!

'Twas wrong. 'Twas unconscionable.

'Twas time someone did something about the matter. Aye, Odo's father had told him once that there comes a time in every man's life when he must choose where he will stand.

As he opened his ledger and carefully inscribed the date, Odo chose.

Chapter 16

BACK ON SALT Spring, things were not going well. At least not for Barb. October had brought its usual chilly rains and autumnal dearth of revenue. On this particular Monday, two days after everyone had left her high and dry without so much as a note, she closed the shop and trudged down to the relative cheer of Joe's bakery. It couldn't hurt to nurse a latte while she mourned over her books.

"Weather sucks, eh?" Joe demanded with false cheer. There was no one else in the shop and Barb guessed he was feeling the same retail fallout as she.

"Among other things." She marked Monty's balance in red, then underlined it twice, just because she was so annoyed with him. Not only had he disappeared but he'd nailed her with an unwelcome NSF charge from the bank.

Ten bucks she could have used for something frivolous, like a deposit against the phone bill. And now, he owed her even *more*, because she'd been dumb enough to let him buy on credit again.

"Seen that Monty around lately?" Joe asked.

Barb grimaced. "He seems to have fallen off the face of the earth."

"No kidding." Joe poured himself a coffee and came to sit opposite her. "Doesn't that figure. You try to be a nice guy and just take it in the shorts."

Barb met his gaze with surprise. "He owed you money, too?"

"Oh yeah. Not a lot, but it grates. Coupla hundred bucks."

"Fourteen hundred and twenty," Barb supplied and Joe winced.

"Yeow! How'd you let him get away with that? I mean, he was a talker, but not *that* smooth."

Barb rubbed her temples, not appreciating the reminder that she'd let her emotions get the upper hand on her good sense. "He paid off his old balance with a boinger of a check."

"And you didn't know it would boing, so you let him charge some more." Joe shook his head. "I tell you, nice guys always finish last." He clinked his mug companionably to hers and they sipped together. "Did he book off with that little redhead you had working there? I haven't seen her much either."

"Yeah, all three of them are gone without a trace." Barb wouldn't think that it was kind of convenient to have no payroll when things were this slow. And she certainly wasn't going to admit that she missed Viviane—let alone the nice masculine scenery. Nope, she was better off without the lot of them.

Wherever they had gone.

"But it's the quiet ones that surprise you. She seemed like a sweetie, that Viviane, though you never can tell." Joe frowned. "Course, you're probably glad to be without the payroll this time of year."

Barb nodded reluctantly. "Except she could really sell books." She sighed and closed her ledger. Barb felt bankrupt, both financially and spiritually, and couldn't imagine how she'd shake herself out of it this time. Maybe she should just let the bank take it all—at least then she'd have nothing left to worry about. The gray slant of cold rain only emphasized the futility of it all.

Her lone iris would probably die.

"Hey, Joe, you got anything else that needs doing?"

A rather interesting specimen of the male gender stepped out of the back of the bakery, wiping his hands on a rag. Barb wasn't down quite so far that she didn't notice.

A small frown marred the space between this guy's dark brown brows and he had to be six four. He had dark brown eyes too, and a serious demeanor. He was built, if looking a bit gaunt and pale, although winter didn't favor everybody. No, this guy looked like he'd rather be outside.

And it was lousy weather for that. Barb sipped and watched him through her lashes.

A harmless treat, after all.

He didn't even glance at Barb, not even out of curiosity, and she tagged him as gay before returning her attention completely to her latte.

A waste, she thought absently. Figured.

Joe frowned. "Sorry, Ryan, I can't think of another thing."

The man shrugged and tossed the rag into the trash. "Then maybe I'll have a look at the truck's transmission again."

He turned and left, even as Joe shook his head. "Poor guy," he muttered.

"New employee, at this time of year? You surprise me."

"Nah, it's my kid brother." Joe sipped as though weighing the merit of explaining, then he shrugged. "Helluva story if you ask me. Busted his ass building a business on the mainland, his wife takes it into her head that he's not good enough for her and packs it up. Gutted his business on the way—getting *her* half—though she did sweet bugger all but spend all those years. Ripped his heart out and ate the sucker warm, if you know what I mean."

Barb nodded. "Read the book and saw the movie."

"No kidding? Well, hey, it's hardly my business." Joe sighed. "Anyhow, he was too good to her, I say, even at the end, and now he's got nothing to show for all his work.

She's living in style, as you can imagine, some fancy hot-shot lawyer sipping champagne at her feet." Joe shook his head. "Another nice guy finishing last."

Barb smiled despite herself. "Runs in the family?"

Joe grinned. "Yeah, yeah, you could say that." He sobered and leaned closer. "Be a while before Ryan heads back onto the field though—he's hurting bad and won't talk about it at all. I tell you, I'm running out of odd jobs around here, though I can understand that he wants to keep busy."

Joe licked his lips, casting a quick glance to the doorway his brother had briefly occupied. "You don't happen to have anything that needs doing, do you, Barb?"

Barb shook her head. "Joe, I'm fresh out of cash. I'm not going to have someone do any work for me when I can't pay them." Barb wrinkled her nose. "It's not in the nice guy code."

But Joe frowned. "No, that's not what I mean. I don't care about the cash and neither does he. He just needs something to keep his hands busy; he's not the kind of guy to sit still and brood. Ryan will work his way through it, he's a pretty balanced guy." He snapped his fingers. "You could think of it as providing therapy."

Barb laughed. "Well, what does he do? I don't have a car, let alone one needing a transmission repair."

"Nah, that's just a hobby. Ryan's a landscape architect and I tell you, he's damn good."

Barb caught her breath. "You mean he designs gardens."

"Yeah, and puts them in. You name it—rocks and patios and decks and trees and pretty posies all in a row. Got no gift for it myself, kill everything I touch. The missus too. She's got African violets blooming on the windowsill for the first time since Ryan moved in and is thrilled to bits. Ryan's even done little waterfalls and I swear to God, when he's done, they look as though they were there all along."

Barb was tempted. Really tempted. But one glance at her books reminded her of the realities of her situation. "Oh,

Joe, I've wanted a garden forever." She sighed. "But I don't know how to do it or even where to start . . ."

Joe saluted her with his cup. "A match made in heaven!"

"But, Joe, I don't have any money for it! The plants will be expensive . . ."

"Hey, not wholesale. And maybe we can cut a deal with someone—Ryan already was talking to some woman down Fulford way who's setting up a nursery for the spring. They're trying to work out a deal to the advantage of both of them. She might need books, or advertising space in your store. I don't know, but it never hurts to ask."

"But . . ."

"But *nothing*, Barb. This is a community and we'll work something out. More goddamn creativity on this island than you can shake a stick at—let's use some. It's not like we're that busy in the winter."

Before Barb could argue any more, Joe raised his voice. "Hey, Ryan! We might have a job for you!"

And Barb felt a tingle of excitement for the first time in years. A garden!

Suddenly, her prospects didn't look so dreary after all.

Chapter 17

'Twas NOT THE first time of late that Niall had awakened with a pounding between his ears, and that recollection did naught to improve his mood.

Neither did the persistent ache in his knee. Aye, he knew where he was without opening his eyes and the chatter of voices told him who else languished here along with him.

And that made Niall of Malloy deeply angry. He had been betrayed by his own overlord, the man to whom he had pledged his loyalty forever.

It seemed the oath was not reciprocated.

Aye, Niall had kept his word and fulfilled his quest, only to learn that the archbishop was not a man of honor. The archbishop dishonored Niall's pledge of fealty and disregarded it, simply for his own convenience. The archbishop had condemned Viviane to death, even knowing that she was not a witch. The archbishop had taken advantage of Majella's vulnerable state.

Clearly, the archbishop was not interested in justice. Viviane had guessed the truth of it but Niall had believed he knew better.

And now, everyone he cared about was going to die for his mistake.

Niall did not want to open his eyes and face yet another failure to his name. He feigned sleep and listened to the chatter around him, almost smiling at the weight of a small hand on his arm. He could readily guess who that was, sitting so close beside him, and did not have long to wait for confirmation.

"But what did Gawain *do*?" Matthew asked, wonder in his voice.

Niall did smile then, just a little, for he knew by that question alone whose hip was pressed against his own. He lay on a hard pallet, his Viviane seated beside him, his nephew keeping vigil.

"Well, he asked the old hag to move out of the road, because he didn't want to run her down." Viviane's voice so close beside him made Niall's heart begin to pound. "He asked very politely, because he was a man who recognized the importance of good manners, but the hag refused to move."

This was the tale of Gawain that was more familiar to Niall, not the version that Viviane had created on her own.

"Did he ride right over her?" Matthew demanded. "He had a big horse, he could have done it."

"Of course not! That wouldn't have been very nice. He asked her what he could do to persuade her to move from the road—because he was too courteous to ride over her!—and the old hag said he had only to answer a riddle." Viviane's voice hushed. "Then she lifted her hand and pointed to the woods surrounding the road, and Gawain saw that the trees were hung with the bodies of dead knights."

Matthew gasped.

"And the old hag told him that they were all the ones who had answered her riddle wrong."

Matthew clutched Niall's hand. "Oh! I would have ridden right over her, right then! She was a wicked woman!"

"Ah, but Gawain knew that she must be a magical being, so he dared not offend her. Gawain knew that when he saw the knights, for there were many there he recognized, valiant men who had ridden off on quests, never to return."

"Like Uncle Niall," Matthew piped up proudly. "But he returned."

"That he did. And Gawain intended to return as well."

"So, he agreed?"

"He did. And the old hag gave him the riddle:

Kings will crow and knights will boast,
Their victories hailed from coast to coast.
But none have named desire innermost:
What is it that a woman wants most?"

Niall could almost hear Matthew thinking.

"A rich husband," the boy decided finally, probably thinking of his mother.

"Ah, that was the first thought of Gawain," Viviane admitted. "But then he wondered if it was too obvious a response. He looked at those fallen knights and knew that all the obvious answers would have been made already. So, he did not say that, and he did not say a fine meal, and he did not say fine clothing and jewellery. He did not even say healthy children, though he considered that possibility long. The word "innermost" made him think there was something more important that a woman might desire."

"Did he guess it?"

"Well, he spent three days and three nights in that horrible forest, feeling the old hag watching him, listening to the rustle of the wind through the cloaks and the mail of the knights all around him. And finally, as he watched the moon rise one night, he knew the answer."

"What was it?"

"Oh, I am not certain I should tell you," Viviane teased, and Niall grinned outright when his nephew cried foul.

"I told you that you had a gift with the telling of a tale,

Viviane," Niall charged and opened his eyes, deliberately avoiding a glance toward his lady. He would not argue with her before the boy, and she had been sorely vexed with him before.

"Uncle Niall!" Matthew hugged him soundly and Niall tousled the boy's hair. "You must know the answer to the riddle, for you know everything."

"Well, I do know this." Niall met Viviane's gaze just long enough to note her minute nod of agreement. "What a woman desires most of all is her own will. 'Tis something any man would do well to recall."

'Twas then Niall realized, somewhat belatedly, that her own will was the one thing he had not given Viviane. She had wanted only to remain on Salt Spring, and he had stolen that choice away from her in his urge to do what was right. And what he had believed to be right had turned out to be dreadfully wrong.

Even beyond that, Niall knew he should have respected Viviane's desire to stay away from Cantlecroft.

Because now she would die. They had come full circle from the first day they had met—not only would Viviane die, but Niall would join her.

That had not been his plan.

And just as before, Niall knew without doubt that he did not want Viviane to die. He could not imagine a world without her sunny smile, or her cheerful insistence that she was lucky; her determination to see matters resolved, or the power of her storytelling. Further, he did not want to awaken and not find her beside him, he did not want to be without her whimsical convictions or her certainty that she could make all come aright, he did not want to sleep without her curled beside him.

He loved her. Against all rhyme and reason, against every conviction that matters tangible alone were real, Niall loved Viviane.

It took him a moment to come to terms with the truth of that, amazing as 'twas.

"Is that the truth of it?" Matthew demanded.

Viviane nodded and smiled for the boy, obviously unaware that Niall had just had an epiphany. He watched her shamelessly, savoring the way her lips curved to form the words, the way her eyes shone as she recounted the tale. "When Gawain gave that very answer, the old hag told him that he was right. She offered him a kiss as a reward—"

"Ewwww!" Matthew grimaced and squirmed with the horror of young boys everywhere for feminine kisses. "I should never kiss a woman, especially a wrinkled old hag!"

Viviane shook a finger at him. "Ah, but you see, Gawain believed it would be rude to refuse her such a small thing. What price is a small kiss? And he felt a bit sorry for her, trapped out in the wild and condemned to ask people this riddle. So he kissed her, and to his surprise, she instantly turned into a beautiful woman."

"Oh!" Matthew's eyes were round.

"And she offered to marry him, admitting that she had been cursed to take the form of this old hag until someone answered the riddle right. Well, Gawain thought he was terribly lucky, because she was very beautiful, so he agreed."

"And they lived happily ever after?"

Viviane shook her head. "Not quite. For the lady confessed that there was one little catch. You see, she still had to be an ugly old hag half of the time. So, she asked Gawain to choose whether she should be a beauty in the day or the night."

"He would not want his friends to think he had married an old hag," Matthew said quickly.

"And he would not want the lady to think that he was wedding her only for his own nightly pleasure," Niall contributed, doubting that Matthew would guess that element of the tale. He was rewarded with a glimpse of his lady's smile.

"Exactly." Viviane nodded. "It seemed to Gawain that this was a test of his character, but he didn't know which to choose. But in the nick of time, he remembered the answer to the riddle."

"The lady must choose!" Matthew crowed and bounced on the pallet.

"Yes! He told her to choose and that completely broke the spell that had been cast over her. So, the lady was beautiful all the day and all the night, and they were married and then they lived happily ever after."

"Because Gawain let his lady have her own will." Matthew nodded happily at this conclusion. "But Uncle Niall knew the answer."

Matthew abruptly gave Niall a hug that brought tears to the knight's eyes. "I am glad you returned," Matthew whispered against his shoulder. "For now we are all together again."

Aye, he had gone soft, 'twas true. Though as he held Viviane's regard, Niall was not certain 'twas such a dire fate. Majella summoned Matthew and with one last squeeze of Niall's hand, the boy scampered away, leaving Niall alone with Viviane.

Niall surveyed her silently for a moment, still marveling at his realization. The liveliness had left her features now that she was no longer telling a tale. Questions lurked in the depths of her eyes and Niall knew he was the knave responsible for their presence.

'Twas not the way he preferred she regard him. Niall frowned and averted his gaze, knowing he needed to repair his error. He had to give Viviane her will, he had to find a way to send her back to Salt Spring. He had to save his sister and her brood from the danger he had cast them into, however unwittingly.

Zounds, but the world was heavy on his shoulders!

"Matthew admires you," Viviane said softly.

Niall snorted and sat up, rubbing his temples with his fingertips, feeling a very unworthy hero for his nephew. "He is young." Then Niall winced at the unwelcome truth.

"Though indeed, he will not have the chance to grow much older."

She leaned dangerously close and placed her hand upon his, her eyes filled with appeal. "Niall, we must talk . . ."

Nay, he must *think*. There had to be a way free of this trouble, a way to see Viviane's desire fulfilled and Niall's family saved.

"Nay, Viviane," he interrupted her crisply. He scowled deliberately and made an excuse. "My head aches overmuch. I fear my companionship would be burdensome." Before she could argue with him—for he knew she would— Niall pushed to his feet and strode across the tiny stone chamber.

The cursed moonstone held the key, Niall knew it well.

And once—*if!*—he retrieved it, Viviane would be gone. The very thought made his innards clench, even though her departure might well see the rest of them released.

Niall could only hope.

He gripped the bars on the window in the door, well aware of Viviane's gaze locked upon him. He hated that he had been discourteous, and heartily disliked that he could not mend matters between them.

But that would only make matters worse when they did part, for part they must. Niall's place was here, he knew it as well as he knew his own name. He had not needed Matthew's reminder of the obligations of his blood. Niall could not simply follow his heart's desire to another place and time, nor could he selfishly change the course of eight people's lives in pursuit of his own happiness.

Which meant that he did not dare give Viviane any hint of his newly discovered feelings for her. 'Twould be better if Viviane despised him for his betrayal, better if she believed him a duty-bound wretch who had used her for his own ends.

Aye, Niall knew that his lady had a weakness for love and its charms. He would not condemn her to the unhappiness of yearning for what she could not have.

He would save that burden for himself, for truly, he would not have to endure it long.

Now, to fetch the witching stone.

Something was wrong.

Viviane didn't know what it was. In fact, she couldn't imagine what it was. It was true that she had questioned Niall's feelings for her—for two reasons.

The first had been proven false—Majella was neither his lover nor wife, nor even pregnant with his child. Niall's obligation was only that of a brother for his widowed sister's children. Viviane liked that he took such responsibility for his family and she had already seen that they were children who would do him proud.

The second had proven to be a miscalculation on Niall's part. Aye, just as Monty had charged, Niall had made a pledge to bring her back to Cantlecroft. He had kept his word, but clearly only because he had believed he could vouch for her innocence. Viviane had seen the truth in Niall's shock at the revelation of the archbishop's deception.

Now that Niall had finally awakened, after a day and a night of laying unconscious while Viviane kept an anxious watch, things should be right between them.

But they weren't. He wouldn't even talk to her.

She wondered whether he was worried about his sister, but he wasn't hovering around her.

Niall was pacing.

And he was avoiding Viviane, as well as a man could in the confines of this cell. He studiously kept from making eye contact with her, he was always on the other side of the small chamber no matter how she tried to end up beside him.

Viviane thought that maybe Niall was insulted that she hadn't given him a chance to explain for himself. She made a point of apologizing, hoping for a kiss, but Niall mumbled an acceptance and turned away.

He busied himself with his nieces and nephews, or scowled out the small window to the corridor. His mood was clearly not good and though he wasn't a talkative man at the best of times, now he positively brooded. Every time Viviane managed to corner him and try to strike up a conversation, Niall mumbled an excuse, ducked and escaped.

It was getting annoying, mostly because Viviane couldn't explain his behavior.

It was only because Viviane was watching Niall like a hawk, trying to sneak up on him one more time, that she even noticed his mumbled conversation with their jailor. Niall had called for water and the little jailor had brought the cup to the door again. This time, Viviane noticed, he came alone, without one of those big sentries hovering behind him.

That sparked Viviane's curiosity. Niall was certainly bigger than this little man and could have pushed past him easily. She supposed there were sentries close by, but then realized that Niall had probably given his word of honor or something that he wouldn't try to escape.

That would be like Niall, she thought with mingled affection and exasperation. And if this man knew him at all, he'd know that as well as Viviane did.

Come to think of it, Viviane remembered that bald little man from the last time she was here. He glanced nervously over his shoulder while he handed Niall the cup of water. At first glance, the two didn't appear to be speaking, but then Viviane saw the jailor's lips move quickly. Either no sound came out or his voice was pitched so low that Viviane couldn't hear it.

She had a funny feeling that something was being decided. She took a step closer and tried to look as though she wasn't straining her ears to listen.

Niall nodded once, quickly, then shot a glance over his shoulder as though sensing that someone was watching the exchange. Viviane hastily dropped her gaze to her hands and hoped he hadn't noticed her attention.

He was hatching a plan! Viviane knew it. Just as she knew

he was going to do something noble and heroic, something that would save them all from death.

She decided right then and there that whatever Niall was going to do, she was going to do it with him. Sticking close by his side was the best way she could imagine to get that chance to talk to him, after all.

And they had to talk.

Niall turned back to the cell, the key grated in the lock, and Majella suddenly screamed. The little man's feet scampered in the corridor outside as he fled back to his station.

"Yowsers!" Monty roared, leaping to his feet from his crouch beside the lady in question. "What is that all about?"

"My water has broken," Majella declared, then lifted her skirts to show the growing puddle. "The babe is coming!" Her beautiful features contorted with pain and she teetered unsteadily on her feet.

Niall was across the cell in a flash, his expression concerned. "Majella, you cannot birth a child in this hovel!"

She gasped as she obviously had a contraction, then managed a wan smile for her brother after it passed. Her fingers gripped his arm tightly. "Niall, we have little choice. Whether you believe 'tis good sense or not, this babe is coming and 'tis coming soon."

Niall swore, then helped Majella to the rough pallet he had recently abandoned. He shoved a hand through his hair and scanned the cell, as though looking for aid unexpectedly hidden amongst them.

"But Majella, you cannot bear a child here," he insisted. "There is no midwife, I know not what to do."

Majella heaved a sigh and winced as she settled on the pallet. "'Tis a boy, no doubt," she said philosophically. "They are most unlikely to heed convenience or the will of others." She grimaced and caught her breath, exhaling mightily when the contraction passed. "And he is hurried. 'Tis a boy, to be sure."

"You cannot do this thing!"

Majella cast her brother a wry glance that made Viviane

smile. "I have done this afore. Niall. Trust my certainty that 'twill happen with or without your blessing."

"But Majella, something could go awry! You could die in such unfitting circumstance. The babe could die in the chill of this place." Niall appealed to Viviane with a desperate look but she had to shrug.

"I have never witnessed the birthing of a child," she confessed, not liking the pallor of his skin. Majella's other children gathered around Niall, and several took his big hand in theirs, though Viviane couldn't guess whether they were turning to him for support or offering their own.

"Well, it's a good job I've done my research," Monty declared, pushing past Niall as he rolled up his sleeves.

"You?" Niall demanded.

"You?" Majella echoed.

Viviane blinked in shock and refrained from comment.

"Yeah, me." Monty surveyed them all, obviously insulted by this commentary on his competence. "Nobody here has like delivered a child before, right?" Niall and Viviane nodded reluctantly. "And I spent two months with a midwife on the island, travelling around to do prenatal and postnatal checkups. We delivered four babies in that time." He held up his fingers. "Count 'em. *Four.*"

"You aided a midwife?" Niall demanded, his incredulity more than clear.

"Hey, it's not off the deep end or anything. Just research. Character research. I had a midwife in a book and wanted to know what she would know, what she'd do, you know?" He shrugged and glanced at Majella. "You don't have a lot of options here, babe. Looks like I'm it."

Majella grimaced and caught her breath, puffing when the contraction passed.

Then she smiled for Monty. "With your count and mine, and this child on the way, we make an even dozen, Master Monty. I welcome your aid—though trust you will not take offense that I heartily pray for an uncomplicated arrival."

Monty winked at Majella. "No offense taken." He

dropped his voice. "In fact, I'm with you. No breech stuff, if you can negotiate it." He looked tellingly around the cell, his gaze lingering on a persistent drip that created a dark puddle in the far corner. "In this joint, we could use all the help we can get."

"Zounds," Niall muttered. He strode to the door and roared anew. "We have need of a midwife here!"

There was a lot of scuttling and heavy footfalls in the corridor, some muted argument and a runner audibly dispatched to the archbishop. Meanwhile, Majella's labor progressed, the child clearly disinterested in what trouble was taken for its arrival. And in the end, no midwife was summoned.

The archbishop forbade it.

This news was received poorly by Majella, no doubt because she had expected better from her lover. "Wretched bastard!" she hissed through her teeth, straining through another contraction. Her brow was damp, her face flushed despite Monty's cheerful coaching.

'Twas bad timing to understand precisely how little the man cared for her, Viviane guessed.

"Don't push yet, babe, you'll just hurt yourself. Breathe, breathe, breathe." Monty puffed, Majella glared and echoed his manner, working in an insult for the archbishop when she could.

Viviane gathered the children in the opposite corner and told them tales, hoping to distract them from their mother's labor. She believed it was the most useful deed she could do, since Monty truly did seem to know what he was doing. Niall paced, his unnatural pallor growing with every passing hour, his limp becoming more and more pronounced as the evening progressed.

Monty was surprisingly calm, murmuring to Majella and even making her laugh at intervals. One at a time, the children fell into restless slumbers and Viviane tucked each in with whatever cloaks she could retrieve.

'Twas late when Matthew's grip finally loosened on Viv-

iane's hand and she was nearly out of tales as his eyes
drooped closed. She brushed the hair back from his brow
and nestled him in beside his brothers. She glanced up in
time to find Niall's considering glance upon her. Viviane
murmured his name and got to her feet, but Niall abruptly
turned to watch his sister.

The single candle had burned low, almost gutting itself in
the residue of wax. There was not much wick left so Viviane
knew it was late. She could hear the silence of the night filling the keep, that curious stillness broken only by the scam-
pering of mice. The cell echoed with Majella's strained
breathing, Monty's encouragement was so low as to be incomprehensible.

Niall was watching the candle and as the flame flickered
and dipped dangerously low, he dropped to one knee beside
his sister.

"'Tis time, Majella," he urged. "You must bring this child
forth with haste."

"First, you want to stop it," she huffed, "and now you
would rush it forth." She rolled her eyes at Viviane. "Is that
not like a man? To want all the world to bend to his desire?"

A contraction seized her and she arched her neck back before Viviane could smile or agree. Majella's teeth gritted in
agony. Niall took her hand, and began to mutter a prayer
beneath his breath. Viviane came to his side and joined his
entreaties, feeling helpless as she witnessed Majella's state.

"I see the head!" Monty cried and Majella visibly summoned her resolve. He shook a finger at her. "Give me a
minute here." Viviane did not know what he did but an instant later, he looked up. Majella was watching him avidly,
her eyes glittering. "Next time, *push*! Push as hard as you
can!"

Majella had only the time to nod agreement before she
cried out again in pain. She gripped Niall's hand so tightly
that Viviane saw her nails cut into his skin. Majella's toes
curled, her back arched and her eyes were squeezed tightly
shut.

"Come on, babe, come on!" Monty urged. "You can do it."

Viviane gasped as the baby's head appeared between Majella's thighs. She heard the children stirring behind her but couldn't look away from this marvel. Monty turned the child with gentle fingers and coaxed it out into the world. Majella screamed fit to bring down the walls, and the children awakened and clung to each other.

And the babe suddenly slipped free of its mother. Its expression was anguished, its skin an angry red; it was the most beautiful thing Viviane had ever seen.

And it *was* a boy.

Monty cooed to the child, stroking the mucus away from his nose, then cast a grin at Majella as he scooped the baby into his own purple polarfleece. "You were right, Majella babe. It's a boy and he's looks just perfect."

"Oh!" Majella clasped her child gratefully to her breast and fell back against the pallet, tears of relief streaming down her cheeks. "He lives!"

"Hey, I'm not like some amateur, you know." Monty fastened the teeth of his chemise so it wrapped around the child.

Niall leaned forward and kissed Majella's brow. "Truly you weep whether the news is good or bad," he teased, a tear making its way down his own cheek.

Majella opened her eyes and smiled at him, the affection between them unmistakable. "A child does not care where he enters the world, Niall. Indeed, the son of God himself came in far worse circumstance than this. We are warm, we are fed after a fashion, and we are together." She sighed, the strain leaving her features. "'Tis enough."

"Aye, Majella," he whispered. "I was worried more for mother than child."

And Viviane blinked back her tears.

"You fret overmuch, brother of mine," Majella teased.

Niall kissed his sister's knuckles and might have straightened, but she seized his hand.

"His name is Niall," she insisted quietly, her tears gleaming on her cheeks as she squeezed Niall's fingers. "In honor of your return to us."

At that, Niall turned abruptly away. He paced to the door again, hung his head for a moment, then took a deep breath. "'Tis precious little my return has brought this child, Majella." His voice was soft. "Indeed, you all are compromised by my deeds."

"Hey, like don't get all serious in such a happy moment," Monty insisted. His cocky grin was back in place and he was flushed with his success. "Everything will come out right in the end. Darkest before the dawn and all that." He grinned at Majella. "Cavalry, right? You've got those do-good kind of guys here, don't you? Robin Hood? The Masked Avenger?"

Majella laughed. "Monty, you speak in the most odd way at times. Indeed, I cannot fathom your meaning."

"Well, hey, this medieval reenactment stuff is seriously freaky. I have no idea how it works, but this jazz puts movie theaters to shame. No wonder you guys get so hooked on it." He looked pertly between Niall and Viviane. "So, like what happens next? Who's got the script?"

"Monty, this is no jest," Niall said solemnly. "We are all sentenced to die."

"Yeah, yeah, but everything's going to be okay, right?" Monty demanded. He gestured to Niall. "Like you have *friends*, right? Three Musketeers stuff? All for one and one for all, take that you dastardly villain. This is *some* kind of game. Advanced 3-D Dungeons and Dragons, right? We're not all like gonna die, are we?"

Niall studied each of them in turn, his gaze lingering on Viviane. He looked oddly grey, very tired and less than happy.

"Nay," he said softly. "We are not all going to die."

Viviane heard the conviction in his tone, and knew with sudden clarity that he was prepared to risk his own hide for the sake of theirs. It was so characteristic of the kind of man she knew him to be that she couldn't believe she hadn't guessed it sooner. Viviane stepped forward just as Niall bent and snuffed the candle with one smooth move.

The cell was filled with a blackness so complete that Viviane could not even see her hand before her face. She heard Majella gasp but knew she had to reach Niall's side.

"Guard!" he cried. "We are without a light and a new babe is arrived. For the love of God, grant us a light at least!"

The baby, as though sensing his cue, began to wail.

And then, just as Viviane feared, things happened very fast.

Chapter 18

NIALL MOVED QUICKLY to the door despite the darkness, having memorized both the distance and all within his path in the last moment before snuffing the light. He caught his breath at the sound of footsteps, flattened himself against the wall and prepared to strike.

The door flew open, and a sentry cursed as a thin ray of light fell into the chamber. Niall ascertained that the man was alone, then locked his fists together and clubbed the guard over the head.

"Niall!" Majella cried, but Niall was not interested in reassuring his sister in this moment.

The guard fell soundlessly. Niall hauled him out of the way and eased the door shut behind him. He divested the guard of his keys, his boots, his helm and his tabard, donning them all in a hurry. He bound and gagged the guard deftly, using the man's own hose to render him helpless.

"Matthew?" he muttered.

"Aye?" The boy's voice wavered in the darkness.

"Hit him again if he so much as stirs. I entrust you with this task."

"Aye, Uncle," the boy agreed, his assent launching a tirade of questions from the others.

"But Niall, what are you doing?" Majella cried.

"Where are you like going? What's happening now?"

"Be *silent!*" Niall commanded, then hauled open the door. He heard a flurry of movement, and someone brushed against him. He assumed 'twas Matthew and hissed a warning to the others. "Stay here and feign sleep. I will not be long." Niall fitted the key the guard had held into the lock once more, then checked the corridor between himself and the exit.

No one but Odo in his chamber. Perfect.

He would fret about the guards in the keep above once he encountered them.

Niall took a deep breath and stepped out into the corridor, feigning nonchalance as he reached back to pull the door closed behind himself. He paused. In truth, he was peering down the hall, growing accustomed to the way the helm restricted his vision. Reassured, he pulled the door shut with a clang and turned the key.

"And be quiet, you miserable lot!" he roared in the very same moment that he saw that he had been followed.

Too late Niall realized that that soft brush of cloth had not been Matthew.

It had been Viviane.

A remarkably determined Viviane. She stood with her arms folded across her chest, undaunted by the glare Niall fixed upon her. Now that he had slammed the door so decisively, he could hardly open it again without drawing the attention of other guards and prisoners.

"You will not escape talking with me," she declared in a heated undertone.

Niall looked desperately down the corridor, finding that mercifully they were yet unobserved. "Viviane, this is neither the time nor the place . . ."

She poked him hard in the chest and her eyes flashed. "Then I will follow you until it *is* the time and the place, until we have talked about what has happened here and until I know exactly what you're thinking! Niall of Malloy, if you think for one moment . . ."

Footsteps sounded in the cross corridor and Niall clapped one hand over Viviane's mouth. She gasped as he hauled her back into the shadows. He stood facing the corner, Viviane sheltered before him, her pulse fluttering beneath his hand. He glared at her, hoping she could see enough of his eyes to believe the seriousness of their situation.

"Be still!" he muttered, daring no more than that. Niall prayed first that Viviane could not be seen, and second that she did not choose this moment to challenge him.

A guard paced past Odo's chamber with heavy footsteps and glanced in their direction.

Niall's heart stopped when that man halted, and he was certain 'twas all gone awry before he had even begun.

"All well, Paul?"

Niall said the first thing that came to mind. "Having a piss in the corner, 'tis all," he retorted gruffly.

The other guard chuckled. "I leave you in peace, then." He saluted mockingly. "Enjoy."

He turned and strode away. Niall did not dare to breathe until his footsteps faded from earshot. And then, he was not inclined to take his hand from Viviane's mouth.

Not until he had had his say. "You are not coming with me," he said, his tone low and savage. " 'Tis neither your place nor your task."

Viviane protested beneath the weight of his hand and Niall gave her an impatient shake.

Time was wasting!

"Viviane! 'Tis *dangerous*! I will not risk your welfare in this!" He dropped his voice to a growl. "The best deed you can do is return to the cell and ensure that all remain calm."

"Never!" the lady uttered beneath his hand. Before Niall could swear, she squirmed and pulled his hand to her chin. "I'm going with you, to make sure your welfare isn't risked," she said with that stubborn tone he had begun to recognize.

"I forbid it!"

"Then I will follow you," Viviane insisted.

The worst of it was that Niall knew she would do it.

"What manner of woman are you to show such disregard for your own welfare?" he demanded with no small measure of annoyance.

To his astonishment, Viviane smiled. "I'm a writer," she said, her eyes twinkling. "And you were the one who assured me that I should do my research."

"What nonsense is this?"

She tapped him in the middle of his chest, that admiration dawning in her eyes yet again and seriously affecting Niall's determination to leave her behind. "I want to see a hero in action. You're going to retrieve my moonstone, aren't you?"

And Niall smiled despite himself. He shook his head but she smiled up at him, so certain of his course that he had to challenge her. "What makes you think as much?"

"It's the only way out." Viviane smiled. "We can all wish upon it and be gone. But there's no way that all of us could retrieve it without being caught. And I know that if anyone can get us out of this, it is you, so you must be planning to fetch the stone and return it here."

Niall studied her, the light in Viviane's eyes bolstering his conviction that he truly could repair all that had gone awry. Indeed, 'twas hard to resist the temptation of spending a little longer in Viviane's company before they were parted for all time.

"You will do as I bid you," he insisted gruffly, knowing full well that she would not. He gripped her shoulders and stared down into her marvelous eyes even as her smile broadened. Indeed, he suspected that he had not fooled her a whit—she seemed just as persuaded as ever that he was her knight.

And Niall could not honestly say that he was disappointed. Still he had to guard his tongue and not give her a reason to be unhappy once their paths parted as indeed they must.

He did not trouble to correct the false assumptions in her summary of his plan. 'Twas true he meant to retrieve the stone, 'twas true that he intended to bring it back here.

But that was so Viviane and Monty could leave as one. Niall briefly considered the wisdom of fetching Monty now, but discarded it immediately. The man could not keep silent and he was too odd in appearance. He would attract attention, the last thing they needed.

To be sure, so might Viviane, but Niall could not deny himself this last indulgence of her company.

"You will heed me, you will do *naught* that is reckless. And you will be silent."

The lady threw her arms around Niall's neck and kissed the tip of his nose through the front of the helm, nearly bouncing in her anticipation.

"I knew you would let me come," she declared gleefully. "Just as I know that I'll get the truth out of you. You must have some feelings for me, regardless of what you say, and I'm not leaving your side until I know the truth of it."

Niall's blood froze that she should be able to read his thoughts so readily as that. He glowered at her, to no visible effect.

But Viviane appeared jubilant and Niall knew there was only one matter that made her so happy as this.

Zounds, but she was going to talk of love again!

'Twas only a matter of time. And Niall knew himself well enough to know that he was a poor liar, certainly poor enough that Viviane would not be deceived.

He had no time to waste.

"Where are we going?" the lady demanded. "And what are we going to do? How are we going to save the others? I just knew you would have a plan, because that's what real heroes do—they have a plan and they take a chance and they put themselves at risk to see the people they care about safe, and you know . . ."

Niall enforced his dictate for silence in the only way that

he knew for certain would work. He caught Viviane's jaw in his hand, bent down and kissed her soundly.

As 'twas likely to be his last taste of the lady, he made it a kiss to remember.

Indeed, when he was done, Viviane clutched his shoulders as though she could not trust her legs to keep her upright. She ran the tip of her tongue across her lips so slowly that he nearly kissed her again. Niall's heart thundered as Viviane stared up at him with wonder, as though he had hung the stars in the firmament.

That sense of invincibility redoubled in a most intoxicating way. Niall grinned down at Viviane and tapped the tip of her nose with one fingertip. Truly, he could not resist teasing her.

"Finally," he said, heaving the sigh of a man sorely tested. "Silence!"

And before Viviane could comment or even gasp, Niall pivoted. He seized her hand and led her down the empty hall at a hasty pace. Truly, they had already lingered overlong.

For Niall knew, there would be no second chances this night.

Viviane realized very quickly that her impulsiveness could cost them both dearly. Niall, after all, looked just like any of the other guards in the keep and could have passed undetected without her presence beside him. But even with Odo's cloak over her shoulders and the hood over her hair, Viviane was an oddity whose presence prompted questions from all they encountered.

After the second intervention, Niall clearly got tired of making up tales, then having to knock out the questioner anyway. He cut right to the chase—as Monty would have said—and took the third sentry down before that man could even open his mouth. Niall had harvested a sword from the first sentry and a dagger from the second, now entrusted Viviane with the dagger of the third.

"Hide it," he instructed tersely, gripped her hand and moved on.

The corridors of the keep were filled with shadows, only lit with flickering torches. The keep was silent, that silence only periodically interrupted with the distant sound of footfalls or snores. The corridors twisted and turned, branching over and over again, and Viviane was glad that Niall knew the way.

And that he certainly did. He moved quickly through the labyrinth, deftly dodging from shadow to shadow, his boots making no sound on the stone floors. Viviane tried to follow suit, though she was sure anyone would be able to hear the frightened pounding of her heart.

But after that third guard, they encountered no others.

In fact, the keep was almost too quiet.

They reached the hall and traversed its brooding breadth, the act of stepping out of the shadows making Viviane understand how wild things felt when they left the underbrush. She was certain that a thousand eyes followed their course from the half-hidden doorways circling the room and knew she saw the gleam of eyes more than once.

But Niall cut a brisk pace to the stairs, then shoved her up them. The sentry at the first floor made a soft cry when he fell, Niall and Viviane freezing for a breathless moment until 'twas clear none would come to his aid.

A pair of servants slept along the corridor here, the very sight troubling Viviane. Niall strode on, his step silent, and just as they passed the second sleeping servant, Viviane tripped. She caught herself and snatched at Niall's back to keep from falling, her inadvertent move prompting him to glance back.

His eyes flashed emerald fire and his arm flew out. Viviane jumped at the close proximity of the clang of steel on steel.

That last servant had leapt to his feet and had meant to strike them down. Viviane gasped and got out of the way, her eyes widening in horror as the men battled.

The fight was swift, that servant equipped with only a small blade. Niall dispatched him with a trio of blows, each harder than the last, and the man slumped to the floor. Viviane eyed his fallen body in shock as she understood fully the danger of their course, but Niall seized her arm, his expression grim.

He jerked a thumb in the direction of the next staircase and urged her onward once more. This time, he kept his blade unsheathed and Viviane knew he expected a challenge.

She remembered that these stairs led to the archbishop's chamber. Niall must be assuming that the moonstone was still there, though how he imagined they would snatch it from under the archbishop's nose, Viviane couldn't guess.

Maybe that man slept heavily.

Maybe he slept elsewhere.

Niall must know something she didn't know.

The stairs were more narrow here, the shadows deeper. In fact, it seemed as though a cold draught flowed down the stairs like a silvery fog. Viviane could almost see it, despite the darkness, and thought it was seeping from under the door at the summit. It glowed faintly, the light increasing as they progressed up the stairs, and reminded her unexpectedly of her moonstone.

But fog didn't spread *within* a keep.

She and Niall exchanged a puzzled glance, their steps slowing of one accord. Niall shrugged and they continued on, their gazes flicking from one side to the other. Nothing but bare stone greeted their eyes, not a sound echoed ahead or behind. A single torch was mounted above the landing at the top of the stairs, its light dancing over the stone.

Viviane's palms were damp, her breathing was short, her heart was pounding. They halted on the tiny landing before the door and Viviane had a very bad feeling about what was behind it.

Not just because this was the chamber where she had most recently been condemned to die.

The fog around their feet now obscured their legs below the knee. It was luminescent and so cold that Viviane shivered involuntarily.

Niall pushed the tip of his sword gently against the door. It was unlocked.

The door opened inward without a sound, yawning wide open just from that single slight touch. The cloud of silvery fog rolled forth to engulf their legs completely, but that wasn't why Viviane gasped in astonishment.

The archbishop stood there, his gaze fixed upon them. "Do come in," he invited amiably, a thread of steel in his tone.

Chapter 19

AROUND THE PERIMETER of the archbishop's room stood all the guards Viviane and Niall had not encountered on their way. The guards' faces were frozen, their stares distant, their bodies did not move. They stood as men enchanted and unaware of all that passed before them.

Viviane shivered anew. She might have hung back, but Niall squared his shoulders and stepped forward, and her hand was still clasped within his.

The door closed with a bang behind them, apparently of its own accord. Viviane jumped and glanced back, but Niall didn't look away from the archbishop.

"I have been expecting you." The archbishop stepped back with a sweep of his black robes to reveal a large mirror. But the image reflected was not that of the room—it was the dungeon far below, where Majella and Monty cradled that woman's new child.

The scene moved. Viviane started when Monty tickled the baby's chin and Majella laughed at his antics.

"Witchery!" Niall muttered and the archbishop smiled.

"I prefer sorcery as a term, myself, but indeed 'tis much the same thing." He picked up Viviane's moonstone pendant and wiggled it, much as a fisherman wiggles a baited hook before his prey. "You will have come for this, I assume."

"It is mine," Viviane asserted.

"Nay, 'twas never yours in truth," the archbishop argued smoothly. "'Twas granted to you for a time, 'tis true, but such a token only ever *belongs* to its maker."

Niall's hand tightened around Viviane's own. "And you know who that maker was." There was no question in his voice.

The archbishop's smile was as cold as the mist obscuring the floor of his chamber. It rolled from a bowl before the mirror, Viviane noted, a bowl of such peculiar hue that she could not look at it for very long.

"No less than the finest sorcerer in all the land," the archbishop declared. He turned the stone so that it caught the light and straightened with pride. "I wrought it, of mist and moonlight and adder's breath." He arched a brow before Viviane could ask how it had come to her. "I wrought it in honor of the birth of mine own spawn."

Viviane was shocked that he could lie about such a thing, just to lay claim to her pendant. "But that's impossible! My father gave this to my moth . . ."

"Oh!" Viviane gasped and took a step backward, her horror complete when the archbishop's smile never wavered.

"Indeed," he said with the satisfaction of a well-fed cat. "I see my intellect has passed to you." He inclined his head slightly. "How very flattering."

Viviane's bile rose. *This* man was her father? It couldn't be!

But suddenly she recalled the moment when her mother had told her the tale of the stone. It had been here, in Cantlecroft, after a procession of the archbishop passed by. That man had been waving at the crowd without truly looking at any of them. Viviane's mother had turned pale, then later instructed Viviane to take the pendant to the archbishop if ever her fortune wavered.

She had died a fortnight later, before Viviane could ask the reason why.

Now, she knew. Her mother had recognized the father of her child. He could not have been the archbishop in the days of Viviane's conception. Perhaps her mother had not known where he had gone.

Viviane wished that they had never found out.

"Viviane is your daughter?" Niall demanded, his outrage clear. "And you condemned your own blood to die? What manner of man is so faithless as that?"

The archbishop folded his arms across his chest and looked impatient. "Truly, 'tis hard to believe that I once thought you keen of wit, Niall of Malloy. Do you know what 'twould do to my reputation to be found responsible for the birth of a bastard?"

"'Twould seem most clever then to refrain from indulging earthly pleasures," Niall retorted, his eyes flashing. Viviane assumed he was thinking of Majella.

"Deny myself?" The archbishop laughed. "I think not." He gestured broadly to the room. "Indeed, I pursued this path to ensure my own comfort, and see no reason to abandon the pleasures of the flesh." He arched a brow. "As indeed, I see no reason to make all aware of my indiscretions. Nay, the moonstone served the purpose 'twas wrought to serve."

"But what of the stone's powers?" Viviane demanded. "Why grant such a gift to a child?"

The archbishop frowned and glanced to the table that the bowl rested upon. Viviane caught a glimpse of the winking stone and knew it still lay there. "I did not know," he confessed in a low voice. "I never guessed it had such power, though indeed the revelation is most useful."

"Grant the stone to Viviane again," Niall urged, stepping forward to make his appeal. "Let her flee Cantlecroft forever. 'Twould be the same to you as if she died."

"Nay, Niall, I could not go alone . . ." Viviane protested, but the archbishop ignored her.

"But she could return at any moment. 'Twould be folly to give another such power over me!"

"She would pledge to not do so! She would swear it, I know it well!"

The archbishop laughed. "And I am to accept a sworn pledge as ample guarantee. 'Tis mockable! And you would have me sacrifice this marvel?" The archbishop scoffed. "I think not. 'Tis far, far preferable that you die and this marvel of mine own creation remains safely here. Indeed, I have a temptation to visit these other centuries and learn their secrets."

"'Tis abominable!" Niall muttered. "How could a man send his own child to die?"

But the archbishop glanced at Viviane. "Nay, 'twas *convenient*. I knew as soon as word came of your arrival, and that you showed such a stone, that you were the fruit of my loins. And that, dear daughter, was why you had to die."

He stepped back and lifted his hands. "'Tis why you still will die."

The archbishop clapped his hands and the guards came to life as one. "Guards!" he cried as they bristled to attention. There were so many of them, even more than Viviane had first glimpsed, a good two dozen ringing the room. "The witch has freed herself and must be killed!"

And he pointed one finger directly at Viviane. The guards brandished their swords, gave a cry and closed in on Viviane as one.

"*Nay!*" Niall roared and lunged forward. Viviane's hand was still grasped in his and he hauled her across the room. He cut down the first attacker with a single blow, his course unswerving and Viviane knew exactly what he was trying to do.

He was going to get that stone.

And she was going to do all she could to help him!

Viviane pulled out her dagger and jabbed at the face of the man who snatched at her cloak. His visor was up and she caught the end of his nose, the sharpness of her blade surprising her. It nicked off the end of his nose and he bled profusely, crying out and grabbing at the wound.

Niall roared and slashed down another, releasing Viviane's hand to grip his hilt and wield his blade like a scythe. He cut a path through their attackers, while Viviane jabbed at all of those who might have fallen on his back.

They were closer, almost within reach of the table. But they were losing the battle, even Viviane could see.

"Kill her, kill him, *kill them*!" shrieked the archbishop.

The guards closed in, Viviane's small blade no match for their heavy swords. She fought as well as she could, trying to be unpredictable and nick whoever came within range.

"Niall," she whispered desperately when four closed ranks against her. They would never make it to that little table in time.

"Duck," he muttered and Viviane had only a heartbeat to follow his bidding before he straightened with a bellow. He pivoted, swinging the sword low and scattered their opponents. One fell, the others danced back.

And Viviane could see the moonstone. She tried to reach it, but Niall roared. Viviane glanced up in time to see a blade glance off his shoulder. She stabbed upright into the neck of the man who dealt Niall the blow, her dagger slipping between his hauberk and helm. He screamed and fell away, Niall straightened and cast her a grateful glance.

The stone winked. Two more guards were closing fast and Viviane had to take the only chance she had. She darted under Niall's arm when he raised his sword again and barely managed to reach the pendant.

Her fingers brushed against it and she scrabbled for a grip. Her heart leapt as she snatched it up. Viviane pulled her hand back just as a wicked blade sliced down like a guillotine. She backed toward Niall, clutching the moonstone over her heart and more than ready to wish.

But Niall wasn't there.

Viviane spun in dismay, only to find that they had been separated. Half a dozen men surrounded Niall, drawing his strikes to one side then another. Viviane saw that they were deliberately forcing him away from her.

The beleaguered Niall glanced up and she knew immediately that he had reached the same conclusion.

"Go!" he cried.

Viviane was appalled. "I cannot!"

"You must," Niall insisted through gritted teeth. He fended off another blow, the near miss making Viviane gasp in fear for his survival.

"But I love you!" she cried, fearing she might never have another chance to tell him so.

"I know," Niall muttered, his low voice audible despite the din. His eyes met hers for an endless moment. "I beg of you, Viviane, do not let me die for naught."

Steel clashed on steel and Niall swore as his hand was nicked. They set upon him with purpose and Viviane could only watch in horror.

"How touching," the archbishop mused at startling proximity.

Viviane jumped, she turned, she found him closing upon her with malice gleaming in his eyes. Two guards were right behind him, another three cutting off Viviane's escape.

And even her tiny blade was gone. Niall still valiantly battled for his freedom off to her right. As much as Viviane wanted to see the outcome of that, she forced herself to watch this most dangerous opponent as he drew near. A lump rose in her throat.

The archbishop halted and stretched out his hand. "Give me the moonstone," he urged, his eyes narrowed. "Give it to me now and I might let you live."

"Liar!" Viviane cried in outrage. His eyes flashed, telling her she had guessed the truth and he stepped forward with no good intent for her.

"Viviane!" Niall roared. *"Flee!"*

With no other choice remaining, Viviane tightened her hand around the moonstone and wished. Her last sight of

Cantlecroft was of the archbishop, his features contorted with fury as he leapt to grab her.

He missed.

Barely.

His anguished cry echoed in Viviane's ears long after the blinding light had surrounded her. She was chilled right to the bone this time, quaking to the depths of her soul. She cried as she had never cried before, knowing that Niall was too heavily beset to survive that battle.

And there was nothing she could do about it now.

She opened her eyes to the blinding glint of sunlight on azure seas, turned and saw the familiar pines and wept anew. It was the beach beside Ganges harbor, Viviane would have known it anywhere.

She was back and she was alone.

But surely she could fix that. Surely she could go back right now and do something, distract the guards or call for reinforcements or somehow save Niall. Surely!

Viviane took a deep breath and fumbled with the pendant as she tried to figure out what exactly to wish. But her fingers were so cold that the pendant slipped from her grip.

And before her horrified gaze, it fell.

She snatched after it, but to no avail. The moonstone hurtled to the earth, struck a stone and shattered to a thousand shards of cold blue light.

No! Viviane fell on her knees, desperate to sweep up the bits. She was close enough to see that eerie light wink out of each and every piece. Even knowing it was useless, she tried to catch the pieces before the next wave swept in from the sea.

But the shards were almost immediately swallowed by the water. They danced before Viviane's eyes and she wept, knowing she couldn't catch them all but still having to try.

In the end, the sea took all of the broken moonstone and Viviane was left shaking on Salt Spring's beach, a heavy piece of silver in her hand and nothing but an ache in her heart.

She sat down on the beach, oblivious to the chill and the incoming waves and cried like a child. For there could be no turning back time again.

Niall of Malloy was lost to Viviane forever.

$\mathcal{C}hapter$ 20

WHAT VIVIANE DID not linger long enough to see in Cantlecroft was the procession of torches heading toward the palace. They flickered in the darkness beyond the windows of the archbishop's chamber, drawing that man's attention away from Viviane's abrupt disappearance.

He stared at the wavering line of fire, the orange flames licking at the blackness of the night, and knew a shadow of dread. Indeed, he had not honed his abilities all these years for naught—though this portent was impossible to miss.

His reign was to be challenged.

The archbishop's lip curled at these peasants having the audacity to defy him. He would see their insurrection brought low! He would see them all executed, slowly and painfully.

"Guards!" he cried and spun to face the room, pleased with the way his robes flared out behind him. The men halted as one, more than one blade held at Niall of Malloy's throat. That man glared back at the archbishop with a rare insolence that irked beyond all.

Later. He would save this one for later and make him writhe. It was Niall of Malloy, after all, who had retrieved the witch who was at the root of it all. And 'twas Niall of Malloy who had compelled the archbishop to condemn a very sweet bit of temptation, taking Majella from his bed.

No matter how he viewed it, Niall of Malloy had cheated him.

The archbishop pointed to the advancing masses, their murmuring already audible, with every vestige of righteous indignation he could summon. "Intruders come to assault the keep! Go forth and slaughter them all!"

The captain of the guard moved to one window, tipped his visor and frowned. "But my lord, this is no army. 'Tis the people of Cantlecroft!"

"Aye! They rebel against my authority. They are sinners, one and all! We have no need of prisoners. I have no obligation to feed and shelter them all in my dungeons at considerable expense. Kill them!"

Gaultier hesitated most tellingly.

The archbishop leaned closer. "Fear not," he said smoothly, "for God will recognize his own."

Gaultier frowned. "But my lord, with respect, there was some trouble in the village after Aaron Goldsmith's demise and it would seem wise . . ."

The archbishop drew himself to his full height. "And you would question my wisdom."

The captain of the guard looked down. "Nay, my lord. Of course not, my lord, but still . . ."

"If you choose to defy me, then you may be the first to die," the archbishop amended with a smile, letting threat slide into his tone. "'Tis unhealthy to foster disobedience within one's guard."

Gaultier's lips thinned and he closed his visor with a snap. "Your will shall be done, my lord." His voice hardened. "As always." He gestured to Niall of Malloy. "What of this one?"

The archbishop settled back in his favored chair, flicked his robes and smiled. "I tire of this digression. Divest him of his blade and kill him."

'Twould be perfect, truly. The archbishop had little doubt that his daughter would return. Aye, those ensnared by love's sweet lie oft made foolish choices at their own expense. She would return for Niall of Malloy.

And the knight's bleeding body would distract her sufficiently long enough for the archbishop to retrieve his moonstone. As an added advantage, Niall of Malloy would interfere with the archbishop's plans no longer.

Perhaps he would "forgive" Majella, once her brother was dead.

"My lord?"

"You heard my command, Gaultier," the archbishop snapped. "I will see him dead by your own hand and immediately." He inclined a hand toward the window and the sound of the approaching hordes. "You have other labor at hand."

One of the guards divested Niall of his sword, though that man released his blade reluctantly. A nick on the wrist persuaded him to surrender it, and he was quickly divested of his other, smaller, blade.

Still Niall stood with defiance, his gaze unswerving from the archbishop's. "You take naught from me," he said in a low voice. "Viviane, who was innocent of your charges, is free."

The archbishop saw the guards turn to look at him, questioningly. "For the moment. 'Tis of no matter." He gestured impatiently to Gaultier.

"Is it not?" Niall demanded, the command in his tone apparently compelling the captain of the guard to pause. "All of these men witnessed her departure, inexplicable by any other than magical means."

He turned to the guards as he pointed to the archbishop. "'Twas *this* man who devised those magical means, this man who has the power of sorcery beneath his hand." Niall fixed the archbishop with a telling glance. "Would you have all these guards killed—as you swore to have me killed—simply for knowing of the truth?"

The archbishop clenched his hands on the arms of his chair. He could nigh feel the doubt sliding through the ranks of his own men. Such impertinence!

"He lies! And he lies so well because he is beneath the spell of that convicted witch. Kill him now, before you are bewitched in turn!"

"How long have you stood in this chamber, Gaultier?" Niall asked crisply. "Do you recall my arrival here? 'Twas you who were enchanted when I arrived and it could not have been by Viviane, who was imprisoned in the dungeons at that time."

Gaultier pushed up his visor again, glancing over his shoulder to the archbishop. His gaze fell tellingly to the bowl, which still exuded the mist necessary for such minor spells.

"Lies!" the archbishop cried, desperate to see his will done. "Can you not see how he undermines your thoughts? 'Tis the way of sorcerers and witches, to make their twisted thoughts seem as your own. Kill him while you can! Kill him afore 'tis too late for all of us!"

"I cannot kill an unarmed man," the captain of the guard said slowly.

"*He is not unarmed!* He casts spells even as you hesitate to do what is right!"

"I know naught of spells and sorcery," Niall insisted softly. "I am but a man of honor, deceived by the man who had the least right to serve me poorly." He arched a brow. "Do not believe for a moment, Gaultier, that you are any less disposable to this one. He would have killed Viviane simply because she was his own child and he wished none to know he had spawned a bastard."

Gaultier's eyes widened in alarm, but the archbishop leapt off his chair. "Nay! You infect their thoughts with lies!" He snatched the blade of one of the sentries and drove it toward Niall's throat.

That man did not step away, his gaze did not waver. Insolence! He deserved to die!

But 'twas not Niall of Malloy who felt the bite of a blade at his throat. The archbishop choked on the cold bite of steel. He looked up the length of the blade, even as his grip on his own faltered, to find disappointment in Gaultier's dark eyes.

"No man of honor kills an unarmed man," he declared quietly. "And no man kills his own spawn." He turned to Niall. "'Tis telling indeed that I do not recall this man's arrival in these chambers, nor do I recall the sun fading from the sky this day." Gaultier smiled thinly. "As you well recall, my lord, I have a fine memory. And I have never liked that bowl."

With that, his lips tightened and the archbishop felt the blade bite deeper.

He knew no more after that, which in the end was good. 'Twould have nigh killed him to see his magical bowl dropped from that window to shatter on the stones below.

He would have been troubled to know that shortly thereafter, peasants flowed freely through his halls and partook of their bounty. He would not have appreciated seeing prisoners released en masse, or Aaron Goldsmith's sons granted many of the gold coins locked safely in the treasury as compense for their parents' untimely death. He would have been sorely distressed to witness those same peasants set fire to his keep and stand back silently to watch it burn.

He certainly would not have been pleased to see Niall of Malloy turn his back on Cantlecroft virtually unscathed, though he might well have savored the shadows in that man's eyes.

Contrary to his own expectation, Niall of Malloy was not dead.

And contrary to a small stubborn hope, Viviane had not returned to seek him out. Niall could not help but be disappointed, despite his own good health. He tended his duties, retrieved his sister, her children and Monty from the dungeon, then led them away from the chaos that had seized Cantlecroft.

"Wowsers," Monty declared as they walked away from the burning of the keep. "This is like some kind of Sensoround experience. How does this work? Where are the projectors? It's like almost *real*. No wonder you people get so hooked on it!"

Majella chuckled and shook her head at his manner, but Niall frowned. "'Tis real, Monty."

The other man blinked, then hastened to match his step to Niall's. "What the hell are you talking about? What do you mean *real*?"

"'Tis truly happening. The archbishop is truly dead, his keep truly burns, those peasants so glad to see the end of him will likely have another unworthy overlord before the year is out." Niall sighed, feeling the world had no promise at all. He could have used a measure of Viviane's cheer, but 'twas clear he was not to have it.

Perhaps she did not truly love him after all.

Or perhaps, love was a fleeting thing for his Viviane. Niall's heart ached with the certainty that his love would not be fleeting. Nay, he would cherish her memory until his dying day.

Alone.

But Viviane was not faithless. Viviane had pledged her love to him. Indeed, Niall's heart still sang a little in recollection of her words. Her ardor had shone in her eyes so that he could not doubt her sincerity.

And Viviane was one who held her course. Nay, if she did not return, then 'twas because she *could not* return.

Though that did little to improve Niall's mood. Six centuries were still lodged firmly between the two and the prospect of matters remaining that way did naught to bolster his spirits.

Aye, he could live *decades*.

"But, but, but," Monty's words and steps faltered. He looked over his shoulder, staring back at the keep as Niall trudged onward. "But that would mean that this really is 1390 in Cantlecroft!"

"Oh course 'tis that," Majella retorted, rolling her eyes and twitching her skirts as she passed him. She was tired and Niall could see the truth of it. He took her elbow and she smiled for him, letting him carry the new babe still wrapped in Monty's chemise. "And what of Viviane?" she asked pertly.

Niall shrugged. "She is gone."

"Not dead?"

"Nay, she fled to another place." Niall had a sense he should not speak overmuch of where he had been and what had happened.

"Is she coming back?" Matthew demanded as he came to hang on to Niall's scabbard.

"I do not think so."

"So, she's just like gone! And I'm just like *stuck*! What is that all about?"

"There is naught to be done about the matter, Monty," Niall said tiredly. "We shall all have to become accustomed to the change."

" 'Twill be no easier for you than for her, Niall," Majella murmured. "That woman did not leave by her own choice, or at least 'tis something of import keeping her from your side. I know a smitten woman when I see one"—she shook a finger under his nose with affection—"not to mention a smitten man."

Niall could not smile, even at his sister's teasing. He wanted only to leave this place behind them. His knee ached with vigor and it seemed that Dame Fortune had not smiled overmuch on him this day.

"But this is all impossible!" Monty cried. "It's nuts. It can't be 1390 . . ."

" 'Tis not impossible if 'tis obviously so," Majella snapped. She rolled her eyes and gave Niall's elbow a squeeze. Monty muttered behind them, but neither spared him much notice.

He would come to terms with his fate, Niall guessed.

'Twas regrettable that Monty had not been able to return to his own time with Viviane, but what was done was done.

And there was naught *he* could do about it. Aye, his life was a failure from one end to the other.

"Where is it we are going?" Majella asked.

"I do not know. Away. As far as possible."

"Hmm. If we continue on to Ledworth, which is just along the way a bit, there is a friend of mine who might see his way to lending us a chamber or two."

"A *friend*?" Niall could not help but ask, his tone chilly. "What manner of friend?"

"Exactly the manner of *friend* you are thinking," his sister declared, her tone so surprisingly sharp that he glanced at her. Her eyes were snapping. "In all honesty, Niall, how many choices do you believe that I have had?"

"You did wed twice."

"Aye, and had five children as a result. How many men do you believe would willingly take on such a number of babes that were not his own?" Majella held up an impatient hand. "You have not to answer that, for I know the answer. *None!* Not a one and 'twas not for a lack of trying on my part! I am not even plain!" she cried. "But it mattered not. Any man who professed his interest changed his thinking when he saw my babes." She flicked a glance Niall's way and her voice softened. "And what was I to do? Abandon my own blood?"

Niall slipped her hand from the crook of his arm, capturing it within the warmth of his own. "Nay, Majella, but you had my aid."

"Oh, Niall, 'twas good of you and I knew it well, just as I knew it could not last. However fond you are of my children, they are not your children. And you can be certain that even if you felt an obligation, many a wife would not have looked kindly upon your support of me."

She reached up and patted his cheek. "'Twas only a matter of time before you had babes of your own and a man's coin can only stretch so far. Nay, I did what I had need of doing. For my babes." She lifted her chin proudly and Niall felt a surge of admiration for her resolve.

He had underestimated Majella, for she was indeed driven by a kind of practicality. 'Twas unexpected and noble, though still he was not enamored of her means. The children could learn that a family should be thus, that a woman should whore to feed her babes, that a father need not take responsibility for the planting of his seed. 'Twas a dangerous example that could color their own futures.

"But Majella . . ."

"Oh, but *naught*! Do not lecture me upon right and wrong in this moment, Niall of Malloy, after the day we have had." Majella granted him a scathing glance. "'Tis true enough that these deeds won me more babes and I know it well enough, but all of them ate well and slept in warm beds at night. A man tends to be indulgent of his mistress, as he would not be of a wife."

"We had fine suppers at Ledworth," Matthew contributed and Niall was horrified that at least he understood much of what his mother did.

Zounds, would Matthew grow up believing that what Majella had done was *right*?

"Look at this babe, Niall," Majella urged, running a gentle finger along the cheek of her brood's newest member. "Have you ever seen such innocence? Such sweetness? When I look at my children, it matters little from whence they have come. They are here, they are my joy"—her voice hardened—"and I will do anything to ensure their welfare." She looked up at Niall, her eyes glittering with determination. *"Anything."*

And Niall realized that he and his sister shared this resolve. He recognized the power of the love that drove her, for he had also felt its bite. Indeed, he would have done anything to see Viviane safe, he had nigh done as much. He had shredded his own hopes to see her granted her own. He would not have regretted his own death, if it had seen her free.

Perhaps he and Majella had more in common than he had oft believed.

"Ledworth, then," he conceded, giving her fingers a squeeze. "As Matthew so heartily recommends the fare."

They trudged in silence, each lost in their thoughts. Niall wondered whether he could find employ as a man at arms in Ledworth, or if he should wait and offer his services to whoever assumed suzerainty of Cantlecroft. Behind them, Monty muttered to himself, his soft swearing periodically interjected with the word "impossible".

"You are dying to know, I am certain," Majella finally said and Niall thought it rude to confess his lack of comprehension. "And I suppose you should know sooner rather than later." She smiled up at Niall, then dropped her voice to a whisper. "This friend in Ledworth is this one's father. I suspect he would like to see the babe."

"But not take responsibility for it?" Niall asked stiffly.

Majella laughed aloud. "Oh, his wife would not care for that!"

And Niall was shocked to silence. He stared at the child who bore his own name and could not think of a thing to say.

Except maybe one.

"And the others?" he asked softly.

Majella sighed. "Timothy is his fruit as well," she admitted, referring to the toddler ahead of them. "'Tis how I can so readily guess his response. He will want to see the child, he will grant me some coin and a kiss." Majella's smile faded. "Then he will return to his wife and the four babes of that match, who know him as their father in truth. I shall be expected to leave quietly, so that his wife is not disturbed by these hints of his indiscretions."

"To another friend."

Majella lifted her chin. "Aye."

Her ensuing silence was telling and Niall knew that she was not so pleased with her situation as she would have him believe.

Before he could say anything, Monty stepped up beside

Majella. He scooped up Timothy when the boy stumbled and the child nestled against his shoulder with a sigh. Monty held the next eldest Elizabeth by the hand. The other children trailed behind him sleepily, except Matthew who was yet fast by Niall's side.

Listening, no doubt.

"Hey, babe, you have like sold yourself way short of the measure," that man said, much to brother and sister's surprise.

"What do you know of it?" Majella demanded. "A man has no obligation to care for his children, he has no need to even look upon their faces when they come into the world."

Monty's lips thinned. "Any man with a soul would be happy enough just to look at your face for the rest of his life."

"Oh!" Majella blushed, then glanced sidelong at Monty. "Oh!" Monty trudged along without looking at her, as though he was embarrassed by his own comment. "I have yet to thank you for your aid."

"Hey, it was nothing. You like did all the tough stuff." He winked at her, his smile tired. "Came through like a trooper."

"Oh." Majella's cheeks stayed stubbornly pink, but Niall was not interested in their mutual admiration. He wanted all the truth laid bare now that opportunity presented itself.

"And Elizabeth?" he asked gently.

Majella bit her lip, her fingers tightening on his as Monty was evidently forgotten. "Oh, Niall, I lied to you and I am sorry."

But Niall had already suspected as much and had for a long time. He smiled at his sister. "That Elizabeth was born overly late of your second husband's seed?"

Majella blinked. "Oh, that as well! I have lied to you *twice* then. Will you forgive me?"

Now Niall was surprised. "Tell me first of the lie."

Majella averted her gaze and her voice dropped low. "Remember when you asked me when I had joined the archbishop in his chamber?"

A cold hand clenched around Niall's heart. "Aye."

"Well, 'twas not recently. 'Tis true that I knew Richard afore, some years ago."

"Nay, Majella. Not Elizabeth."

'Twas indicative of that child's exhaustion that she did not even glance up at her name. Monty, Niall noted with approval, eased Elizabeth slightly further away from her mother that there might be no danger of her overhearing what was said.

The two men's gazes held for a significant moment and Niall saw a new seriousness in the man he assumed to never be serious.

Perhaps 'twould serve Majella well to know a man with midwifery skills.

"Aye, Niall, 'tis not a pretty tale. Richard came to the funeral, indeed he read the Mass, and he was such an elegant man. He was so very charming to me."

"I recall his presence," Niall acknowledged, though at the time, he had assumed grieving Majella unaware of such details.

Majella heaved a sigh. "Truly I had never seen a man so finely wrought and he was such endearing company. And you know, that match was not a good one. 'Twas difficult to mourn its passing. And Richard was so marvelous. He visited me numerous times . . ."

"Spare me the detail," Niall interjected.

"Well, there *was* a child, you might as well know it all. From the marriage. I was carrying it at the funeral. But I lost it and was so upset. A babe lost! 'Twas devastating—yet Richard came and was so compassionate, and well, I suppose 'twas not within me to refuse a little affection when so much had gone so recently awry . . ."

"And then you conceived again."

Majella bit her lip and nodded. "I could not see the harm

in insisting 'twas the same child come late. Indeed, 'twas how I preferred to think of it."

And no doubt how the archbishop preferred to think of it, knowing now his distaste for bastards. Niall could not help but look back at the girl.

Elizabeth was the archbishop's child.

She was Viviane's half-sister, which was a most curious thought.

Niall halted suddenly and seized Majella's elbow. "Did he ever grant the child a gift?"

Majella looked flustered as the babe in Niall's arms began to stir at his abrupt move. "Well, he did, but 'twas no large thing and certainly not appropriate for a small child . . ."

"A pendant. He gave her a pendant." Niall's voice rose in his excitement. "'Tis mounted with a moonstone."

Majella stared up at him, her confusion clear. "How could you know that?" she demanded and his heart began to pound. If Viviane could not come to him, then Niall would go to her! It could be done! "Niall, what is this about? You look most fevered, which is not like you in the least."

"Did he or did he not give the child a pendant?"

"You sound as Richard did," Majella said crossly. "He insisted on knowing what had happened to that cursed stone and I lied to him, for I did not like the look in his eyes. And I did not like how he looked at Elizabeth. But how could you know of her pendant? The child has not even seen it herself . . ."

"Where is it, Majella? Where is the stone?"

She huffed and glared at him as the baby fussed, then plucked the child out of his arms. "I left it at our lodgings when we came to wish you well. 'Tis in the care of the keeper . . ."

"Do you trust this man fully?"

Majella smiled ruefully, then cooed for the baby. "As much as any. What ails you so? Why is this of such import?"

"We must retrieve it, Majella."

"We cannot. 'Tis too far. And indeed, it belongs to Elizabeth," Majella insisted with a stubborn heft of her chin. "'Tis hers by right and it shall remain hers for as long as I have anything to say of the matter."

Niall halted and pulled his sister around to face him, letting her see his determination. "Zounds, Majella, it cannot be too far! I shall carry each and every one of you upon my shoulders, if needs demand it. We must retrieve the pendant with all haste!"

"This is of great import to you."

"'Tis all to me," Niall acknowledged. "But you speak aright in that it belongs to Elizabeth. Truth be told, this pendant could win her much, far more than her father ever believed when he granted it." Niall smiled encouragement when his sister looked astonished. "Let me tell you a tale, Majella, and at the end, you shall make the choice of what is to be done." He squeezed her shoulders once. "I swear it to you."

Chapter 21

THE THIRD REJECTION letter was the last straw.

Viviane opened the package from New York with shaking fingers, hoping that it held better news than the last two had, then sighed with disappointment.

Maybe she wasn't a good writer, after all. In fact, the third publisher had taken three pages to enumerate all the things they disliked about her tale. Viviane shoved the letter back into the envelope with the dog-eared manuscript and left the store, feeling Barb's sympathetic gaze follow her. Viviane was glad Barb didn't say anything because she probably would have just started to cry.

In the end, it didn't seem that she was such a lucky person after all.

Maybe she just couldn't believe in her father's goodwill anymore, not after having met the nasty person in question. Maybe the moonstone had been her good luck talisman, despite her father's malice, and losing it had ended Viviane's lifelong streak of good fortune. Maybe it was really about attitude—as so many books insisted—but Viviane couldn't summon the energy to care.

It had been six weeks since her return and she missed

Niall every bit as much as that first day. Maybe more. It certainly wasn't getting any easier to be without him, despite what some of the books in Barb's shop insisted.

It was being without Niall, without her one true love, that ate away at her and Viviane knew it.

Just as she knew there wasn't anything she could do about it.

She didn't have to like it.

Viviane lay awake at night, wondering whether Niall had even survived that night and hating that she would never know. His armor taunted her from the floor where he had left it, tormenting her with the fact that its presence *here* could have been responsible for his death *there*.

She had finally worked up the gumption to check one of the books in the history section, which only referred to Cantlecroft as a footnote in the peasant rebellions of the fourteenth century. Cantlecroft had ceased to be in 1390, as Monty had once said, though pertinent details were unavailable.

Nothing was going right for Viviane anymore.

She turned away from the glow spilling from Joe's bakery, avoiding what little bustle there was in Ganges's sleepy core. The last thing she wanted was company. Viviane returned Ryan's nod as that increasingly familiar man passed her on his way to Barb's, a tube beneath his arm that Viviane knew contained yet more drawings for Barb's garden.

The amazing Mouats held no fascination for Viviane these days—in fact, going there just reminded her of Niall and the glow in his eyes when she tried on those rubbers. The green rubbers themselves had been consigned to the darkest corner of her room, a room that trumpeted memories of Niall from all sides. She couldn't bear to part with his armor, let alone his array of pristinely packaged toothbrushes.

It began to rain, a lazy, soft sort of rain which suited Viviane's mood perfectly. It seemed to her that the sky was weeping sympathetically for her plight.

Her dragging footsteps turned of their own accord to the beach and soon she found herself standing on the very spot where she had returned to Ganges. The sea lapped at her toes, its surface shimmering silver and pewter as far as she could see.

If this had been a tale of any merit at all, Viviane concluded with annoyance, the sea would have returned what it had stolen from her. Right now. A mermaid would have appeared from the mist to grant her a gift, or a clamshell would have opened at her feet to display her shattered moonstone pendant, magically repaired.

Viviane waited, but nothing happened.

She was confusing fanciful tales with the truth again. Viviane couldn't help that she found such tales much more appealing. She heaved a sigh and folded her arms across her chest, watching a little crab scurry out of the way of the gentle roll of the waves.

She supposed she should figure out a way to get on with things, to make a new start, to put the past behind. She couldn't summon a lot of enthusiasm for the idea and looked for a helpful mermaid one more time.

The crab started at a sudden flash of blue light, then darted in the opposite direction. The light came from behind Viviane, but before she could look, a familiar voice carried down the beach.

"*Yes!* Yes, yes, *yes*! Kowabunga—it worked!"

Viviane spun around to find Monty dancing a wild jig on the sand behind her. Monty!

Just Monty.

He punched his fists at the sky, then fell on his hands and knees. "Man, oh man, I can like *relate* to the Pope," he muttered inexplicably, then noisily kissed the beach. He did it twice more then bounced to his feet, hailing Viviane with a wave. "Viviane, babe, how are you?"

She didn't want to hurt his feelings by pointing out that

sand clung to his whiskers. He looked even more disreputable than the first time she had met him but she was glad to see him all the same.

"Monty!"

"Yeah, babe, it's me!" He let out a hoot, then ran to her and scooped her up in a hug. "And man, it's good to be back in ye olde Salt Spring."

Viviane couldn't help looking past his shoulder, but Monty was clearly alone. Her heart twisted and she remembered a little too vividly that Niall never had confessed to having any feelings for her.

Maybe she *had* been wrong about him.

"Hey, like why the long face?" Monty playfully jabbed his fingers into her cheeks and forced her lips into a curve of a smile. "Miss me?"

Viviane wrinkled her nose, seizing an excuse she knew he'd understand. "My tale of Gawain was rejected today, for the third time."

"No kidding." He gave her a quick hug. "That's some bitch. Was it like a form letter? Those are the worst." He affected a haughty tone and matching pose. *"Dear Author. Unfortunately we find absolutely no merit in your work and find its presence in our offices singularly offensive. Good luck finding a sucker elsewhere. Sincerely, the Editors."*

Viviane smiled despite herself. "Not quite that bad." She folded her arms across her chest, wondering how she would ask what she really wanted to know without sounding desperate. "Although they did take three pages to tell me everything they disliked about the book."

Monty's expression brightened. "No kidding? A real letter? You got like a *real* letter? And it was three pages long?"

Viviane nodded. "The letter made it clear that they didn't want the book, Monty—let alone all the reasons why."

"Viviane, babe, that's like *gold*!" He grinned like a madman. "You're *in*. People would kill for a letter like that. It's good news, a good rejection. Make those changes, and you'll have a sale." Monty rubbed his hands gleefully together. "Do you want an introduction to my agent? He's a shark at the negotiating table and with this kind of interest, you'll need . . ."

Viviane put her hand on Monty's arm as he showed no signs of stopping soon. "Monty, how did you get here?"

Monty fell silent midsentence. He studied her, his expression as serious as Viviane had ever seen.

She guessed that he saw more than she would have liked, because he tapped the end of her nose with a gentle finger. "Hey, you already know how I got here," he said quietly. "And you're right—ah, I saw you look!—I came *alone*." He wrinkled his nose. "What can I say? Everyone wants a guinea pig and"—he deepened his voice in obvious mimicry—"'tis only good sense to ensure . . ."

"But . . ."

Viviane's question was cut short by a second shimmer of blue light. She winced even as her heart started to sing and peeked through her lashes as soon as she could stand the brightness.

But it was only Majella. She wavered on her feet, her arms full of young children in various stages of disorientation. Monty quickly stepped forward to help her, extricating children and setting them on their feet, sparing Majella a hearty buss.

"Hey, babe, like welcome to my world. You okay?"

Majella conjured a trembling smile. "Oh, Monty, I shall never become accustomed to your strange speech."

"We'll work on it," Monty insisted and Majella flushed slightly beneath his intense gaze, looking suddenly like a young girl. They exchanged greetings and Viviane noticed that there were only four children with her. She dared to hope one more time.

Monty and Majella exchanged a smile, then Majella glanced over her shoulder expectantly. All of them closed their eyes against a brilliant shimmer of light. Viviane was running into the light even before she could see where she was going. She knew who was coming last, she knew who would ensure that everyone was safely departed before he followed, she knew that her luck was changing back to the good side one more time.

Viviane knew her hero was coming back to her.

And she wasn't disappointed. Niall appeared before her very eyes, looking as golden and as hale as she recalled. Matthew clung to his hand, and Elizabeth held Matthew's hand. Mark hung from his uncle's shoulder and another wide-eyed toddler was nestled in the crook of Niall's arm.

And in his left hand, a moonstone pendant remarkably like Viviane's own reflected the shimmer of the sea and the rain. Its chain was knotted around his fingers, the pendant swinging free. Viviane immediately understood that they had each held it to make their wish, then Niall snatched it back in the nick of time.

"Niall!" Viviane cried and fell upon him. He divested himself of children and caught her against him with a chuckle, lifting her high in a bone-crushing hug.

"My Viviane," he whispered against her throat, a thread of uncertainty in his tone. His cheek was pressed to hers and Viviane felt the anxious thunder of his heart.

He hadn't been sure.

They might as well have been alone. Viviane pulled back and framed his face in her hands, needing to touch him to know for certain that he was here. "You came back," she whispered, suddenly shy. She was painfully aware in this moment that there was no sweet pledge between them.

"Aye," he whispered, his green gaze searching. "I had a confession and a question for you that could not be denied."

Viviane parted her lips but no sound came out.

"I love you, Viviane," Niall declared. "I love you as never a man has loved a woman before." A vulnerability dawned in his expression, the sight tearing at Viviane's heart. "Will you wed me now, knowing the truth of it?"

"Oh yes!" Viviane laughed, she cried, she rained kisses all over Niall's face even as he began to chuckle.

"Tears," he mused moments later, brushing one fingertip tenderly across her cheek. "You should know that I cannot bear to see a woman weep." He arched one brow, mischief lighting his eyes as he tugged her even closer. "I shall have to coax your smile, my Viviane. Be warned that you may have need of your rubbers."

"No," she whispered. "Not anymore."

Niall's eyes flashed, he laughed aloud for the first time in Viviane's experience. He looked younger, yet more vital, a man filled with the promise of the future.

Her man and the promise of their future.

Viviane's heart sang as Niall interlaced their fingers and lifted his other hand high. The moonstone glinted as he swung it by the chain. He looked once to Majella who nodded emphatically, then he flung the stone far out to sea. It flashed once before it splashed in the distance, then it was gone, swallowed by the sea forever.

Majella applauded, Monty gave a hoot of delight, and they two continued their course toward the town. The children trailed behind them, full of questions and earthy demands now that they were recovered from the transition.

"We begin anew, my Viviane," Niall declared, his intent gaze fixed upon her, his fingertips on her jaw. "The past can haunt you no longer."

He brushed his lips across hers and Viviane shivered. Niall smiled down at her and she reached up to trace the curve of his firm lips. "I like when you smile," she confided and his grin broadened.

"Then we shall have to ensure each other's happiness," he teased. "Aye, I shall pledge it to you."

To seal that vow, Niall dipped his head and kissed Viviane so thoroughly that she thought her heart would burst. Her knight was a man of his word and she had no doubt he would keep his pledge.

In fact, the warm certainty of Niall's love proved to Viviane that her luck had never faltered despite her doubts. He had loved her all along. She knew now that she should have never doubted it, just as she knew she would be blessed with good fortune for all her days.

Not to mention her nights.

Epilogue

IT WAS THE Tuesday before Easter, on a misty April morning, that Ryan saw the electric blue blossom.

He had just come up to tuck a few more plants into Barb's new flower beds when she wasn't looking—a columbine with three perfect blossoms, a lady's mantle with its yellow blooms just in bud. He knew that Barb would like the shape of the columbine flowers—they were like fragile trumpets—and the ruffling on the edge of the lady's mantle leaves.

Ryan was starting to have a pretty good idea of the kinds of things Barb liked. And he liked being able to make her smile once in a while. She looked as though she hadn't done much of that in the last few years.

He could relate.

He could also relate to how surprised she was whenever anyone did something unexpected and nice for her. Ryan had a feeling that he and Barb were slowly going to get to know each other a whole lot better.

That was fine by him.

He felt as though he was walking through clouds as he climbed the hill to her place and the morning mist swirled around his ankles. Ryan paused more than once to look over the silent harbor, glad for a hundred reasons that he had come here. It was early. Even the birds weren't up, but he had to catch the first ferry from Fulford this morning.

And he wanted to do this first, so he could spend the day imagining Barb's surprised smile. Ryan stepped into the garden, hoping he was earlier than her today, and the vibrant blue immediately snared his eye.

It was gorgeously vivid and he knew exactly what had bloomed. Barb was going to be over the moon! Ryan crossed the garden, circumnavigating the pond he had installed and pausing beside the stones he had worked into place.

It was the Siberian Iris that she had tried her damnedest to kill. Ryan shoved his hands into his pockets and grinned at the stubborn little sucker.

This was a far better surprise than what he had brought. Ryan quickly added the young plants to the beds, deciding where they would look best with an ease born of experience. He turned to leave, then stopped to look at that iris again.

It was so beautiful, all the more so because the plant reminded him of Barb. This little iris had toughed it out, dumped in soil and light conditions completely wrong for it, thriving despite the odds. All it had needed was a little TLC to coax it to bloom.

Ryan was good with TLC, at least the kind plants needed.

He liked to think that the plants people picked said something about the kind of person they were, and Barb's choice spoke volumes. The iris leaves were like swords, their edges sharp enough to cut. A Siberian Iris was a tough plant, bred to survive brutal conditions and harsh winters.

Yet still it made a fragile and beautiful blossom, one of stunning color that was carefully sheltered behind those sharp leaves. A delicate core. Ryan bent and studied the bloom, impressed as always by the detailed craftmanship of Mother Nature.

He smiled when he saw the next bud lurking below, just a tip of blue that would emerge into splendor by the end of the week. That was all the encouragement he needed to pull out his shears.

There was a vase in Barb's kitchen with a fantastic surface texture and millions of metallic hues depending how the sunlight caught it. It held a place of honor on the kitchen shelf, even though it was always empty, and Ryan had a pretty good idea what Barb was saving it for.

Spring was a time for fresh starts.

An hour after the ferry chugged out of Fulford Harbour, Barb yawned on her way into the kitchen. She always slept late after the sabbat. She plugged in the kettle sleepily, and pulled back the drape to study her new garden. She still couldn't believe it had come to be there, and had to prove it to herself a couple of times every day.

Making a garden had been quite a process and a lot of work. But it hadn't cost as much as Barb had feared— mostly because of Ryan's connections and the hard labor both of them did, moving rocks and soil. In the end, the effort made the garden feel more like Barb's own.

And she had enjoyed Ryan's company. He had a way of listening, *really* listening, that she liked. He didn't make her feel impractical and foolish for wanting a garden, or even for her reasons why she wanted one, though Barb hadn't parted with those secrets easily.

And the resulting garden was exactly as she had always imagined it would be—with a few critical improvements. Ryan had done such a beautiful job. It looked as though it had always been there. Barb smiled slightly at the nodding white flower that *hadn't* been there the day before, and knew very well who had put it there. She'd look closer after her shower, but she already knew she'd like whatever he had brought.

He was a man who paid attention to little things. Barb liked that.

She turned and caught her breath when she saw her special vase in the middle of the kitchen table, exactly as she had always envisioned it. Her hand rose to her lips and she crossed the room slowly, hardly able to believe what she saw.

Her iris had bloomed!

And the flower was so beautiful. It was delicate and faintly ruffled, a fantastic hue that proved on closer examination to be shades upon shades of saturated blues. There were tiny beard hairs on three of the petals and they were of brilliant sun-drenched yellow.

Barb touched them with one finger and was amazed that such beauty could come from one plant, especially one that had until recently been so very unhappy.

There was a note tucked beneath the vase, the bold masculine printing very familiar to Barb after all the garden sketches she had seen.

BEAUTY TRIUMPHS!
CELEBRATE WITH ME—AND DINNER—TONIGHT?

Barb chuckled to herself and traced Ryan's strokes with one fingertip. She supposed that accepting the invitation was the least she do after the man had saved her plant.

And coaxed it to be happy again.

But it wasn't the blue iris blossom on her kitchen table that made Barb greet Ryan with a smile.

It wasn't because Viviane finally had a call from a publisher who wanted to buy her manuscript. It wasn't even because Monty paid his balance that afternoon—a vigilant Majella by his side.

It wasn't even—as Barb insisted—that Viviane and Niall were going to move out or that Niall's apprenticeship with Derek was working out so well. She tried to convince her date that all of these things were responsible for her buoyant mood.

But Ryan, a keen observer of details, knew better than to believe her.

Author's Note

AFTER ALL THESE references to Gawain and his adventures, you may be wondering why the full tale of that legendary knight is not included in the book. Part of the reason is that there are so many stories about Gawain and they have been fitted together in many different ways over the centuries.

According to Arthurian chronicles, Gawain was the nephew of Arthur, the son of Arthur's sister Morgaine (sometimes called Anne). Like Arthur, there is some question that the character may be modelled after an historic figure, an illegitimate son of a king of Lothian and Orkney who was denied by his father. Some tales call Gawain the son of a fairy, cast out by his parents and raised by a childless fisherman and his wife.

There is also speculation that Gawain is the medieval version of a Celtic solar hero. This is evidenced by Gawain's strength waxing until midday, then waning thereafter in several tales, and can also be supported by the persistence of unusual elements in stories about Gawain.

No matter his origins, Gawain was reputed to be the champion of women, a courteous and fearless knight who was both noble of spirit and golden-tongued. He crossed water to win an island ruled by women (Avalon?) and besieged the Castellum Puellarum (Castle of Maidens) in several tales. He also is often portrayed as the diplomat who reconciles differences at Arthur's court. His symbol is the pentacle (a five-pointed star often associated with paganism); his sword was named Excalibur; his destrier was named Gingalet ("of good staying power").

Gawain figures prominently in three different stories of the Arthurian cycle, though his role (like that of most of the players) changes in each version. It has also changed over time, several of his stories being rolled into Arthur's mythology.

The first tale is that of Gawain's rescue of a woman of otherworldly origins. After a series of ordeals—battles with demons, the "terrible kiss" of a serpent, and nightmares—Gawain rescues the lady in question and she gratefully bestows her sexual favors upon him.

The trials here are somewhat bizarre, even in medieval terms—hand-to-hand combat was a much more typical test!—the kiss of the serpent in particular hinting at the old association of snakes with the Goddess. The besieged lady's characteristics suggest that she may not be mortal. In many versions, she grants Gawain a token or talisman which magically protects him from harm after his success. It has been suggested that this tale is one of Gawain being tested as the earthly consort of the Goddess and that winning the challenge makes him her champion.

The second tale of Gawain is that of the Riddle Test, much as Viviane tells Matthew in the archbishop's dungeon. Medieval people loved riddles so that part of the tale isn't unusual, although the riddle is. Those familiar with pagan symbols will recognize the two aspects of the Goddess in this tale—that of the Maiden and the Crone. Hers is not a passive role, either, for she challenges knights—who bow to her will!—and demands Gawain's kiss. Additionally, courtesy is given greater weight than military ability, though this story purportedly predates the romances of courtly love by a number of centuries.

The final tale involving Gawain is perhaps the most telling one in terms of exhibiting his Celtic pagan history. "Gawain and the Green Knight" tells of the arrival of a large knight completely green in hue (yes, even his hair!) at Arthur's court during the Yule festivities. He challenges the knights to cut off his head—none take the wager except Gawain. To Gawain's astonishment, the stranger doesn't defend himself (although he is much larger than Gawain) and Gawain successfully beheads him with a single blow.

To everyone's surprise, the Green Knight then scoops up his head, and demands that Gawain meet him in a year so that he can return what he was given. Gawain keeps his word, even knowing that he will be killed. In several versions, this tale is entwined with the other two above, so that the token given by the lady saves Gawain's life.

Of course, the Yuletide festivities at Arthur's court would coincide with the Celtic pagan celebration of the winter solstice. Traditionally, the day of the solstice (the shortest day of the year) was considered a day "out of time"—in Gawain's story, this is the date of his meeting with the Green Knight. This contest with a much older (albeit green!) knight also echoes the sacrifice of pagan kings, a ritual which ensured that the Goddess's consort was always a virile champion.

Hopefully, you found Niall of Malloy a suitably honorable consort for Viviane and her otherworldly token. Viviane, incidentally, is the beauty in the Arthurian cycle who begged Merlin to teach her all of his magical tricks. In this case, the pupil excelled the master, and Viviane imprisoned Merlin with a spell when he grew displeased with her prowess. She has also been associated with the Lady of the Lake, the keeper of Excalibur, which makes a nice little circle back to Gawain.

FRIENDS ROMANCE

Can a man come between friends?

❏ **A TASTE OF HONEY**
by DeWanna Pace   0-515-12387-0

❏ **WHERE THE HEART IS**
by Sheridon Smythe   0-515-12412-5

❏ **LONG WAY HOME**
by Wendy Corsi Staub   0-515-12440-0

All books $5.99

Presenting all-new romances—featuring ghostly heroes and heroines and the passions they inspire.

❤ Haunting Hearts ❤